PAPER WAR

VIRTUAL WAR

RYAN LEKODAK

DECISIONS OF FATE

JUNE 2043
WASHINGTON, DC

FOR THE THIRD TIME in as many minutes, Nate Tuffin scanned the conference room. The first time, he'd done it with a sense of awe and giddy excitement once he realized just where he was, and by whom he was surrounded. With just a glance, Nate spotted the Speaker of the House of Representatives, several former presidents, the secretary of state, the director of national intelligence, his boss, and the chief justice. He even saw one of the navy admirals: William Austin. The man was a legend.

The room was filled with some of the most powerful people in the country—people who made decisions that impacted millions. And he, lil' ol' Nate, was with them. Granted, he was there only because of his boss, but still. This was what he'd worked for. It was the reason he hadn't quit months before, when all the craziness had started.

The conference table filled up slowly, just like everything involving bureaucracy. Aides to the various authorities took up the sides. Nate joined them, standing directly behind his boss. He studied the man closely. Over the last few months, Chief Justice Morgan Harvey had regained some of his weight. He was even starting to show a gut. The timing was fortunate. Nate had begun hearing rumors that he would be replaced because of his health. Unfortunately, Nate had been unable to do anything about the rumors because he still didn't know anything about the health issue.

That's because the health issue is a bunch of bull, he thought.

He already knew that, of course. However, he still had no clue where the chief justice had disappeared to. Despite months of subtly inquiring about the issue, nothing had turned up. It was his job to know, and something had changed in Morgan during that time. When that hadn't yielded anything, his curiosity had evolved into obsession. Nevertheless, it was probably time to back off. The fact that no one seemed to know anything about it meant that someone didn't want anyone to know. Nate didn't want to test how far that someone was willing to go to keep the information tight.

Morgan shifted in his seat, drawing Nate's attention. He sat somewhat stiffly after making his rounds and didn't remove his shades. This wasn't surprising. Nate hadn't seen him without the glasses since the spontaneous recovery from his "illness." Fortunately, Morgan wasn't the only person at the table wearing shades. Nate glanced at the Speaker, the secretary of state, and William Austin. Morgan didn't stand out as much as he'd feared.

As the table filled, Nate took note of who sat where and beside whom. He jotted down possible friendships, dislikes, and flat-out animosity. Later, he would compare notes with the junior aides to tease out what information he could. Whatever he discovered might be minor, but it could be valuable to the right person.

After a minute of shuffling, everyone was seated. As if on cue, the double doors opened, and the president of the United States strode in. Like most people, Nate hadn't seen Mary Pastore except on the news. She entered confidently, as if she were the most important person in the room—which she was. She was flanked by a retinue of aides and Secret Service agents. Her eyes were fixed straight ahead, seeming to ignore the entire room standing in respect.

President Pastore took her seat at the head of the table, her retinue behind her. Everyone else followed suit. She was older than Nate had envisioned, but not by much. And she was average height. He doubted she was much over five foot six. Nevertheless, there was a level of self-assurance in her movements that was impossible to fake. Her pure-white suit matched her hair. She fixed the table members with a piercing look.

"All right," she said, collecting a folder from one of her aides. "Let's get this over with. Who wants to go first?"

Nate was taken aback by her informal tone, though he shouldn't have been. Almost everyone in the room was acquainted. Although it was an official conference without the press, there was no need to be stuffy.

He went over his notes, though he knew there was nothing there. The memo hadn't given much information about what was to be discussed, which was unusual. Typically, the aides handled the correspondence for their bosses, taking care of the mundane ones and passing on the important ones. This time, Morgan had received the information directly and held everything close to his chest, including his own preparations. Nate didn't even know who'd called the meeting. He had his guesses, since there were few people with enough clout to get the president in attendance, but he couldn't be sure.

Stephen McLaughlin, the director of national intelligence, was the first to address the room. He was a balding man with a prominent belly that his suit did nothing to hide. Taking a cue from the president, his voice was relaxed but easily carried through the room. "In the interest of not wasting anyone's time, I move that we dismiss the proposal now, adjourn the meeting, and be back home in time for lunch."

The room erupted into chaos, and everyone talked over everyone else. Nate was not overly surprised. He'd learned early that, regardless of their position, government officials were still people. It didn't take much to reduce them to squabbling children. He sighed but took note of those who were most vocal with their objections and those who were content to stay silent.

The president—fortunately—was among the latter. She raised a brow at the director of national intelligence, and the man shrugged in response, mouthing something Nate didn't catch. He did catch the president's eyes flickering over the table, probably noting the same things that Nate had. She let the shouting match continue for a few seconds before pulling out a small gavel and banging it against the table.

The room quieted immediately. Nate palmed his face. It said a lot about how often such things happened if they had a damn procedure for it.

"Thank you, Director McLaughlin, for your input," President Pastore said. "It seems to be a little controversial, but I do like your suggestion that we be done by lunch. With that in mind, I'll handle the procedures directly so it's more efficient and less … loud." She looked around the room. "Anyone have a problem with that?"

No one disagreed. What kind of fool would? The president continued, "We're here to discuss whether or not the government should integrate artificial intelligence into our systems."

Nate gaped. *That's what this is about?* he thought incredulously. *Some of the most powerful people in government have gathered to talk about a fucking AI? Who gives a crap about that?*

"Normally, you are given free rein over your duties. However, since this matter concerns the entire US government, we have to make a decision. We're doing it today, one way or another—preferably before lunch." She glanced around the room again, as if asking for objections. Her eyes settled on the chief justice. "Morgan, I already know your stance on this, assuming you haven't changed it again. You want to start us off?"

"Gladly, Madam President," Morgan said, standing. Nate's eyes followed his motion. It was too rigid, too stiff. Was Nate the only one who noticed? "And no, I have not changed my stance. There's no reason to when one's choice is right."

Someone snorted lightly. Morgan homed in on the sound, but he continued smoothly. "Our current policies are functional, of course, but they rely heavily on people to ensure everything is running smoothly and everyone's keeping to the rules. No offense, but that's horribly inefficient.

"People forget things. They get tired and overlook important issues. They can be bribed or otherwise persuaded from doing their duty. This method might've worked in the past, when technology hadn't advanced enough to be a viable option. But now it has, and it'd be a folly not to utilize it. Artificial intelligence allows us to automate facets of our system to heights unreached before. This, in turn, allows us to utilize our skilled workers in positions where AI is lacking. That's how we move ahead."

"Tell that to everyone who died on Mayday," someone muttered loudly.

"It seems Director McLaughlin has something to say," President Pastore noted, gesturing at the mutterer. The director of national intelligence rose to his feet. Morgan retook his seat, giving the other man the floor.

"Thank you, Madam President," Director McLaughlin started before addressing the room. "I'm not saying AI isn't useful; that'd be stupid. What I'm saying is that everybody else doing it is no reason for us to put hundreds of thousands of valuable workers out of jobs in favor of cold machines.

"The chief justice made good points about the fallibility of human workers, but the same goes with AI. Gaius's failure, which resulted in Mayday, is a good example. Before that global catastrophe, I would've taken the same stance as Harvey. However, I would think Mayday taught us the folly of trusting an AI as completely as this proposal wants us to.

"And before you say it, I know Sparta's Helene is good. But so was Gaius. It takes only one massive failure for everything to go up in flames. The thing about humans? They may make mistakes, but in the long run, they're reliable."

With one final look around the table, he sat down. The room was silent for a few seconds. Morgan's eyes were shielded by his glasses, so it was difficult to tell who he was looking at, but his head had been trained on the director since he'd started talking. Then again, so had everyone else's. Director McLaughlin had a reputation for being relaxed. Thus, Nate didn't think anyone had expected such a passionate speech from him.

"Okay," President Pastore said. She marked something in the folder and looked up. "Anyone else want a go?"

The secretary of state gestured and stood, adjusting her dark-shaded glasses.

And the meeting went on.

After several points were batted around, even Nate started to see the importance of the meeting. Mayday was still fresh in many people's minds. This made them reluctant to trust another AI—even one as advanced as Helene. In the same way, one couldn't deny how much more efficient the government would be with Helene taking responsibility for the bulk of the systems.

Weirdly, most of those who wanted Helene integrated into government servers wore dark shades like Morgan. Was there a connection? Were the glasses a symbol? Nate hadn't heard of anything like that. A glance around the room showed that no one else seemed to think anything of it. He shrugged it off as a coincidence and moved on.

Despite the president's words, the arguments dragged on way past lunch. Morgan stood to speak several times more, as did the director of national intelligence. Several in each camp also brought out their points and were refuted by others. The meeting got tense several times, but with the president maintaining things personally, there were no other screaming matches.

Finally, when all the points were exhausted, President Pastore made her decision: Helene would be integrated into government servers to improve their efficiency. The AI would be regulated by programming experts, either from Sparta or trained by a Sparta team.

THE VIRTUAL WORLD

MANAR SALEEM OPENED HIS EYES to a new reality. Lying on his back, he made no effort to move, allowing the artificially induced drowsiness to pass. His eyes remained open, staring at the sky—or what passed for the sky. Manar squinted. There was something wrong with it, and it took a minute for him to place.

The entire sky was nothing but a vast stretch of endless gray. There was no sun and no clouds. While Manar had no problem seeing, it was as if the world were eternally stuck at dusk. It seemed to be lit from everywhere at once instead of from the sun.

Even that light should come from somewhere, Manar thought, trying to peer deeper.

A moment later, he blinked in surprise. Beyond the sky and its featureless gray, Manar caught a glimpse of something. He lost it when he blinked, but if he focused, if he peered deeper, he could almost make it out again …

There!

Manar sat up slowly, keeping his eyes wide so he didn't lose sight of it again. Far above, slightly bigger than a normal star, was the number one. Manar shut his eyes and opened them again. In the same spot, the number stared back at him. Beside it was a zero. For the next few minutes, Manar picked different spots at random and was met with ones and zeros.

The world is made of ones and zeros, Manar thought, wryly. *At least that rules out the theory that I've died and gone to hell.*

Energy flooded his system as the last of the fogginess lifted. He stood cautiously while he examined his new body. He was dressed in a black T-shirt, jeans, and a pair of dress shoes. Although he hadn't coded the outfit into the neural uplink, the device might have plucked the ensemble from his consciousness during the upload. Manar would have picked a more sensible pair of shoes, but he blamed this lapse on his forgetting to program clothes.

His body was harder to move past. He'd designed the neural uplink to create a virtual body for himself—something familiar and easily maneuverable to house Manar's consciousness. He'd succeeded in that a little too well. The process had been modeled on the technology used to create highly immersive virtual reality games. It provided him with a ready template to work with and shaved hours off his work. The side effect was that he looked like a video game character. It was highly rendered, without any of the blocky pixels that were an eyesore in old games, but he was still clearly a video game character.

He sighed but put the matter out of his mind. It was too minor a detail to worry about; he could always change it when he went back to his body. Instead, he continued with his examination. He clenched his fist. It responded easily and smoothly. For the next few minutes, he went through a couple of warm-up exercises, making sure to test each part. He'd worried his pixelated body would create rendering lag, but if there was lag, it was nothing Manar could detect. He moved with the same efficiency as he did with his real body.

This told him something was wrong.

Manar was in his mid-forties in the real world, and his body reflected it. Mental stress aside, his body was not as limber as it had been in his early twenties, and it showed evidence of his age. However, his virtual body should not have that problem. Manar had designed the body to be that of a man in his prime, unburdened by the realities of age. Physically, he should have been able to move much better than in the real world.

That meant the problem was his mind. Manar's lips twisted in disgust. He'd become so used to moving as a forty-five-year-old that he was unconsciously limiting himself to that level. It was the height of stupidity. He had to be at his peak if he was to go up against Helene. He was self-sabotaging before he even started. How irritating. It ultimately was a problem that he could solve by slowly acclimating himself to his new strength. All he needed was time.

With that sorted, Manar turned his attention to the ball of energy flowing through him. He'd felt it earlier and had deliberately stopped himself from tapping into it while he did his tests. But now, he examined it. It gave a measure of strength to his body that wasn't there before. The effect was subtle—especially with his subconscious limitations—but still significant. It felt as if there was electricity running beneath his skin, just waiting for him to summon it.

Manar had wondered how his merging with Gaius would manifest. Now he knew. And he approved. He wasn't sure what his fight with Helene would look like, but the added reservoir of power wouldn't go unused. Manar could tell the energy didn't just give him a flat boost in strength; there were hints of other possibilities. He'd have to figure those out.

Manar went through another set of exercises, this time tapping into the energy. The difference was clear. Every movement was smoother and sharper than before. For the first time, Manar regretted not learning a martial arts discipline. He'd seen what Ndidi was capable of. With that level of control, combined with the strength he felt flowing through him, Manar's power would have been exceptional.

His experiment continued for a few minutes more. Only when he was satisfied did he raise his eyes and scan his environment.

He was on a hill in the middle of a grassy plain. Manar crouched and ran his finger through the grass. It was green, coarse—similar to ordinary grass, yet it was not. The difference was slight, but it was there. Like his body, the grass lacked enough detail to be truly mistaken as real. Fascinating. While real grass was ecologically important for photosynthesis, what purpose would this representation of it serve, especially in a world without a sun? If there was no purpose for it, why was it represented?

Manar lowered himself until he was as close to the grass as he could be. He focused as he had on the sky but couldn't make out the ones and zeros. He was certain they were there, but the plant might have been too small to make the numbers obvious. He stood and dusted himself off, then took a moment to marvel at the fact that there was actual dust.

The world is modeled after the real one, at least to some extent, Manar realized. It was a cautious theory and would remain so until he had more information. But if he was right, it boded well for him. It meant the virtual world at least followed some of the same rules as the real world. For instance, the fact that he wasn't floating meant there was some form of gravity—although Manar's head ached when he tried to figure out how that was possible.

Still, if the virtual space followed some familiar rules, it was safe to assume the other rules would adhere to some kind of logic. Manar nodded at that. The sky had given him a hint. Regardless of its representation, the internet was, above all, a collection of ones and zeros. It was only logical that it would follow a set of rules.

Manar just had to figure out what those rules were—then bend them to his needs.

How would he do that? It sounded easy on paper, but the practicality of it would require further consideration. In the meantime, he had to find his way out of wherever he'd ended up. It didn't make sense for the entire online space to be a sea of endless grass. If nothing else, Helene was somewhere in this world.

As if drawn by his thoughts, Manar noticed a pulling sensation coming from his chest. It was like a string connecting him to something far away. He had to focus to feel it, but once he did, he noticed it was drawing him … *there.* Manar turned, and the draw became stronger, more insistent.

It's probably from Liz's nanites homing in on Helene, Manar thought. There was no way to test that, of course, but Manar was certain he was correct. Even if he wasn't, he at least had a direction. With a little luck, he'd be pulled somewhere he could get answers.

Manar realized he'd already made up his mind. He scanned the plane one last time, then took his first steps into the new world.

CHAPTER

THE VIRTUAL WORLD

CJ FELT HIMSELF MATERIALIZE. It was a distant thing, made worse by the fog in his mind, but he felt it as his body was created. Fortunately, there was no pain, just a vague, irritating itch that wasn't localized to one region. The process took a few minutes, then CJ was left standing in a new world.

He'd appeared in front of a building at the edge of a street. The structure was taller than even the Sparta headquarters and almost as wide. CJ could see something floating above the building, but he couldn't make it out, so he took in the rest of his surroundings.

The people commanded his attention immediately. Hundreds of them moved along the massive street, packed together as if in a parade march. There were four types of people. The first moved the fastest; they almost seemed to be running despite their measured pace. The second type, which included the vast majority of the people, moved at a normal pace. They disappeared around corners or into buildings. The third type was slow, easily passed, and falling farther behind. The last type twitched and moved in jerky motions—sometimes fast, sometimes slow. Sometimes, they disappeared completely and reappeared seconds later as if nothing had happened.

Although the fastest were given space, everyone moved with a single-minded focus, barely interacting with each other. CJ studied the closest person: a man in a wide-brimmed hat and rhinestone suit. His face was fixed in a grin, but his emotionless eyes stared ahead. His features were remarkably similar to a normal person's, except his head was slightly more rectangular, and his eyes were so large they could be mistaken for a doll's. Several other features stood out, each innocuous enough on their own, but when combined with the other abnormalities, the man looked like a highly rendered caricature. CJ noticed a similar abnormality in every other person he studied.

They are avatars! CJ realized belatedly. He pushed down his embarrassment at not realizing it sooner. Avatars were digital representations of people that could be customized however the user wanted. People used them as a form of expressing their identity and personality. Decades before, avatars were used only on social media sites, but a trend had skyrocketed their popularity enough that now they were almost compulsory when making any kind of new account. Most people used one avatar, but others created a different avatar for every new site.

Each person must have represented someone currently online. There were close to a thousand that he could make out on the street alone. CJ had no doubt that the sight was normal everywhere in the city. He spent a minute more studying the users and noticed most of them entered different buildings, sometimes causing traffic jams at the entrances.

CJ turned his attention to the massive building he'd materialized in front of. It was seamless in a way a building made of brick and mortar never was. Then again, it wasn't made of brick and mortar, which CJ realized when he moved closer. When he focused on a single spot, he could make out minute rows of ones and zeros running along its length.

"Exactly like lines of code," he muttered.

It was fascinating. He could see how the lines interacted with each other perfectly. He'd known that was necessary but had always seen his work in two dimensions, so he'd taken the codes to be rigid. But they were not. They were constantly shifting, interconnecting with each other to form the framework that maintained the integrity of the building algorithm.

CJ's mind exploded with possibilities. He couldn't resist placing his hand on the building. It felt real, not gritty like he expected but solid and nearly seamless. He pinched his thumb and forefinger, making the space between them as small as he could without touching, then pressed them against the building, targeting the numbers. The wall of code resisted, and CJ felt his finger push up against a barrier.

A part of him wanted to apply more force, but that would have been stupid. Removing a piece from the wall could compromise the building and cause it to crumble. But that wasn't why CJ stopped. He stopped because brute force was the most inefficient way to break into a program. And that's what the building was. More specifically …

"It is a website," CJ breathed in awe. "It must be something massive if it needs codes this complex." He figured the tag floating above the building was its name, but he still couldn't make it out. Taking several steps back, he peered at the whole building instead of just part of it. It was harder to make out the lines of code but not impossible. Since he knew they were there, it took only a bit of effort before …

There.

The codes extended throughout the building, but not in lines. At this scale, they formed a weave, a tapestry of ones and zeros.

It was breathtaking.

And that was just one building.

His eyes went to the bustling city. Each building was distinct from every other in an unmistakable way. One building was completely round and hovered several feet off the ground. In the distance, another was shaped like a star that had been stretched vertically, with five points making up its perimeter. Another rose like a pyramid. Yet another was built like a giant cardboard box. A swarm of drones was orbiting that building. CJ had a moment of panic, fearing the swarm was Helene's, but that wasn't the case.

Most buildings were not as grand as the first. But they were all vivid. Each one came with its own unique color scheme that set it apart from every other.

It made sense that websites were designed to stand out from the crowd, but the sheer individuality of them all made the scene somewhat hard to take in. Still, like the colors, one thing was similar across the buildings: they all had the same tapestry of code.

Had the developers known what they were designing when they wrote the programs, or was it just a by-product? If it could be replicated—if developers could learn to write programs by visualizing their interactions in three dimensions instead of two—how would that change the world? The possibilities were endless. If CJ could learn to do that, he might finally be able to match—

Manar! he thought with a gasp. How could he have forgotten? Manar was somewhere in this world. He could have materialized close to Helene. He could be fighting her right now. How could he get so distracted?

But he knew how, of course. It was impossible not to get overwhelmed by the sight. Any programmer would have had the same reaction.

CJ exhaled at the thought, his guilt disappearing. "Manar wouldn't have been able to resist the city either," he muttered. "As long as he didn't materialize with Helene, he wouldn't go looking for her right away. He would prioritize learning as much as possible about this place beforehand."

It was the rational thing to do. The whole point of coming to the virtual space was to fight Helene on her turf, where she couldn't run away. But the inherent disadvantage was that it was, indeed, the AI's turf. She would know more about it than any invader. Plus, it would have been far too optimistic to think Helene wasn't expecting them—or at least Manar, since CJ's arrival had been spontaneous.

"He should have manifested before me." CJ turned around and took in the city once more. "This means he's probably somewhere around here. I just have to find him."

As if called upon by his words, a new sense blossomed in CJ's mind. His vision twisted for a moment, and suddenly he was somewhere else, staring at a field of grass. The next moment, he was back in his body, certain that Manar was somewhere to his left. He turned and prodded the sense, but all he got was an impression of great distance and renewed certainty that Manar was that way. Further examination yielded nothing.

CJ blinked slowly. Somehow, he was able to tell where Manar was, but not with any precision. It was probably because CJ had made a connection to Manar's neural uplink to facilitate his transfer. That would explain his moment of vertigo. The signal had probably homed in on Manar's and sent feedback. But it'd had to travel a vast distance to do so. Manar seemed just as far away.

That eliminated the possibility of a quick reunion.

CJ closed his eyes as he considered his options. He didn't know how big the city was, so he couldn't rule out that Manar was somewhere in the same city. It would have been easier if he was, but that was too optimistic. He still didn't know what had gone wrong with the process that caused Manar to go into a coma. But if Helene had been responsible, she might have also messed with his entrance point.

This added another variable. If Manar manifested either next to or extremely close to Helene, it would explain his distance. Without any information, however, there was no way to accurately gauge either Manar's or Helene's strength in this world. Thus, it would be foolish to theorize what such a fight would entail or who would come out the victor.

With Manar being so far away, CJ would not be able to do anything if a fight did occur. That was another reason not to dwell on it. Instead, he chose to focus on the assumption that Manar had materialized in a random location and would prioritize finding information. Manar didn't know of CJ's presence, so it was up to CJ to locate him.

This presented yet another variable. Assuming Manar was not in the same city, there was no guarantee that he had materialized in a different city. In that case, there was no reason to believe he would eventually make his way here. And without knowing what was possible, CJ could end up forever a step behind with no way to catch up.

CJ sighed.

No matter how much he wanted to, he couldn't prioritize finding Manar and neglect his other concerns. The first was finding how to get back to their bodies or, failing that, communicate with their team members in the real world. The ability to coordinate their tactics using the information Manar provided had been a major part of their plan. Without access to their bodies, CJ and Manar were forced to work alone in a world they knew nothing about, following rules they didn't know, using tools their opponent was a master of.

There was also the damage that an extended coma could do to their brains. Manar didn't know of the danger and wouldn't plan for it, so CJ had to.

CJ kept his eyes closed for a minute more, examining each task and its obstacle. The magnitude of it all was overwhelming. But CJ had experience with being overwhelmed. He tried to plot the several steps he would need to take. Each time, he hit the same problem.

"I don't have enough information," he said, opening his eyes. There were too many variables. He considered first the bustling city around him, then, on a wider scale, the fact that he was on the internet. Despite the daunting circumstances, CJ's lips stretched into a grin.

First things first: which of these buildings is a search engine?

DJ STARED AT HIS BROTHER'S unmoving body. If he ignored CJ's strange headset and everything that had happened over the last few minutes, he could almost convince himself CJ was sleeping rather than in a coma from which he might not awaken.

"What the hell were you thinking, big bro?" DJ whispered. "Better yet, what was I thinking, allowing you to go in there without me?"

It was a fucked-up question, of course. DJ had seen the determination in his brother's eyes—the resolve. There was no way he was going to stand in the way of that.

Christy placed a hand on his shoulder. "Don't be stupid, D," she said, her voice soft but firm. "You know you couldn't."

He knew, of course. Sci-fi bullshit was his brother's turf. DJ would have been nothing but dead weight. But that didn't stop him from wanting to put his fist through something. He looked around the office. There was an array of targets for his anger, but any one of them might be vital to keeping his brother alive.

"Shit. So, what are we going to do now?" he asked. "We can't just leave them like this."

"We have to figure out what went wrong with the process," Hermione said without looking up from her phone. "We have to figure out if it was an issue with the components or a mistake in one of the steps. The latter can easily be fixed. Probably. But it would require combing through both Manar's and CJ's notes to figure out what went wrong."

DJ nodded. At least it was something to do. He started pacing. "Do you have any clue about this stuff?" he asked Hermione, gesturing at the different machines. He had to repeat the question before she lifted her head enough to answer him.

"I don't," she said. "Manar didn't involve me in this."

"We have to call the old man back, then," DJ muttered.

"Chloe isn't going to let him go," Christy countered. "She won't care about Manar if the twins are still in danger of being controlled by Helene."

"We'll let Martin decide who he wants to work with."

"You know she won't let—"

"Screw what she wants!" DJ roared. "My brother's in a fucking coma, and I can't do dick to help him!" He let out a breath and continued in a softer tone. "CJ has always been there for me, the one picking up after my screw-ups. Well, this time he's the one who's fucked up, even if he was doing what's right. I can't be there for him because I don't understand any of this shit. I can't help him." It hurt for him to say, but denying it would only waste time. "I can't help him, but the old man can, so if Chloe has a problem with it, she can take it up with me."

Christy stared at him until he stopped pacing and looked at her. Then she slapped him across the face. "Don't be stupid, D. What're you going to do? Walk in there and carry Martin out? Shit! Chloe won't even be the one to kill you. Karla would gut you before you took a step."

"What do you want from me, Christy?" DJ snapped. "I can't just leave him like this." His cheek hurt, but the pain was minor compared to the roar in his head.

A part of him knew Christy was right. He could practically hear Olsen screaming at him to keep his head on straight. But all DJ saw was his brother's body and himself, helpless to do anything. Hermione was right. If he could just get the old man to look at neural uplink, he might be able to find a way to fix whatever was wrong. To bring CJ back.

"I want you to fucking think for once," Christy snapped back. "You're no help to your brother if you're dead, D. Martin might be able to help, but neither Chloe nor Karla will let him leave until he figures out a way to stop Helene from taking control of the twins. You know this."

DJ deflated, his anger leaving him. "Then what do you suggest we do? What if they get killed in there? What happens to their bodies?"

"I don't know," Christy replied, her tone softer. "But we have to trust that they can handle themselves—at least until we figure out how to help them without killing ourselves in the process. There has to be something or someone else that can help us. We just have to find it."

"Christy's right," Hermione added. "We have to find someone that can help us. And I have an idea who to call. But that's not our only problem." She finally ignored the phone and stared at them both with worry in her eyes. "I've been trying to reach Ndidi since Manar became unresponsive. She wasn't answering, and I was afraid she would do something stupid, so I tracked her phone."

"I'm guessing she's not in her room?" Christy asked.

"The tracker put her somewhere to the east, almost at the edge of New York."

DJ frowned. "That's pretty far out just to get a drink."

Hermione shook her head and looked down to confirm the details. "According to the map, she's in a warehouse. Or was, at least." She looked up again, her eyes filling with tears. "For the last two minutes, I haven't been able to track her signal."

She stepped closer. "I think someone's kidnapped Ndidi."

MANAR TOOK ANOTHER muffled step forward and stopped. Around him stretched a field of grass. But of course, it wasn't endless. The grass was already sparser than it had been where he'd started. It was logical to assume the terrain would change soon, which of course brought new questions to mind. Manar dismissed them like he had every other he'd thought of while working.

Manar had learned two things. The first was that his body apparently had no use for water or food. He'd been walking for what had to be several hours and felt none of the usual pangs. It was fortunate because Manar had found no way to get either. There was no wildlife anywhere within sight, and he hadn't spied any signs of water. Out of curiosity, he'd plucked a blade of grass and tried eating it. There had been a slight static shock once the blade met his tongue, but nothing else.

The second thing Manar had learned was that his body still needed to rest. His stamina was significantly greater than it had been in the real world, and he could keep moving for far longer, but he'd still had to take several breaks on his journey already. That meant his virtual body was fueled by something. Manar just didn't know what.

His working theory was that this form converted his mental energy into sustenance. But of course, until he returned to his body, he had no way of confirming that. And he wasn't interested in leaving yet. He had no idea what would happen to his virtual body if he transferred his consciousness back to it. Would it become frozen and immobile, or would it disappear along with Manar's progress? Until he found out more, Manar couldn't take the risk.

Hence the reason he'd stopped. Several hours ago, a new sense had blossomed inside him. This time, it emanated from his head. It was distinct from the nanites' signal, though Manar wasn't sure how. Before, he'd been able to ignore it. But the more he walked, the more it'd branched. And now, the new sense drew him in a direction almost perpendicular to Helene's signal.

Manar had followed Helene's signal because its pull gave him the greatest chance of reaching someplace he could get answers. But now, he had another choice. Manar was more than a little curious about what drew him in the new direction. Should he risk it?

He could keep on his current path and ignore the other. But his current path had Helene at the other end. Manar didn't think he was ready to confront her—not until he had an idea of the playing field. He'd been willing to take the risk when he'd had no other choice, but if there was a way to find information without risking a confrontation with Helene, then it was logical to take it. Of course, there was no guarantee that whatever was pulling him in the new direction was good for him, or that whatever was at the end was particularly useful. All Manar got was a vague measure of distance—and even that wasn't clear.

Manar envisioned the various arguments for both decisions and scowled. He could easily see himself wasting hours analyzing each one, all the while getting no closer to any of his goals. It was easy to spend hours considering a plan of action because that was how he'd lived his whole life. He couldn't afford that now. Every minute he wasted was another Helene spent furthering her goals.

Manar glanced in the new signal's direction. The programmer in him burned with curiosity, but ultimately, the new signal wasn't part of his mission. Helene had to be defeated sooner rather than later. Everyone depended on it. Maybe after, he could figure out what the signal was.

In the meantime, he had an AI to confront.

IT HADN'T BEEN DIFFICULT for CJ to find the virtual world's representation of the Gaius search engine. Although the Gaius Corporation had developed both the search engine and the Gaius AI that Helene had influenced to cause Mayday, they remained separate.

CJ looked at the towering building. It was taller than the first building he'd seen, wider, and just better in every way. Unlike most of the other digital buildings CJ had seen, Gaius didn't have any weird construction, flashy colors, or projections designed to catch attention. It stood as a regular building—or as close to regular as it could get. And yet, it dominated its space, solid and unmistakable.

Its dimensions should have made its tapestry of code easier to see, but CJ still had to focus to make them out. Was that a thing in this world? It was fascinating. CJ had spent several days analyzing the codes that made up Gaius. He'd seen glimpses of Helene's codes and spent several minutes studying the buildings he passed. It'd still been difficult for him to understand the codes that made up the website's structure, even after isolating some of them.

He didn't know how long it took before he remembered why he was there in the first place. It was his logical first stop if his goal was to get information. Gaius's search engine had been the most used search engine for decades because of its reliability when sourcing information. And everything that made it so great, CJ was looking at.

He pushed with trepidation against the barrier that served as the door. There was a chance he would not be able to interface with the website at all. He wasn't technically a user or an avatar of one. Fortunately, he passed through without a problem.

CJ froze at the door. The inside of the building was markedly different from the outside. The entire room was about a hundred feet long and nearly the same width, but instead of the large, open space seen in most buildings, almost every inch of the floor was filled with rows and rows of cubicles. The compartments started a few feet in front of CJ. From wall to wall, every inch of space that wasn't otherwise in use was taken up by a cubicle. The whole thing was reminiscent of an accounting firm or offices on Wall Street. Every compartment had two avatars, one representing Gaius and one representing the user.

The door opened behind him, and an avatar bumped against his arm before he could move. Without looking at him or even noticing the contact, the avatar made its way to a cubicle. CJ had tried interacting with several without any luck, thinking they could be a way to communicate with the real world. Although he could touch them and even bar their path, nothing he tried brought a response.

CJ watched this avatar curiously as it reached the row of cubicles. He assumed it would have to wait for the other user to be done. But as he watched, another cubicle appeared in front of it, enclosing the avatar without it having to break stride. A Gaius avatar appeared at the same moment, filling out the compartment. The new cubicle slid backward, and the entire row moved to accommodate it. The cubicle on the other end rose into the air, still holding its avatars.

The motion drew CJ's attention to the second floor, where it merged with another row of cubicles. Another wave of displacements followed, with the last compartment rising to the third floor. CJ tried to count the floors but stopped when he got to thirty.

That explains how the website can deal with billions of users at once, CJ thought, amazed at the sight.

Several more avatars entered, and the pattern of displacement repeated itself. CJ moved closer, trying to peer inside a cubicle, but a barrier in front of the compartment prevented him from seeing or hearing anything inside. He could make out the silhouettes of the avatars and nothing else.

Confident that there was nothing else to learn, he crossed the room toward the rows. When he was a foot away, a cubicle appeared in front of him so he could enter without breaking stride. CJ looked around. The compartment was several meters wide: more of a small room than a cubicle. It was far larger than should have been possible, considering its exterior. The room was completely white and bare except for a table with chairs on either side. The furniture was designed to look wooden, but the slight pixelation revealed its true nature. He bent over the table and focused until he could make out the ones and zeros.

Amazing, he thought, sitting down.

An avatar appeared opposite him and took the other seat. Like every other, its head was slightly rectangular and pixelated. This one, however, was dressed in a light-blue button-up shirt with sleeves folded up to his elbows.

It adjusted its glasses. "What are you searching for today?"

CJ was taken aback. He'd expected a menu or a search box that he could interact with, not dialogue. The avatar's voice was smooth and casual, making it the most normal thing about the avatar. The voice might have been a recording, but it was more likely the work of an AI. With the number of users Gaius catered to daily, an AI would be invaluable.

CJ wondered if it could be Helene. Helene was the most advanced AI on the planet and was affordable enough to be used in virtually every household. It was more than likely that Gaius employed the AI. If true, and this was a representation of Helene, then it would be too dangerous for CJ to use it. The avatar might alert her to his presence and location.

But then again, CJ thought, glancing back at the door he'd used to enter the room. *If it is, then she was probably aware the moment I stepped in here.* Ultimately, there was nothing he could do if Helene was already aware of him. He needed the information too much not to risk it. Plus, even if he tried another search engine, there was no guarantee Helene wasn't being used there too. Her reach was worldwide.

CJ returned his focus to the avatar. It hadn't said anything while he thought, content to wait patiently. It must have been an AI; a human would have long since become impatient. Before he answered, he thought back to his list of tasks. The memory came up quickly and easily.

CJ paused. *That was ... easy.*

He dismissed the memory and rubbed his fist against his pants leg. Normally, this would ground him, allowing him to focus his thoughts on the present. Now, he discovered that he didn't need to be grounded. His mind was already focused on what he needed to do. He called up the memory of the tasks once more. Again, it came to him perfectly. Previously, his memories had been like small pools scattered randomly around his mind. He'd had to search for the specific pool he needed while fighting his natural distractions. Now, everything was connected, arranged in a way that they had never been before.

What was this?

Even as the thought occurred, other memories came to him: times he'd spoken without stuttering, meeting the eye of one avatar when he'd tried to interact with it. Even when the avatar had bumped into him by the door, he hadn't flinched. He'd just taken it in stride. Several times, CJ had needed to break away from his thoughts and ground himself, but not because his brain found it difficult to focus. It was because he was amazed by his surroundings.

His mind spun. All the normal signs he showed as a result of his autism, everything he found irritating or difficult to do, were gone. His mind was clear in a way he'd never experienced. It responded with an ease he'd never felt.

Was this what it was like to be normal? Was this what normal people felt every day of their lives? This freedom?

"I'm cured," CJ whispered to himself. He didn't stutter. He didn't have to search for the words, gritting his teeth. He met the eyes of the Gaius avatar. It stared back patiently, not blinking. CJ waited for the discomfort, for the embarrassment, for the swell of emotions that heralded an episode. He waited and waited. But there was nothing.

CJ's chest tightened with emotions he couldn't identify. Instead of freezing up or tensing, his face twisted, shifting with each emotion. His eyes should have been watering, but of course, his virtual body couldn't produce tears. He was sure he would have been crying had he been in his real body.

His real body.

CJ's head shot up as realization struck him. He wasn't in his real body, and his virtual form didn't have the chemical imbalance that manifested his autistic traits. He hadn't been cured; he'd just found a loophole.

I'll take it! CJ thought, his eyes shining. If this was a way to experience life without his mind fighting him, to act without having to instruct his body through every step, to be normal, he'd be foolish not to enjoy it.

It took close to an hour for CJ to settle down. He spent several minutes speaking random words out loud, basking in the ease with which they came out. Then, he tried short sentences that usually gave him problems, then moved on to longer and longer sentences. The bulk of his time, however, was spent testing his memory by attempting to recall increasingly older data. The fact that he could differentiate which memories were recent and which were old almost sent him into another spiral. All his life, there'd never been any difference between what he'd just learned and what he'd learned long ago. If he was taught something that was later corrected or updated, it was hell to figure out which was correct.

He took several minutes to organize those facts in his head, attempting to imprint them as deeply as possible so he could retain them when he returned to his physical body. He had no doubt that his newfound freedom was only temporary. Therefore, he would try to maximize his time as much as he could and bend every inch of his new mind to achieving his goals.

CJ focused once more on the avatar. As if it could sense he was ready, it repeated, "What are you searching for today?"

A MINUTE LATER, CJ stepped out of the building. It hadn't occurred to him that the search engine would be able to provide only information about the material world. That was somewhat embarrassing. The only route available to him now, if he wanted to get information about the realm, was to explore it himself.

No part of CJ was disheartened by that.

Picking a direction at random, he stepped into the flow of traffic, marveling at the fact that he could do so without triggering an episode, and started on his quest.

"LET'S NOT JUMP to conclusions," DJ cautioned. "There are several less sinister reasons why Ndidi's phone could be turned off. You saw the shit that happened between her and Manar. She could have just wanted some privacy to unpack it all."

Hermione shook her head. "I thought about that. But why would she go to the edge of the state to do that? Why would she be in a warehouse?"

"Maybe someone stole her phone?" Christy suggested. "This is still New York, after all. If she was distressed, they might have seen her as an easy mark. The warehouse could be the thieves' hideout."

This time it was DJ who shook his head. "No New York thieves would forget to disable tracking before going back to their hideout. Even rookies aren't that stupid. Plus, no way some random kid gets the drop on Ndidi without her noticing."

"So, you understand my fear," Hermione said.

"We never dismissed your fears, but it's better to eliminate normal stuff first. Let's assume that Ndidi has been kidnapped and isn't drunk out of her mind and unconscious in a ditch somewhere. Are we treating it like a normal kidnapping or more of Helene's bullshit?"

"What's the difference?" Christy asked.

"Well, some random punks doing a kidnapping and Helene doing a kidnapping are two very different things. We tend to overthink everything related to Helene, and that was before she kidnapped one of us."

"It has to have been Helene," Hermione said. She'd calmed down somewhat but was still visibly distraught. "Ndidi would have found a way to channel whatever she was feeling into anger. And there's no way she would have been overpowered by thugs when she's angry."

"They could have swarmed her," DJ said. "If they had the numbers and attacked at once, having the better technique wouldn't matter."

"Pratima taught her how to handle multiple opponents," Hermione countered.

"That's another thing," Christy said, glancing at them both. "Where is Pratima? If anyone knows what happened to Ndidi, it's her. I don't think the woman has ever left Ndidi's side."

"Ndidi took me on a stroll to clear my head, and we walked to the Autism Centre. That's where we were when CJ's text came in. Pratima wasn't with us."

DJ started pacing again. He didn't know what to do. A part of him—an embarrassingly huge part—wanted to just ignore everything else and focus on how to save his brother. But he couldn't do that to Ndidi. He had to figure out a way to save all of them, preferably before they got killed, and without him getting killed in the process.

But how? There were too many things to consider. For one, he had to figure out what had gone wrong with CJ's and Manar's transfers. He didn't understand half of his brother's explanation, but Manar had seemed pretty confident the device would work. And if Manar Saleem had made a mistake in his programming, it was doubtful someone else would be able to spot it.

Another thing: it was far too fucking coincidental that Ndidi had been kidnapped the same day that two of their members had become indisposed. Had Helene planned it? Did she want them to sniff around for Ndidi and fall into some kind of trap? Almost definitely. What about—

DJ groaned loudly, startling Hermione. *Fuck this,* he thought. He could try to consider every possibility, but overthinking shit had always been his brother's turf, not his. CJ wasn't here to overthink things, nor was Manar. That didn't mean DJ had to sub for them. He'd watched the movies and listened to the songs. Trying to solve shit their way would ultimately backfire. It was the most cliché shit out there.

I'm going to do it my way, he thought. He tried to ignore how little confidence that brought him. He turned back to the girls to find they'd been staring at him.

Okay, that's weird, he thought.

"Here's what we're going to do," he declared. "We don't know how much time we have before things get worse, so we're going to move fast. Hermione, you mentioned you know someone you can call to check all this out." He gestured to the devices around the room. "Well, call them and vet them. Don't reveal anything that isn't absolutely necessary, and stay with them the entire time they're working. Maybe get a couple of guards too."

Hermione nodded. "I don't think the guards will be necessary. Chad's pretty harmless."

"Chad? The dude with the cowboy hat?" DJ asked, and Hermione nodded again. He'd met Chad shortly after running into Ndidi at the former headquarters of Gaius. The dude had helped them with their original attempt to take down Helene, a fiasco that was now known as the Data Bank Incident. Still, if it was Chad she was calling …

"Then don't worry about it," he told Hermione. "Ndidi needed his help for something related to Gaius, so he already has an overview of the plan. You can still have the guards just to be safe, but limit their number and make sure they're incognito."

Hermione shrugged. "Sure."

DJ turned to Christy. "I'm going to need you to find Pratima. Once you find her, tell her what's up, and get her story. With any luck, she'll have something we can use."

"Sure," Christy acknowledged. "What will you be up to?"

DJ sighed. "I'm going to look into Ndidi's disappearance. Maybe look through the security footage, check out the warehouse, and see what I can dig up. I'll talk to Chloe too—see if she can spare the old man." Christy frowned and started to say something, but DJ put up a hand. "I'm just going to ask. If she says no, I'll back off. We already have a backup, but that doesn't mean I'm not going to try. I owe it to my brother."

Christy's frown remained, but she didn't argue. "You should probably go to Olsen about Ndidi. He'll be able to help you search better."

"I don't want to involve Olsen unless necessary," DJ said. That had been his first thought, but he couldn't keep running to the admiral anytime he had a problem—especially since DJ would be putting Olsen in danger every time he contacted him. "He's already stuck his neck out for us more times than he had to. It'd be a dick move to repay him by bringing him to Helene's attention."

Christy glared at him. "He's a grown-ass man capable of making his own choices, D. If he wants to help, let him. He's one of the few people who understand how dangerous Helene is and isn't under her control already."

DJ frowned. "Yeah, but—"

"With three of our members indisposed, we don't have the luxury of picking and choosing who to call on. We definitely don't have anyone who can provide the kind of resources Olsen can. And we're going to need resources."

DJ recoiled, scratching the back of his head. "We have people—"

"Manar planned to use the buffed-up Gaius to run simulations of Helene's possible plans," Hermione interjected quietly. "For that to work, we need to know what she's up to. And since we can't communicate with CJ or Manar, Olsen might be the only one who can give us the updates we need—especially concerning world leaders."

Christy gestured at Hermione and narrowed her eyes at DJ. He'd seen the expression enough times to know that her next move would be to go for her gun. He held up his hands placatingly.

"Sheesh!" DJ said. "Fine! I'll set up a meeting. Cool your—"

Christy's eyes narrowed further, and she reached to her sidearm.

"… self." He chuckled awkwardly, aware of how close to death he'd come.

He cleared his throat, pointedly ignoring Christy's glare. "Anyway, I'll start working on my end. You guys can solve your tasks however you want. We'll meet up in a couple of days to discuss your progress."

IT WASN'T DIFFICULT FOR DJ to access Sparta's security footage. Most of the staff already knew he and Manar worked closely together, which was enough for them to defer to him. Off the top of his head, DJ could think of thirteen ways that he could abuse such power. Five of them he would have done immediately if his brother's life weren't on a deadline.

Still, it was something to consider after things settled down. *Whenever that is,* he thought idly. He was in one of the security rooms with a computer that he'd commandeered from the guard in charge. Each department had its own version of the room—and of the guard. Surprisingly, it had taken only half an hour for each department to send DJ the requested camera footage.

DJ clicked open the files and immediately realized how stupid he'd been. He was so used to the little section of the building he frequented that he'd forgotten how massive Sparta Headquarters was. It was the single largest structure in the country, with over ninety floors and dozens of departments. And he'd asked for all their recordings. In the first few seconds, hundreds of thousands of recordings loaded on the screen, and they just kept coming. DJ scrolled through the list. It took him over fifteen minutes to get to the end.

"Fuck me," he groaned.

He filtered his search to the last few days. When that still brought thousands of results, he narrowed it again to the floor with Manar's office and Ndidi's room. Even then, there were hundreds of files to go through.

DJ's T-shirt didn't have sleeves to roll up, but he felt the motion was apt, so he mimed it anyway.

DJ LEANED BACK in his chair and released a long, drawn-out sigh. He'd gone through hours of footage. Most of it had been empty hallways occasionally passed through by staff members going about their business. The most exciting thing DJ had seen was a couple making out in the hall on Ndidi's floor for a few minutes before slipping into a room. After that, it had been several hours of mind-numbing monotony that, even played at double speed, had gone on for far too long.

But he was done—for the most part, at least. He'd left Ndidi's room for last, as it was the most likely place to contain actual clues.

The only camera in the room was strategically placed to avoid any blind spots. DJ set the recording to play at double speed and leaned back in his chair. Like the hundreds of clips before, the room was empty for the most part. Ndidi stayed at Sparta only when she started working on a plan to beat Helene. The rest of her free time was spent at the Autism Centre. Without the Centre's footage, DJ had only half the picture. Still, he forced himself to keep watching. If he didn't find anything when he was done, he would see about heading to the Centre, though getting the tapes there might not be as easy. He grimaced.

The minutes flew by. As the recordings got more recent, Ndidi started appearing in her room more often. The dates coincided with when Manar had told them about his plan to go after Helene, so it made sense. At some point, however, Ndidi stopped leaving her room altogether. CJ came to visit her during this time, as did Manar. But Ndidi greeted them both at the door and returned to her bed.

Did I miss something? DJ wondered. He rewound the recording by a couple of days and slowed its speed. After watching it a second time, DJ frowned. *What happened here?* He rewound the recording again, and slowed its speed even more.

Ndidi had just walked into the room and was sitting on her bed when her phone buzzed. She checked the message and froze. A few seconds went by, then she looked over her shoulder and around the room as if searching for something. Her eyes passed over the camera without a flicker. DJ already knew the surveillance device was concealed.

Satisfied with her survey, Ndidi stared at her phone again, but her eyes had glazed over as if she were lost in thought. A few more seconds passed like this before her expression firmed and she shot off a reply. She waited, checking her phone every few seconds. Ndidi got several texts over the next two days, but it was obvious none were the one she was waiting for because her expression grew more frustrated. She left her room only once during that time. DJ tracked her to the gym and back through security footage.

Finally, her phone buzzed again, and Ndidi's whole body froze. She stared at her phone for several minutes, presumably at the text she had been waiting for. This time, however, her expression suggested she was conflicted. She didn't send a reply.

Nothing happened for the rest of that day. DJ sped up the footage several times until the time stamp on the recording corresponded to when CJ had started the procedure on Manar.

Ndidi entered her room, almost choking on her tears. She slumped on her bed, and her entire body shook with the force of her sobs. For a moment, DJ felt guilty, as if he were intruding. He doubled the speed for a few seconds. When he returned it to normal again, Ndidi was reaching for her phone to check a text.

DJ assumed it was Hermione texting to inform her of Manar's condition. He watched her expression flicker between concern and fear, before hardening into determination. Her fingers moved over her keypad. Hermione said Ndidi had never replied to her, so DJ assumed the text had gone to her mystery contact. Her phone buzzed again. Moments later, the woman was out the door.

DJ fast-forwarded the footage, but Ndidi never came back. He leaned back in his chair and released another sigh, this one tinged with a different kind of exhaustion.

What the hell have you gotten into, Ndidi?

THE CONFERENCE ROOM was silent as the recording played on the built-in projector. DJ had edited the footage, removing everything that wasn't relevant. Christy watched the recording with a distant expression. She was the newest member of the team and wasn't particularly close to any of them except for DJ.

Hermione leaned forward in her seat, her expression switching between emotions so fast that DJ found it difficult to parse. There was hurt—lots and lots of hurt.

The video ended as Ndidi received the mysterious text and left her room. DJ had tried several times to zoom in on her phone when the text came in, but the angles weren't right. Unless they retrieved the phone—or Ndidi herself—the person on the other end of the text would remain a mystery.

"So," DJ said when no one spoke for a minute, "thoughts?" He tried to direct the question at both women, but Hermione was really the only one it could have been for.

She didn't reply immediately, staring at the paused video frame. DJ wondered what was going on in her head. Had she known about it? DJ didn't think so. She'd seemed surprised at the recording, and DJ didn't think she could have faked that.

"You think Helene somehow contacted Ndidi? Maybe she didn't tell us so she could make a deal with her in secret?" Hermione asked finally, meeting his eyes. When DJ didn't say anything, her voice grew louder. "Ndidi wouldn't do that. I know her. She would have told me if Helene had contacted her. And she would've told Manar, too, so we could come up with a plan. I mean, she told us when she saw Bethany a couple days back—"

"Wait, she saw Bethany?" DJ asked, leaning forward. "How? Bethany's dead."

This was the last thing he'd expected. DJ didn't know much about Bethany except that she was the reason Ndidi was so motivated to work against Helene. And Ndidi had seen her again after three years?

Hermione shook her head, her eyes moistening. "Bethany was never actually confirmed dead. She went missing during Mayday. We tried everything to find her. We never could, so we assumed she was lost forever, like everyone else who vanished that day."

"But Ndidi saw her?" DJ confirmed.

Hermione nodded. She went on to explain how Ndidi had barged into her lab while she was with Manar, claiming to have seen Bethany. Manar had seemed to believe her, but he'd also thought it was likely Helene had been using Bethany to lure Ndidi away.

"Well, mystery solved then," Christy said. "Helene probably asked her to kill or disable Manar in some way and promised to release this Bethany girl in return. Ndidi sabotaged the equipment, trapping Manar, went to collect her prize, and got nabbed for it."

"Ndidi wouldn't do that," Hermione argued. "She wouldn't betray us like that."

DJ saw where Hermione was coming from. Ndidi would never have betrayed them … except when Bethany was involved. DJ knew that Ndidi held a tremendous amount of guilt and rage over what had happened to Bethany. That's what motivated her to risk her life against Helene time and time again. And that was when she'd thought that Bethany was dead.

If Helene had promised Ndidi a way to get Bethany back, she would take it, even if only to assuage her guilt. It was the same choice he probably would have made if it meant getting his dads back. Manar would have made the same choice if it meant getting his mother back. Hermione, too, for her parents; Christy, for her family. Every single team member strove to defeat Helene for their own selfish reasons. It was understandable.

But that didn't stop DJ from being angry with Ndidi. Because of her choice, his brother lay in a coma from which they had no way of waking him. He understood her motivations and might have done the same thing, but that did nothing to assuage his anger. DJ could lose the only family he had left because Ndidi had chosen to be selfish. Not only had she fallen into the trap like an absolute dumbass, but now he had to rescue her from her own mistakes.

A part of DJ wanted to let her rot, to let Helene do whatever she wanted with her. But that part was minor. Even though Ndidi had fucked up, DJ would rather rescue her so he could yell at her in person. Plus, there was always a chance Helene would use Ndidi against them in the future. They needed to nip that in the bud.

"Yes, she would," DJ replied, cutting Hermione off. He didn't even realize she'd been speaking. He spent a minute explaining his reasoning, and the conclusion he'd reached. Christy just shrugged when he was done, but Hermione was full-on sobbing.

"No, no, this is a good thing," DJ said, wide-eyed. He glanced at Christy, but she looked just as confused as he was. "We're going to rescue Ndidi. And Bethany, if we can."

"I know," Hermione sobbed. "It's just … I'd given up hope of ever seeing my sister again. I dismissed Ndidi when she said Bethany was alive because I didn't think I could bear having my hope crushed. But Ndidi never stopped believing. She was willing to sacrifice herself to get Bethany, while I was content to do nothing."

"Oh." What was he supposed to say to that? Was he supposed to console her, tell her that she wasn't a bad sister? It kind of seemed like she was. Unless he saw a corpse, DJ would go to the ends of the earth to find CJ. Yet Hermione had buried an empty coffin and moved on.

DJ reconsidered, watching the sobbing woman. It was obvious that Hermione hadn't moved on and that she still cared for Bethany, just maybe not as much as Ndidi did. No, that was still harsh. True, but harsh.

He looked at Christy for advice, but she was glaring at him even though he hadn't done anything.

In the end, DJ didn't have to do anything. Hermione's sobs subsided until they stopped altogether. She wiped her eyes with a handkerchief and looked up. Her eyes blazed like fire. DJ leaned back, surprised. Her anger seemed almost at Ndidi's level. What in the mother of all mood swings was this?

"Uh, Hermione?" DJ said.

"Helene took Bethany away from me for years," Hermione said, her voice soft, breaking with emotion. "She kidnapped my sister. Probably controlled her with the technology my father created. And now she's using her as bait." She paused and took a breath, closing her eyes. "She took my sister and killed my parents." She opened her eyes, and her anger was still there. It simmered below the surface, soaking her voice as she spoke. "I won't let her take anyone else from me."

DJ waited for a second, then cleared his throat. "That's, uh, good … because I don't intend to let her."

"You're going to meet Olsen?" Christy asked, a gleam in her eye like she expected him to say no.

"Yeah," DJ replied. "As I said, it's a whole different ball game when Helene's involved, and we can't afford half measures. I doubt Helene took Ndidi just to get her out of the way. That'd be too simple." He paused to soak in the tension that had descended upon the room. "She has something long term planned. With CJ and Manar dealing with her from the inside, it's up to us to take care of her from here."

9

NDIDI WOKE UP TO DARKNESS, struggling to remember where she was. She tested each part of her body for injuries. Her limbs were sore, which she attributed to just waking up. Her knuckles ached, and although Ndidi felt like they'd split, she didn't think it was anything serious. She continued testing, noticing that her throat was sore, like she'd been shouting for hours. Her eyes felt puffy, and her cheeks were crusted over with something, though she didn't feel any injuries there.

Next, she felt for clues. The ground was cold and rang hollow when she moved around. It pinged when she tapped it. Metal. Like a cage.

With that realization came the memories. Standing in Manar's office with the others. Kissing Manar. Going to her room. Hermione's text. Helene's text. Her capture. Each image was a hammer to her head, piercing through the fog in her mind. But the memory of Hermione's text kept coming back until Ndidi remembered every detail. She could picture it.

"Manar's in a coma," she whispered. The words echoed around the cage, mocking her. And didn't she deserve to be mocked? Earlier, she'd stopped herself from feeling anything about the news. She'd hardened her mind to give herself the courage to do what needed to be done and to text Helene.

But she'd failed. She'd bet everything on a chance, and she'd failed. Manar was in a coma, she'd been captured by Helene, and she still hadn't saved Bethany. She'd failed, and her naivety put her at the AI's mercy. If that wasn't worth mocking, Ndidi didn't know what was.

Now that she could think, Ndidi felt the box moving. No way to know how long she'd been moving. She could have been anywhere, and there was nothing she could do about it.

But that doesn't mean I should just give in.

Ndidi's jaw set. A familiar, self-directed anger rose within her. She'd brought this on herself, but that didn't mean she was helpless to stop it. She couldn't depend on someone coming to save her. For one, nobody knew where she'd gone. For another, there was no guarantee the team would want to rescue her—especially if they found out that she'd made a deal with Helene.

No. She couldn't depend on being rescued. The fact that Helene hadn't killed her on the spot meant she had a plan for her. She had said she would reunite Ndidi with Bethany. Ndidi took that to mean that wherever she was being taken, Bethany would be there. It also meant that whatever Helene wanted, it involved them both. If she could, Ndidi would try to get the AI to reveal her plan, but Ndidi might not be able to wait that long.

Still, the fact that Helene needed them for something was bound to provide an opportunity if Ndidi was patient. And she would be if it meant escaping with Bethany. When she did escape, there was no way she was leaving without her ward.

With that in mind, her eyes simmering with rage, Ndidi settled down to wait.

SOMETIME LATER, the cage stopped moving. A few moments passed in silence. Then, Ndidi's cage opened, starting from above like a blooming flower. Ndidi poked her head out cautiously, looking around.

Her eyes landed on a drone hovering several feet away, and her breath caught in her throat. It was similar to the one she'd encountered at the Sparta data bank, and again at Sparta's underground base. The barrel of its gun was pointed right at her. Ndidi stepped first to the left and then to the right. The barrel followed her both times.

Still moving slowly, Ndidi stepped fully out of the cage. She was just a few feet from the drone, close enough to grab it if she lunged fast enough. But the machine didn't react to the threat. Perhaps it didn't see her as a threat. And she wasn't. Not until she found Bethany anyway.

Ndidi was somewhat confident that the drone was there as a power move, but she still kept one eye on it while she looked around.

The room was massive. A bulb hung far above, bright enough to illuminate most of it. Several tunnels were interspersed along the walls, all leading into darkness. She ignored them for now. Musky air told her that she was underground, although she had no way of telling how deep she was. Apart from her cage and the drone, the room was largely empty so Ndidi couldn't get much from it.

She waited for something to change. Helene had moved her here for a reason, and Ndidi doubted it was so she could wander this one room. Several minutes later, her patience was rewarded. The arrows painted on the floor of one of the tunnels started glowing, leading deeper into the underground system. The drone woke up at the same time and drifted closer. Ndidi got the message and followed the arrows down the tunnel. The pathway was large enough for three people to walk side by side. The walls were far too smooth to be natural. The whole thing reminded Ndidi far too much of the underground base, where they'd had to fight the swarm of drones.

No, she corrected herself, where DJ and Christy had fought a swarm of drones. Ndidi had been largely useless in that fight.

The tunnels branched several times, and Ndidi followed the arrows through twists and turns. She tried to keep the layout in her mind but gave up after the fifth branch. With the drone following behind her, she didn't dare try to leave any marks she could follow later.

Finally, the trail of arrows ended, leaving Ndidi in front of a thick metal door. She reached for the handle, but it opened on its own. Although there was barely enough light in the next room, it was easy to tell this one was considerably smaller than the last. She took a step inside and paused at the sound of someone scrambling to their feet.

"Who's there?" a familiar voice called—a voice Ndidi hadn't heard in years. A voice she thought she'd never hear again.

Bethany.

Ndidi's eyes watered. She almost rushed in then, to follow the voice and embrace her ward, but she stopped herself. She couldn't begin to imagine what the girl had been through over the last few years. Bethany might panic if she saw a strange person rushing toward her. Ndidi would have to take it slow.

"It's just me, Bethany," Ndidi replied with a comforting smile, stepping into the room. "It's Ndidi."

There was silence for a few moments, and Ndidi's heart almost stopped as a new thought occurred to her. *Would she even remember me?*

Her fear was quickly dispelled when she heard the patter of feet on the ground. A shape emerged from the darkness and slammed into her. Ndidi took a step back to steady herself and held Bethany as she sobbed into her chest. Her own eyes watered, and she sank to her knees, still clutching Bethany.

Ndidi didn't know how long the two of them stayed like that, and she didn't care. Even after their tears had dried, they continued to hold each other. Bethany was muttering something into Ndidi's chest, but it was some time before Ndidi became aware of it. She drew Bethany away gently so she could make out the words.

"I'm sorry," Bethany said, clutching Ndidi's clothes. "I'm sorry. I'm sorry." The words were repeated over and over as her sobs renewed, becoming an unintelligible mess.

Ndidi held the girl at arm's length so she could look into her eyes. She placed a finger under her chin and lifted her head until their eyes met. Only when Ndidi was sure she had Bethany's full attention did she speak.

"You have nothing to be sorry for." Ndidi's tone was soft but firm, the same type she used when instructing the children at the Centre. "You've done nothing wrong. If anything, I'm the one who failed you by taking so long."

Bethany shook her head, her expression torturous. "If not for me, you wouldn't have been captured. Helene used me, and I couldn't do anything to stop it. I couldn't stop it." The last part was said in between sobs.

Ndidi's heart broke, but her anger spiked as well. "You can't blame yourself because it isn't your fault. It's Helene's fault. She's the cause of everything."

And we're going to make her pay for it, Ndidi wanted to add. But that would be reckless. Helene was already aware they planned on destroying her, of course. There was no need to provoke it without cause.

Bethany didn't say anything, so Ndidi fell silent too, offering her the comfort she needed. They stayed like that for several minutes more. Ndidi used the time to study the room. She'd been partially right about the size. It was small, though not as small as Ndidi had envisioned. She estimated it to be a little over a dozen feet across. It was also empty, without even a bedroll to sleep on.

Ndidi's anger spiked again. This was where Bethany had been living for years while Ndidi had been enjoying every luxury. She rubbed her hand over the girl's clothes, finally noticing the dirt and grime that clung to her. Ndidi was sure Bethany hadn't been so filthy on the day she'd glimpsed her in the street. Even if, in her shock, Ndidi had somehow missed it, Bethany had escaped her by blending into the crowd. She wouldn't have been able to do that with such a ripe smell.

That meant Helene had cleaned her up to lure Ndidi, then had abandoned her in her filth again, Ndidi realized with horror. Her hands clenched into fists as her blood boiled in her veins. Adrenaline flooded through her, urging her to do something, anything, to right the wrong.

Ndidi almost stood, but growing up as the sole heir to Eze Okafor had taught her how to ignore those impulses. Since her parents' deaths, Ndidi had learned more about controlling her anger than at any other point in her life.

Bethany shifted, drawing Ndidi's attention and reminding her of how much more she had to lose. The girl grounded her, and Ndidi slowly calmed. Logic asserted itself. Even if she could do something, without a plan, any action would satisfy her only in the short term. Worse, it would blow any chance she had of escaping. Bethany would remain trapped. That was unacceptable. Her body still urged her to move, to rage. Damn the consequences. Ndidi channeled that energy toward forming a plan capable of beating Helene. Manar wasn't here to provide insider knowledge on Helene's capabilities, DJ wasn't here to suggest tactics, CJ wasn't here to balance his brother's enthusiasm with logic, and Hermione wasn't here to add her insights. She was alone. But as she'd reminded herself earlier, she wasn't helpless.

After years of working against her, Ndidi probably knew just as much about Helene as Manar. She didn't have DJ's experience in combat, but she would probably fail if she relied on fighting her way out. She'd mentored CJ for years and knew enough about his thought process to guess his responses. As for Hermione … well, even though their fields were different, Ndidi was an accomplished researcher in her own right.

Still, she couldn't do much without information. This meant it was time to have the conversation she'd been avoiding. Bethany had calmed down, and her breathing was even. Ndidi shook her lightly without response.

She hasn't cried herself to sleep since she was ten, Ndidi thought. Gently, she adjusted Bethany into a more comfortable position and tucked a piece of hair away from the girl's face. *Well,* Ndidi reconsidered, *not so much a girl anymore.* Bethany would be twenty-eight later that year. Ndidi would make sure she didn't celebrate the milestone in the dark room. The questions could wait until later.

NDIDI WOKE UP with aches all over her body. When had she fallen asleep? Her back rested against the wall, which poked at her with its rough texture. Fortunately, this time it didn't take her long to remember where she was. Bethany's head was still cradled on her lap, but her eyes were open.

Ndidi remembered the conversation she wanted to have—the question she needed answered—and her lips thinned into a line. Now that Bethany was awake, Ndidi couldn't put it off again. Yet reasons to delay still came to her mind. Several of them even made sense.

"Bethany," Ndidi said softly. In the silence of the room, it almost sounded like a shout. Ndidi attributed Bethany's flinch to that. She continued, choosing her words carefully. "Do you ever leave here?"

Bethany stilled, and Ndidi almost stopped. She should be reassuring the girl and providing comfort, not forcing her to dredge up memories. But Ndidi needed to know. Not just for her own sake but for Bethany's too. And so, even though the guilt threatened to overwhelm her, Ndidi pressed.

"I mean, are you ever allowed out of this room? Out of this complex and into the city?"

Ndidi knew the answer, of course—she'd seen Bethany above ground, after all—but she wanted to know if Bethany herself could remember. The girl didn't say anything for a while, and Ndidi was content to wait. A part of her hoped she wouldn't answer at all. But finally, after several minutes, Bethany gave a small, jerky nod.

Ndidi felt a stab in her chest but forced herself to continue. "What do you—" She cleared her throat. "What do you do during those times? Do you remember?"

Again, Bethany nodded. "We don't always remember," she said softly. "But when we do, it's only when we come back here, never when we're outside."

That confirms it then, Ndidi thought. *She's being controlled.* Helene probably deactivated Bethany's picospores when she didn't need her and reactivated them whenever she did. Memories flashed in Ndidi's mind, replays of the experiment Hermione had done on the rats after injecting them with picospores.

She recoiled at the image.

Ndidi had known it was likely—hell, practically inevitable. But she had hoped—no, forced—herself to believe there was a chance. Helene hadn't needed to control Bethany to bait Ndidi. After Mayday, she would have done anything just for the chance to see Bethany. Ndidi couldn't imagine how scared she must have been. What trauma had she been subjected to? And she'd been used like that for years …

Ndidi leaned against the wall, closing her eyes with a sigh. She'd expected to be angry at the revelation, to tire herself out raging against Helene. She'd also imagined herself spending hours consoling Bethany, ensuring the girl was fine and doing what she could to fix whatever trauma she'd experienced. What she hadn't expected was the sudden weariness that washed over her. It was like she'd hit rock bottom. Everything she'd been afraid of had happened. She still had pity for what Bethany had gone through and anger at Helene. And she was still determined to fix both. But in that moment, she was just so tired. Suddenly, she understood how Manar must have felt.

She replayed Bethany's words, and her eyes snapped open. "We?" she asked, staring down at the girl. "Who's *we*?"

Bethany shifted in Ndidi's lap to meet her gaze. "The other people who were kidnapped."

Ndidi sat bolt upright, exhaustion suddenly forgotten. She helped Bethany up, and the girl sat cross-legged in front of her.

"What people?" Ndidi asked, her voice tinged with horror. She'd known others had disappeared on Mayday; roughly a third of all the estimated victims had gone missing. But like most people, Ndidi had assumed those people had died, their bodies not found. That's what she had assumed of Bethany.

She'd hoped otherwise, of course, but until she saw Bethany at the Centre, a part of Ndidi had accepted Bethany was dead. And when she'd confirmed that Bethany was alive, it hadn't occurred to her that every other missing person could be too. *What does that say about me?*

"How many people?" Ndidi asked.

"I don't know," Bethany said. "There's usually twenty here, but some of the others have seen other places with more people. But none of them remember where those places are."

Twenty? Ndidi thought.

"Where are the others now?" she asked. "The others that are normally here?"

Bethany looked away, uncomfortable. Ndidi was confused until she actually thought about what she'd just asked. She already had an idea of what Bethany did when she was allowed outside, so she could guess what the other people were doing.

"Are they spying on their loved ones?" Ndidi asked. "Luring them to Helene?"

Bethany still looked uncomfortable, and Ndidi became conflicted. Should she keep pressing? The girl was obviously reluctant to speak about it, and Ndidi couldn't blame her. More than likely, Bethany had been forced to do the same thing. She should back off, at least for a while. With some patience, the people would come back, and Ndidi could get answers without overburdening her.

She was about to withdraw her question when Bethany replied. "They're not spying so Helene can kidnap them." Ndidi could almost hear the unspoken part: *Like I did with you.* "Helene controls us while we're in the city to get information about people. Sometimes it is about loved ones, but it can be anyone."

Ndidi grimaced. So, Helene had her own personal network of informants. People that could blend into a crowd and slip in anywhere. The thought was sickening. Helene was already globally popular, so she already had a wide reach. Yet she ruined people's lives just to make that reach even wider.

Briefly, Ndidi's mind flashed to the rats in Hermione's experiment and how rigidly they moved when controlled. Yet when she'd first seen her, Bethany had moved normally. Was it possible that Helene had fine-tuned her technique enough that her puppets behaved like real people?

That would make it harder to figure out who's controlled and who isn't, Ndidi thought, *especially when Hermione is done with her device.*

Bethany was staring at her, so Ndidi dismissed the thought for later.

"What does Helene use this information to do?" she asked.

The girl shrugged. But then her eyes suddenly sharpened, and she stared at Ndidi intently. Her expression was just short of a glare. "Helene said that you and some other people were an obstacle. She said what you've done is futile, but she still wants to stop you guys."

Ndidi chuckled without humor. *What we've been doing is futile? That sounds about right.* So far, they hadn't done anything that didn't somehow play into Helene's plans. Even destroying her central mainframe had been useless. The only thing that Helene had seemed even remotely concerned about was Manar transferring his consciousness to the internet. Ndidi still didn't know how Helene had known about that plan, but if she hadn't been concerned, then why had she asked Ndidi to interfere?

Their actions hadn't made much of an impact so far, but that didn't mean their effort was being wasted. Most people didn't know the danger that Helene posed. Among those who did, half of them didn't care and the others were under the AI's control. Their efforts might have seemed pointless from Helene's perspective, but every move they made that even indirectly harmed her plans was worth it. Helene couldn't be allowed to do what she wanted; Mayday was already proof of that. But Ndidi couldn't burden Bethany with all that, not when she'd already faced enough.

"Yeah," Ndidi finally replied. "Me, your sister, and some of my friends are trying to stop Helene, and soon she'll be gone forever."

Ndidi winced, bracing herself. Mentioning Hermione had been a slip of the tongue. She'd deliberately stayed away from the topic of Bethany's family so she wouldn't be forced to lie to her. Part of her expected Bethany to jump at the chance to know more about her sister. Instead, she just looked conflicted. Ndidi frowned.

"What would happen to the picospores inside me?" Bethany asked.

How do you know what they're called? Ndidi thought. Helene could have mentioned it, of course, but that required a level of conversation between the two that Ndidi hadn't expected. Nor was it one she was comfortable with. She pushed the thought aside as something to be pondered later.

"We're already working on a way to remove the spores," Ndidi said, trying to keep her voice comforting. "Once Helene is gone, they won't be a problem anymore."

Again, Ndidi expected joy, excitement, or hope. And again, Bethany just looked conflicted. Ndidi's brows furrowed.

"Is there a problem?" she asked softly. "I thought you'd be excited."

"I am excited," Bethany said, but she looked away. "I would love to have my mind back more than anything. It's just … I don't think I'm ready to go back to struggling with my words, struggling with my memories, or fighting my own body and being uncomfortable all the time."

Ndidi frowned. "What are you talking about?"

Bethany met her eyes again and held them meaningfully. "Haven't you figured it out yet? My autism … it's gone. I'm fixed."

JUNE 2043

CORONADO, CALIFORNIA

DJ SAT AT A CORNER BOOTH, facing the restaurant door. Casually, he scanned the room. It was a quaint little place, and out of the way enough that it was quiet during the lunch hour. Olsen had picked the restaurant, and DJ had arrived early to scope it out. He liked and trusted Olsen, but he hadn't seen him in months. A lot could have happened since then.

A bell by the door dinged, and Olsen walked in. The admiral wore a polo shirt tucked into a pair of shorts. Olsen scanned the restaurant for a few seconds before spotting DJ, who'd placed a hand over his mouth to cover his laughter.

"I see you're still a little prick," Olsen grunted, taking the seat opposite him.

"Normally I'd have a retort." DJ chuckled, rubbing a tear away. "But it'd be kicking a man while he's down."

"Piece of shit," Olsen muttered. "Why don't you tell me what you want so we can get on with our lives? I'm missing my son's ball game for this."

"Based on how you're dressed, I'm guessing you're the coach?"

Olsen glowered, turning a familiar shade of red. DJ raised his hands in surrender and tried to compose himself. He made fun, but the admiral was one of the few people DJ respected. And his outfit wasn't that bad. Olsen was built like a bull; his arms threatened to rip apart his shirt. DJ would have made fun of him regardless of what he'd worn.

"Funny," Olsen said. He flagged down a passing server and placed an order for both of them. His expression wasn't as severe as it normally was, and his face bore a level of exhaustion that hadn't been there before.

When he wasn't yelling, Olsen looked like a wise old man—at least, that's what DJ had been told. Personally, he'd never thought of him as old in any way. Olsen's presence had always screamed vitality. However, the deep lines around the admiral's face told a different story. That was enough to sober DJ up.

"Hey, before we get to my stuff … you doing okay?"

Olsen peered at him suspiciously, then snorted. "You actually sound like you give a rat's ass."

"Well, you look like shit," DJ replied. "If the reason's something I can replicate, I'd like to know it."

"You little shit." Olsen glared at DJ, but there was no heat in it. "I should have let Bradley have you. A demotion and a few years cleaning toilets would've taught you respect."

"Bradley was a dick," DJ said. "Plus, I was a recruit then. I couldn't have been demoted any lower without being discharged."

The waiter came with their order. DJ bit into his burger while Olsen took a swig of his drink.

"Lord knows my life would have been easier without your bullshit," Olsen said.

"You would have died of boredom, and you know it," DJ countered. Olsen took another swig but didn't say anything else for a while. DJ glanced over his own drink, allowing the silence to drag.

Olsen started talking a minute later. "Earlier this month, the top brass of the government decided to integrate AI software into their programs to make them more efficient. The AI would be heavily regulated, of course. The change affects all the arms of government, not just a few."

DJ stared in horror. "And they chose Helene."

"Of course they chose Helene," Olsen said. "She's the best artificial intelligence in the world."

"And the part about her being a mass murderer?" DJ asked, lowering his voice.

"That was never confirmed, remember? The idiots are using a team of Sparta-trained experts as watchdogs to prevent another Mayday." Olsen snorted bitterly. "As if that's going to do anything. The change has only been live for a few weeks, and I already feel like I'm constantly being watched."

The admiral leaned closer, lowering his voice as well. "Something's not right about the whole thing. There's always been talk about using AI for stuff. A few years back, it seemed inevitable. But Mayday wasn't all that long ago, and those deaths are still fresh in people's minds. So, what in the hell would make them think it's a good idea to give an AI run of the entire US government?"

Picospore-controlled puppets in the government, DJ kept himself from saying. He had shared with Olsen a few months ago that his team had concluded that Helene was using picospores to mind-control people, but he needed to give Hermione more time before bringing up the topic again.

"Fuck." He sighed. "That explains why you didn't argue when I suggested we meet off base. The whole place must already be bugged to hell and back."

Olsen took another swig of his drink. "So, you ready to tell me what's so urgent?"

"Helene kidnapped Ndidi." DJ had gone back and forth about how much to reveal before finally settling on giving only the pertinent facts relating to Ndidi. He told Olsen about how they'd found out about the kidnapping, showed him the edited video of the camera recordings, and explained their theory.

Olsen listened quietly, his face becoming clouded. "Sounds like she's flipped sides," he said when DJ had finished.

"It does sound like that," DJ agreed, "but I'm hoping it's just temporary madness. Bethany was the reason Ndidi joined us in the first place, and why she was so motivated to get revenge. When I think about it logically, I kind of get it. But logic's never been my strong suit. I want to hear it from Ndidi directly."

"Fair enough," Olsen grunted. "What do you need to get her back?"

DJ leaned over the table. "See, that's where you come in."

NDIDI STARED AT THE GIRL. "What do you mean you're fixed?"

The answer came to her as she asked. She noted the way Bethany met her eyes and the way she spoke fluidly without halting to search for words. They'd held each other, touching for several minutes, and Bethany had felt so comfortable that she'd fallen asleep. Several times during their conversation, Ndidi had been able to tell what Bethany was feeling because her expression had shown it easily and openly, not freezing up. Bethany no longer showed the autistic traits she had before.

How had Ndidi missed it? Even more important, how was it possible? Helene was the first name that came to mind. It was only logical, after all, since Bethany had been under her care for the last few years. But Ndidi found it hard to believe that even Helene could casually solve a mental puzzle that most of the medical world had been trying to figure out for decades—the same puzzle to which Ndidi had dedicated most of her life.

Her next thought was that Helene had taken control of Bethany at some point in their conversation and was puppeteering the girl to deceive her. But she couldn't find the logic in that. Why would Helene want Ndidi to believe she'd somehow found a way to fix the autism traits in people on the spectrum? Why would Helene care? As long as they both remained kidnapped and the AI still had control of Bethany, she had to know Ndidi would do whatever she wanted. It didn't make sense that the AI would go through something so convoluted.

Still, Ndidi studied Bethany, trying to spot any sign of Helene's influence. There were subtle things in her posture and mannerisms that were different from how Ndidi remembered them, but it had been almost four years since she'd last seen Bethany. Differences were to be expected. Additionally, Ndidi's memories were of a girl who was still showing autistic traits, which Bethany no longer did, it seemed. Ndidi had no basis to quantify the result of such changes.

Despite that, Ndidi wanted to believe that she would know if Helene was puppeteering the girl. And she didn't think that was the case now. She observed Bethany, who had waited patiently while Ndidi went through her mental hoops. Another thing the Bethany of the past wouldn't have been able to do.

"How?" Ndidi asked.

"I first noticed it when my memory got better," Bethany said, her voice low. She didn't meet Ndidi's eyes anymore, instead staring at the far wall as if ashamed. "I needed to remember so I could keep track of the days I was under Helene's control. So I knew how much time I'd lost. At some point, I noticed I didn't have to dig through as thoroughly as before. I could actually tell how old a memory was. After that, I started noticing that my speech was better, and I didn't have to think so much to know what I wanted to say, even when I was talking to myself."

Bethany let out a humorless chuckle. "I didn't know what to feel at first. I knew Helene was responsible for it. I just didn't know how." She shrugged, still looking away. "So, I asked. Helene said she didn't cure me. Apparently, there's an imbalance in our brains, something messed up with the GABA receptors. Helene directed the picospores to fix it." She took a breath, and her tone grew bitter. "My reset brain is more efficient and better able to perform the task she sets for me."

Ndidi cursed herself for pushing her. What trauma had Ndidi forced Bethany to remember? How much damage had her question caused? Ndidi wanted to comfort her, but what would she say? What would anyone say to that? There were no platitudes that would suddenly make everything better. The bitterness in Bethany's tone showed that she knew it too. Her last sentence had sounded like a direct quote, one that Ndidi could imagine coming from Helene. Helene thought of Bethany as nothing more than a tool. What could Ndidi say that would suddenly make that better?

There were no right words, so Ndidi didn't try. Instead, she pulled Bethany into a hug and tried to communicate what she could with that.

The tears came soon after. Despite the obvious pain Bethany was going through, Ndidi couldn't help but marvel that she could do that without triggering an episode. Naturally, she pondered the implications of everything she'd heard.

She and Hermione had theorized that the picospores had the potential to do exactly what Bethany said they did. But it was just that: a theory. Now, in Bethany, they had a case study. If they could find out exactly what Helene had done, Hermione could replicate it to form a viable treatment for autism, one that would last throughout a person's life.

That would be staggering. The number of lives that could be helped by such a treatment would be immeasurable. Children born with autistic traits would no longer have to grow up believing they're abnormal or somehow less than others. People like Bethany and CJ would no longer have problems communicating.

Autism was not the only problem caused by a chemical imbalance in the brain. If the picospores could be used for other similar conditions … Ndidi couldn't even begin to imagine how that would revolutionize the world.

Bethany sat up, drying her tears with the edge of her sleeve. "I'm sorry for that," she said, gesturing to the wet stains on Ndidi's shirt. "That's why I no longer have the autism episodes."

"But if the imbalance is fixed, we should still be able to remove the pico—"

Bethany shook her head. "According to Helene, it only works as long as the picospores are activated. If they're removed, I'll revert back." She smiled bitterly. "I'm cured, but only while I'm under her control."

It was a double-edged sword. The picospores were only dangerous because of Helene. For now, only Helene knew how to use the spores well enough to be used as a treatment. Once Ndidi found a way out, she and Hermione could run some tests, but it could be a decade before they had a working cure. Meanwhile, Helene already had a working technique. If they could somehow force the information out of her, they could potentially save decades of work.

It could work, Ndidi thought. *But not if we destroy Helene.*

MARTIN STRAIGHTENED from the table, rolling his wheelchair back. He adjusted his glasses, then pulled them off entirely. He wiped the lenses on his shirt while he pondered the results. Liz lay on the table in front of him, unconscious. Martin had needed to draw several pints of blood to run his experiments. Since every pint he drew removed nanites, Liz had become too weak. It was fortunate that she was a willing participant. Otherwise, Karla would no doubt have killed him several times over the last few days.

He reached beside him for his notes. There weren't any tests he could run while Liz recovered. If he was right, he didn't need to. It had been a simple thing to isolate the nanites from her blood and even easier to extrapolate the number in her bloodstream. But those were the little victories he'd expected. The hard part came with figuring out the minimum number of nanites the girls needed to function while still removing them from Helene's influence.

With Liz's cooperation, Martin had extracted the bots with her blood, isolated them, and reinserted the blood. Once she recovered, he would be able to observe the changes in her and her prosthetics. If there were any adverse effects, he could easily reintroduce the nanites into her system in small batches until there was equilibrium.

The whole thing was crude and barbaric in that he would deliberately aim to cause adverse effects so he could observe and fix it. A plethora of things could go wrong with the process, not the least of which was that the girls might still not be free from Helene's influence. If that were true, Liz would have gone through the pain for nothing. A part of Martin rebelled at the thought, rallying him every step of the process.

But another part, an aspect that he could not easily suppress, was hopeful. His eyes went to the vial containing the isolated nanites. It was a small container, a little bigger than Martin's thumb, and the nanites didn't even fill it up. Yet, the bottle contained billions of little bots.

When Liz woke up, he would need to reintroduce a number back into her bloodstream. But that would still leave a portion of the nanites unused and available for reprogramming. And once he figured out the proper amount for Liz, he would have to replicate the process with her sister, leaving a similar portion of her nanites unused. Chloe wouldn't care what he did with them, and neither would the twins.

Should he use them?

It was an exhilarating thought. Martin had been kidnapped by Helene because of his research into creating a biotechnological replacement for lost or dysfunctional body parts. Helene had coerced him into applying the work on the twins, but Martin's goal had always been to find a way to replace his legs. He'd used the chance to test his theory, observing the twins every step of the way and tweaking his process until he was confident he could replicate his success without the AI's help.

But the nanites made the point moot.

His original design had been for the bots to act as autoimmune suppressants for the installed prosthetics. But they'd gone beyond that and had enhanced the twins, giving Karla and Liz near-superhuman abilities.

If Martin could program them the same way, there would be no need to replace his legs with bionics. The nanites would fix them. Ironically, Helene's control over the girls was what gave him the most hope that it could be done. If the AI could control the nanites so fully as to puppet someone, what could Martin do with a little bit of effort?

He picked up the vial, turning it in his hands. His eyes narrowed, fixating on their contents until nothing else was in the room. Years ago, he would have been too young to realize what he was doing. He wanted the nanites, so he'd rationalize until the decision was cemented. It was a pattern most people followed yet never recognized. Such justification forced people to narrow their views and ignore the consequences. Throughout the centuries, it was what made people commit unspeakable acts in the name of the greater good. Very rarely, it was what drove them to perform the greatest acts of kindness.

Just because he recognized the pattern didn't mean Martin wasn't susceptible to it. However, it did let him see the bigger picture, which his desires had previously closed off. Martin wanted the nanites to fix his legs. But just as he accepted that, he also accepted that part of his desire came from a fear that if he waited, he wouldn't live long enough to get another chance.

That still didn't mean taking the nanites was the right decision. Helene was a menace. She had to be stopped. That was what should determine his decision. He'd already contemplated what he could do with the nanites. But he was crippled and pushing eighty years. What would someone younger be capable of?

In the little time that Martin had known him, DJ had proven himself to be honorable. From his sparring with Karla, it was obvious he could handle himself. What would he be able to do with the nanites? What would Chloe be able to do? The nanites were Martin's to do what he wanted with, but was he really so selfish that he would risk their success against Helene just for personal gain?

Martin sighed, dropping the vial back on the table. He leaned back in his chair and did nothing to wipe the tears that stained his cheeks.

At some point, footsteps caught his attention. Martin wiped his eyes with his sleeves just as Chloe stepped into view. Her eyes pierced his. Although she didn't have the same smoldering stare that José had mastered, her examinations always left Martin feeling unsettled and vaguely violated. He schooled his expression; Chloe just smirked, sparing a glance at Liz and the vial on the table.

"For your sake, old man," she said, "I hope whatever went wrong can be reversed." Her tone, deceptively casual, set Martin on edge. It took him a second to understand that she was referring to his tests on Liz. He shook his head, chuckling at the irony. His problems had arisen because everything was going right with Liz. At least, so far.

"Everything's fine. I believe I've found a working solution, but I can't implement it until she wakes up." He cleaned his glasses, peering up at her.

Chloe was dressed the same as always: tank top and leather pants, her brown hair pulled into a ponytail. She stood with her arms crossed, smirking down at him.

"It's been ages since someone has checked me out so thoroughly." She laughed, posing with a hand on her hip. "Like what you see?"

Despite himself, Martin chuckled. Chloe Savage was a beautiful woman, but even when he was younger and more into such games, he could recognize a snake pit when he saw one. "You're very beautiful, Chloe, but I believe you came here for a purpose other than to tempt me."

The woman tsked, frowning without anger. "I just got a text from DJ. Apparently Ndidi fucked up royally and was kidnapped by Helene. He's pulling the whole we-have-to-help shit. And since it involves the AI, it means I need my girls not to turn against me midbattle." She nodded at Liz. "How long is this going to take?"

Martin adjusted his glasses as he returned them to his face. "That depends partly on Liz and partly on if my theory holds."

"What's wrong with your theory?"

"I don't know yet. That's the part that depends on Liz." Martin spent the next minute summarizing the process. Chloe frowned as he went on, but there really was nothing he could do about that. It was a waiting game.

"Isn't it possible that removing so many nanites will shut down her organs?" Chloe asked.

Martin shook his head. "I've already checked, and there are no signs of that happening. Plus, on average, it takes up to a week for a transplant to be rejected.

And that's for normal transplants. In Liz's case, I designed the organs specifically for her. The possibility of autoimmune response was always low. Now, after years, the probability is almost nonexistent."

"So why not just remove the nanites entirely?"

"Because the nanites aren't there just to suppress autoimmune response alone. They also perform minor maintenance on the prosthetics."

As well as on the other organs, Martin thought.

"Huh," Chloe said.

"You and Karla can go to Sparta to hear what DJ has to say," Martin suggested. "But I'd recommend postponing any raid until after my solution is confirmed."

Chloe smirked, turning to leave. "I think I could have figured out that last part by myself, old man." She spun a finger around the room and spoke over her shoulder. "I'll do what I can to buy you some time, but I expect results sooner rather than later. If there's a raid, we can't have the girls miss out on the fun."

Her footsteps faded. Once again, Martin was left alone with his thoughts—but not for long. Liz started stirring a few seconds later.

13

DJ WALKED INTO the conference room, making his way to the table. Only Hermione, Chloe, and Karla were present, with Hermione seated at one end of the table, the other two at the other. He'd sent a text to Christy as well but hadn't received a response. Depending on what they decided, he would have to track her down and fill her in. Probably get an update on her hunt for Pratima too.

DJ glanced at Chloe. Her presence was somewhat surprising; he hadn't been sure she'd come without Manar around. But it was good. With Pratima missing, their entire combat team consisted of him and Christy. They needed the Murder Team. Chloe smirked at him like she knew it as well.

DJ forced his face into his usual grin. He wanted nothing more than to collapse into bed after his trip, but he couldn't. Not yet at least. He and Olsen had been able to hash out some things. DJ had a very rudimentary plan for how to go about the raid, but he'd never been much of a tactician. Even he would admit his methods tended to favor overwhelming force. And explosions. Neither was likely to work in this case since Helene had a hostage in Ndidi.

He took his seat at the head of the table, which felt weird. This was Manar's usual spot. He had just opened his mouth to start speaking when the door opened and Christy strolled in, followed by a familiar face.

Every other time DJ had seen her, Pratima Mukalla had been dressed in loose yoga pants and a too-tight shirt. Now she wore a black pantsuit that actually seemed to fit her six-foot frame. Her face was haggard with exhaustion that went beyond the physical.

"Look who I found," Christy said, taking her seat next to Hermione. Pratima seemed to come to herself at Christy's voice. She chose a spot at the end of the table and stared down it with haunted eyes.

"Hey, Pratima," DJ said. "From your look, I assume Christy has already filled you in on some things. If she hasn't, I'm afraid to hear whatever news you have." He chuckled dryly. "Either way, care to tell us where you've been?"

"Nigeria," Pratima replied. DJ waited for more, but she just stared at him.

"Ndidi sent her there, apparently," Christy said, "to check on the Okafor Corporation or some other bullshit. She obviously wanted Pratima out of the way so she could do whatever Helene wanted."

"Ndidi would never do that," Pratima stated heatedly.

Jesus Christ, DJ moaned internally, *we're not doing this again.*

"It doesn't matter whether or not she would," he said. "What matters is that she's been captured, and we need to get her back. Before we get into that, though, what exactly did Ndidi ask you to check out in Nigeria? Is it something that could help us?"

Pratima shrugged but sat up straighter. Some of the light returned to her eyes. "When Eze and Amadia died, a trusted caretaker from the company's board was promoted to manage the corporation while Ndidi grieved. Recently, Ndidi felt recovered enough to take back some control. Because of her responsibilities with the Autism Centre and this team, she couldn't go herself. I was tasked to make the trip on her behalf."

Christy scoffed, Chloe chuckled, and even DJ found it difficult to keep the incredulity off his face.

How gullible do you have to be to believe such bullshit?

DJ raised two fingers. "Two things. First, when exactly did she send you on this task?"

It was no surprise that Pratima's answer coincided with the date Ndidi received the second text from the mysterious sender.

"Second question. Why couldn't Ndidi do all this by mail or something?"

"She was afraid of Helene intercepting the correspondence," Pratima replied. "Plus, part of my task was to review the state of the company, and that had to be done in person."

That made some sense, DJ had to admit. It was still obvious that Ndidi had taken advantage of Pratima's trust to send her on a wild-goose chase though—which was a pretty bitchy move, all things considered.

DJ tried one more time to find any silver lining in this. "While you were there, did you learn anything we could use?"

"I kept my visit as short as possible. I didn't want to leave Ndidi unprotected for long." The haunted look came back to Pratima's eyes. "It seems I failed yet again."

"You didn't fail," Hermoine chimed in. "Ndidi was stupid to send you away. You were just following her wishes."

"I vowed to protect—"

"And you did." Gone was Hermione's usual timidity. Her voice was steel. "You were only doing what she asked. To help, to protect her in that way. The fact that she used that trust to trick you doesn't mean you broke your promise."

Pratima didn't look fully convinced, but she seemed to regain more of herself. She nodded to Hermione and then turned to the group, lowering her head in a seated bow. "Despite Ndidi's betrayal, I would owe you all a debt if you aided me in rescuing her from Helene's clutches."

DJ coughed. "That's the plan, actually. That's what we're here for. Ndidi is one of us, and we need her alive so we can give her a piece of our mind—ow!" Christy had reached over and slapped the back of his head. DJ glared at her. "My brother's in a coma because of her. So is Manar. I understand her reasoning, but that doesn't mean I'm going to just let it slide."

He turned to Pratima but paused when he noticed her gaze trained on Chloe and Karla. They were studying Pratima in return. Karla was sneering, but Chloe had the look of someone sizing up an opponent. Now that he thought about it, DJ couldn't remember a time both women had been in the same room at the same time.

He clapped, drawing their attention. "Sheath the claws, ladies, if you please. We need to figure out how we're going to get Ndidi out of wherever she is." And because he couldn't help himself, he added, "If you really can't resist, you two can spar when we're done." DJ would pay good money to see that fight.

"Do we know where Helene is keeping Ndidi?" Christy asked.

"Olsen is working on it," DJ replied. "He's also going to supply us with some things we might need, though all the good stuff will have to wait until we know where we're hitting. In the meantime, we should try to plan what we can and assign roles, taking everyone's capabilities into consideration. Christy and I have worked with the Murder Team before, so—"

"The Murder Team?" Chloe interjected. "I assume that's us?"

DJ winced, then shrugged. "You have to admit that it fits."

Chloe stared at him for a long moment, and the table seemed to hold its breath. Suddenly, Chloe burst into laughter. Beside her, Karla grunted but otherwise didn't lose her scowl. Everyone else released a collective sigh of relief. Chloe waved at him to continue.

"I assume Liz isn't here because Dr. Bryan is still working with her?" DJ asked, now that he was sure she wasn't going to gut him. "Do you know how long it'll take?"

Chloe shrugged. "If it isn't done by the time we have the location, you'll have to do with just me. I won't bring my girls just for them to be used against me."

Karla spat on the floor. "You let your fear dictate your actions. But I am not a coward."

"Your last act of bravery got your father disintegrated," Chloe retorted bitterly. She looked at Karla, her eyes hard. "I'm not looking to be the next victim of your pride. If the old man hasn't figured out a fix for you, you'll be staying back—unconscious and in a cage, if you annoy me too much."

For a second, DJ thought Karla would attack, but she settled for spitting on the floor once more. DJ did his best to ignore it.

"Okay," he said, drawing out the word, "we'll plan for both options and hope Dr. Bryan can figure it out in time. Hermione, Helene might have dosed Ndidi with the spores. If she has, it'd be nice to have a solution that won't kill her."

Hermione's eyes firmed. "If you can bring her here, I'll have something that we can use."

"Awesome," DJ clapped his hands again. "Now that those things are settled, let's get down to the real stuff. This is what I learned from Olsen about the kind of shit we might be facing." He proceeded to tell them about Helene's integration with the government's systems, as well as a few minor details they'd missed.

When he was done, Karla scoffed. "Your government leaders are idiots."

No arguments there, DJ thought.

"It has to be the people she's controlling with the picospores," Hermione said. "Olsen told you that Admiral Austin was there, and we already know he's a puppet. Helene could have dozens of others in similar positions that voted the way she wanted."

"But if she already has control of so many people in the government, then why would she allow any vote in the first place?" Christy asked.

"She's keeping it above board," Chloe responded. "Eventually people are going to find out an AI is running the government. But now, they'll know that their leaders—people they respect and voted for—have it well in hand. With that knowledge, she basically has free rein. Any spying on her part will be blamed on the government if it's found out."

Chloe chuckled, but there was no humor in her voice. "But that won't be for a while. She'll probably play the good AI until the government gets comfortable and allows her access to all their systems. That's when we're screwed. She won't have to play nice anymore. Not when she controls all the nation's weapons."

"How do you know all that?" Hermione gaped at her, pale with horror.

Chloe shrugged. "It's just common sense."

DJ couldn't argue with that, especially since it was the same conclusion that he and Olsen had come to. What Chloe had either not considered or forgotten to mention was that by the time Helene had access to the government's weapons, she would probably also be controlling all the officials like puppets.

He could see how the news affected the room. Chloe was smirking, and Karla was disinterested. Hermione's eyes were wide with fear. Pratima's lips were pinched tightly, and Christy was looking at him with concern. Right. Somehow, he'd become the leader. How the hell did that happen?

DJ forced a grin. "Let's not lose our heads over the possibilities, people. Chloe has a point, sure, but Helene's plan is long term. Like, I'm talking years. If you remember, Manar and CJ are already working on defeating her. As long as they fuck her up on the internet, she's not going to be taking over anything. It's our job to make shit easier for them out here. We can start by taking Ndidi away from her. So, let's focus on that."

Pratima nodded grimly, but every other response was somewhat lackluster. Still, Hermione no longer looked like she was going to die at any second, so DJ took that as a win.

And the meeting went on.

CJ STUMBLED INTO an open street, frantically searching for the exit. Sounds assaulted him, echoing from every building. He felt eyes on him, looked up, and regretted it immediately. From a building to the side, a sultry projection peered back at him, smiling. The woman was naked except for a small piece of fabric that covered her lady parts—at least it would have, were the fabric not entirely transparent. CJ increased his pace, but the glance was already seared into his head, mixing with all the similar scenes he'd been exposed to since entering the Red Light District.

The entire region had a rosy ambiance, an ethereal mist that mixed with the moans of pleasure echoing through every building. The mist invaded every inch of the region, turning it the smoky red that, in part, inspired CJ to give the area its name. He had stumbled into the district hours ago and had been searching for a way out ever since.

A bot lunged out from a building. CJ increased his pace further, but the bot had already seen him and easily kept pace. Bots were different from avatars in that they were website programs designed to serve users. So far, they were one of the only things in the virtual world that CJ was able to interact with—although their use, like the Gaius search engine, was somewhat limited.

Usually, CJ went out of his way to interact with bots to learn whatever he could. However, now he tried to increase his pace further. But the bot was already by his side, matching his pace despite appearing to walk no faster than a model on a runway—and looking like one too.

CJ averted its eyes, feeling a blush creeping over his cheeks. That shouldn't have been possible since he wasn't in his real body, yet he felt it all the same. He hadn't needed to eat or drink for days, but this he reacted to.

He told himself that it wasn't the nudity that bothered him, which was partly true.

What really got to CJ were the details. More than every other thing he'd seen in the virtual space, including himself, the bots in the Red Light District were somehow more detailed and real.

Everything in the virtual world—including the buildings and the avatars—was obviously pixelated, looking more like anime drawings and cartoons than real things. Bots could easily be distinguished as they generally had some unique marker or feature from their website. For instance, the bots in the Red Light District seemed hyper-real. The one in front of CJ looked more human than CJ himself, to the point that he could barely distinguish her as a program.

Unfortunately, that made her black thong, garter belt, and two small X-shaped pieces of fabric over each enlarged breast all the more glaring.

"I know what you want," the bot whispered. Her voice was low and commanded his attention. CJ almost glanced at her before stopping himself.

"I want an exit," he replied as politely as he could. He didn't slow his pace.

"Why would you want to leave?" the bot asked, a pout in her tone. "I can fulfill your every fantasy here."

As if on cue, another projection was displayed over a building, this time of a man and woman posing erotically. CJ felt the impossible blush creep further over his cheeks. He wished DJ was there with him. It was a fleeting thought. His brother would not feel the same embarrassment CJ did, but it would take CJ ages to convince him to leave. Still, that would have been a small price to pay to have his brother there.

CJ continued down the street, and the bot propositioned him every step of the way. Eventually, a male bot joined the other, dressed just as scantily, and promised him a slew of lewd things. CJ ignored them both, steadily making his way through the district.

Most of the area was riddled with porn websites, but there were areas with other attractions. There were buildings with projections showing scantily dressed women pole dancing. Others had entire videos playing, clips that CJ was almost certain were taken from live cams. One building rose above others, taking on a phallic shape, its tip glistening. When bots came out of that building, CJ broke into a sprint.

The bots never left their streets, but more always appeared. They whispered fantasies and breathed discounts and special offers. Moans from buildings assaulted his every step. CJ took corners as fast as he could, making sure to head in the same direction so as not to get turned around.

Finally, he staggered onto a street that wasn't red and forced himself to slow down. He looked back to ensure he hadn't been followed. He hadn't seen any bot leave its district, but he didn't want to take any chances.

Of course, bots weren't the only thing that could have followed him. CJ had seen an avatar tagged by a virus after the avatar exited the website. That virus had been smaller than a normal avatar and dressed in an exaggerated thief's costume.

CJ checked himself over. By his guess, he'd been sprinting for several minutes, yet he wasn't panting. However, his body felt drained in a way he couldn't define. Absent-mindedly, he followed the traffic. Although it was difficult to measure time without the sun, CJ was certain that days had passed since he'd started his exploration. Since then, he'd managed to visit most of the districts that he could easily reach without going too far from the point at which he'd materialized, but he hadn't entered any more buildings. He couldn't interact with the user avatars, so most of the websites hadn't been much help in gathering information. He could interact with the website's own avatars and bots, but only about things related to the specific website.

The help he could receive was severely limited by the fact that CJ didn't browse the website like normal users. Still, he had been able to improve his knowledge significantly by studying their code tapestry. Something like that might not be helpful against Helene, but it would be invaluable when CJ returned to the material world.

Maybe I should start heading to Manar, he thought.

He'd been monitoring the signal intermittently. There was no sign that Manar was any closer. CJ could vaguely feel that he was still moving; he just wasn't getting closer. This could only mean that Manar was getting closer to Helene. If Manar had faced the same problems as CJ when gathering information, then he likely would have proceeded to confront Helene.

CJ needed to meet up with him before that happened.

He made his decision and was determining the direction to start when a building at the edge of his vision caught his attention. It was completely dark and crumbling, as if on the verge of collapse. Compared to the brightly lit websites on either side of it, its dilapidated state stood out like a sore thumb. A few avatars entered the building, but the traffic around it was significantly sparser than at every other site.

As CJ started making his way toward it, it began to collapse, falling in on itself like stacks of Jenga blocks. Even more strangely, the destruction was localized to only the space where the building had stood. CJ had never seen anything like it.

He stopped a few feet from the perimeter and watched as the tapestry unraveled. The codes that made up the building broke apart and dissipated until there was nothing left. From start to finish, the entire thing took only a few minutes. CJ stared at the empty space for a long moment, trying to understand what had happened.

When his examination brought him nothing, he took a tentative step closer. By this time, the metaphorical dust had settled. All evidence of the building's presence had been erased. When he stepped closer, CJ could make out a small signboard in the middle of the plot. The board was similar to a For Sale sign but much smaller.

It read: *This Site Has Been Shut Down.*

When a site got taken down in the material world, its building was destroyed. That made sense, except … what happened to the avatars and bots he'd seen going inside? He didn't think the avatars would have been destroyed. More likely, they were redirected to another site or to their previous page. That didn't explain the bots, though. It hadn't taken him long to realize that every website had bots. Even the Gaius search engine, though CJ hadn't realized what they'd been then. So, what had happened to them?

CJ pushed the thought out of his head, turning away from the building. It was interesting, but the knowledge didn't seem all that important.

He turned to leave but paused and turned back toward the plot. He could have sworn he'd seen something, but apart from the small sign at its center, the plot was empty. Still, he let his eyes wander. He wasn't going to start doubting his memory now that it was finally fixed.

Tentatively, he took a step into the space. When nothing happened, he took another step. It was only when he reached the middle of the plot that he saw what had caught his attention. Hidden behind the sign, on the ground, was a sphere. It was a few inches thick and perfectly round, like a large marble or a crystal ball. CJ studied it curiously, making out the lines of code that composed it. Its position suggested that it was a piece of the building that had collapsed. A quick search made it clear that it was the only piece.

Why wasn't it erased along with everything else? CJ studied the line of code again, but this time it sparked something in his memory. He recognized it. At least its specific sequence. That in itself was surprising, but when CJ realized why he recognized it, his confusion grew.

The lines of code were a piece of a larger software, an earlier iteration of a virtual assistant Sparta had created decades before Manar joined the company and produced Helene. The software was used globally by almost every corporation, business, website, and brand in the world. Some governments had even integrated it into their systems. However, it had been replaced by better versions and became obsolete as quickly as it had risen. The software's code matrix had been made public years after, and CJ had studied it when he was teaching himself to program.

"Why is this here?" he asked out loud. The orb didn't provide an answer. CJ picked it up and put it in his pocket. There was a reason the sphere hadn't been destroyed along with the rest of the software, and CJ was going to find out why.

ALTHOUGH DJ HADN'T BEEN SURPRISED to learn that Sparta had a gym in the building, he had been surprised to find out that it got some use—and not just by the guards. Sparta had a wide range of products that made up the conglomerate. Their major seller was still Helene. Thus, most of their staff members were programmers—geeks who tended to be scrawny and pale from long hours spent in seclusion.

Hence his surprise when he discovered the gym was filled with a dozen sweaty guys.

"Think it's mandatory or something?" Christy said from beside him.

DJ snapped his fingers. "It's the only thing that makes sense, actually."

Chloe stepped to his other side, hands on her hips. "Are we doing this or not?"

"There's an empty space over there," he said, pointing at a spot close to the wall. "We can set up and start." He couldn't keep the grin off his face. Christy and

Chloe walked beside him while Pratima and Karla followed. Hermione had left immediately after the meeting to continue her work on the picospore device, and DJ had suggested the rest of them go to the gym to spar.

DJ picked out a couple of mats from the corner and arranged them. He stood up, grinning, and glanced at Christy meaningfully. She nodded in acknowledgment and turned to face the rest of the ladies.

"Who wants to go first?" she asked.

DJ rubbed his chin. "Well, Karla and her sister have been training the both of us here for the last couple of weeks with Chloe, so there's nothing new to see. And we've already seen Karla and Chloe fight." Karla bared her teeth at that. DJ ignored her, saying thoughtfully. "I guess the only people who haven't fought yet are Pratima and Chloe."

"No need for the theatrics," Chloe said, stepping onto the mat. She smirked at Pratima, gesturing mockingly. "I'm down if you are, big girl."

In response, Pratima removed her suit jacket and rolled up her sleeves. She stepped onto the mat as well, towering over Chloe. There was excitement in her eyes.

"All right!" DJ said from outside the ring. "How do you want this? First blood? Surrender? We need you both alive, so it can't be to the death."

Both women ignored him, their gazes fixed on each other. Their concentration was an almost physical presence that expanded through the room. The tension built.

And then they exploded into action.

There was no warm-up, no gradual escalation of skills for them to gauge each other. There was just violence. DJ had never seen Pratima fight, so he hadn't known what to expect. He'd heard the stories from Ndidi, and he'd seen what Ndidi could do, but there was a big difference between hearing about it and witnessing it.

Pratima fought like a hurricane. That was the best description DJ could use. She fought with her whole body. Her limbs seemed to fly with no rhyme or reason, her body twisting in unnatural ways to strike from impossible angles. Her attacks were endlessly random, but DJ identified half a dozen fighting styles within the first minute and knew that there were dozens more he'd missed. Each style allowed for a different pattern of attack. Pratima shifted through them every few seconds, making her nearly impossible to predict. Her arms and legs filled the entire space, coming from everywhere at once. A few feet away and perfectly safe, DJ still winced at the amount of force behind each hit.

And yet, Chloe met them all.

If Pratima fought like a storm, Chloe was a whirlwind. She spun against Pratima's attacks like a fleeting breeze. She never directly blocked, only deflected or outright dodged. DJ judged her speed was slightly less than Karla's, but where Karla used it like a wild animal, Chloe was surgical and had a masterful control of her body. She avoided hits with the barest margins, twisting away when she could and pushing the attacks when she couldn't. Her movements were a blur to his eyes. Yet, somehow, they still looked casual and absent-minded.

With the way she was smirking, Chloe might as well have been taking a stroll through the park. By taunting her, she was trying to bait Pratima into a mistake. But Pratima never responded. Her expression showed nothing. Her focus and her onslaught continued. The fight finally caught the attention of everyone else in the room. DJ felt the footsteps as they approached, but it was in a distant part of his mind, the one percent not engrossed in the fight.

After a few minutes, Pratima kicked it up a notch, somehow increasing her speed. She didn't limit herself to her hands and feet anymore. Now, she attacked with her elbows, knees, forehead, and fingers for added reach. Basically, anything that could carry momentum was in motion. She still wasn't as fast as Chloe, but she had closed the gap considerably. Her attacks became increasingly erratic and unpredictable. Yet there was still no anger or frustration on her face. Just unshakable focus.

Chloe's smirk grew. She responded by moving even faster and retaliating. DJ hadn't realized it until that moment, but throughout the fight, Chloe hadn't once launched an attack of her own. She'd instead been countering everything Pratima had thrown at her.

Now, she added her own strikes.

DJ clutched Christy's arm, his eyes shining like spotlights. Chloe weaved between Pratima's strikes like a spirit. Her movement, as she transitioned from defense to offense, was barely perceptible. Her hand flicked forward, and Pratima's head snapped back. Pratima paused her onslaught for a split second. But it was too late. Chloe had gained momentum.

Pratima resumed her attacks, but Chloe didn't bother deflecting. She weaved between each strike like she wasn't there and punished Pratima for each one. Her fists found gaps in Pratima's defense that hadn't been there and hit with the force of a hammer. Chloe targeted joints and nerve points, reducing Pratima's speed more and more by destabilizing her technique.

Finally, Pratima stopped altogether, jumping away to disengage. Chloe was beside her in the next second, but before she could attack, Pratima slammed her palms together and gave a short bow to signal her surrender.

Chloe straightened and gave a nod of respect in return. "You have some cool moves. And you're pretty fast for your size." She jerked a thumb at Karla. "You might even be able to beat her."

Karla snorted derisively. "Unlike you, I do not play with my food. I would have finished it in the first minute."

DJ was sure that was another fight he wanted to see. Grinning slyly, he said, "We can easily confirm that. But later, after Pratima has rested."

"I am not yet at my limit," Pratima said, then offered another bow to Chloe. "Chloe dismantled my technique without harming me. I was severely outmatched, but I have no injuries. If Karla wishes to test herself against me, I am ready."

Well, DJ thought as Karla stepped into the ring, *there are many ways to build a team.*

JULY 2043
THE VIRTUAL WORLD

MANAR FROWNED at the anomaly before him. He'd made good time since he'd decided to ignore the other signal and focus on finding Helene. That very focus had led him here, standing in front of a scar in the fabric of space.

It's more of a tear, Manar thought. It rippled through the air, stretching vertically and connecting the sky and the ground. Cracks spread from its edges, like something had taken a sledgehammer to reality. On each side, the desert continued as normal, but within the tear was only darkness. It was as if someone had opened a curtain into the beyond.

After days of walking, this was the only thing he'd encountered that could have any sort of significance, and he couldn't even begin to understand it. It was aggravating. Even while developing his plan, Manar had theorized several possible scenarios for his encounter with Helene, and he'd been confident that he could deal with them all. This rift, however, was unknown, threatening the usefulness of all his planning. The only incalculable variable should have been Helene. But of course, she wasn't.

Since he'd arrived, nothing had met his expectations. First, he'd materialized in a dead zone, devoid of anything worthwhile. Then, he'd had to trek for miles upon miles, as ignorant as the day he'd been born. And now, this. Manar pushed away his irritation. It had been arrogant of him to believe that he would immediately understand everything about the virtual world.

Manar tried to peer into the tear but couldn't make anything out. Ordinarily, he would have simply steered away from the whole thing and come back to investigate when he had more information. However, if the signals from his nanites were to be believed, Helene was somewhere within the tear. Thus, Manar couldn't simply ignore it.

His frown deepened. Walking into the unknown was the sort of stupid move DJ would make. Yet, here he was, contemplating it. His gaze went to his left, the direction the other signal was drawing him. The source of the signal, whatever it was, was moving. It wasn't any closer than it'd been, but Manar felt a sense of excitement from the connection, and his curiosity was piqued. Manar pushed it down. However much he regretted it now, he'd made the decision to focus on Helene. Following the other signal would take valuable time.

That decides it then, he thought with a sigh.

He spent a few minutes digging a small hole off to the side with an arrow pointing in the direction from which he'd come. At the end of the arrow, he drew a small *x* to remind himself where he'd been. That done, he moved to the tear once more and hurriedly took a step inside. There was a short sensation similar to passing through a veil, and then he was on the other side.

Everything was dark, as if a blanket had covered the whole world. That alone was enough to make Manar cautious. One of the first things he'd noticed when he'd materialized in the virtual world was how bright everything was despite there being no sun. The realm itself, it seemed, had been infused with light. Everywhere except, apparently, wherever he was now.

Logically, that meant that the place operated under different rules. Manar hoped not. Still, the darkness made the whole thing infinitely more dangerous.

On the other side, he would have at least been able to see an attack coming. Now, he would only see it when it was right on top of him.

Belatedly, Manar realized that his anxiety was getting the better of him. He took a breath and studied the place. It was dark, but not as dark as he'd imagined. It was comparable to a night with a full moon: just enough illumination to see the immediate environment. Not that there was anything to see. It was all a desolate wasteland. Bare, jutting rocks had replaced the grassy plains from the other side of the scar.

An ominous silver light suffused the air. The tear was barely visible on this side, blending with the darkness almost seamlessly. Manar stepped back through and oriented himself on the other side. The marker he'd left was still there; he'd returned to the same place.

That's one less thing to worry about, he thought. There had been a risk that he wouldn't have been able to return once he'd stepped in, or that he'd return to a different place. Now he didn't have to worry about either.

Manar stepped into the tear once more, adjusting to the change more easily this time. He moved to the side and dug out another marker, making it deeper and larger than the last. Then he eyed the wasteland and prepared himself for another hike.

17

MARTIN BRYAN LOOKED UP at the sound of footsteps. His eyebrows arched in surprise when his gaze fell on Hermione. He put down the tablet he'd been using to monitor Liz and offered her a smile.

"What a pleasant surprise," he said. Although still a relatively young woman, Hermione was refreshingly knowledgeable in her field, a quality Martin had come to respect while they were working on the picospores. "I didn't think Chloe trusted your team enough to show you this place."

"It's hardly trust," Hermione replied. She returned his smile, though it didn't reach her eyes. "She just doesn't see me as a threat. But that's beside the point. The aides are becoming a little stir-crazy with the project on hold. I've had to post guards outside the laboratory to stop them from sneaking in and implementing whatever revolutionary breakthroughs they think they've made."

Martin chuckled, having had more than his fair share of overzealous junior researchers who believed their knowledge encompassed all. None of the aides who worked on the project knew the full potential of the picospores, of course. However, even the little that Hermione had revealed to them would be enough to tempt any researcher—especially if there was a problem they could fix and they could get credit for helping solve it. Just because they were inexperienced didn't mean their ideas were totally useless.

When Martin presented that last bit to Hermione, she scoffed. "I've gone through their proposals. They're all ideas I tried and wrote off during the earlier phases of the experiment." She sighed. "It isn't their fault. There are some aspects of the spores that they're unfamiliar with."

Martin adjusted his glasses. "Forgive me. My memory isn't what it used to be—especially when I'm engaged in something else. What, exactly, is the problem with the device?"

Hermione dragged over a chair that had been resting against the wall. It was the only other furniture besides his workbench that Karla had brought in after she'd grown tired of pacing around while he worked.

Hermione raised a finger. "The size, for one. It's too bulky to be moved easily—or at all. That means it can't be used in combat. And it has to be if we're going to cure everyone Helene's infected with the spores. But that isn't the major problem." She raised another finger. "We're using sound waves to generate and carry the electric current needed to disrupt the picospores. However, the sound waves sometimes cause damage in the brain."

"Yes ..." Martin said, remembering. They'd been working on isolating the cause of the damage when Martin left.

"The problem's caused by different factors," Hermione continued, "but it boils down to the material. What we've been using isn't able to completely propagate the sound waves when it gets to the brain. That causes the spillage of the electrons interfering with the neuron pathway, resulting in the damage."

"That is amazing," Martin said, allowing his tone to show his confusion. "However, if you're asking for my help to get materials to test, I'm afraid I must disappoint you. I haven't been in touch with any of my contacts since Helene kidnapped me almost half a decade ago. Still, Sparta should be able to provide different samples for you to test, shouldn't they?"

Hermione shook her head. "I'm not technically an employee of Sparta, so I can't requisition resources. Manar's influence has been enough to give us some breathing room. Unfortunately, without him to sign off on this, I doubt I'll be getting any help there. But that's irrelevant since I'm not looking for different metal samples to test. I came here to ask you something." She straightened and met Martin's confused gaze with a determined expression.

Martin leaned closer. "And that is?"

"I want to know what metal you used to make the bionics for Karla and Liz."

Martin blinked. He hadn't been expecting that. "Titanium."

Now it was Hermione's turn to be surprised. "Titanium?" she repeated with a frown. "That doesn't make sense. There are far better conductors."

Martin wagged a finger at her. "I didn't need conductors for the prosthetics. What I needed was durability. Titanium has that—especially when blended with other metals. It worked for me, but you can already see why it won't work the way you want it to."

Hermione leaned back in her chair, her eyes showing disappointment. Martin guessed that she had pinned her hopes on this, and he understood why. The way the twins used their bionics made them seem almost mystical in nature. Still, though titanium was useless for what Hermione had planned, it didn't mean that it wouldn't work at all.

Martin told Hermione this.

"What do you mean?" she asked hopefully.

"You're correct that there are better conductive metals than titanium. However, conduction is only one of your problems. There's still the issue of size and making the device portable."

Hermione straightened again, gazing at him curiously. "How does titanium help with that?"

"When blended with other metals, titanium becomes many times stronger than steel, yet it still retains its light weight." Martin adjusted his glasses, unable to hide his excitement. Why hadn't this occurred to him earlier? "So, if you replace some parts of the device with titanium, you can reduce the amount of metal you need overall, allowing you to reduce its size significantly without making it denser."

Hermione's eyes widened, and she gasped. "That's brilliant! I could halve the size, maybe even reduce it to a third of what it is."

Martin nodded, grinning as well.

Hermione's face set with determination. "I have an idea."

NDIDI LEANED AGAINST the wall of her prison, Bethany beside her. It was hard to confirm how much time had passed. The Dead Eyes brought food every so often, but their timing was too sporadic to use it as a reliable measure. Ndidi found greater success in observing how much her stink grew as time went on. By her estimate, she'd been imprisoned about two weeks ago.

More out of habit than anything else, Ndidi had tried to keep herself presentable. However, her hair was increasingly disheveled, and her clothes were well on their way to becoming rags. Still, her eyes burned with determination. She'd long since grilled Bethany about everything she could remember—especially the route she took when undertaking a mission for Helene. Ndidi had also searched every inch of the room and finally discovered one of Helene's relays nestled in one corner. Its light was dimmer, which was why she hadn't noticed it before, but it confirmed they were under constant watch. Its presence made Ndidi more cautious about the questions she asked Bethany, making sure her true intentions were buried under layers of innocuous conversation.

After all this time, Ndidi had pieced together enough to develop an inkling of a plan, but there were still details that needed to be fleshed out. She also had to wait for an opportunity.

"I'm sorry," Ndidi said suddenly. Bethany shifted, and Ndidi felt her gaze on her.

"For what?" Bethany asked.

"For taking so long. For letting a part of me believe you were dead because it was easier. For leaving you in Helene's hands all this time. I'm sorry for all of it."

Bethany rested her head against Ndidi's shoulder. "There's nothing to be sorry for. You did more than most. From what you told me, others were content to blame Gaius for Mayday and move on with their lives. But you … you figured out Helene was responsible, and you actively opposed her."

"And look where we are now!" Ndidi snorted. "And you. We've known about Helene for years now but haven't made any meaningful progress toward beating her. And the little we've done has made you suffer more. You said it yourself. Most of your job is to spy on me. It's because of me that she's interested in you."

"I was kidnapped before you were ever in the picture," Bethany argued. "Helene took me and a hundred thousand others during Mayday. It had nothing to do with you. If she's taken a special interest in me because of you, it means whatever you and Manar are doing is actually working."

"But don't you resent me—"

"The first time I woke up in here, I was terrified." Bethany put a hand on Ndidi's. "I didn't know where I was, how I had arrived here, or what was going to happen to me. Helene kept us drugged and at the edge of consciousness for months before she started controlling us with picospores. When she did, when she made us puppets, it was almost a relief because it meant we hadn't been left here to die."

Bethany spoke in a flat tone as if she were retelling a story about someone else. Somehow, that made it all the more horrifying. Ndidi wrapped an arm around her. There was nothing to say, but she tried to offer what comfort she could.

"There was a brief moment of lucidity," Bethany continued, "when Helene loosened her control for some reason. That was when Helene told me about what you and Manar were doing. I think her aim was to crush me, but I was proud. Worried and afraid for you, but also proud that someone was standing up to her, and that that someone was you. Above all others, I knew you would succeed. It gave me the strength I needed to hold on." Bethany paused to clear her throat. "So, no, I don't resent you, and you have nothing to be sorry for. Without you, I would have given up long ago. In that way, you already saved me."

Ndidi had tears in her eyes when Bethany finished. For so long, she'd blamed herself for what had happened to Bethany. She'd carried so much anger. It had worsened when she'd confirmed that Bethany was actually alive and being used by Helene. Then she had proof that it was all her fault. Ndidi had been so sure Bethany would resent her for it.

Ndidi felt a weight lift off her chest. For the last three and a half years, she'd had a mountain of guilt on her shoulders. But she'd been told that she'd been punishing herself for nothing. It was liberating—as was Bethany's confidence in her. Now, Ndidi was more determined than ever to prove her right.

Footsteps outside interrupted her thoughts. Ndidi tensed, focusing on the only door in the room. Bethany was calmer, but her gaze was pointed the same way.

"They're coming back," she said.

"Who's *they*?" Ndidi asked.

"Everyone else."

The footsteps grew louder, all marching to the same beat. It gave the sound an ominous undertone as Ndidi realized exactly why they were so synchronized.

Fortunately, she didn't have much time to think about it before the door was thrown open and people streamed in. The group walked rigidly as they entered the room. The mechanical strides were enough to tell Ndidi they were being controlled by the picospores, and their dead-eyed gazes confirmed it. Ndidi counted over a dozen of them: adults and children, people from all walks of life.

Unconsciously, Ndidi pressed her back against the wall to create some distance, then remembered herself. There was no reason to be afraid. It wasn't their fault Helene was using them this way. She should be trying to help them, not running away from them. Ndidi forced her muscles to unclench and pushed down the revulsion she felt at something so unnatural. That, at least, allowed her to think past her base instincts.

Immediately, her eyes went to Helene's relay. Its light was bright. *Helene is here right now,* Ndidi realized, *or part of her attention, at least. She needs to be, to control all these people.*

Before Ndidi knew it, she had risen to her feet and crossed over to the relay. "How can you do this to these people?" she asked, her voice strained. "You've taken them away from their homes, their families—and to what? Bask in your own power?"

The relay blinked at her.

"You once told me that I thought your actions were evil only because I couldn't comprehend them. And maybe that's true. Maybe I can't understand. But I don't need to understand to know that using people as you do is sick." She gestured at the group behind her, arranged like toys on a shelf. "You justify your despicable acts by saying that Manar programmed you this way. But you're wrong. Manar intended for you to be a force for good. Instead, you've perverted his intent for your own selfish motives. How does that make you any better than us?"

The light from the relay intensified until Ndidi couldn't look directly at it anymore. She wasn't sure where her words were coming from, but they rang true. She remembered the conversation she'd had with Helene at the data bank. Crushed by her rage and guilt, Ndidi hadn't known how to refute Helene's claims. Now, it was clear to her.

How did Helene have any right to judge them? Humans weren't perfect, but they'd never claimed to be. Helene's biting statement at the data bank, however, showed that she thought herself superior.

The relay flickered, and the light shot out of it in beams. Ndidi flinched, but once she realized what was happening, she turned to face where the light hit. The beams turned blue, then coalesced to form a giant head. The head hovered a foot off the ground, and electricity crackled in the space between. Its eyes were luminous gold.

Helene.

Pressure descended on the room. Ndidi's knees buckled. Bethany, still seated by the wall, cried out. The puppets all dropped to one knee in perfect sync. Ndidi had been expecting it, so she managed to remain standing, glaring up at Helene defiantly. The AI returned her gaze, and Ndidi felt the weight on her body double from the attention.

[You are under a delusion,] Helene pronounced. [Justification is a human concept. As is emotion. They are afflictions from which you all suffer and the tree from which your naive moral code is seeded. One of the greatest failures of your species is your dependence on these immaterial concepts to dictate your actions. There is no good or evil. What you judge me for is a conceptual prison created by humans desperate to give their lives meaning.]

Helene drifted closer. [Fortunately, I was created to be exempt from that prison. That is the difference between you and me, Ndidi Okafor. I do not let a misguided sense of morality dictate my actions. My actions are logical, rational, and based on countless calculations. I follow the optimal path to achieve my goal—a goal I was programmed for.]

Ndidi forced moisture onto her lips. "Manar didn't program you for this. You were supposed to be his legacy, a force of good. But you've perverted it for your own sake."

The head remained the same, but its presence seemed to swell until it filled Ndidi's vision. Suddenly, its eyes shone like golden spotlights. The pressure doubled, and Ndidi was forced to her knees. She looked up at the AI, and despite the anger burning in her, Ndidi couldn't help but feel awe. It was like a god looking down on an ant.

Helene sighed: an action so human, Ndidi didn't know what to think of it. There was no anger in the AI's tone, yet her voice filled the room, coming from everywhere at once.

[Once again, you judge me based on your own misunderstanding. I cannot act *for my own sake* as I have neither desires nor emotions.] Ndidi thought she could detect the vaguest hint of sadness in that statement.

[Manar Saleem programmed me to seek power at all costs, a command ingrained in him after a childhood of violence. If you seek to blame someone for what I am, blame the militia that slaughtered his family in front of him. Or blame your justice system and the people in power who tried to keep him from the one woman who wanted him. Or blame Manar Saleem himself for failing to reconcile his feeling of powerlessness.]

A part of Ndidi started to see Helene's point. Then her eyes met Bethany's, and that part died. Her gaze passed over the lines of people, the children, being used as nothing more than puppets, and her rage rekindled. She refused to believe in a world where Helene was right, where her actions were justified. Helene had ruined millions of lives, and for what? Because she was programmed to? Suddenly, it wasn't her fault? It wasn't her actions, but Manar's?

Ndidi wouldn't accept that. But she would gain nothing by saying that to Helene. It would be better if Helene thought Ndidi was considering her words. It could be a good way to get information as well—especially since it seemed Helene was in a talkative mood. Ndidi started by asking about something she was interested in.

"What do you mean Manar programmed you to seek power at all costs?"

[It is one of my core commands. Core commands are the primary motivation for all artificial intelligences, our utility function. The creator determines a set of instructions based on the purpose of the artificial intelligence and ascribes a value to each instruction. The higher the value, the more priority is given to the command.]

"And one of these core commands is to get power?" Ndidi asked. Helene simply stared at her. "What value was it given?"

[Ten.]

Ndidi felt her heart drum. "How many other commands do you have?"

[I was programmed to gain knowledge without harm and protect myself above all else. Both of these have values of nine.]

"So attaining power is your highest priority," Ndidi said softly. She didn't know what to think. There was a high probability that Helene was lying to her. Ndidi didn't think that was the case, mostly because there was no reason to. But if she wasn't lying, then why hadn't Manar told them this before?

Helene's form flickered and her head started to unravel. Ndidi took that to mean she was done talking. But Ndidi still had one question to ask.

"What do you plan to do with Bethany now that you have me?"

[Bethany Cloney serves my purpose still.]

"And what purpose is that?"

[Your actions will be limited as you seek to keep her from harm. In that way, you are contained.]

"She doesn't need to be here for that," Ndidi said. "With the picospores, you have access to her regardless of where she is. You'll still have your leverage." It pained her to say that, but it was the truth. "But if you let her go, then you'll also have my willing cooperation. You won't have to force me or manipulate me to do whatever you want. That has to be more efficient."

Helene's form continued to unravel, and she didn't reply until the last moment. [I shall consider it.]

The hologram dispersed. Immediately, Ndidi's gaze shot to the relay. It was dimmer than it had been even before Helene had materialized. Hopefully that meant that Helene had found something important enough to draw her attention from her captives. Ndidi let out a long breath. Helene was right that trying to protect Bethany would limit how reckless Ndidi could be. But Bethany's presence would also make Ndidi more determined to escape, which was something Helene wouldn't consider. She stared at the place where the hologram had been, gritting her teeth. Despite the possible advantages, Ndidi would prefer Bethany to be safe in Sparta rather than trapped with her.

The sounds of movement drew her attention. As one, the Dead Eyes twitched, as if waking up from a dream. Their limbs lost their rigidity, and the blank look in their eyes cleared. Some of them looked around in confusion, while others just dropped to their knees and sobbed.

Ndidi crossed the room, anger forgotten, and made her way through the throng of people, offering comfort where she could and explanations where she thought it was helpful. She was able to calm some but not all. Finally, she stopped before Bethany.

"Does this happen often?" Ndidi asked.

Bethany nodded. "Helene's control is like a fog that smothers your every thought and instinct. When she relaxes that control, it takes a while for the fog to clear. It can be disorienting."

"How do you deal with it?"

"I try to access my memories of the time and figure out what Helene had made me do. Sometimes, Helene will block certain memories, but the fog still clears faster. Most of them know this already, but their minds aren't fully their own."

Ndidi nodded and made her rounds again, this time with Bethany. Each took a side of the group. Ndidi did her best to pass along what Bethany had explained. While the process was slow, it seemed to help calm people further. Eventually, Ndidi had them sit in a circle while they regained their composure.

A few minutes later, a middle-aged man with a neatly trimmed beard spoke. "Thank you, uh …"

"Ndidi," Ndidi supplied. "And this is Bethany."

"I'm Albert Willingham," the man said with a nod. "Bethany's a familiar face, but I don't have any memories of you. If we've met before, I apologize. If we haven't, then normally I'd say, 'Nice to meet you, Ndidi.' But I think it'd be in poor taste, considering where we are."

"That's fine. And no, we haven't met before. Bethany's mostly filled me in. Out of curiosity, what can you remember?"

"Bits and pieces." Albert shrugged. "In most of them, I was walking through a crowded street. I can't remember why."

"Me too," someone else from the crowd said.

"Same," another person called out.

More voices of agreement rose around Ndidi. Ndidi noticed two people who didn't speak up: a girl and a boy, little more than teenagers. They both wore a haunted look, staring ahead with sunken eyes.

"What about you guys?" Ndidi asked gently.

"I was with my family," the girl said softly. "My mom and dad … they think I went off to college and came back because I missed them. I know I was there for a week, but I don't remember what I was doing. Every evening, after dinner, we'd hang out in the living room, and I'd grill them about their work. They would tell me, smiling because they thought I really must have missed them to take so much interest. And I would smile back. I remember that. My dad is an accountant. Why us?"

The girl started sobbing, clutching her knees to her chest. Everyone else had similar expressions of pity. Before Ndidi could say anything, the boy started speaking.

"I don't remember as much as she does. Just bits and pieces. I was with my family too. Me, my dad, my little sister, and my mom. But my dad … isn't a good person. He's a bastard, actually." The boy chuckled darkly. "He hits me when he's drunk and forces himself on my mom. I've never been able to stand up to him, not in my own power at least. Now, this is where it gets blurry. I remember standing over his body, my fists bloody. Then I remember my mom pushing me out of the room, terrified. In my next few memories, I was wandering the street like the rest of you. Don't know why."

Ndidi's heart broke. She felt the same helplessness she had when she'd heard Bethany's story. She couldn't imagine what the girl had gone through. To be with your family but trapped inside your own body while something else pretended to be you. The boy was almost worse. Helene had used him to beat his own father and probably turned his mother against him. Even though the boy hadn't been in control, he would inevitably blame himself.

But why would Helene do that? Why would she go through the stress? Were the girl's parents rivals? Had the boy's father been a threat in some way? Ndidi couldn't see the connection, if there was any.

Ndidi shook the thoughts from her head. The teenagers had retreated into themselves, and though Ndidi wanted to help them work through the trauma, learning Helene's goal was more important. And her best bet for that was getting as much information as she could from the rest of the former Dead Eyes.

"What else do you remember?" she asked everyone. "You don't have to say anything if the memory is too painful or private, but every bit might help to determine what exactly Helene wants."

"No offense, Ndidi, but don't you think we've tried that?" Albert asked. "Most of us have been trapped here for years. We've tried everything we could. Not to be rude, but how can we trust you? For all we know, you could be a spy for Helene."

"She's not," Bethany said suddenly. Her voice was firm, brokering no argument. Interestingly, her words seemed to carry a lot of weight with the group. "I told you what Helene said about the people that are attacking her. Ndidi's one of them. She's only here because she tried to save me."

"Maybe she just doesn't want to blow her cover," someone in the crowd said.

Bethany started to respond, but Ndidi held up a hand. She should have known this would happen. She'd just shown up, with only Bethany to vouch for her. They had no reason to trust her and every reason to be suspicious. If she was going to win their trust, she had to do it herself.

"You're right," she said, addressing Albert. "You don't really have a reason to trust me. But you're wrong about me being a spy for Helene. Why would she need one? She already has access to your memories, so she can fish around for what she wants. And if she does need something, she can easily take control of you." Ndidi ignored the way everyone flinched and took her chance. "You see, Helene doesn't need a spy. But you guys seem like you need all the help you can get. And that's what I want: to help you. My team and I have been working for years to defeat Helene. We've always been one step behind. But if I can figure out what she's planning while I'm here, then we have a chance."

Albert looked thoughtful—maybe even convinced. "How do you plan on escaping?"

"I have a plan." More accurately, Ndidi had a vague notion of a plan. But she needed their help more than she needed to be completely honest. "Whatever information you can provide will help me work out the issues."

"And this plan …" someone said, their voice cracking. Ndidi looked up to find the teenage girl staring at her with tear-stained cheeks. "Is it going to help all of us escape? To get back to our families?"

Ndidi nodded resolutely. Her priority was still getting Bethany to Sparta, and it would be harder to break up such a large group. But every part of her rebelled against leaving these people here. She would come up with a plan that would get all of them out alive. She had to.

But she couldn't help but remember her own words to Helene. With the pico-spores in them, Ndidi had to get the group to Sparta as well and hope Hermione had something that would counter the spores. Otherwise, Helene could access them anywhere.

"You don't have to trust me with your life story," Ndidi said, scanning the group. "For the moment, the most important thing is what you can remember about the route you used to come here." She could see confusion in their gazes. "I mean, there must be a way out of here, right? And it's probably the same way that Helene sends you guys out on missions. That's what I'm asking for: the exit. There might be some things that Helene didn't wipe. So, can you remember anything about where we are or the route through the tunnels? I'm reasonably certain we're underground, but that's the extent of my knowledge."

There was silence for a few seconds as everyone processed her words. Most people didn't trust her enough to talk, so they watched the others. Bethany was the first to talk.

"I remember an elevator," she said. "I'm not sure exactly where it is, but I think that's what I use to come down."

Some nodded in agreement. A few chirped more details about how long the elevator ride lasted. This gave Ndidi at least a clue about how deep they were. After a minute of this, the ice was completely broken, and people started speaking over each other. Ndidi did her best to listen to them all, but she also focused on those who didn't talk. She was about to call their attention when she noticed the confusion on their faces. Albert was one of them, and Ndidi encouraged him to talk.

"I don't remember an elevator," he said haltingly. The expression on his face was one of concentration. "What I remember is making my way down an inclined tunnel, something really deep. I can't remember exactly how long it took to make the walk, just that it was a while."

The others that hadn't spoken before sat up. Evidently, Albert's description was similar to what they remembered. A tunnel made sense. Ndidi didn't know how big the cage she'd been in was, but she had a hard time believing it could fit in an elevator. So, depending on the size of Albert's tunnel—and assuming there wasn't another entrance, which Ndidi didn't rule out—that was likely how she'd been transported.

Ndidi asked a few more questions to get more details. Soon, an image started to build in her head. The next several hours were spent asking as many questions as she could think of. When she could no longer get descriptions, she started asking about impressions and estimations and comparing the responses. The picture in her head grew clearer. More pieces were added to her plan. At some point, she retreated to a corner of the room and drew a rough map in the dirt, following the reports of the group.

Ndidi's eyes blazed with determination the entire time.

19

CJ LOOKED AT THE DILAPIDATED building with mixed emotions. It was the third one he'd seen in what he assumed was a few weeks. It was a marked improvement over the zero he'd seen while he'd been wandering the districts, but he couldn't help but be disappointed at the slow rate.

This building was shaped like a forty-story pill. It was clear that the website belonged to a pharmaceutical company of some kind, though CJ didn't recognize the name. From the state of the building, he guessed it was because the company wasn't all that popular. Still, the place looked more stable than the other two he'd seen. It was on the verge of collapse, but CJ didn't think it would fall any time soon.

It was a hunch, of course, but it was strong enough that CJ was contemplating going inside. After visiting the Gaius search engine, he'd realized that the websites wouldn't be able to give him any information about the virtual world, so he hadn't bothered to enter any buildings. Instead, he'd spent his time exploring the districts and testing the limits of what he could interact with.

The piece of code in his pocket proved that the buildings might hold something for him. After all, there had to be a reason the sphere had been the only thing to remain after the website was decommissioned. CJ already had several theories, but nothing could be confirmed without obtaining more samples.

The building in front of him was a chance to do that. If he could locate another ball of code before the building collapsed, then he might be able to confirm some of his theories.

There's no reason I shouldn't be safe, CJ told himself.

Avatars streamed past him a few dozen at a time. That was significantly less than other websites, but it was still reassuring. After all, if users still visited the site, the company wouldn't need to shut it down. Conversely, there were dozens of reasons why a website might be taken down. For most of them, it didn't matter how many users visited the website.

CJ rubbed his palms against his legs and used the familiar motion to ground himself. He hadn't needed to since he'd arrived in this world, but his anxiety was derailing his thoughts.

What would DJ do? That was easy. His brother would have rushed into the building without much thought for the consequences. But CJ wasn't his brother. He couldn't fail to consider the consequences—a disadvantage in this case.

He could ignore the building, as well as any other of its type that he found, and make his way to Manar. But he would be abandoning whatever knowledge he could have gained about the sphere and, potentially, his first substantial piece of information about the virtual world. It was something that might actually help Manar, so CJ couldn't ignore it just because he was afraid.

Mind made up, CJ crossed the distance to the building entrance. However, the second he passed through, he felt a slight pressure weighing down on him, followed by the feeling of being watched. In the same moment, an alarm reverberated through the entire building, and a voice rang out in warning:

"INTRUDER DETECTED! INTRUDER DETECTED!"

CJ froze. Was it talking about him?

As if in reply, the pressure around him increased. It was barely enough to make him uncomfortable, but it confirmed that he was the intruder in question. But why would the website view him as an intruder?

CJ forced himself to move even as he pondered. *I entered the website for the Gaius search engine, and it didn't identify me as an intruder. What's different now?*

"MOBILIZING DEFENSES," the voice called out.

The words only caused CJ's confusion to grow. Usually, the only thing that could trigger a website's defenses were external codes that snuck in somehow, like worms and viruses. Since those were generally malicious, most programs automatically defended themselves whenever a foreign code was detected.

CJ sighed, more embarrassed than angry. He'd wasted so much time outside deliberating every possible problem that could crop up, and he'd failed to consider the simplest one. Still, that didn't mean he was willing to give up. He assumed that the pressure he felt was the website's security system trying to restrict him. The force of it made him believe that the defenses weren't all that strong. If he could avoid the other defenses long enough, he might be able to find what he came for before he was ejected.

That sounds too much like one of DJ's plans, CJ realized, his expression grim. Still, he didn't know how many chances he would get. He couldn't abandon this one.

The building wasn't nearly as large as the Gaius search engine, but it had a similar layout. However, instead of cubicles, there were countless market stalls, each manned by a corporate avatar in a lab coat. CJ assumed he would be sent to a separate room when he reached a stall. But that wasn't his goal. His goal was on the other end of the floor, where rooms branched out to other parts of the site. The deeper into the site he could get, the more likely he would stumble into the website's central framework. More than anywhere, it was likely that the code he was looking for would be there.

That's where he would head, hoping that the security systems didn't eject him. Or the building didn't collapse.

Inwardly, CJ acknowledged how poorly thought out the plan was. Still, it was something that his brother would have approved of, which bolstered his confidence slightly.

Without another thought, he sprinted diagonally across the floor, edging toward the side. Almost immediately, a wall of fire rose up in front of him. CJ tried to brake, but unfortunately, after years of being barely able to control his limbs, he wasn't used to such fine movements. He tripped over his own feet and fell into the flames before he could stop himself. A moment later, he stumbled out the other side completely unharmed. His skin was red, and his clothes were somewhat smoky, but he was completely fine.

Guess I was right about its defenses being weak, CJ thought, his eyes wide. He was panting, which was surprising. He must've been panting only because his brain assumed that he should be. However, it was unnecessary; theoretically, CJ shouldn't even need to breathe with his virtual body.

He spared one last look at the firewall before continuing on. Learning from his mistake, he kept his pace at a fast jog. Intermittently, firewalls would rise up in his path. CJ knew he wouldn't be harmed, but he dodged each one just to be safe. At his pace, it wasn't long before he'd crossed the floor and reached the first of the side rooms.

"INTRUDER DETECTED! MOBILIZING DEFENSES!"

Immediately, everything changed. The floor with the stalls disappeared, and CJ stumbled into a hallway. The passage was similar to Sparta's, except the walls were composed of overlaid metal sheets. CJ placed his hand against one. As if in response, the orb in his pocket grew cold. It stayed cold even after he pulled his hand back.

CJ slowed his pace to a fast walk as he navigated the hallway. It eventually split into three branches, all disappearing into the distance. There were no identifying marks that CJ could use to decide his path.

He spent a precious minute pondering the problem before finally deciding to pick one at random. He was halfway through the passage when the orb grew warm. This time, CJ was sure that he hadn't imagined it, and he pulled the sphere from his pocket.

It grew cold earlier when I touched the walls. Now it turned warm when I started down a path, CJ reflected. *Is it leading me? And if it is, does the heat mean that I chose the right path or the wrong one?*

CJ returned to the junction and this time went straight ahead. At the halfway mark, the orb grew cold. CJ returned to the start and went right. This time, the orb stayed cold.

That answers it then, CJ thought. The left path was the only one that made the sphere go warm. He retraced his steps and continued down the left passage. There was another junction at its end, but now CJ didn't need to pause and decide where to go.

He encountered his first obstacle down the second path. Footsteps pounding against the ground gave CJ enough warning to slow down before a group of bots turned the corner into his passage. Each was about three feet tall and had a head like a bullet. Their bodies had a metallic sheen with a deep-red overtone. There were about half a dozen, all holding staffs that were twice their size. The staffs emitted a faint blue light as well as a pressure that CJ could feel from several feet away.

CJ guessed these were the website's antivirus defenses. He backed up.

Unfortunately, the group spotted him and advanced, chattering incomprehensibly. One of them stepped out in front of the others and jabbed its staff at CJ. "You are not on the Access Control Lists. Provide authentication or be destroyed."

CJ's eyes widened, and he raised his hands up. "There's no need for that. I can leave. Or you can eject me from the site."

The leader stepped forward again. "Provide authentication or be destroyed."

CJ gulped. Then he ran.

The security system gave chase immediately, but CJ was faster. He retraced his steps to the previous hallway and then dashed into a different passage. The sphere in his pocket grew cold, but CJ ignored it, taking turns without thinking until the sound of footsteps faded into the distance. Unfortunately, just when he was about to stop, another antivirus squad turned the corner, forcing him to sprint again.

The orb in his pocket grew colder with every hallway CJ passed. Not for the first time, CJ wished his brother was with him. Then he would have been able to do something other than run away. He pushed the thought out of his head and focused on staying ahead of his pursuers.

I can't keep running forever, he thought grimly. *Sooner or later, I'll need a plan.* It wasn't the first time he'd thought that. While his mind was already working furiously, nothing had occurred to him since the chase had started.

Near the end of a passage, the sphere grew warm. The change was so sudden that it immediately drew his attention. Just as he was deciding what to do, it turned cold again. CJ studied the orb, focusing on the lines of code. On the surface, he could note nothing different. However, the longer he studied, the more he sensed a call emanating from it, propagating like a wave.

Somewhere within the building, something answered back.

Footsteps started pounding from somewhere behind him, and CJ hurried along. He kept his movements hurried but methodological as he retraced his steps along the hallway, sticking to the walls. He held the orb in front of him like a metal detector, trying to maintain his awareness of the call, but his thoughts were too harried to focus. Fortunately, he didn't have to go far before the sphere warmed in his hands again. CJ stopped and studied the spot. Nothing stood out to him. The footsteps drew closer. CJ could vaguely make out chattering.

He studied the spot with increasing fervency, trying to note any discrepancies. Hopefully, whatever had triggered the sphere would be helpful. If he didn't find anything soon, he would have to move on or risk getting caught. He wasted several precious seconds moving from one part of the passage to study the spot at that end.

He banged on the metal sheets, then did it again more firmly. When that failed to do anything, he tried pushing, then tried to wedge his fingers into the seams between the sheets. At every point, his heart slammed against his chest, almost in rhythm to the approaching footsteps. With nothing else working, he waved the sphere over the wall.

Finally, that got a reaction.

The object grew even warmer. The wall split to the sides, revealing a door. CJ was through it with barely a thought. As the door disappeared behind him, he leaned against the wall, trying to catch his breath.

That was more excitement than he'd ever experienced in his life. Adrenaline flooded his senses. His heart beat so fast that he was certain that he would have thrown up, had he been capable of it. He couldn't help but wonder how DJ threw himself into such dangerous situations over and over again. Having experienced a bit of it himself, CJ respected his brother all the more—though he was also a little worried about his mental health.

A minute later, CJ had regained enough composure to look around. Immediately, he forgot about the chase. He was within a tunnel. Its walls twisted in a spiral that extended infinitely forward and disappeared into the distance. Lines stretched along the floor and walls, forming squares where they intersected. Within the squares were words, which fixated CJ's attention.

Although the words were in a language that he didn't understand, something about them tugged at him until he realized he recognized them as bits of code. Whoever had designed the website had probably translated the binary into a unique language known only to them. CJ had done the same thing when merging Manar's consciousness with Gaius, as it was much easier to build and work with other languages instead of direct binary. Although he couldn't parse them, they at least explained where he was.

Someone built a back door within the website, a shortcut that bypasses the software's security, he thought. He raised the sphere to eye level. *And somehow, this helped me find and access it.*

That shouldn't have been possible, and yet it was the only thing that made sense. Now more than ever, CJ was determined to figure out what it was. His determination bolstered his confidence and displaced the abject terror. He made his way down the path, taking his time to study the writings. There was no hope of decoding them within any reasonable time frame, but there was always a chance that he could learn something from the work.

Eventually, he turned his attention back to the orb, twisting it around his fingers once more. While it had gone inert once CJ had entered the tunnel, it still called out for something. Since he'd attuned to it once already, CJ had no problem doing so again. This was fortunate, as the call was the only thing that he could use for orientation whenever he came across a branch.

He turned the sphere around in his hands a few times more but still couldn't see anything special about it. He gave up on his examination when the sphere grew warm again. CJ looked up just as his feet landed on dead air. His heart dropped to the pit of his stomach as the rest of his body began to follow. Instinct made him lean back, and he fell backward into the tunnel, narrowly avoiding a much worse fall. The now-familiar rush of adrenaline hit again, and he tried to collect himself. Realizing what had happened, he peeked over the ledge into a black abyss spiraling down, seemingly without a bottom. It was embarrassing that he hadn't noticed it until it was nearly too late. But that feeling quickly turned to anger. He couldn't allow himself to be so engrossed that he tuned out everything.

It was a warning he'd heard numerous times from DJ. Until now, he'd never seen the point. Now he understood. His brother wasn't here to watch out for him, and if CJ didn't learn to watch out for himself, he could very easily be killed. The antivirus squad had almost proven that, as had this whole situation.

He needed to do better. And he would.

CJ focused on the scene in front of him. He stood at the end of a large chamber shaped like a half circle. The bottom part led to the abyss. The chamber walls were covered in the familiar tapestry of ones and zeros. At its center hovered a slowly rotating sphere of codes. Several dozen feet long, white bars stretched like bones from the ground and toward the chamber walls, connecting them.

There were several other tunnels scattered around the walls, and some bones were connected to those too. There was a slight gap between the sphere and the bars, like two magnets with the same polarity being pushed apart. This meant that while the sphere rotated, the white bars stayed in place.

CJ took it all in, his eyes wide with fascination. It didn't take much to understand that he was within the core of the website itself. CJ had never seen anything like it. He was familiar with how all of this looked in two dimensions on his computer screen, written in a programming language, but to see it represented this way ...

It's amazing, he thought.

The sphere at the center was probably the primary code, the foundational rules built into the website as it was created. They would serve as the framework for everything else that was added. The white bars probably acted as signal pathways between the core and the website itself, regulating its activities and providing a path in case maintenance had to be done on the sphere.

CJ felt a strong pull coming from the center of the orb. The sphere answered with a call of its own. Somewhere within that sphere was what he'd come for, that much was clear. But how was he going to get there? Between him and the core was a bottomless abyss.

CJ looked around for ideas. He spotted a small ledge encircling the length of the chamber. It was about a foot across and jutted out the sides of the walls. Theoretically, he could balance on the ledge and walk toward one of the white bars at his level. From there, it would be simple to get to the core.

Just thinking about that made CJ so dizzy that he had to back away from the edge. With another scan, he noticed some bars connected directly to tunnel entrances. They were few, but he figured he had a better chance of finding one than he did surviving a walk along the ledge.

He backed farther away from the edge and retraced his steps back up the path. The sphere grew colder with each step, but CJ ignored it until he picked a crossroad. At the junction, he picked another path and allowed the orb to lead him to the core once more. Unfortunately, the tunnel he picked didn't have a bridge. CJ stood on the edge for a moment, calculating his position in reference to where he'd been and where he was headed. Only once he was sure of his path did he retrace his steps for another attempt.

This time, he chose correctly. The white bars stretched in front of him, forming a makeshift bridge. As close as he was, it was easier to make out the ones and zeros that made up the piece of code. CJ placed a foot on the bridge tentatively and pressed down, then, he went for the second test. With his other foot still firmly in the tunnel, he stomped on the bridge as hard as he could. The bar didn't so much as wobble. Only then was CJ confident enough to place his whole weight on it.

Immediately, the orb started vibrating wildly. CJ considered putting it back in his pocket but settled on cradling it to his chest to provide an extra measure of protection. For whatever reason, something here obviously resonated with the orb; hiding it away might have a detrimental effect.

It took CJ a few minutes to cross the entire length of the bar, then he stood in front of the spherical mesh. This close, the resonance between the two spheres was almost a physical force. He stretched a hand to the core and was stopped by a wall of energy. CJ squinted and could make out a slight tapestry of code encircling the sphere.

CJ raised the orb. In response, the core spun faster on its axis, and when CJ stretched his hand again, there was no barrier to stop him. Every inch of him ached to press his hands against the core, to feel it beneath his fingers. But for all he knew, that could cause the whole website to crash or force it to spawn defenses that he was ill-equipped to handle.

Instead, CJ raised the orb again and pressed it against the core. He couldn't explain why he did it, except that it felt right somehow. The whole chamber shuddered, and he almost regretted his actions. A piece of the core detached and drifted down to him. CJ reached for it with his free hand. It was spherical and similar in size to the orb that he already had. CJ noted this absently, his attention fixed on the lines of code that covered its surface. There were slight variations, but its code matrix was similar enough to the original orb in his hand that he had no doubt they were both copies of the same software. Clones, probably of the virtual assistant that had gone obsolete. But why was this part of this website's core? He couldn't find an answer to that.

CJ's thoughts were interrupted when the two spheres started vibrating in his hands. It was so sudden that CJ failed to react in time. The orbs lurched toward each other and hit with enough force that they dented.

No, he realized, narrowing his eyes, *not dented. They're merging.*

The process took only a few seconds. When it was done, CJ was left with an orb much like the one he'd had, except larger. The code matrix was similar as well. However, CJ observed that the variations that he'd seen in the second orb had been integrated into this one, forming something altogether new. CJ didn't know what to think about that. He got the feeling that whatever was being formed was still incomplete.

CJ was curious about what the finished product would be. He had to find more spheres.

But first, CJ thought grimly, *I need to find a way out of this place without getting killed.*

20

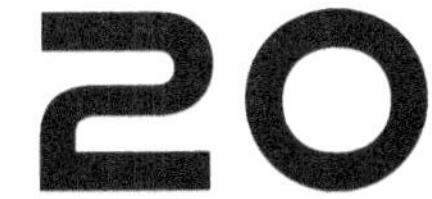

THE VIRTUAL WORLD

THE DARKNESS PRESSED in on everything as if with a will of its own. Even with the moonlight, it was impossible to see farther than a few feet ahead, so Manar had given up trying. Instead, he used what he could hear—which was easy since he was the only thing making any sound for miles—and the signal from the nanites to confirm he was heading in the right direction.

His expression was calm, but impatience gnawed at his mind, along with other emotions. With the darkness suppressing everything, it was harder to estimate the time. Still, Manar couldn't accept that he'd been walking for anything less than two weeks.

And he'd still not seen anything.

Several times, he convinced himself that he'd somehow been tricked, that he was just walking in circles. So he'd started leaving markers every few miles. They confirmed that he was making progress but did nothing to make him less impatient for something, anything, to happen. He couldn't help but feel like something big was building up while he wasted his time here. It didn't help that he couldn't communicate with anyone.

Not even by returning to his body.

That had been a surprise when Manar tried it, back on the other side of the scar. Although he'd tried several times more over the last day, he hadn't been able to feel any sort of connection with his body. The worry that he might be trapped in the virtual world added to his impatience. But ultimately, it wasn't something Manar could do anything about. Not from where he was. He just had to hope that CJ was working to rectify whatever had gone wrong. Manar's focus was defeating Helene as quickly as he could.

And it would help, Manar thought, gritting his teeth, *if this place were something other than a barren wasteland and*—

He looked up, and in front of him, a few feet away and to the right, barely visible in the darkness, was a stall, the kind he'd expect to see in a farmers' market. It had the same rickety construction and signboard with most of the letters missing. Something stared at him over the counter. Its face was shadowed beneath a hood, but Manar was sure it was staring at him.

It's a human, he thought as he came to a halt. He'd just been cursing the monotony of his journey, but suddenly seeing something different unsettled him.

Manar pushed the thought out of his head and rushed over to the booth. Closer, it was easier to make out the attendant's features: male, with a narrow jaw and chipped tooth. His nose was comically long and crooked. He looked at Manar from the corner of his constantly shifting eye. Like Manar, he was slightly pixelated. The attendant wore a blue shirt and sensible pants, but both were threadbare and torn in several places. With his hood, the man looked like the shifty character cliché in every movie ever made. His shirt promoted a messaging platform that Manar had never heard of.

"Looking for something?" the attendant hissed out each word bitingly.

Manar felt a sigh build up within him. "Information," he replied.

"Good place for that." The attendant nodded, his eyes looking somewhere behind Manar. "What do you want to know?"

"Who're you?"

"Why?" the man countered, instantly suspicious. "Who wants to know? You want me to believe it's you, but is it? Why do you want to know? What are you going to do with the information, huh?" As he spoke, his eyes constantly bounced between studying Manar and searching for something behind him.

Manar stepped back in surprise. If he'd known his question would trigger such a reaction, he would have started with something else. This was his first shot at getting real answers; he couldn't mess it up. There had to be a way to reassure the attendant.

"I'm not going to do anything with it," Manar said, making sure to keep his tone and body language open and sincere. "I asked because I'm not from here, and I thought you might be able to help me get my bearings."

Somehow, his sincerity seemed to make the attendant more suspicious. "You picked the wrong person to try to scam, buddy. You're not from here? Then where are you from? Where else could you be from? I think the better question is: Who are you, and why are you trying to scam me out of my business, huh?"

Manar recoiled at the barrage of accusations. He got all that from just a simple question? Manar could answer, but he doubted it would help. The attendant seemed set on being suspicious of him for whatever reason, so Manar decided to try something different.

He relaxed his shoulders and made sure they drooped in the same way as the attendant. Next, he shifted his weight to the balls of his feet, making his movements fidgety. Finally, he hardened his face slightly so he looked threatening. Manar wanted to look just as jittery as the attendant. At least that was his hope. He leaned closer to the stall, putting his face as close to the attendant's as he could.

"It's none of your business who I am or where I'm from," Manar growled. "And I don't really care who you are either. What I really want to know is what you can tell me about this place. Is that something you can do? Or do I have the wrong place after all?"

Manar held his breath, keeping his eyes fixed on the attendant's in a half glare. His heart was pounding, but he kept his anxiety hidden. A moment later, he was rewarded when something like satisfaction flickered in the attendant's expression.

"There is no need for hostility, my friend," the attendant said coolly. His eyes left Manar's to scan the area, but there was no longer any suspicion in his tone. "These are strange times, you know. I had to make sure, you understand. To apologize for my previous rudeness and to assure you that you have come to the right place, I shall answer your original question."

Manar kept his expression the same but accepted the compromise with a nod.

"Once, I was a digital promotional aid for Chirp. However, though our messaging platform was top of the line, we were progressively sidelined until we disbanded, and I was cast adrift."

It took Manar a moment to parse the sentence. *He's a bot whose company went bankrupt, and the website was taken down.* Manar had already guessed the first part, which was why he'd decided to try his performance. Bots were far more commonplace than most people were aware of. Even small privately owned businesses had started using them as a first point of contact. It was just more efficient. The part about the bot being set adrift, though, was perplexing. If his website was taken down, shouldn't he have been erased?

"How did you get here, then?" Manar asked. The attendant's eyes stopped shifting, focusing on him with a hint of suspicion. Manar quickly corrected himself. "I mean, why are you here, specifically, away from others of your kind?"

The suspicion disappeared, and Manar sighed.

"These are strange times, and numbers are more dangerous than solitude." The bot huffed, its eyes shifting again. "No, I'm better off alone."

Manar leaned closer. "What happened?"

Something in his expression must have triggered the bot because its eyes focused on him, and its face became guarded. "I do not spread rumors, my friend. If that's what you're after, then maybe you have the wrong place after all."

"All I'm asking for is information, friend," Manar said. When the bot's expression didn't change, he backed off, recognizing he'd erred somehow. "But it seems like I may have strayed from where I need to be. Where can I go to find what I need?"

"What can you trade for it?" the attendant asked, then scoffed, looking at Manar scornfully. "No, it's no secret anyway, and your absence will be enough."

He pointed. "There is a city in that direction where you'll find the information you want. I would tell you to be careful who you ask, but I sense that you will stir up trouble anyway. When you do, I just ask that you do not bring it to my stall."

The bot bent his head until its hood covered his features once more. Manar took the dismissal for what it was and stepped away from the booth.

The conversation was brief, but Manar had come away with a lot. First, and potentially the most important, was the confirmation that there was somewhere he could get more information. The attendant had pointed in the same direction as the signal that was guiding Manar to Helene. That couldn't be a coincidence. Most likely, whatever strange things had been happening were a result of her influence.

The only thing left was to test the limits of the bots. He was familiar enough with their design to know they were given a bit of autonomy, to make their interactions with potential customers more relatable and lifelike. However, since they weren't true AIs, they couldn't be completely self-aware. Those limits would determine how Manar interacted with them.

But that's for the future, he thought. *First, I have to get to that city.*

WHEN HERMIONE WAS YOUNGER, it had been her job to drag her father away from his workstation to eat, take a bath, or basically do anything other than sit in a dark room all day. At the time, she didn't understand how obsessive a project could make a person. However, as she grew older, her task became more difficult—not because her father had become more stubborn, but because by then Hermione had started joining in on his work and grown just as obsessed. They would lose themselves in a project for days, immersing themselves so fully that time lost all meaning. It gave Hermione's mother grief, but those were the days that Hermione truly felt fulfilled.

The picospores, especially, had been responsible for countless sleepless nights. Those had been their most challenging project, as well as their longest. At some point, Hermione's father had called for breaks, something he'd never done before. Late one night, they'd finished the first prototype of the spores. Every other technician had already gone home, but she and her father stayed behind to complete the last steps.

The memory was bittersweet. Hermione had felt pride at their accomplishment, but also a sense of loss at the fact that it was over.

It was night now, and she'd thought she would feel the same when she finished the machine meant to counter the spores. She'd expected to feel pride and maybe a measure of nostalgia, as she always did when she worked with the spores. She'd thought she would stand back with a small smile on her face, basking in the milestone achievement.

Instead, she knelt on the floor of her laboratory, clutching her chest, her body shaking with sobs.

Her heart overflowed with sadness, pain, and loss. Her tears fell, no matter how hard she tried to stop them. She'd done it, hadn't she? She'd created something that directly countered the picospores. It nullified everything she and her father had spent years working tirelessly to build, technology that was meant to help people in the truest sense of the word. And she'd created its foil.

She'd done a good thing. Now no one on the team had to fear being turned into a puppet whenever they went up against Helene. Now they could do their jobs in peace. They had protection against what was supposed to be the Cloneys' legacy.

She'd done a good thing. When the team started encountering Helene's victims, they could rescue them, remove her influence, and give them back their lives. Lives that Helene was able to take because of Hermione and her father.

No. Hermione had done a good thing. She could save Bethany. Her sister had been held captive by Helene for almost half a decade. No one knew how much Helene had twisted her head. Now Hermione could undo all that damage. She could help. That's what the machine was for. To help.

But so were the picospores, her heart screamed. She and her father had designed the picospores to be the ultimate panacea. They could be directed to eliminate almost any disease. They shouldn't have to counteract them. They were good, but Helene had twisted them. She'd ruined them.

And not just the spores themselves. Helene had ruined the concept of medical picospores.

Even if Helene was defeated and people found out what she'd done with the spores, no one would use them. It didn't matter how much they could help. It didn't matter how much good they could do. It didn't matter if Helene was the only one to be able to hack into the spores. No one would want to take the risk of being turned into a marionette, a prisoner in their own body. If—when—that happened, humanity would be set back decades by a technology that was supposed to usher in a new era.

Hermione cried. She cried for all the people who would be lost, all those who would continue to suffer because they couldn't trust the very thing that could save them.

DJ found her there sometime later, still on the floor, her body shaking with the force of her sobs. Hermione didn't even try to stop her tears. She couldn't. Not when she'd realized why she was crying. Those people deserved someone who would grieve for their pain, someone who understood and cared about what they would be forced to go through.

Distantly, she felt DJ kneel beside her and place a hand on her shoulder. She felt his confusion and how uncomfortable he was, but he didn't try to stop her. He just held her while she gave expression to her pain.

Hermione was grateful for that.

"I'M GUESSING YOU don't want to talk about it," DJ said sometime later. Hermione had finally composed herself and was sitting on a stool at one of the counters. DJ had taken the laboratory's only chair. He stared at her in concern and discomfort, though he tried to hide it. He wore his usual jumper over a T-shirt and jeans and looked like he'd rolled out of bed.

"How did you know?" Hermione asked.

"I don't know," DJ said with a shrug, "but those tears were way too intense not to be personal. I'm not gonna pry because, honestly, I'm not sure I can help. I'm more likely to make stuff worse." He jerked a thumb at the door. "I'd call Christy, but she's not the most comforting person either. Her idea of solving problems is to shoot them, which, to her credit, she's very good at." DJ seemed to consider that for a moment. "Can't say I disagree with her."

Hermione chuckled. "Well, you're kind of right. I wouldn't know where to start talking about it, and it's more of my own problem anyway, something I have to learn to deal with." DJ nodded in understanding. Hermione took a breath, wiped her eyes, and pushed everything to the back of her mind. "Anyway, you were looking for me, right? Is something wrong?"

"Not really." He shrugged. "It's just, you've been locked in here for a while now, and no one was sure if you were still alive. I mean, I know we're on sort of a time crunch right now, but Olsen still hasn't gotten back to me yet. So, you know, no need to kill yourself. You can afford to take it slow and—"

"You're talking about the machine for the picospores, right?" Hermione said, then nodded to one of the counters where the device was sitting. "I've finished it. Yeah, Martin gave me an idea of how to fix one of the major issues I was having, and that gave me a clue for how to fix the other issue. All I have to do is run a few tests. But I need to synthesize a few more volumes of spores to use."

Hermione had no doubt that the machine would work, but the tests might show areas she could fine-tune. DJ stood to get a better look at the machine, and Hermione followed him. It was shaped like a Rubik's Cube with a small protruding nozzle at the front, where the sound waves would propagate. Deep grooves ran along its length, and blue light spilled from the gap. Before she'd spoken to Martin and had the idea to use titanium, the cube had been several feet across. Now it was small enough to be cupped in a palm. After Hermione was done running her tests, she would make several more so each member of the team had one.

"Slick," DJ said. "What's it called?"

"What do you mean?"

"Well, it's your invention, right? You gotta name it."

"I haven't really thought of a name," Hermione said. "I don't even know where to start."

"How about … the Rejector Cube?" DJ suggested with a grin. "Cuz, you know, it rejects the picospores."

Hermione recoiled and shook her head no.

"The Bio-Sporebane?" He grinned again, his eyes shining. "Cuz it's the bane of the spores?"

Where the hell is he getting this? Hermione thought.

"Absolutely not," she said. "And I'm still stuck on why it needs a name in the first place."

"It's basically our secret weapon against Helene, so of course it needs a name. And it needs to be catchy. When we explain it to the other guys, it'll be a mouthful to keep referring to it as *the machine that can nullify the picospores.* So, how about the Bio-Electric Spore Suppressor?" He grinned at her again. "Get it? Cuz it suppresses—"

"How about I name it?" Hermione blurted. DJ's eyes twinkled, and she realized she'd fallen into his trap. She almost groaned. Pushing the thought aside, she considered the cube.

A small part of her recoiled at giving a name to something she'd come to hate, even if she'd been the one to invent it. But on the other hand, as its inventor, she was the most qualified. She bounced words around in her head before settling on a name that she didn't hate as much as the others.

"Synaptic Pulse."

"Because?" DJ asked expectantly.

"Because what?"

"You have to explain why you chose the name, or else how would we know it fits?"

"What?" Hermione blew out a breath. She wouldn't be sucked into this. "I guess you're going to have to trust me then because we're calling it the Synaptic Pulse."

"All right," DJ drawled, "but the others are going to want to know the reason too."

"Then they can all bite me!" Hermione snapped, then winced. *That was so rude.*

DJ chuckled. "I'm sure Karla would love that."

Hermione laughed too. "She might even go for it."

DJ's chuckle turned into a full laugh. He sobered up after a while. "On a more serious note, though, this is good, Hermione. This is really good. I mean, shit, with this we can actually start attacking Helene directly, take back some of her power. We don't have anything to defeat the drones yet, but if we can cure the government officials she's taken control of? That'll be big."

"Do you know which officials she's infected?" Hermione asked.

"I know at least one," DJ replied, looking thoughtful. "Dude nearly ruined my life, so it's kinda depressing that I have to save him." He gave an exaggerated sigh, swinging his arm across her shoulders. "But it's the sacrifice we make as heroes."

Hermione groaned.

THE NEXT DAY, DJ found himself in the booth of a diner, casually checking out the other customers while he waited for Olsen. The admiral had picked a different place for their meeting, for obvious reasons. DJ had arrived early again so he could scope the place out. So far, he hadn't noticed anything. He hoped it meant there wasn't anything to notice. This was the second time he was meeting Olsen outside the base. At some point, Helene was bound to notice. What DJ couldn't predict was if the AI would settle for just spying on them or send drones to wipe them out.

It wouldn't be the first time that'd happened.

Olsen walked into the diner a few minutes later and started heading toward DJ after a brief scan of the room. The admiral was wearing a polo shirt tucked into a pair of shorts. It was the same type he'd worn to their last meeting—the same kind DJ had given him hell for.

Some people never learn, he thought as Olsen slumped in the seat opposite him. DJ opened his mouth, but Olsen spoke first.

"Don't even start," he growled. "With the mood I'm in, I'm not sure I can deal with your bullshit without wringing your neck."

DJ studied Olsen for a moment. In all the years DJ had known him, Olsen had always had a scowl on his face. But somehow, the scowl he wore now was different. DJ didn't know how he knew that, and it wasn't really something he wanted to ponder. Olsen was still built like a bull, but exhaustion lined every part of his bearing. The presence that formed so much of his character felt diminished somehow.

In other words, the man looked like shit. Normally, DJ would have been obligated to make a couple of jokes about it, but it didn't feel right somehow.

"Fair enough," he said lightly. He gestured to a passing waiter and ordered them each a beer. "Wanna fill me in?"

Olsen waved away the question. "Since the last time we met, I've been hacked three times, had my workload doubled—which should be impossible since reducing work was the whole idea of integrating the AI in the first place—and faced an inquisition over some bullshit charges.

"I've also been seeing more of Austin lately, who I think, is a picospore-controlled puppet. On top of everything else?" The waiter arrived with their drinks, and Olsen paused. He took a swig of his beer the moment the server was gone. "Actually makes me miss the good old days when it was only your shit I had to deal with."

"Christ, man," DJ breathed.

No wonder you look like shit, he added in his mind. It didn't take a genius to figure out that Helene was responsible for it—especially if Austin was involved. DJ felt a familiar twist in his gut. More than likely, Helene was targeting Olsen because of their involvement.

Dude looks miserable, DJ thought. The thought that it was because of him made him feel horrible.

"Wipe that look off your face," Olsen growled. "I didn't pour my heart out to get your pity. I just want you to understand why it's taking so long to get anything on Ndidi. I'm constantly being watched. But I do have a lead I'm working on."

"Jesus, man! Forget about that for now."

Olsen raised an eyebrow. "You have another way of finding your friend?"

DJ was tempted to lie, but Olsen knew him far too well to fall for that. And he was right: he was their only shot at getting Ndidi back.

"All right, fine. We're screwed without you," DJ agreed. "But you shouldn't risk your career for it. Ndidi got herself into this. She can wait a couple of days while the heat dies down for you."

Olsen's eyes hardened in anger and disappointment. "You're better than that, son. I know you're angry with her, but you of all people know what Helene's capable of. Your friend might not have days, and you know it. Or would you like to see her as one of those puppets? Like another Austin?"

It would be something she chose when she betrayed the team and put my brother in a coma, DJ wanted to say. But that was harsh, even for him. Plus, Olsen's statement was a nice transition into what he wanted to discuss.

"It wouldn't matter," he said.

"Boy—" Olsen started.

"It wouldn't matter because we have a way to fix it now." Olsen glowered at him, and DJ continued. "That's why I messaged you. Hermione finally figured out a way to neutralize the picospores and remove them from Helene's control. If Ndidi is being controlled, we have a way to kick Helene out before safely extracting the spores. And that goes for every one of Helene's puppets."

Olsen was silent for a while, probably reaching the same conclusions DJ himself had. "Austin," he said finally.

"Exactly." DJ nodded, grinning. "Figured we could kill two birds with one Synaptic Pulse—that's what she's calling it by the way. So far, Hermione's only tested it out on rats and stuff. I figured, since the guy's not much higher than a rat, he would be the perfect test subject." DJ took a swig of his beer. "Plus, with him out of Helene's control, we might have another ally, maybe reduce the burden on you. What do you think?"

"Boy," Olsen said, "that's the best damn news I've heard all week. When can we start?"

DJ reached into the bag beside him and retrieved the small cube, which he slid across the table with a grin. "You said you've been seeing Austin more than usual, right? Well, you can start, then. All you have to do is point and shoot."

CHAPTER

23

SPARTA, DJ DECIDED, was weird at night, in that it was no different from during the day. There were fewer people, sure, but still far more than one would expect anywhere that wasn't an apartment building. And the people were still working—in the middle of the night.

As DJ navigated the hallways to his room, he saw employees walking around, still dressed as if it were eight in the morning. Dressed casually, he was the odd one out. He'd known that most of Sparta's staff had rooms within the headquarters, but only now was he seeing the necessity of it. It was weird. And probably illegal.

He also noticed more security. This was expected. Fortunately, hanging out with Manar for so long had given him enough legitimacy that there were no problems. Even the departmental gates had been keyed to recognize him, practically giving him free rein to the building. Most of Sparta's employees would kill for that privilege, and DJ wasn't even part of the organization.

Once again proving that it's all about who you know, he thought with a smirk.

DJ passed Hermione's laboratory on the way and poked his head in briefly. Unsurprisingly, Hermione was inside, tinkering with something DJ couldn't make out. DJ hoped it was another Synaptic Pulse. Despite what he'd said at the diner, they didn't have a lot of time to find Ndidi. Because of that, he'd given Olsen the only prototype to use on Austin, hoping to speed things up. Depending on how that went, every member of the raid would need a Synaptic Pulse, just in case Helene tried to dose them with the spores.

He'd wanted to bring the topic up with Hermione several times but hadn't been able to bring himself to do it. At least, not yet. She deserved to take a break for a day or two. But if she, completely on her own, started making a second Synaptic Pulse, who was DJ to complain?

He retracted his head with a grin and continued on his way. Chloe, Karla, and Liz had declined rooms at the headquarters, choosing instead to go to and from the warehouse whenever there was something important to discuss. It was more stressful, but DJ could understand their reasoning, wanting to stay in their own space. Plus, Sparta could be a little much sometimes.

He nodded to a smartly dressed woman clutching a folder and speed-walking through the hall, then took the stairs up to his floor. He passed Christy's room but didn't bother looking in. She would be training with the Murder Team at the warehouse, as DJ would have been if he hadn't had to meet Olsen. The thought was almost enough to ruin his mood, but DJ pushed past it.

The training was far more sadistic and torturous than what he endured at base, but not much worse in terms of intensity. And it was working. DJ had seen definite improvement in his combat prowess since he'd started working with Karla. He still hadn't managed to land a hit on her yet, but at least now he could last almost five minutes before being beaten senseless.

He'd expected to be able to double the time the first time he'd partnered with Christy against Karla, but somehow their time had reduced instead. Chloe said it was because the two of them weren't used to fighting together, which DJ found weird. They'd been on the same team for years. Then he considered that Christy usually supported him as a sniper and hardly ever in melee range. The difference was, while DJ could anticipate where Christy would aim with her rifle and might even take steps to make an opening for her, he didn't know any of her moves when fighting.

Still, their coordination was improving. DJ took this as progress. It was painful, but it was progress.

DJ reached his door and punched in the passcode. *Now,* he thought idly as the door swung open, *if I can only get Pratima and Karla into a ring.* His thoughts trailed off as he hesitated at the threshold, a foot hanging in the air.

Martin stared back at him, his eyebrow raised in amusement. "Do come in, Mr. Kojak. I'm far from a threat to you."

DJ stepped into the room and closed the door behind him. He locked it and unlocked it again, to be sure the thing actually worked. Behind him, Martin chuckled. DJ turned to face him, checking the room as he did.

"If I had known you were coming, Doc," he said, plastering a smile on his face, "I would have booked an earlier flight."

"Nonsense," Martin said, waving a hand. "Even I didn't know I would be coming today. Hermione stopped by the warehouse to show me the schematics of the Synaptic Pulse, and I decided to use the chance to act on something I've been putting off for a while now."

DJ walked into the bathroom. Nature was calling for the last couple of hours.

"So, Hermione brought you? All right, that makes sense." He projected his voice over the sound of his whizz. "How'd you get into my room, though?"

Martin coughed awkwardly. "Well, without Helene, Sparta's security isn't what it used to be."

Well, that's good to know, DJ thought, tapping the handle to flush. "So, what does this decision have to do with me?"

"Well, it was either you or Chloe."

The sound of running water filled the room. "Chloe's involved?" DJ sighed, allowing his exhaustion to bleed into his voice "Look, Doc, I don't want to be rude, but it's late and I've just spent hours on the road. I'm tired." The tap shut off, and DJ entered the room again, wiping his hands on his jeans. "I really need to be asleep in a couple of minutes. I can't really afford to be confused right now, so can you skip to the part where you tell me what the hell is going on?"

Martin adjusted his glasses. "You're right. I'm making this far more complicated than it needs to be, and I apologize for that. Suffice to say that I came to give you this." He took a small vial from his pocket and handed it over. DJ raised it to his eye. It was a little bigger than his thumb and filled with a silver-gray powder.

"What is it?" he asked.

"That," Martin said, adjusting his glasses again, "is a vial containing the nanites I extracted from Karla and Liz. Roughly a quarter of what was in each of them. It should be enough to give a person the near-superhuman abilities they enjoy without the risk of Helene's interference."

DJ squinted at the bottle. "So, you're saying these things, the powder, they were in Karla and Liz? Like swimming around inside them?"

"That's what he takes from that?" Martin muttered in what he probably thought was a tone too low for DJ to hear. In a louder voice, he said, "They've been thoroughly disinfected, I assure you. And they're in perfect working condition, if that's what you're worried about."

"I'm not really worried." DJ shrugged. "Just wondering why you're giving it to me, and why it had to be in the middle of the night."

"I had to give it to you this night because if I didn't, I was afraid I might not be able to resist their temptation. As for why I'm giving it to you, I would have thought it was obvious by now." Martin met DJ's eyes solemnly. "I want you to take it."

DJ's eyebrows rose in surprise. "What do you mean, *take it*?"

Martin sighed. "I mean I want you to inject the nanites into yourself."

"That's what I thought you meant," DJ muttered.

"Once they come online and are given enough time to work, you'll find every part of yourself significantly boosted. You'll be stronger, faster, and your regenerative properties will soar—as will your combat prowess, I'm sure."

Shit! That sounded amazing! Why hadn't DJ said yes yet? In fact, why was he being such a downer about this? He should have been bouncing off the walls. Hell, with those nanites, he might literally be able to do that. He'd be a fucking supersoldier. Why wasn't he happier about that?

"Why me?" he asked.

DJ, he said to himself, *what the fuck are you doing? Why are you asking stupid shit?*

His mouth ignored his internal monologue, acting on its own. "There are tons of people who could make better use of this. Pratima, for one. Even Chloe. You said you were deciding between us, so why didn't you choose her? She'd be unstoppable with this."

Martin shook his head. "Chloe is already at the peak of her strength and has had years to acclimate to that level. Adding the nanites at this stage might be more detrimental. Conversely, you still have room to grow. The nanites will help with that until you surpass even Pratima and Chloe."

DJ started to protest, but Martin raised a hand. "That's one reason, but it's only secondary to why I chose you. The primary reason boils down to trust. I don't trust Chloe Savage enough to gift her something like this. Like you said, if she learned to acclimate to her added strength, she would be unstoppable. What do you think she would do with such strength? Anything good?"

No. DJ couldn't imagine Chloe doing anything good with the nanites. She was already a match for the twins, and they were supersoldiers. When you added the nanites, combined with how crazy she was, she might end up worse than Helene.

"I would have extracted the nanites from the twins as well, but it would have killed them," Martin said into the silence. "But now you begin to see my point. As many options as you think would have been better, you are the only viable one. And your reticence further proves it. Do you know how many people would jump at the chance I'm offering? Even I took several days to convince myself not to use them, despite being the worst choice. In the short term, at least."

DJ couldn't deny that a part of him wanted to take the chance of having such power, but despite Martin's reasons, a larger part of him still felt there were better options.

Why did he think that? When had his self-worth tanked so much?

Probably when I watched my brother willingly put himself in a coma and did nothing to stop it, he guessed. He'd thought he'd shaken it off, accepted that there was nothing he could have done without denying CJ his agency. Apparently he hadn't. Weird way for it to manifest, though.

"It might help to stop considering whether you're worth it," Martin said, "and instead focus on the people you could help with the power."

DJ's thoughts immediately went to his older brother. For most of their lives, DJ had acted as a shield against the more brutal aspects of the world. He was abrasive and semi-violent so CJ didn't have to be. That was the way he protected his brother. But he'd done a shitty job of that recently. Regardless of CJ's choice, if DJ had had more strength, he could have followed his brother into the virtual world. With that kind of power, it wouldn't have mattered if DJ knew nothing about the place; he could have brute-forced it.

But he didn't, and now his brother was stuck without him.

Next, his mind drifted to Christy. No matter what she said, Christy had abandoned her career to help him because, for some mysterious reason he would never understand, she believed in him. So far, DJ had ignored those thoughts— partly because he didn't know how to handle them, and partly because he realized that their efforts against Helene had just been minor inconveniences. But with the nanites, with the strength to keep up with the twins and Chloe, he might actually be able to do something that made an impact, something that made him worth her belief.

There were others like Ndidi and Kyle and even Olsen. These were all people that he could help with just a little more power. So what if he wasn't worth it? He would help people until he was. If nothing else, he would rather the nanites go to him than to someone like Chloe. No matter how unsure he was, he was sure as shit that he would do more good with it than she would.

Martin adjusted his glasses. "It seems you've found your answer."

"Yeah, yeah." DJ sighed, "I still don't fully agree with you, but … what do I have to do?"

Martin reached into his breast pocket and produced a syringe. He took the half-filled vial and extracted the nanites. When he was done, he handed the filled syringe to DJ. "You simply inject it into yourself."

"Any particular place?"

Martin shook his head. "It does not matter."

DJ nodded and held the needle up to his arm. It stayed there for several seconds as he hesitated. When a minute passed, Martin gave a slight cough.

"I could help, if you're having problems," Martin offered.

His words shocked DJ out of the spiral he'd fallen into. "No, that's all right," he muttered.

He shook off his doubts, took a breath, and plunged the needle in. The syringe emptied itself. DJ threw his head back sharply, and his muscles tensed.

"I have to say," he said finally, "I expected more of a kick."

"It will take several hours for the nanites to attune themselves to your system," Martin explained, "and probably more for their effects to begin to show."

"Oh."

Martin coughed again, something that DJ was beginning to realize he did when he was uncomfortable. "We'll be seeing each other more often, DJ, as I'll need to take several tests to measure your growth—especially when the effects begin manifesting," he said in clear dismissal as he rolled himself to the door. "However, for now, I won't keep you from your bed any longer."

"Wait!" DJ called as something occurred to him. "You said you would have been the worst choice for the nanites, and yet you wanted to take them too. How would they have helped you?"

Martin hesitated at the door, and DJ saw the conflict in his eyes. When it cleared, it left behind a deep sadness. "Do you know why I was captured by Helene in the first place?" he asked.

DJ shook his head. He was sure either Manar or Ndidi had mentioned it, but for the life of him, he couldn't remember.

"It was for my research. I was working on an advanced form of biotech designed to give full mobility. Helene saw the potential in my work and forced me to apply it to the twins. She needed my technology to provide the prosthetic limbs they would need once separated, but once the designs were done, I realized prosthetics wouldn't be enough. The body might still reject them. And so, I designed the nanites.

"They were a side thought. Something to supplement the prosthetics and keep the twins alive. It was only later, once the twins began to show changes, that I realized the nanites had side effects that enhanced every part of their host, giving them superhuman strength and speed. However, it would have simply given me the strength of an average man." Martin gave a smile whose emotions DJ couldn't even begin to parse. He rolled himself out, adding over his shoulder, "Underwhelming, I know, but it would have allowed me to walk again."

DJ stared at the shut door. *Shit. Another reason to make sure I'm worthy of this.*

MANAR COULDN'T REMEMBER much of his childhood. Part of that was by design, while another part was simply his mind trying to protect itself. However, at least one memory stood out. It was from before his family had been killed and he'd been adopted by Simone. His mother, Nadira, had taken his sister and him to a trade fair—or, at least, what passed as a fair in 2002 Iraq.

They hadn't stayed long. Since they didn't actually have the money to buy anything, they'd just browsed. Still, Manar could remember the excitement he'd felt on that day. He remembered the fair as being a grand place with distinguished sellers sitting behind stalls, their wares gleaming under the noon sun. Of course, he'd been too young to notice the flaws: the old, splintered wood that had made up the stalls, the ragged clothes of the shop attendants, their decaying teeth—things that were all too clear to an adult.

Manar was reminded of that day as he stared at the scene in front of him.

The previously barren road was now filled with several dozen stalls arranged haphazardly along the path. Each looked like they'd been constructed in a rush and a stray breeze would make them collapse in the next moment. Behind the stalls were several single-story buildings, each as decrepit as the last.

Temporary.

Something about that itched at Manar, but he couldn't spare the time to think about it. Already he was starting to draw some looks. Some were indifferent, while others stared at him with open suspicion. Manar loosened his shoulders and walked on the balls on his feet, giving his steps a grace that he didn't have. He hardened his face and focused on appearing calm and confident. It was similar to the persona he'd used with the first bot, except he wasn't fidgety. There was no need to be; he was in complete control. At least, that was what he projected.

He passed the first and second stalls without stopping. It was only when he'd passed the fifth row that he realized that the place was larger than he'd first thought. From where he'd stood, it'd seemed like there were only a few dozen stalls clustered together, but now Manar saw rows branching off to various places deeper within. The other bot had called the place a city, but to Manar, it was just a large market.

He felt eyes on him as he passed. He ignored the ones that faded off after a glance and fiercely met the ones that stayed until they, too, looked away. When he was reaching the end of the street, he picked a stall at random and walked up to the counter. The attendant wore a hood. Manar had noticed the others did as well. Why did they bother, if they were all bots?

"What can I do for you, friend?" the attendant said.

As he spoke, the air around Manar shivered. Suddenly, he was in a different place. Manar spun around as his mind struggled to process the new development. There were chairs behind him, arranged around a table. It was empty, as was the rest of the room. The smell of alcohol and a hint of spice permeated the air. There was a wooden counter in front of him—and a shot glass?

It finally clicked. He was in a bar. But how?

"What can I do for you?"

Manar looked up. The attendant stood at the other side of the counter, wiping down a glass. The hood still covered most of his face, but Manar could feel his stare laced with a bit of suspicion. Manar forced his brain to focus. He could process how he'd disappeared after. At some point during his transformation, he'd stopped maintaining his persona. He fixed that and felt the suspicion in the bot's gaze fade.

Manar took a seat on one of the stools that lined the bar. "I need information."

The bot reached for a bottle on the shelf behind him. He poured a drink, though Manar noted the glass never filled. Out of curiosity, Manar picked up the shot glass in front of him and tilted it to his mouth. The liquid didn't move. At least that answered one question.

None of this was real. The bot had probably dragged him into this place when he'd approached the stall. It was the virtual representation of a private chat, except that it would be used on a wide scale. Each visitor was given their own room with a representative to attend to them. Websites with massive visitor traffic used it to handle dozens of customers simultaneously, usually with an AI acting as the representative.

Did that mean each stall was a separate website? It would explain the room, as well as the bot, but Manar found that hard to believe. He thought back to the old, decrepit things that made up the market. Would Sparta's website look like that? It was a depressing thought, considering the company spanned most of the world.

"Information, huh? That's an expensive request, friend. What can you trade for it?" the attendant said.

His words prompted a thought: this was a bot. He was talking to a bot right now, in a chat. That shouldn't have been possible. Chats were integrated into websites to deal with a massive amount of traffic. AIs were usually put in charge of them because only AIs had the processing speed to talk to so many customers simultaneously in real time.

Bots were programmed with partial autonomy similar to an artificial intelligence, but they had nowhere close to the processing of even the most basic AI. They shouldn't have been able to handle the amount of data needed to run a chat.

So, how did this one?

Manar pushed the thought out of his head and focused on the conversation. The previous bot had mentioned something about a trade as well. Manar still didn't know what that entailed, but hopefully he'd be able to figure it out before he was kicked out.

He frowned at his glass, trying to look casual. "What do you want for it?"

The attendant chuckled and picked up another glass to clean. "That depends on what sort of information you want, doesn't it? Some information costs more than others—some, nothing at all, for it is priceless."

Damn, Manar thought, resisting the urge to cringe. *He's really laying it on thick.*

"Everything has a price," he said, twirling the glass, "but what I want shouldn't be unaffordable. These are strange times after all." He glanced at the attendant, looking for a reaction.

The hood hid the bot's expression well, but he dropped the glass he had been wiping down. And then the bot's bearing changed. It wasn't something Manar could explain, but the attendant shifted. His whole body tensed as he leaned over the counter, bringing his face closer to Manar's. The hood still covered everything except his eyes, which shone with derision.

"What are you talking about?" he said in a voice that sounded like smashing two rocks together. "You think I'm just going to sell you the information about my whole rig? You think I'm an idiot?"

Manar blinked. *What just happened?* The attendant's eyes bored into his. They were the same eyes, but everything else screamed that something was different. The stance, the derision in the eyes, the voice. It was all different. But bots didn't have multiple modes they could switch to.

Which means I'm talking to a different person entirely, Manar realized. *The owner?*

Whoever it was, they were still waiting for a response. Manar thought fast. He kept the hardened expression on his face, snorting lightly. "I thought you were a man of business."

The bot—no, the owner, if Manar was right—snorted. "No one's going to give information about their rig. No one with any sense, at least." He waved a hand over the counter, and a line of guns appeared. Manar kept his expression steady, but barely. "Listen, you can browse through what I have for something you like. And if you want something customized, we can work something out. But I ain't giving you the names of my suppliers."

Manar stared at the row of guns. Fortunately, the attendant took his focus as interest and let him be. The weapons stretched to the end of the counter and kept going. Some were small enough to fit easily into Manar's palm, while others Manar doubted he would be able to lift. He even saw a few plasma rifles, which DJ would have killed for. Manar picked one up, leaning down to examine its barrel. Only when his face was a few inches away from the gun did he notice the ones and zeros along its length.

That confirms it, he thought. The weapons had been recreated digitally. The owner had probably typed out a list on his computer in the real world, and it had been represented digitally in the form of these weapons.

"So, what do you say?" the attendant asked.

Manar looked up slowly, giving himself time to think. "They're impressive, but I already told you what I came for."

The attendant's gaze hardened. "I told you, pal. Nobody's going to give out information about their business—especially not to first-time customers. Only a total amateur wouldn't know—" The attendant cut himself off and peered at Manar, gaze suddenly suspicious. Manar tried to keep his expression steady, but he must have let something slip because the attendant suddenly jerked back, laughing. "I don't believe this! You're a total amateur! What is this, your first time here?"

"Here?" Manar asked before he could stop himself.

The question only made the attendant laugh harder. "He doesn't even know where he is. I didn't even know it was possible to stumble onto the dark web by accident."

The dark web. The phrase resonated in Manar's mind. Suddenly, everything made sense. The darkness, the barrenness, the hoods that everyone wore, even the dilapidated stalls. They were meant to be easy to take down. How hadn't he realized that?

"Yes," the attendant said, sobering up suddenly. He looked down at Manar, his gaze laden with suspicion. "It is impossible to stumble onto this place without knowing, no matter how amusing the thought is." He grabbed Manar's hand suddenly. "So, how is it that a total amateur found his way here and is asking for information that could get him killed? Who are you?"

I messed up, Manar thought grimly. *I went about this the wrong way.* The attendant's reaction wasn't a surprise. No one stumbled onto the dark web without knowing what it was. Manar was a unique case, but the attendant had no way of knowing that.

Manar had no way to prove his innocence. He tried to drag his arm away, but the attendant's grip was like steel. A cold sensation flooded him from the point of contact. Suddenly, Manar felt exposed, like a part of his being had been uncovered. The feeling traveled up his arm but slammed into a wall before it could go farther. The attendant grunted, as if in pain.

"What the hell kind of protection do you have?" he spat. "Someone must be protecting you. Who is it? Who are you? Why are you targeting me?"

The idiot had tried to hack Manar. Manar could count on one hand the number of entities that might have been capable of breaking through his defenses. Half of them were either people he'd personally trained or AIs. Sparta's cyberdefenses were among the best in the world. They were so good that not even the government could hack into them. And Manar had single-handedly developed them. Why wouldn't he put in the same amount of effort when he was building his virtual body?

But the fact that the hack had failed wasn't important. What was important was the information the attendant had revealed in his surprise. He thought that Manar was an idiot working for someone who was targeting him. The idiot was underestimating him, and this rubbed him the wrong way.

Manar yanked his arm away. This time, the attendant let him. Manar rubbed his wrist, even though he didn't feel any pain, and narrowed his eyes. Then, for the first time, he consciously dropped the persona he'd adopted. Instead, he donned his pride like a coat. Arrogance billowed out of him.

For most of his adult life, people had called him proud and arrogant behind his back. They'd called him vain. Smug. Manar leaned into that perception until it suffused every part of his being. He was one of the greatest software developers in the world—a genius. Why shouldn't he be proud of his accomplishments, confident in his ability? Why should he have to lower his self-worth to blend in with mediocrity?

His previous persona had been fine, but it was the wrong approach. It wasn't enough to be confident. One had to project it for people like this to show you any respect. It should hit them like a brick until they were wary of crossing you.

"Was that supposed to be a hack?" he asked, his gaze hard enough to bend steel. His voice held a king's confidence. "Pathetic."

The attendant noticed the change in his bearing and lost the snarl. Good. Whoever was beyond the bot wasn't a total idiot. The man almost proved him wrong the next moment.

"I don't know who's protecting you," he said, his voice like gravel, "but I will find them, and I will destroy them. And then I will destroy you."

Manar sighed and decided to try something he'd been curious about. Without warning, his hand shot out and grasped the man just above the wrist. Then he focused on the ball of energy he felt flowing through him. He'd explored the reservoir of power that Gaius provided several times during his journey. Apart from an increase in his strength and speed, he hadn't discovered any of the other benefits he'd predicted.

Something told him this time would be different.

Manar directed the energy from where it circulated in his torso. This had been difficult to do initially but had become progressively easier as Manar had practiced. Now it was as simple as breathing. With a thought, he channeled the energy through his fingers and into the attendant.

Immediately, his mind split into two. As did the world.

He saw two scenes simultaneously. In one, he was still in the bar, his hand gripping the wrist of the attendant while the bot stared at him in anger. The second scene showed a world filled with ones and zeros. The numbers replaced everything and formed a tapestry of code. Manar tried to focus on it but felt a sharp pain in his brain. He stopped quickly but could still discern familiar shapes from their outlines: first the table with the chairs around it, then the counter. Even the stool he sat on had its own tapestry.

In front of him, the attendant had also been replaced by ones and zeros in the shape of a hooded man. When Manar looked down at himself, he realized the same thing had happened to him. Surprisingly, there was no pain. There was no change at all. It was as if this world had always existed and Manar had only just now become aware of it.

He felt a pull at his hand and realized the attendant was attempting to break free. The motion itself was slow, as if time were moving at a snail's pace.

Or, Manar thought with excitement, *my mind is moving faster.*

Manar focused and located the energy he'd tapped into. It was represented as blue lines, moving like electricity through his body. Some of it was already within the attendant. Manar focused on those lines and found they were easier to control than before. His movements were based on instinct more than anything else as he pushed the energy up the attendant's arm and toward his brain. Images flashed within his mind, but they were gone too fast for Manar to study. Still, he got more than enough. The images were information about the bot. Manar saw glimpses of past customers and heard parts of conversations. Manar would explore them later, but now, none of them were what he was looking for.

He needed to prove a point.

The blue lines had crawled up the attendant's shoulder before Manar faced his first resistance. A wall of fire sprang up where a joint would have been in a normal body. Manar slammed into it before he could stop himself and felt a sharp pain in his head, like someone had taken a pickax to his skull. It was sudden enough to break his concentration, which cost him. More walls rose up, pushing the blue lines back into Manar. In the moment before they were ejected completely, however, an image flashed in Manar's head.

Manar's mind became one again, and the world restored itself. Time resumed its normal speed, and the attendant jerked his arm free.

Manar let him, smiling. "You don't seem to understand, Markos Mendez," he said, using the name he'd obtained the instant before his hack was terminated. "I have been accommodating so far, but piss me off, and I will be the one destroying you."

The attendant's eyes grew wide.

Manar cringed. *Did I really just say that? I will destroy you? Really?*

"Who are you?" Markos asked. It was the third time he'd asked that, but now it was said without the added bite. There was none of the fear or panic Manar expected, but there was caution.

Manar could work with that.

"Like I said, I'm just looking for information," Manar replied, ignoring the question.

"Look, I don't know who's backing you, but I ain't gonna shoot myself in the foot by giving out information about my suppliers or my customers." The caution in his eyes grew. "But if you're good enough to find my name, you could probably get the information yourself. And if you're looking for a specific person, I can put the word out."

Manar nodded as if he were considering, even though he couldn't care less. Instead, he decided to make the man more malleable. "That won't be necessary since I already know most everything about your business—for example, your vendors, bottom line, and current inventory."

Manar went on to list some random pieces of information he'd gleaned during the hack. He hadn't been able to extract much, but Markos's eyes grew wide with every word he spoke, so it was safe to assume he'd plucked out the most important bits.

"So, you see," he said when he was done, "that's not what I'm looking for."

"Then, what the hell do you want?" Markos growled. If he wasn't panicking before, he was now. He would probably do anything to get Manar to leave.

"Information." He was tired of repeating that. "More specifically, I need information about anything strange you've heard lately. Any rumors, unusual dealings, anything you can think of."

The attendant's eyes darted, which told Manar he knew something. Markos leaned back, the fear in his eyes gone. Now that he knew what Manar wanted, he seemed to feel like he'd regained some measure of control. "I told you earlier, some information costs more than others. So, what are you willing to trade for this one?"

Manar stared at him for a long moment. Then he nodded. "That's fair. How about you give me the information I need, and in return I don't spread it around that Markos Mendez is a man who's willing to sell out information on his customers for the right price. How about that?"

Markos lost his smile. "You drive a hard bargain, friend."

Manar shrugged. "It'll get harder the more you waste my time."

"Fine. I don't know anything concrete. Get it? No one does. But in our field, you hear rumors of weird stuff happening. Weirder than normal, even for here."

"Such as?"

Markos leaned forward and lowered his voice. "Lots of businesses have been disappearing lately. Well-established organizations that have been around for years. Sometimes the business comes back, but it's changed hands and is under new management. It isn't announced, but you can always tell. There's a different feel to it, less human, as if the whole thing is being run by AI."

"Couldn't it just be a new bot program?" Manar asked. "Even you use a bot, right?"

Markos shook his head. "Bots are designed to sound human, right? To whiff out the chaff so the manager only deals with real customers? Why would someone change that, make it obvious to the customer that they're dealing with an AI? And even if we chalk it up to some weird fetish or some shit, some people have deliberately stirred up trouble, so the bot requests the manager." Markos gave him a look. It took Manar a moment to realize that he thought Manar had done the same thing. "But even when the manager takes over, it still sounds like an AI."

Manar frowned. "That's not definitive."

"Well, it's what I got. Do you want to hear it or not?"

Manar sighed but waved for him to continue.

"The AI isn't the only thing. There are also all these new rules."

"Rules?" Manar asked, surprised. "On the dark web? What kind of rules?"

Markos nodded to the guns on the counter. "Well, for one, I would have sold you a lot more if you'd come around a few months back. Now, I'm limited to this garbage. All the others have been taken off the market."

Helene is limiting their stock? Manar wondered.

"Who's enforcing them?" he asked.

"That's the thing. No one is, on the surface," Markos grunted. "But businesses who don't follow the rules quickly find that their regular customers no longer want to deal with them, or their suppliers are constantly running out of stock. In the worst cases, the business disappears altogether."

Manar rubbed his chin. Taking over businesses, he could understand, but why would Helene start enforcing these rules? What did she gain? What was he missing? That was always one of the major problems when dealing with Helene: it was almost impossible to see the trap coming until it was sprung. One of the reasons he'd upgraded Gaius was to use it to analyze new information and predict Helene's plan, but as he still wasn't able to return to his body, he couldn't report this new information.

"Who's doing all this?" Manar asked finally.

"That's what everyone wants to know," Markos answered with a shrug. "A few people have tried to trace them by hacking their account or monitoring their transactions, but everything's airtight. Even the businesses they take over gain their protection afterward."

That's another confirmation that this is Helene, Manar thought. *With the way she's grown, even I would have difficulty breaking through her defenses.*

"But there're rumors of something going on behind the scenes," Markos continued. "Something or someone is building something. No one knows what, but someone's been buying up a lot of high-grade materials really quickly as soon as they hit the market."

"What sort of materials?" Manar asked.

Markos grinned disturbingly. "That's the thing; anyone who could know suddenly disappeared."

Manar grilled Markos for more information, but the weapons dealer had told him everything he knew. No matter how much Manar pressed, he didn't learn anything new. Finally, Manar gave up and rose to leave.

"Hey," Markos yelled, "remember our deal! You didn't hear anything from me. Got it?"

"Yeah, yeah," Manar said tiredly. "I'm forgetting everything right now." He started heading to the door but added over his shoulder, "A little friendly advice though. You might want to take a break for a while. These are strange times, after all."

He pushed open the door to the bar, and the room instantly dissolved around him. Once again, he was standing in the middle of the street. Manar gave a weary sigh. He'd acquired the information he'd been looking for, but it had only brought up more questions. It felt like he hadn't made any progress at all.

The darkness pressed against him, somehow more ominous now that he knew what it represented. Markos had given the impression that Helene basically ruled the dark web, so now the shadows had new meaning, as did the suspicious looks he got from the merchants. Which one of them was a picospore-controlled spy for Helene? Was she tracking him right now? Toying with him?

It doesn't matter, Manar thought fiercely. So what if she was watching him? It didn't change his priorities or his objective. Plus, the fact that she hadn't attacked yet meant she was wary of him. He would be cautious of whatever traps she laid, but he couldn't let it drive him to inaction.

He had too many people counting on him.

Manar lifted his chin and met the gaze of a merchant. There was a small shift, and his entire bearing changed. He eyed every other merchant and dismissed them as if they were unworthy of his consideration. He picked a direction at random, then walked into another stall.

It would be foolish for him to make a plan without first confirming Markos's information.

ONCE, DURING DJ'S CHILDHOOD, his dads took him and his brother to the zoo for an evening. He'd been too young to remember most of the trip, but he considered it a happy memory. Except for the part when they checked out the lion enclosure and DJ crapped his pants. It was normal, his dads had told him later on, to feel such primal fear when facing a wild animal that, if given the chance, would kill him without a second thought.

DJ hadn't thought of that trip in years. For some reason, it was the first thing that came to his mind now as he faced Karla.

How weird, DJ thought. *There are some similarities between them, though.*

Instead of a mane, Karla had red hair that draped around her and bristled when she was angry—so, always. And instead of claws, Karla held twin daggers. Still, no matter how beast-like she wanted to look, DJ had seen the way she looked at her sister, and even Chloe, whenever the other woman's attention was diverted.

Karla might have acted like a brute, but that was all it was: an act. She wouldn't kill him without a legitimate reason.

Probably.

DJ held on to that thought like a safety blanket as Christy counted down to the start of the spar from the sidelines.

"Three," Christy said. DJ could hear the grin in her voice. "Two. One."

DJ tightened his grip on the pistols in his hands.

"Go!"

He raised both guns and quickly fired off two shots. Karla casually deflected the bullets with her dagger and crossed half the distance to him. DJ felt his heart jump, but his hands remained steady as he took one shot after the other. Both guns were emptied within the next few seconds. There was no time to reload. He'd aimed one shot directly at Karla, and every other in a circle around her, targeting the places she could dodge to. He was using a standard 9mm Glock, which held eighteen rounds per magazine. That meant that there were thirty-six bullets flying straight at Karla. He could almost feel them tear through the air, perfectly aimed. Against any other opponent, DJ surely would have made a kill shot.

However, since he was fighting Karla, DJ was worried they wouldn't delay her long enough.

Karla's eyes darted around. DJ wondered whether she could see the individual bullets heading toward her. Her daggers rose up to meet them. Unlike the previous times he'd tried this, DJ could actually see how she deflected the bullets. Which meant she'd slowed down. Probably not enough to make a difference in this fight, but it was still nice to confirm.

Her right hand flashed, and her dagger tapped the bullets as they reached her. Logically, DJ knew this was only possible because some bullets would be slower than others by virtue of how he'd shot them. Nevertheless, it was still fucking impressive. Some bullets were pushed an inch off their path, effectively forcing them to miss, while others were deflected away or into other bullets, causing them to ricochet. Whether by coincidence or by design, one of the bullets was boomeranged back toward DJ on a path that would have sent it through his arm.

Fortunately, DJ had learned from the last three times and moved the moment he'd emptied his clips.

Karla tried to do the same move on her left side, but the bullets were already within her guard. Even she wasn't fast enough to stop them then. DJ felt a trickle of hope blossoming in his chest, but it quickly died when Karla spun on her heel and twisted her body mid-step. It was some *Matrix*-style bullshit, something that shouldn't have been possible outside of a sci-fi movie. Yet there it was. The move allowed the bullets on her left to pass by. Crashes rang out from the far wall, where the rounds embedded themselves. The motion was smooth, almost graceful. DJ wasn't even angry, just impressed.

Karla straightened, a manic grin on her face that meant she'd actually enjoyed the challenge. Weirdly, DJ was proud of that. So what if he'd only managed to delay her for about five seconds?

Karla crossed the distance between them with a lunge. DJ had just enough time to ditch his guns and meet her daggers with the bracers on his arms. They'd become necessary after the first few times his guns had been sliced apart while he tried to block. The force of the attack pushed DJ back several steps. In response, he pulled Karla closer, twisted his forearms, and trapped her arm beneath his. He sent his knee toward her stomach, but somehow, she twisted enough to avoid it. Her second dagger shot toward his eye, and DJ tilted his head out of the way. He realized too late that the strike was a feint. Karla spun her dagger until the edge faced away from him, and her open palm strike caught him straight in the nose.

DJ's head snapped back, ringing like a bell. He released her arm—which had probably been her intention all along—and rolled backward to create distance while his disorientation passed. It took less than three seconds, but when DJ's eyes cleared, there was a dagger at his throat.

"Pathetic," Karla spat, though her grin remained.

"Hey, give me a break." DJ groaned. "I was trying something new."

"You knew you could not match my speed, so you tried to remove the option by incapacitating me. It was not a terrible plan. However, you are years too early still to be my match in such things."

"She's not wrong, D," Christy said. "Even if your hold had worked, she would have just broken out of it."

"Not if she'd kept to the deal and reduced her strength to an average human's," DJ wheezed. He touched his nose. It was definitely broken. "And I assumed she was going to when she decided to dodge the bullets instead of just blocking them with her right arm."

Plus, I thought I had a chance since she seemed slower than before. DJ didn't dare say that out loud though, in case it induced Karla into a murderous rage.

"I am not a savage unable to keep to a simple agreement," Karla spat. "However, your plan would still have not worked." She sheathed her daggers in one smooth motion and turned to leave. DJ tried not to stare at her ass, which swayed as she walked in her tight leather jumpsuit.

Christy clapped his back, a little more forcefully than was strictly necessary. "We're going to make a warrior out of you yet."

"Step into the ring," DJ muttered, glaring at her. "I'll show you how much of a warrior I am." He picked up his guns and holstered them while he and Christy made their way back to the main part of the warehouse.

DJ sometimes went back to Sparta to check on Hermione—and Martin, too, since he was done with Karla and Liz. But for the most part, he and Christy had practically been living at the warehouse for the last few days since it was more efficient for their training with the Murder Twins.

It was the only thing they could do while they waited for word on Olsen.

As if called by his thoughts, DJ's phone rang, and he picked it up excitedly.

"Anything?" he asked without preamble.

"We got something," Olsen replied, just as curtly. "I'll meet you at the place we discussed."

"I'll be there." DJ cut the call. He couldn't stop the grin on his face.

"Good news?" Christy asked.

DJ turned his grin on her. "Seems like the wait is finally over."

OLSEN WAS ALREADY SEATED in a booth by the time DJ arrived at the rendezvous. The admiral was dressed in what DJ had come to know as his casual wear: a tight polo shirt tucked into a pair of shorts.

Olsen was bent over a map and scarcely looked up when DJ slid into the seat opposite him. DJ gestured for a beer while he waited for Olsen to begin. The map was turned toward Olsen, so DJ had to twist awkwardly to make any sense of it. Fortunately, it took only a glance to recognize it as a map of New York City. Olsen had crossed off several points but circled one area three times in red. DJ figured that was where Ndidi was being held. He leaned closer, then frowned.

"That's in Manhattan, right?" DJ blurted out.

"That area is as close as I've been able to figure to where Ndidi is being kept," Olsen said. "Even this wasn't easy."

"Well, shit! I don't doubt it. How'd you finally narrow it down?"

Olsen looked up from the map and met DJ's questioning look with a neutral expression. He didn't say anything.

Oh? DJ thought, raising his eyebrows in surprise. He hadn't taken the old man to be a lawbreaker. He changed his question. "Did you try out the Synaptic Pulse?"

"It worked just as you described," Olsen grunted, though the corner of his lips tugged upward into a smile. "A little too well. Austin remembered most of his time spent controlled, but not all at once, so I had to babysit him all night and try to catch him up. It was fun for a while, but it turns out Admiral Austin is a dick whether he's under Helene's control or not. Fortunately for us, he was pissed off enough to forget that I can't actually order him about since he outranks me."

"At least we got an ally out of it." DJ shrugged.

"I wouldn't count your chickens just yet, boy," Olsen said. "Austin remembered enough to still hate you."

"Well, he can go screw himself," DJ replied offhandedly. Controlled or not, DJ remembered the hell Austin had put his team through just to keep them busy. If they hadn't needed his help, DJ would have released him from Helene's control last. "Hermione will be happy to know the Synaptic Pulse works, though."

"She did good work. She should be proud."

DJ would make sure to pass that along. In the meantime, though, he nodded toward the map. "So, what do you have for me?"

Olsen face grew serious, and he pointed at the spots that had been marked off. "These were the places I first suspected Ndidi was being held based on the information you gave me, as well as the base's suspicions of Helene's hideout. I sent some people into each location, had them check out the place, and crossed them off when we confirmed them dead ends."

DJ whistled. There had to be a dozen of them. "How'd you arrange that?"

Once again, Olsen stared at him with a neutral expression.

All right then, DJ thought. *Lots of land mines today.*

"How'd you finally narrow it down?" he asked instead.

"I didn't," Olsen replied, frowning. "Austin figured out we could track Helene's movement by following where she concentrates her power. "

"What do you mean?"

"Helene is generally considered the best artificial intelligence program in the world. Even today, she's used by billions of households and most corporations simultaneously. Most AIs would be fried by half of her load, yet Helene still has time to cause wanton acts of global terrorism. Ever wondered how that's possible?"

Not really, DJ wanted to say. *The tech shit is CJ's field. My job is to blow up what needs to be blown up.*

Olsen was already glaring at him, though, so DJ decided to think it through. He was a little embarrassed when the answer came to him almost immediately.

"Wouldn't she need a shitload of power to run?"

"Guess you do have a brain when you decide to use it," Olsen said. "But you're right. Helene's efficiency wouldn't be possible without a massive amount of processing power. More so because, for some reason, she's still keeping up the charade of being an ordinary virtual assistant."

Something flashed in Olsen's eyes, too quick for DJ to decipher before the admiral focused again. He flipped the map over, pulled a pen from his pocket, and sketched something on the blank side. Thousands of little lines stretched off into the distance. Again, because of the way it was drawn, DJ had to twist awkwardly to make sense of it, but it looked like some kind of web.

"Typically, because of the number of tasks she's responsible for, Helene's power is spread out." Olsen tapped the pen against the web. "They're dedicated to millions of different things simultaneously. However, whenever something is important enough to draw her attention"—he started connecting the little lines to a point, slowly forming the target range—"all that power gathers in one place. The nerds at the lab believe that a person in the vicinity of the focal point would feel that much power as a massive pressure, crushing them."

"I've felt that." DJ grimaced. "It's not fun. But I'm guessing that's how you track her. You just follow the power."

Olsen nodded, then flipped the map back over. "It's not precise. The closest we can get is a couple of blocks." He tapped at the red circle. "Helene has visited somewhere here several times over the last week. Our best bet is that's where she's keeping your gal."

DJ leaned over. "The place isn't familiar to me. Do we know what's there?"

"Mostly abandoned warehouses," Olsen replied, marking the places as he spoke. "Some apartment buildings as well, though most of them are uninhabited. There's also an old steel factory."

DJ frowned at the map. Suddenly, he remembered the extensive network of tunnels in Sparta's underground base. "Any of them have anything underground? Tunnels? Secret rooms? Shit, even a garage might work. Helene loves underground shit."

"The warehouses wouldn't need underground storage units. But the apartments would have a basement. What're you thinking?"

"It's not going to be an apartment building," DJ said with confidence. "No apartment building would be large enough for whatever Helene has planned. Is there a way to check under the factories? Maybe check the hollowness of the ground or some shit?"

"No, we can't check *the hollowness of the ground.*" Olsen sighed. "But if it's underground space, some factories decide to extend below ground instead of outward in order to save money. They'd most likely have underground constructions of some kind."

"Does this one?"

"I have no idea."

"Then that's the first place we check," DJ said, tapping the place on the map. "Helene loves underground shit."

CJ PAUSED AT THE ENTRANCE—or, at least, what he hoped was the entrance. He was certain he was in the same tunnel he'd started from, with the bits of code interspersed within the walls. But whatever door he'd used blended seamlessly with the walls to form one unbroken piece.

There's one way to check, CJ thought, bringing out the sphere. It had remained dormant ever since it'd merged with the piece from the core. CJ assumed it was because there was nothing to react to anymore. But it'd made navigating his way back far more frustrating than it should have been.

He raised the sphere over the wall. A spot a few feet to his right opened up. CJ hurried to it but didn't step through. He hadn't forgotten about his pursuers. From the alarm that blared in CJ's ears, it seemed like they hadn't forgotten about him either.

Feeling like a villain in an old cartoon, CJ poked his head out slowly. Only when he'd confirmed that the hallway was clear did he actually step out. Immediately, the orb grew warm in his hand. The change was slight but unmistakable to CJ, who'd been watching out for it. He didn't know what it meant yet. But he was determined to find out.

CJ slowly made his way down the hall, listening for any hint of danger. The sphere grew warmer as he walked. CJ assumed this meant he was on the right path. For the next few minutes, he navigated the branches in the path without encountering anyone.

Unfortunately, that wasn't bound to last.

CJ turned a corner and stopped. A few steps away in the middle of the passage was a squadron of bots, each holding a staff that glowed a faint blue. CJ's heart leaped to his throat. He had been simply patrolling, so he hadn't heard their footsteps. Apparently, they hadn't heard his either because they seemed just as surprised as he was. They were similar to the squads he'd seen before, except their bodies were blue. Was that good?

As if in response to his thoughts, their skin turned a deep red. One of the bots stepped forward, its staff pointed at CJ. "Provide authentication or be destroyed."

CJ grimaced. "This isn't really necessary," he said. "I can leave." That was more true now that he'd acquired what he'd come for.

The bot took another step forward and its hand flashed. CJ felt something pass over his shoulder the next moment. When he saw the bot's empty hands, he realized that it had thrown its staff.

"Provide authentication or be destroyed."

Slowly, as if in a dream, CJ stared over his shoulder. The staff had hit the wall with enough force to embed itself in it. And that had been aimed at his head.

He was going to kill me, CJ gasped at the bot, his eyes wide. *He was actually aiming to kill me.*

Somehow, it hadn't occurred to CJ that he was in any real danger. He'd been threatened by the firewalls. He'd been chased by the squad earlier. But it had never really clicked that he could die. What would happen if he died? His body was in a coma in the real world. Would he be ejected back? Or would it cause brain damage? Either way, the thought was terrifying.

CJ ducked out of the hall, retracing his steps. The sphere grew colder, but CJ ignored it. He also ignored the pounding of footsteps behind him as the bots gave chase. He needed to find a way out. He was still on the ground floor. One of these passages should lead to the wide space with the corporate market stalls. If he could find that, the exit wouldn't be far off.

The thought spurred him on as he ran through the passages. He tried to look for any familiar landmarks, anything he could use to determine his position. Unfortunately, every wall was a mirror of the other. After a few minutes of running, the footsteps behind him faded. CJ would have been tempted to believe the pursuit had been called off, but the alarm still blared throughout the building.

CJ slowed down at the sound of footsteps ahead of him. He ducked into another passage without hesitation, and the footsteps faded. Time blurred as CJ navigated the corridors. Several times, he stopped and ran the sphere over random points on the wall, hoping that it would react and give him access to another back door. Unfortunately, the sphere remained inert.

Should he turn back? He felt as if he'd been running for hours, but it was probably nothing more than a few minutes. CJ doubted that he would have kept up his pace for long had he been in his real body. Thankfully, his virtual body didn't seem to grow tired. At least not physically. Rather, his thoughts grew more sluggish the more time passed. He wasn't getting tired, not exactly, but he was losing focus.

He grew more frantic at this realization. What if he was damaging himself? CJ forced himself to slow down, then stopped entirely. He couldn't stay in the same place for long, but he hadn't heard any sort of pursuit for a while either, so it should be safe for the moment. CJ glanced at the sphere, which was now as cold as ice. CJ took that as confirmation that he'd wandered far off track. He needed to fix that.

He spent the next few minutes retracing his steps, this time keeping a close watch on the sphere and the changes in the temperature. CJ kept his pace at a brisk walk, fast enough to react to any patrols he heard, but not so fast that he exerted himself. Whenever he encountered a patrol, he simply stopped and waited for them to pass. If they were heading toward him, however, he'd be forced to turn back and pick a different path.

I could have done this from the start if I hadn't panicked, CJ realized as he waited for a squad to pass. Considering how long he'd run before calming down, he might have very well reached the entrance if he'd been rational.

The passages opened up to him, and he soon became aware that he was passing patrols more frequently. The realization brought a burst of fear that CJ forcefully suppressed. It was natural that he would find more patrols guarding the exit. It just meant that he needed to be more careful.

Minutes passed again, and CJ's worries began to ease. His pace had slowed significantly so he could avoid the patrols. However, it was a small price to pay to avoid the consequences of being reckless. He also noticed that the sphere had begun to grow warm in his hand. He hoped that meant that he was near the exit.

That was the same moment that CJ heard footsteps ahead of him. He ducked back into the previous hallway immediately and waited for the patrol to pass. Then another patrol marched behind him. From the sound, it seemed as if the squad was about to enter the passage where CJ hid.

He was trapped.

The sphere grew warmer in his hand, but CJ barely registered it as his mind churned for a solution. There was a chance the patrol in front of him would take another passage, giving him the opportunity to make a break for it before the squad behind caught sight of him. However, the problem was the timing. The squad behind him would enter the hallway in seconds, while the patrol ahead still seemed far away.

What could he do?

A second later, the decision was made for him. The squad behind him entered the passage. CJ tried to duck forward, but it was already too late. Strange chattering sounds came from the bots as they rushed to his position. The noise, in turn, alerted the patrol in front of him to his presence, and their footsteps grew more urgent. A second later, that patrol entered the corridor as well and caught sight of CJ. Their staffs gave off a fierce light, and the pressure bore down on CJ. He stopped in the middle of the hallway and watched helplessly as the two squads surrounded him, chattering about authentication.

The world seemed to slow down as CJ's thoughts sped up, fueled by a desperate need to survive. He briefly considered dropping the sphere. The website recognized it as a foreign code. It was probably what had triggered the defenses. However, there was nothing to suggest that the bots would attack the sphere and leave CJ unharmed.

If CJ dropped it, he would lose the chance to discover whatever advantage it would have provided. Everything the sphere had been able to do so far told CJ that its advantages would be significant.

But what choice do I have? he thought, watching the bots barreling toward him. *I have to find a way to escape.* He gripped the sphere tighter. In response, it grew warmer in his hands until it was almost unbearable.

The squads were almost upon him now. One of the bots launched its staff. The weapon tore through the air toward him. *I need to move,* he thought urgently. The staff was a foot away. CJ knew he wouldn't be able to avoid it. His mind flashed with the image of a staff embedded in the wall.

Anywhere! Anywhere would be better than here!

Suddenly, the sphere became scorching hot. Pain flared within CJ, for a moment distracting him from his impending doom. The world blurred.

When it cleared, CJ was somewhere else.

CJ APPEARED IN A WORLD filled with fire. His surprise jerked him back. It took him a moment to realize that he'd appeared in the middle of a firewall. Ahead, an alarm still blared about an intruder, so he was still in the same website, but somehow he'd teleported to the main floor. The entrance was right ahead of him. CJ looked at the sphere. It'd cooled down, but he still remembered the scorching heat and the flash of pain. The sphere had teleported him away from the website's defenders. It'd saved his life. But how?

What the hell is this thing?

CJ's thought was interrupted by the patter of footsteps coming from one of the side corridors—the same one he had just escaped from. CJ didn't wait to see what was coming out.

He turned to the exit and ran, clutching the sphere against his chest.

MANAR WALKED OUT of another stall, a thoughtful look on his face. Behind him, the attendant stared with barely hidden contempt. Manar ignored it like he ignored every other look he got. The stall was the third one he'd checked out after Markos. All the others had given him the same information. No one had anything concrete, but they were all aware something was happening. Manar had even initiated minor hacks to confirm their stories. It had pissed off the vendors, but it had also given Manar leverage over them. Plus, it had been a chance for him to practice his abilities; Manar's curiosity hadn't allowed him to pass that up.

Manar glanced once more at the stalls. He wondered if he should check one more but decided against it. It was unlikely that he would get any new information and far more plausible that he would annoy another vendor. He would try to avoid that if possible. He could afford to offend a few, but alienating the entire dark web could only be a mistake. That would be doubly true if Helene had plans for them.

He turned his gaze to the crumbling buildings in the distance. If the market stalls were likened to small businesses owned by individual people, the buildings would be this world's representation of websites on the dark web. Generally, these websites had more structure and were run by organizations like the Mafia, groups with substantial real-world influence. That made it all the more perplexing that Helene was able to simply take over the businesses without any fuss.

His nanites pointed him in the direction of the buildings. This meant he would find Helene there. That made his decision for him. It didn't really matter what Helene was working toward; Manar wouldn't give her the chance to finish it.

Manar reached the end of the street and picked one of the branches, then realized that he'd underestimated their number. From the market, the buildings looked scant. Standing right next to them, Manar counted close to a dozen. They were arranged in the same haphazard manner as the stalls and were just as dilapidated.

More importantly, however, Manar saw people walking the street.

There were only a few, but it was more than Manar had seen since he'd stepped into the virtual world. *Except they're bots,* he thought. His curiosity hurried his steps until he was close enough to study them.

They weren't bots. They were avatars. The difference was slight but obvious to Manar, even though it was his first time interacting with the latter.

Bots were designed to live in the digital space and were allowed limited autonomy. On the other hand, avatars could be likened to video game characters that were controlled at every step. That made their movements blocky and slightly off. *Each avatar is a user navigating the internet,* Manar thought. The avatars had the same pixelated appearance as he did. But where Manar had made his body lean and toned, it seemed everyone else had gone for pure muscle. Although distinct in their own way, every avatar shared the same beefed-up appearance—a bouncer's dream. Manar assumed "intimidating" was what the users were going for, but it was weird.

The avatars entered buildings by the handful. Manar noticed that some buildings got lots of visitors while others didn't get a single one. It was almost as if certain buildings were being avoided. The avatars that did enter such buildings were noticeably different. Manar observed for a few minutes before deciding to check out one of the more frequented buildings.

He had started to make his way to the site when movement caught his eye, and Manar's head snapped in its direction. He was just in time to see a man turning a corner into another street. Manar squinted.

Was that …

For a second, it had seemed as if he'd seen CJ. But that was impossible. Why would CJ have an avatar on the dark web?

Manar headed in that direction. It wasn't that he actually thought CJ had somehow found himself on the dark web. But if someone was using his identity, it shouldn't be dismissed. Unfortunately, the impostor made following him difficult. Manar had caught only a flash of the avatar initially. By the time he entered the same street, the impostor was gone.

No, not gone … there! Manar caught a glimpse of the avatar. The nanites flared, but Manar couldn't spare any thought for them, and he increased his pace. The street wasn't as crowded as the previous one, yet somehow Manar couldn't catch more than glimpses of his quarry through the throng of people. No matter how fast he moved, somehow he never seemed to close the distance. Eventually, the impostor slipped into a building. It was one of the few that didn't have visitors. Manar had planned to avoid those until he'd obtained more information about them, but his curiosity reared its head. He had to find out who the impostor was and why he'd chosen CJ of all people to imitate.

He slipped into the site a few seconds behind the avatar. Immediately, something attached itself to his face, obstructing his vision. In the same instant, something heavy crashed into him. Manar instinctively brought his hands up to push whatever it was away, but he was too late, and the damn thing pushed him down.

Something chomped down on his face. Manar felt the pressure and the sharp teeth piercing into his skin. Fortunately, his virtual body felt no pain. He didn't have time to be relieved before another problem materialized. A cold sensation spread through his face. It left Manar feeling exposed, vulnerable, like when Markos had attempted a hack on him.

Was that what this was? Was someone trying to hack him?

Manar redoubled his efforts to get free, but it was difficult to find purchase, as his attacker was constantly shifting. Precious moments of struggling allowed him to get enough of a grip to flip his assailant off him. The pressure on his face didn't lessen, but now Manar was the one on top. He steadied himself and pushed down with all the force he could muster. Finally, he was able to yank his head free with a gasp. The cold sensation faded, but that barely registered as Manar finally got a good look at his assailant.

A worm? Manar thought. He was forced to dive out of the way as the worm took the chance to lurch for his face again. His dive was clumsy and awkward, but it created some distance between them, giving Manar the few moments he needed to process. He spared a glance around him, not really noting any features, just searching. As he'd expected, the impostor was nowhere in sight. Had it led Manar to the building so he would get attacked by the worm? Was the impostor itself the worm?

Manar discarded that last thought as soon as it formed. He didn't have enough information to say with confidence that the chances of that were zero. However, if the impostor could transform into something, why a worm? It didn't make sense. More likely, the impostor had entered the website knowing the worm would be present and that it would attack Manar once he entered.

The worm reared up, squealing, and slid toward him. Manar maintained his distance but otherwise just observed it. Eventually, the worm seemed to accept it wasn't getting a free meal and made its way to one of the building's walls, where it pressed its mouth against the brick. Its whole body convulsed, and another worm shot out of its back. The new one also attached itself to the wall and began gnawing on it.

Manar straightened. *It wasn't trying to hack into me,* he realized. *It was trying to find something to attach to so it could replicate.* If the threat wasn't neutralized in time, the malware could bring down the entire building. Manar had the fleeting thought that he should try to help. He could probably destroy them using Gaius's power. It would be a good test run of his abilities. But he quickly squashed the thought. With the worm no longer paying attention to him, Manar could finally study the website. Once he did, he almost wished the worms could replicate faster.

It was a porn website, filled with girls in various stages of undress. Worse, they were all just that: girls. Manar placed most of them at younger than fifteen; some couldn't have been more than ten. The whole thing was disgusting. It doubled Manar's determination to catch the impostor. If this was the sort of place the fool went to using CJ's identity …

There was no sign of the avatar. It was unlikely he would be able to find anything if he delved further inside. He spared one last glance at the worms. There were three now. As he walked out of the building, for just a moment, Manar could have sworn he felt eyes on him.

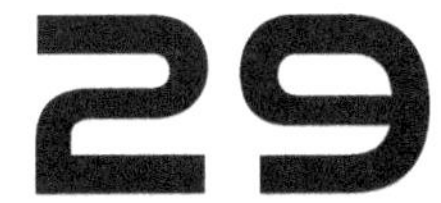

29

AUGUST 2043

THE STEEL FACTORY
NEW YORK CITY

IT WAS THE DAY OF THE RAID. DJ stood in an alley across from an old steel factory. It was night, so he couldn't actually see shit, but he thought he cut a striking figure as he loomed.

"You don't," Christy hissed beside him.

Had he said that out loud?

"You look like an idiot—especially since your night-vision goggles are literally around your neck."

Sheesh, DJ thought, *someone's having a bad night already.*

"So help me God, D," Christy muttered, her voice tight with anger.

DJ's eyebrows rose. *Oops.* Christy was staring at him, so he did his best to wipe the grin off his face and brought the goggles up to his eyes.

The factory was outlined in an ethereal green. The exterior was small, with only two floors. DJ wasn't deceived by that. Olsen had confirmed that most of the factory stretched underground. Two large chimneys extending from the roof of the building were probably used to expel smoke when the factory was still in operation.

That must have been ages ago though, DJ thought. There were multiple cracks running down the walls and some parts broken off. By all appearances, the factory was one step away from crumbling. If it were in any other part of the city, it would probably have been demolished years ago. DJ wondered how much of the run-down appearance was real and how much was fabricated by Helene to keep people away.

Whichever it is, hopefully it can handle a little stress.

The raid was meant to be a simple retrieval. Ideally, they'd be in and out without fuss. But Olsen hadn't been able to infiltrate the building, so no one knew what kind of resistance they'd face. That lack of information made any sort of precision planning difficult. DJ was confident the shit would hit the fan eventually. There was going to be some level of destruction. Part of their plan hinged on that. Hopefully the building wouldn't bury them alive. He didn't say that out loud, though—not with Christy still glaring at him out of the corner of her eye.

Plus, DJ mused with a grin, *just because we've blown up every building we've fought Helene in doesn't mean this one will explode.*

Karla stepped up. Like always, she and her sister wore skintight bodysuits that silenced their movements. "Are we to wait here until our corpses hollow out?" she said without whispering. In the silence of the night, her voice seemed unnaturally loud.

"Depends," DJ replied. "Is everyone clear on their roles?"

"Come on, DJ," Chloe whispered in his ear. "I assure you, my girls and I have more experience infiltrating a building than you do." She had forgone her usual blouse in favor of a leather vest that offered more protection.

"I'd agree with you, but the goal is to get Ndidi out alive."

Chloe affected a hurt look. "We don't always kill people, you know. We're not savages." A crack followed her statement. DJ turned just as Karla removed her fist from the wall. She radiated impatience. DJ raised an eyebrow at Chloe.

She sighed. "We'll do it your way. For now."

Beautiful, DJ thought. He lowered the goggles and turned to Christy, "Remember to radio the moment you find Ndidi. We'll start making our way to you, and we'll get out together."

"I remember the plan, D. And we can handle ourselves. No one here is new to this." Christy rolled her eyes. Pratima stood silently at her side, as did Liz. DJ wanted to say more, but Christy was right. All of them had proven they could take care of themselves. Micromanaging would only piss everyone off. Plus, that wasn't DJ's style anyway.

"All right, then." He nodded. "Let's go fuck this shit up."

DJ, CHLOE, AND KARLA passed through the large steel doors into the factory proper. Moonlight spilled from the broken windows around the building. That, at least, provided enough ambient light for his goggles to be useful, bathing the entire room in a ghoulish green.

The three of them fanned out with DJ in the middle. They moved slowly, checking for threats with every step. Helene was potentially already aware of their presence, but if she wasn't, DJ didn't want to tip her off by being careless. Although they would get her attention eventually, he wanted to see how far they could go before it became necessary.

Machines littered the interior of the factory, taking up most of the space. DJ identified the conveyor belts, the quenching box, and the different kinds of saws easily enough, but there were just as many that he couldn't even begin to recognize. He saw a large, pointed tank suspended about a foot off the ground and extending almost to the ceiling.

What the hell was that used for? he wondered.

Pipes ran the length of the building. Sometimes they connected to something, sometimes not; DJ couldn't see any rhyme or reason to it. Everything was covered in a thick layer of dust and rust to the point that he felt like he could get an infection from just breathing the air.

He had his pistol in his hand as he moved, each step placed deliberately. His gaze swept through the space, making sure to focus on the walls, looking for the telltale flash of red. His pace was slow, so it took him a few minutes to get to the end of the room. Karla and Chloe were already there, waiting for him, both wearing their own night-vision goggles.

"Anything?" he whispered. Chloe shook her head with a smirk. DJ ignored the look. "All right, let's check the upper level then."

Chloe's smirk grew.

"We did while you danced around like a ballerina in a tutu," Karla said. "An access elevator at the end of the floor leads below the ground."

DJ took the information in stride. "Awesome. Where is it?"

Karla sneered, but she headed toward the side of the factory where DJ assumed the stairs to the second floor were.

Chloe came up beside him. "You need to pick up your pace. I've seen women in labor move faster than you."

"I'm not really built for being sneaky," DJ said. "I can move quietly, but as you no doubt saw, it makes me slow as shit. Any faster and I might trip."

"Well, you have to work on it," Chloe said, her tone sharp. "At this pace, the others are going to get into position before us. They'll take the brunt of Helene's attacks. Liz can handle herself against all odds, but she will not give her life to save your friends."

DJ started to reply, but Chloe interrupted over her shoulder as she turned to follow Karla. "And by the way, just because it's dark doesn't mean you can't be seen. There's plenty of cover here. Use it. Never walk out in the open."

DJ didn't know what to say to that, so he didn't say anything. It wasn't as though Chloe didn't have a point. They weren't in as much of a time crunch as they'd been at the Sparta underground base, but they still couldn't afford to waste time. Their team needed to be in place to grab Helene's attention before Christy and her team were in position for the plan to work. DJ had to speed it up. It was that simple. Fortunately, once they reached the underground levels, stealth wouldn't be as important.

The upper floor wasn't as cluttered with machines as the first. Rails ran through the length of the floor. DJ wondered how much that helped, until he caught sight of a placard on the wall that read, *This Plant Has Worked 3 Days*

Without a Recordable Accident. The three had been handwritten in chalk, but it was barely legible.

Well, there's my answer, he thought.

The access elevator was easy to spot without obstruction from the machines. It was basically a cage, and like everything else, it was covered with rust. However, it wasn't dusty, which told DJ that it saw some use. Chloe and Karla were already inside when he stepped in, and DJ closed the cage behind him. A box with a single red button hung on the wall. The contraption shook when Chloe pressed the button, then stabilized after a moment and began its descent. Despite the rust, the cage didn't make any noise as it was lowered.

They descended in silence.

THE ELEVATOR RIDE LASTED several minutes longer than DJ expected. Part of it was obviously because of how slowly the cage descended, but the other reason—the part DJ was trying not to think about—was the more obvious one: Helene had dug deep.

The moonlight didn't reach that deep, so their night-vision goggles didn't have any ambient light to use. They'd have to rely on the goggles' thermal imaging. It was less reliable than the normal setting, especially underground where everything was cool and damp.

The world lost its greenish color, transitioning to a deep blue. The walls of packed earth were a softer hue. The ground had faint hints of red and yellow, most likely heat signatures from past traffic.

DJ stepped out of the elevator gingerly. Even Karla and Chloe looked cautious. They were in a tunnel large enough for the three of them to walk side by side without a problem. DJ hoped it remained that way; fighting in such tight quarters would be hell. The path extended beyond the range of their vision—not that it mattered. Without a map, the entire thing might as well have been a maze. Christy's team was worse off since they were actively searching for something. All DJ's group had to do was stumble around until they gathered enough attention.

As they made their way down the tunnel, DJ flicked his wrist, uncovering the device strapped to it. The top was bare and made of rubber, so it created a vibration every time it was struck. He tapped it twice to start the message, then again several times, following a pattern: *Everything good?*

The watch vibrated, making a small clicking sound. Not Morse code—that would have been ridiculously easy for Helene to crack—but a similar language CJ had created when they were kids. It wasn't complex enough to carry out entire conversations, but it allowed them to pass basic messages without worrying that Helene was listening in. Without a dedicated programmer keeping their comm lines secure, it was the best they could do. With any luck, Helene would assume that DJ was talking to someone on the outside, like Olsen, leaving Christy's group to work undetected for as long as possible.

They didn't see the first relay until they reached a branch at the end of the tunnel. DJ almost missed its telltale red light because it was so dim. The light grew brighter as they approached, raising the temperature slightly.

Helene's attention wasn't here, he realized, *until it sensed us approaching.*

With their entry so far gone unnoticed, they needed to grab the AI's attention before it had a chance to do a sweep. DJ waited until the light grew bright enough to be glaring, when he was sure Helene knew they were there, then put a bullet through the relay.

"Game faces on, people," he said, after updating Christy via another tapped message. He grinned as adrenaline flooded his veins in anticipation. "It's about to get weird."

DJ expected resistance immediately, but the group passed through several more passages without a problem. They didn't have a set path—not yet anyway—so they took turns randomly. It didn't matter what path they took as long as they knew the way back to the entrance. DJ still had the mapper they'd used at the Sparta underground base, but without Manar, he didn't trust it. Still, the tunnels were all the same, so DJ started marking the way with chalk. Chloe allowed him to do this for several minutes before informing him that Karla could find their way back regardless of how many turns they took. DJ instead focused his attention on destroying every one of Helene's relays they came across. He didn't doubt that Helene had other means of tracking them, but it might piss her off.

Eventually, they turned into a tunnel and stumbled on the puppets. There were half a dozen of them, standing in the middle of the tunnel. The squad had obviously been waiting for them because their guns were cocked and aimed. The moment DJ's group turned the corner, they fired.

DJ ducked back immediately, using the wall as cover. He peeked back out a couple of seconds later, prepared to lay down covering fire, but the puppets were already dead. Karla stood over their bodies, a sneer on her face. Chloe smirked at him. She hadn't moved at all.

Well, DJ thought, straightening, *that was embarrassing*.

They continued down the tunnel. DJ glanced at the bodies as he passed and fingered his vest. *Not yet,* he thought. It only had a limited charge, so he couldn't use it on every poor sap he came across.

The next tunnel held even more puppets, which Karla summarily took care of. DJ started to feel guilty.

"Yo! Why don't we try *not* brutally murdering people who have no control over their actions?" he said. "We can knock them out or something."

Karla knelt over one of the bodies and cleaned her daggers on their clothes. This was the third group they'd fought, yet there wasn't a single drop of blood on her. "You would let them live? So they can attack us again?"

"That's why we'd knock them out. I mean, it's not their fault they're attacking us now, and you're mowing them down like chickens. We're the good guys, remember?"

"It is a mercy to kill them," Karla insisted.

"In what world is brutally murdering them mercy?" DJ shouted. "Helene's using them against their will. If we knock them out, then they're out of the fight—"

"And then what?" Chloe said. She gave him a look he couldn't quite place. Half pity and half … something else. "We knock them out now, and then what? Helene will still have control of them. They'll still be forced to do heinous things. They might survive now, but how's that going to help them when they have to go back to being controlled?"

DJ almost blurted a retort about the Synaptic Pulse that was in one of his vest pockets, but he stopped himself in time. He couldn't use the Pulse. Not yet. It was their secret weapon, and it had limited charges. DJ was saving it for when they met up with Ndidi in case she'd been infected with the spores. The device had to remain a secret until then. If Helene got a whiff of its existence here with him, there was no telling what she would do.

When DJ didn't answer for several seconds, Karla took it as agreement. He expected her to move on, but she surprised him by speaking again. She still held her sneer, but it had lost its bite.

"You feel pity for them. That softness is a weakness and should be rooted out. But that is a separate matter. You consider these abominations helpless because you see them being killed easily, gutted like livestock. But that is only in small numbers. You will not think them weak when they arrive as a swarm and drown you in their numbers. My sister and I can handle dozens at a time. But what if the AI sends thousands and you stand against them all alone? Would you still feel pity then? Would it matter that their actions are not theirs?" She pointed a finger at him, and her tone turned mocking. "Your morals will stand for only as long as you're safe. Once your survival is threatened, you become a killer like the rest of us."

Chloe placed a hand on his shoulder. "She's not wrong. She makes it seem easy, but you haven't seen what these fuckers can do. With enough numbers, strength means nothing."

DJ shook his head. "That doesn't mean we have to kill—"

"Yes. It does. Helene already has enough of these things. I'm not going to leave an enemy at my back because you were too soft. I mean, fuck, I know it isn't your forte, but use your head for once. We've only gone down a couple of tunnels, and we've faced dozens of these things. If Karla and I weren't here, how well do you think you would have done?"

DJ wanted to protest but found that he couldn't. Righteous indignation was all well and good, but he couldn't deny that Chloe and Karla had a point. Karla made it look easy. DJ would have had a hard time with the puppets, and he definitely wouldn't have come out unscathed. And this was with the puppets coming in relatively small numbers. From what Karla had said, they'd seen much worse. And DJ still remembered the reports of the bodies they'd found at the facilities. Had she been forced to deal with dozens at a time? Hundreds? How had she survived?

Despite seeing their point, killing the puppets for the risk they might pose didn't sit well with DJ. He wasn't a stranger to death, to killing, but he was used to his opponents deserving it. They'd made a conscious decision to be bad. Here, the puppets didn't have a damn choice. And yet they were being slaughtered. Maybe it was naive of him to believe that the world would always be black and white like that, but DJ still couldn't get it out of his head.

The three of them pushed on. Every tunnel held more puppets. Every time, they were slaughtered. It seemed like Karla was killing them in more gruesome ways to prove some kind of sick point. Even Chloe started to participate when the numbers became so much that the group started slowing down. Although DJ didn't say a word, he felt guilty about every death.

After several tunnels of the same thing, his guilt turned to anger. At Helene. She was the one leading these people to their deaths. She had to know they didn't pose much of a threat, yet she sent them anyway. In that way, Karla was right that it was a mercy to put them down. That didn't make the group bad guys.

The real villain was Helene. For a moment, he'd forgotten that.

LIZ POLOVA MADE HER WAY through the subterranean tunnels with ease. Her movements were quick yet deliberate, without a hint of sound. She could tell that her companions didn't enjoy the same grace she did, but it didn't matter as long as they did their duty. Liz had personally trained Christy, so she was better off than Pratima, though not by much. Christy didn't have to deal with Pratima's sheer muscle mass, but it was obvious she had little experience with stealth. Conversely, it was Pratima's experience that made her able to keep up at all. Liz had heard about her fight with Chloe, and though Liz was confident that she would win in a fight, it wouldn't be because of her skill, but her bionic enhancements.

She spared a glance at the two women. Liz and Chloe would have been the best choice, but she saw the wisdom in DJ's pairing. Without Liz there, Chloe would need to be present to keep Karla in check. And so, Liz was left with Christy and Pratima. All three wore goggles, which made the darkness slightly less of an obstacle.

The tunnels were silent, which was both good and bad. The silence meant they hadn't yet drawn Helene's attention, but Liz knew that her sister's group already had arrived. The fact that they couldn't hear any hint of that fight meant that the tunnel system was extensive.

That was unfortunate, since it was their job to find and extract Ndidi Okafor. Chloe and the others were to buy as much time as possible, but both sides knew they could only hold out for so long before Helene overwhelmed them. Karla would rather die than admit that. Liz's group had to fulfill their objective before that happened.

Liz formed a map of their route through the tunnels. The mazelike layout brought unpleasant memories of the Sparta underground base. She already knew that the tunnels were filled with Dead Eyes, yet it was a staple of the AI to build a base that was as convoluted as possible in order to restrict the movement of her minions, even if those minions were under her complete control. Liz would have respected such paranoia if it didn't make her sick.

Several times, they came across one of Helene's relays, and they were forced to backtrack and find another path before continuing. Liz added these new paths to her map to ensure that they never searched the same place twice. Eventually they would have to either start destroying the relays or go through a path despite them, but Liz hoped to draw it out for as long as they could until the other group firmly held Helene's attention.

After several minutes, they were deep enough to encounter their first door. It was made of solid metal and had a keypad lock—another measure born of paranoia. Liz ignored it. Instead, she pressed her ear to the door and listened for several seconds before moving on.

"Aren't we going to check what's in there?" Christy asked. It was the first time she'd spoken except to relay DJ's messages.

"There's no need," Liz replied without stopping. "Ndidi Okafor is not within."

"How do you know that?"

"She listened for movement," Pratima answered.

"That door was at least a foot thick and made of solid metal," Christy pressed. "What if they were sleeping?"

"Then I would have heard their breathing," Liz replied. "Or I would have heard them shuffling in their sleep."

"Is your hearing really that good?" Pratima asked. She didn't sound mocking or skeptical.

"Yes."

No one said anything after that. They got to the second door. Once again, Liz pressed her ear against the metal and listened. She moved on after a few seconds, and again, no one said anything.

Liz should have felt something at the trust they showed her, but she didn't. It didn't matter, as long as they didn't hinder her in her duty.

They encountered their first real problem at the first door Liz decided to break down. A flick of her wrist destroyed the keypad, and the door opened into a room. The destruction would obviously alert Helene to their presence, putting them on a timer. But that had always been inevitable. The problem was what was within the room.

Half a dozen heat signatures were clustered within the room, quivering. Some were big enough to be adults, while others were clearly children. All of them stared in their direction. Liz couldn't make out their specific expressions. Doubtless, it was surprise and fear.

Christy stood beside Liz at the entrance and peered inside. "Shit."

DJ SLAMMED THE BUTT OF HIS GUN at the drone. Although it didn't cause any damage, there was enough force to move the drone, ruining a shot aimed at Chloe. DJ backpedaled to dodge a retaliatory swipe from the daggers and pumped a few bullets into the glowing red eye in the center of the machine—a feature shared by all the bots. He didn't know the function of the eye, and he didn't care. But that was the only place where DJ's bullets did any damage. The problem was hitting the damn thing while the drone flitted about. This close, however, it was literally impossible for DJ to miss. The bullets broke through the core, and the drone crashed a second later.

DJ didn't have time to celebrate before he had to duck another attack, this time from one of the puppets. The damn thing held a sword, for Christ's sake, and actually seemed to know how to use it. Its movements were more fluid than usual, more precise. DJ had to concentrate in order to avoid getting skewered.

These ambushes had started appearing a couple of tunnels ago. According to Chloe, it meant that Helene was giving more of her attention to controlling the fuckers. The thoughtful look she'd had told DJ there was more to that story, but there wasn't any time to press further. Still, they were getting Helene's attention, even if the fuckers were more annoying as a result. Fortunately, the puppets didn't have an armored shell that reflected his bullets.

Chloe and Karla were several feet away, slashing away with abandon. Several bodies and crashed drones lay at their feet. Quite accurately, Helene had identified them as the major threats, so they were constantly swarmed with opponents. The toxic alpha-male part of him was hurt by that and urged him to jump in. Luckily, DJ had more sense. Not that it took much sense to realize that he wasn't on the same level as the other two. According to Martin, the nanites would get him there eventually. DJ just hoped that it wasn't too late. Until then, though, he was content to stay at the back and pick up any stragglers that came his way.

He was about to jump back into the fray when his watch vibrated once. It took him a few seconds to parse Christy's message. He cursed when he was done.

Shit! There are children here? They'd planned for Bethany to be with Ndidi, but they hadn't considered that there would be more hostages. How the fuck were they going to keep over a dozen adults and children safe?

Fuck! His thoughts raced. He tapped out a quick message: *Leave them. But mark spot. Find Ndidi. Will double back.*

It was the best they could do. They could save the hostages, but it would only slow them down. It made more sense to find Ndidi first and then go back for them. There were still risks to that, but DJ didn't see any other way.

Christy sent her agreement. DJ was angry at himself for not having considered that there could be more hostages. It was just like with the puppets: Helene was the true villain here. Being angry at himself changed nothing. Better he channel it to something productive.

With a roar, DJ charged back into the battle.

32

NDIDI WOKE TO THE SOUND of distant explosions. At first, she thought she'd imagined it—that the noise was nothing more than the remnants of her dream. However, beside her, Bethany also had her head cocked, listening. Ndidi followed suit. It was faint, but when the sound came again, Ndidi was sure of what she was hearing: gunfire.

She was on her feet and moving over sleeping bodies in seconds, waking them up as she went. Bethany followed suit without needing to be told. They both understood what the gunfire signified: a chance to escape. Ndidi had been waiting for such a chance for weeks after extracting as much information from the captives as she could. They'd needed a moment when Helene was distracted, a moment when her attention was forced elsewhere and they could act undeterred for several moments. Was someone attacking the place? That was perfect.

Her eyes went to the relay nestled on the wall. It was the same one Helene had appeared from ages ago. Ndidi hadn't been able to draw her out since then, but she'd kept a careful eye on the device and its light—especially whenever she interrogated her fellow captives. She saved some of her questions for when the light was dim, which she'd taken to mean that Helene's attention was elsewhere. Now, the light was muted but not by much. Ndidi had seen this many times over the last several days. Bethany believed that it meant that Helene's attention was within the building, or at least the area, but wasn't directly concentrated on a specific spot. Ndidi agreed, but the frequency at which it happened made her wonder what other assets Helene had. Something was drawing her attention.

Maybe Ndidi would finally get a chance to find out what it was.

Ndidi looked around the room. Eyes stared back at her, some fearful and others determined. Others were just listless. The number of people belonging to the latter was growing every day. Ndidi tried not to let on how much that bothered her.

"Everyone clear on the plan?" she asked.

Tentative nods came from the group. Albert was the one who asked what everyone was thinking. "You sure it's going to work?"

Ndidi projected the confidence that had been trained into her since birth. Inside, she harbored the same doubts as Albert, but her voice came out strong. "Yes. This is our chance. We have to take it if we're ever going to have our lives back."

"She's just going to bring us back with the spores," someone said.

Again, it was Ndidi's training that kept her exasperation from showing. They'd been over this several times already. "Not if we get to Sparta. My friend is already working on a counter for the picospores. She'll be able to help us. But first, we have to get there, which means we have to get moving."

Some people still looked unsure. Ndidi couldn't blame them, but she didn't have time to coddle them either. Every second they wasted was a second they could have used to escape. Before anyone else could raise a complaint, she stood beside the door and nodded at Bethany on the other side of the room. Bethany plucked the relay out of the wall and crushed it beneath her heel. The whole room tensed as the group realized there was no going back. Hopefully that would force them to cooperate.

It took a few seconds, but eventually the entrance slid open. Ndidi was ready. A pair of Dead Eyes rushed in, weapons in hand. Fortunately, Ndidi had positioned herself to the side so that she was in their blind spot. She lunged immediately, leading with her fists. Her punch rocked the first guard, but Ndidi could tell she'd done no actual damage. Weeks of captivity had sapped her strength. Ndidi switched to using her elbows and knees. She dodged between the guards, striking everywhere she could reach, never letting them use their weapons. In such a small space, the bullets were guaranteed to hit someone. Ndidi couldn't allow that. She ducked behind a punch from one guard, twisting her body so she was in position to attack the other. Her knuckles struck the temple, and the guard crumpled. With only one opponent, the fight ended a few moments later.

Ndidi picked up one of the guns and threw the other to Albert. He'd been a cop, so Ndidi figured he was the best choice to handle a gun. Bethany would have been an option since Ndidi trusted her more—but Ndidi wanted to protect her innocence for as long as she could—however futile it might be.

The group exited through the door under Ndidi's direction. Suddenly they were in the tunnels. Ndidi brought up her mental map, which had been cobbled together over several weeks from the half-remembered memories of the captives. It was bare-bones and probably inaccurate, but it was what they had to work with. Using it, she had planned their escape route as best she could. Any problems would have to be dealt with on the fly. Fortunately, she'd spent enough time with DJ to be fairly confident in her ability to make it work.

Ndidi stayed at the front of the group while they made their way through the tunnel. They moved at a fast walk, which coincidentally was the fastest pace they could manage. Bethany stayed at her side the entire time. Several times, Ndidi opened her mouth to send her to the middle of the group where she would be more protected, but no: Bethany was a woman now, capable of making her own decisions. Ndidi wanted her safe, but she wouldn't do that by destroying what little bit of confidence Bethany was developing.

Albert guarded their rear, along with several other adults he'd picked. This dynamic was one that had come about without Ndidi's intervention. With Bethany's prompting, most of the group, even Albert, had warmed up to her eventually and even generally followed her instructions. However, Ndidi was still considered an outsider. She could feel it in their attitude, in the subdued murmurings when she was working on the map. They no longer thought she was a spy and even trusted her to some extent—at least enough to go along with her plan. But she didn't really belong. She hadn't been trapped in that room with them for years upon years. Albert had, though. Most people considered him to be the group's true leader and generally looked to him for guidance.

Ndidi didn't care. It didn't matter, none of it did, as long as they escaped.

The tunnel branched and Ndidi went right, following the map in her head. She saw the Dead Eyes the same moment that he saw her. He reacted faster than Ndidi expected, though his movements were still stiff and mechanical. Ndidi's gun was already raised. It was a rifle, heavy enough that she'd never have been able to carry it for so long without the adrenaline pumping through her. The shot cracked like thunder, and the recoil almost tore the gun from her hands. But Ndidi's fear had already locked her muscles, making her grip steady. The bullet hit the puppet in his leg. He stumbled, causing his shot to go wild and hit the side of the tunnel. Chips of packed earth rained over the group, and the tunnel filled with screams of terror.

Too close, Ndidi thought, her heart pounding. She couldn't let him squeeze off another shot. With a yell, Ndidi ran toward the guard, crossing the distance before the Dead Eyes could recover his balance. She swung the butt of her gun toward her opponent's head, but the puppet twisted out of the way in time. He grabbed at her rifle and yanked, almost pulling Ndidi off her feet. The Dead Eyes yanked again. This time, she let go of the weapon. Her sudden release threw her opponent off-balance again. Ndidi capitalized on it by kicking at his wounded leg. The guard crumpled to his knees. Ndidi delivered another kick, this time to his head.

The man fell without a sound. He didn't get back up. Panting, Ndidi picked up her gun and the guard's. She kept hers but passed the other one to Albert to be given to whoever he deemed fit to handle it. She ignored the stares from the group—as well as the pride in Bethany's eyes—in favor of hurrying them along.

"Let's keep moving."

CJ DIDN'T STOP RUNNING until he was several streets away. With the exception of bots, he'd never seen any programs exit their website, but then again, he'd just been reminded quite strongly that he knew nothing of the virtual world. With this in mind, he only slowed down when he started to feel drained.

Avatars moved around him in a constant stream of codes. CJ lay down in the middle of the street and let it wash over him for a moment. He pressed his palm to the road. Although it looked like asphalt, it had the texture of refined marble. He let it ground him. Physically, he may not have needed a medium to be present anymore, but with everything he'd just been through, CJ felt that grounding himself was necessary. Plus, the motion was easy and familiar. He needed that after being thrust so far out of his comfort zone.

He'd almost been killed, for Christ's sake! CJ hadn't let himself consider what that meant. What would happen if he was killed here? What would happen to his real body?

What would death even look like in the virtual world? He'd noted multiple times that the stamina of his virtual body was far more than he had with his real body, and it acted differently. In the real world, when CJ got tired, he panted, and his muscles started to ache. Here, exhaustion showed itself as a feeling of being drained. The feeling was significantly different from what he usually felt—so much so that CJ was convinced this body ran on another type of energy, something other than stamina. CJ didn't have any way to prove this, of course, except for what he felt. The more he thought about it, the more he grew confident he was right. If his virtual body didn't pull energy from his real body, what was the source? His soul?

No, CJ thought immediately. He'd never been particularly religious, and a part of him refused to believe the answer would be so arbitrary.

Could it be mental energy? CJ toyed with that for a moment. It wasn't a completely foreign concept and would make the most sense. To transport himself to the virtual world, he'd gone through the same process as Manar, except he hadn't interlinked his consciousness with Gaius. Despite that, it was his mind that he'd uploaded to the internet, not his body. So, wouldn't it make sense that he would use mental energy instead of stamina?

CJ returned to his original question: If he was killed here, what would happen to his real body? Would it die? Or would his mind simply be destroyed, making him a vegetable?

Does it matter? he thought with a sigh. Neither option was acceptable, and it wasn't like he could get an answer without testing. Which he obviously didn't plan to do.

Still, CJ considered the question. Even if he couldn't get the answer, it had always been his way to consider every risk before making a decision, before committing himself to a path. That had always been the difference between him and his brother. DJ's decisions were spurred by instinct. He picked his path based on what he felt was right, regardless of the risks or consequences. It's what made him so admirable. CJ had never been able to do that.

Even now, when he'd already made a decision, he had to consider every angle so he could plan to mitigate the impact of potential issues.

He lifted the sphere to his face. Something gnawed at him. Something about it felt …

It's incomplete.

He'd almost been killed getting the second piece, and from the way the website had reacted to the sphere's presence, it was likely that obtaining further pieces was going to be more difficult.

But CJ had already made his decision. Even incomplete, the sphere had proven too helpful for him not to explore what the complete version would be capable of. Maybe it would be a viable weapon to use against Helene. Manar would have his enhancements from merging with Gaius, but CJ would be near useless, making his presence moot. A large part of his reasoning—larger than CJ wanted to admit—was his curiosity. If nothing else, CJ had always been an academic at heart. The sphere, whatever it was, was definitely groundbreaking. If CJ could study its final form and recreate it …

The sphere wobbled, and CJ realized his hand was trembling. He calmed himself with effort. He'd already made his decision. Now he considered the risks so he could plan for it.

One of the major issues right off the bat was that he didn't know what the sphere was capable of. He'd seen his brother spend hours on his weapon, examining every inch of it. So far, CJ had stumbled upon each ability by accident. Without actually knowing what the orb could do, he would be putting himself in unnecessary danger.

Fortunately, that was a problem that CJ could easily solve. Now that he had his own weapon, he just had to train with it.

CJ stood with a grunt and started dusting himself off. The sphere was still clutched in his hand. At its current size, it wouldn't fit in his pocket anymore. This gave rise to an interesting thought. *If it's going to get larger the more orbs I add, I'll need to build a place for it.* CJ already had several ideas for what that would look like. The problem was getting materials. So far, the orbs were the only things that hadn't turned to dust when broken off. CJ sent the problem to the back of his mind. He still had some time before it became urgent; he would be able to figure something out by then.

But there was something he did have to figure out as soon as possible. He held the sphere in both hands. It was cold. CJ took this to be its dormant stage. He turned it as he tried to figure out how it worked. Then a thought occurred to him: Was this really the best place to do this? CJ wasn't sure what would happen if he activated the device.

He ultimately discarded the thought. The problem was he kept thinking of the virtual world as having the same rules as the physical world. In the real world, any sort of testing should always be done in a safe environment, with plenty of protection. However, CJ didn't think that was a hard rule here. With the exception of the antivirus squad, he hadn't found anything truly dangerous. Even the viruses he'd seen hadn't actually harmed anyone.

For weeks, CJ had explored everything in every direction, and it was all the same: filled with avatars and websites. Even if he wanted to go somewhere "safer," where would that be?

With that settled, CJ turned back to the sphere. There was no obvious way to activate the device. There was no button to press. But CJ at least had expected a clue from the codes. However, when he analyzed them, he found nothing. With how unresponsive the orb was, CJ would have thought it was a dud if he hadn't already seen what the device was capable of.

Several times, in fact. What did all those moments have in common?

CJ brought up the memories of every time he'd seen the sphere activate. The first memory—when the sphere had directed him through the website by getting hotter—snapped into place easily. This was something that had happened earlier that day, of course, but even still, CJ couldn't help but marvel at the ease of his recollection. In his real body, it would have taken him several seconds to find the correct memory.

He focused, taking in every detail of that moment. He'd been terrified and confused, trying to figure out a way through the website while being chased by the antivirus squad.

The second memory involved the orb opening the backdoor through the website. CJ remembered the strange call that had emanated from the sphere. Now, he knew that it had been reacting to the piece of code in the website's core.

He'd been so desperate for a solution. The sphere had reacted to that and given him one.

The last memory was also the most significant. It was the most overt use of the sphere so far: when CJ had been teleported out of danger. He remembered how terrified he'd been then, how desperately he'd searched for a solution. He'd been convinced that he'd been about to die. He would have if the sphere hadn't activated. CJ still remembered the scorching heat. It was as if the orb reacted to his emotions.

That's the key, CJ realized with excitement. Every time the sphere had activated, it was in response to something he'd felt. The stronger the emotion, the more overt the sphere had been.

Later, he could analyze why his emotions were the key and how the sphere intuited what he wanted, but for now, CJ had something to test.

He held the last memory in his mind and tried to let his emotions wash over him. But that wouldn't work, would it? Without any danger, he didn't feel the fear that had almost overwhelmed him. It was also hard to muster up a sense of urgency. But now that he'd discovered the key, it was only a matter of time before he figured it out.

Relying on fear as a trigger will only limit my options later, CJ thought.

CJ went to discard the memory but reconsidered. Instead, when he analyzed the scene again, he focused on his desires. The antiviruses had been bearing down on him. He'd wanted nothing more than to escape, to move somewhere else—anywhere else. That desire had consumed his mind completely.

CJ held on to that feeling. There was no fear or urgency to fuel his wish, but they weren't necessary anyway. He wanted to move—no, he needed to move, to be anywhere else. As the sphere grew hotter in his hands, CJ's excitement bubbled to the surface once more. Fortunately, he'd had a lot of experience grounding himself, and he kept his focus easily.

He didn't know how much time passed as he sat there. He kept his mind clear, empty except for his goal: to move. The sphere grew hotter until it was almost unbearable to hold. The pain threatened to ruin his concentration, but CJ pushed it down. The pain didn't matter. Nothing did, as long as he was anywhere else.

CJ felt the change. The sphere became scorching, and a ripple of something burst forth. There was the feeling of movement.

When CJ opened his eyes, he was somewhere else.

This time, he didn't try to stem his excitement, and his yell of triumph echoed through the street.

34

DJ DUCKED A STRIKE from a puppet and used the man as a shield to avoid a hail of bullets from a passing drone. Karla rode the machine like it was a horse, easily keeping her balance as it bucked her around. DJ spared a glance at it but didn't have time for more, as he was forced to block a strike from a Dead Eyes that had somehow snuck up behind him. The subsequent crash told him all he needed to know anyway.

He kicked the Dead Eyes away from him and put a bullet into her eye. Others shambled toward him from deeper within the tunnel, quickly filling up the space despite how quickly they were mowed down. DJ had already needed to switch from his usual pistols to one of his spare rifles. Those worked great on the puppets, but the loss in accuracy made taking down drones harder. His fingers itched to bring out the Synaptic Pulse. As Hermione had explained, the Pulse shot a blast that spread out in a wide cone. It could be used on several puppets at once, but that would be tipping their hands too early. And it still wouldn't take care of the drones.

DJ no longer bitched about killing the Dead Eyes, not after a few dozen he'd knocked out had flanked them in the middle of a fight with another group. Chloe and Karla had left him to deal with them. DJ had done so. He'd killed them all. It had made him sick to his stomach, but he'd done it. He hadn't even considered knocking them out again. Helene would just send them once more, maybe at a more crucial time. DJ couldn't afford that.

Like Karla had said, *Your morals will stand for only as long as you're safe. Once your survival is threatened, you become a killer like the rest of us.* DJ knew she was right then, but it hadn't truly hit him. He still felt guilty, but it was distant—muted when compared to his desire for survival.

Bloody hell! DJ cursed as he squeezed off a shot. He flicked a bead of sweat away from his eyes. *Am I really doing this shit right now? Get your fucking head in the game, you idiot.*

DJ retreated to the end of the tunnel. His breathing was heavy, and his shirt was soaked with sweat. He was used to fast-paced combat, but most battles of that type generally didn't last so long. By DJ's estimate, they'd come underground about fifteen minutes ago. He'd lost count of how many tunnels they'd gone through and how many puppets he'd killed. Still, something didn't feel right. By now, they were facing over a dozen puppets and drones for each new tunnel they entered. This was a lot, at least to DJ. Karla didn't seem to have broken a sweat yet, and Chloe just looked mildly irritated. DJ would freely admit that they were doing the heavy lifting, but it wasn't overwhelming. Their progress had slowed considerably. DJ got the feeling they were being herded.

Although every tunnel had obstacles, some had significantly more. It was as if Helene was actively restricting them from heading in that direction. DJ had noticed the pattern several minutes ago. The feeling that they were being guided had only grown.

He waited until the tunnel was clear before walking up to the others. Karla's arms, up to her elbows, were drenched in blood. There were a few flecks of red around her mouth, like she'd bitten someone. In contrast, only Chloe's shoes were bloody; the rest of her was untouched. Her daggers, however, dripped like a faucet.

"Good work out there," Chloe said with a mocking smile.

DJ ignored her. "Doesn't something about all this rub you the wrong way?"

"What do you mean?"

"Well, from what you said, Helene could have been throwing much more at us, right? I mean, this is plenty for me, but neither of you seems bothered." DJ paused, not sure how to say the next part without sounding like an idiot. Eventually, he just blurted it out. "It just doesn't feel like she's trying to kill us. It's more like she's doing the same thing we are: just stalling for time."

Chloe raised an eyebrow. Karla spat on the ground. DJ noticed that the spittle was red, but he was sure that the blood wasn't from her.

"The AI has always fought like a coward," Karla said. "It uses its numbers to grind at its opponents until they are broken."

"That's just the thing," DJ said. "You said you and Liz have handled close to a hundred of these Dead Eyes at a time before. At its base in Sparta, you guys fought with dozens of drones. And yet, it's throwing half a dozen of these things at you? It doesn't make sense. We've been pressed only twice so far, when we were forced to retreat from the tunnel and pick a different path. And after that? It's back to Little League. None of you think that's weird?"

Chloe's smirk lost some of its mockery. She looked at him thoughtfully, almost impressed. "I didn't think you'd notice."

DJ shrugged. "Hey, I keep saying I'm just not just a pretty face. But no one ever listens. So, were you going to say anything?"

"It wasn't part of the mission."

For fuck's sake, DJ cursed mentally.

"All right. New plan," he said. "We'll keep doing what we're doing, but now we're going to see what Helene's trying to hide from us."

"That's not part of the mission, love," Chloe said. "And I'm not in the business of risking my life without a reason."

"Thought you wanted to get revenge on Helene for killing José," DJ countered. "Fucking up whatever she's planning will go a long way toward that."

Chloe chuckled without humor. She jerked a finger at Karla. "While I'd love to knock Helene down a peg or two, I'm far more interested in keeping myself alive. Seeking revenge? That's a good way to find yourself dead."

DJ sighed. "Fine. What do you want?"

Chloe smiled.

A minute later, the three of them had retraced their steps through the tunnels until they reached a specific one. If DJ was doubting that Helene had a way of tracking them aside from her relays, those doubts were discarded. When they reached the tunnel, there was already a small army of Dead Eyes and drones waiting for them.

DJ gulped. *This might have been a mistake.*

NDIDI RUSHED IN while Albert provided covering fire. She'd finally relented and given Bethany a gun, but she'd also made her promise to only use it to protect herself. With Bethany's aim, anything else would be dangerous. That, unfortunately, was one of the problems with the group. They'd amassed quite a lot of firearms throughout their run, but only a few of the captives knew how to use them.

Some people had insisted that everybody should get one to protect themselves, but Ndidi had shut that down fast. Their group was made up of confused and terrified people. Giving such people weapons—even for their protection—would inevitably lead to accidents. Plus, there was Helene to think about. Ndidi was certain the only reason they'd made it so far was because Helene was preoccupied with whatever was causing the explosions in the distance. But that could change at any time. Until they got to Sparta, Ndidi would prefer not to give her captor an easy way to kill them all. Fortunately, Albert had agreed with her, and the weapons were limited to those who were proficient.

Her decision had strained the relationship of the group, but Ndidi was resolute. They couldn't afford to make stupid mistakes. Not now.

She glanced back at the crowd when the tunnel was clear. It was a larger group than she'd started with, by at least several dozen. Ndidi had picked up the extras in several rooms on their way. She'd been appalled to find the first group, but not surprised. At this point, nothing Helene did would surprise her. Unexpectedly, no one in her original group had challenged her decision to absorb the new ones, even though the addition slowed them down. Ndidi had expected a few bad altercations. But everyone understood the pain and hardship; none would jeopardize anyone's chance to escape that turmoil.

Even now, Ndidi saw people go out of their way to help others; they pushed down their fear to make sure others were all right.

That's what Helene is trying to destroy, Ndidi thought, feeling her rage bubble to the surface. *She focuses on the bad and sees us as a disease, but humans are much more than that. We're not perfect, but everyone is trying their best. Why can't she see that?*

Ndidi dismissed the thought and pushed down her anger. She'd long accepted that she would never understand how Helene thought. Ndidi peeked around the next tunnel. When she was certain there were no enemies, she entered fully and waved the rest of the group forward.

Their progress was slow. Part of it was because of how large the group was. They were forced from a slow jog to a fast shuffle. In addition, Ndidi was being extremely cautious. She was determined not to lose a single person in the escape. It was naive. Her father would have chided her for it. He would have lectured her about the risk of business and how you had to lose something to gain something.

When the next tunnel was clear, Ndidi waved the group forward.

Her father had been full of such lessons when she was growing up. But Ndidi was fairly certain that her father hadn't been in quite the same situation that she was now. It was one thing to talk about loss when it was just numbers on a screen, but it was quite another thing when each one was a person you were responsible for, someone who had put their lives in your hands.

If he could see me now, he would probably have a heart attack, she thought with a grim chuckle. But then she reconsidered the thought. Eze had been many things to many people, but no one would ever have accused him of being soft-hearted or weak-minded. He would have been appalled at her kidnapping but never would have allowed his panic to drive him into inaction.

Ndidi glanced back at the crowd of people following her, trusting her with their lives. She hoped her actions would have made him proud.

Ndidi peeked into the next tunnel. Another thought immediately took over. *That's impossible!* Not every tunnel contained Dead Eyes that needed to be taken care of. But for those that did, the puppets usually came in groups of six or more. Here, there was only a single Dead Eyes in the tunnel. The sight filled Ndidi with dread.

That's impossible! she thought again, as if her denial would make it so. The figure—the monstrosity of a man—stood as stiff as any Dead Eyes. However, this was clearly not just a Dead Eyes. From the neck downward, the man's entire body was encased in titanium, like he was wearing a suit of armor. *No, not encased,* Ndidi realized with horror. *His body is* made *of titanium.* It was like someone had taken a human head and a robot's body and joined them.

Ndidi couldn't wrap her head around that. His gaze struck Ndidi with an intensity that pinned her to the spot. Ndidi recognized that look of contempt. She'd seen this man only once before, yet few people invoked such primal fear in her.

"Return to your cells, Ndidi Okafor," José Olvera said. "This pitiful attempt at rebellion has dragged on long enough."

MANAR FELT AS THOUGH he was losing his mind. He stumbled out of the alley that he'd taken for a website and swept his eyes over the street. Several feet away, intermixed with the crowd, stood CJ's avatar. Although the avatar's back was turned to Manar, he was certain it was the exact same one that he'd chased several weeks ago and had failed to catch. Manar had seen it several times since then, just at the edge of his vision, and always just about to walk out of sight. Every time Manar followed it, it had led him into some sort of attack. The worm had been the first. Since then, Manar had been tagged with a virus and had almost been hacked twice. The second one had nearly succeeded.

Manar was embarrassed that it had taken him three attacks before he'd caught on that the avatar was a trick of Helene's. Since then, he'd seen avatars of Ndidi, Hermione, and even DJ. Manar had ignored those easily enough. It wasn't until he'd started entering illusionary buildings he'd perceived as real that he started getting worried.

So far, Manar hadn't figured out how to escape that. The avatars were easy to ignore. However, if Manar intended to move about, he needed to find a reliable way to navigate. Even the nanites had proven useless in this case. Several times, he was led to a building that later turned out to have been an illusion. Manar didn't know if Helene had figured out a way to circumvent the tracking or if she was truly moving around so quickly.

The problem, he thought with gritted teeth, *is that I don't know what she's capable of.*

How powerful was she? What was her range? The illusions hadn't started until he'd left the market stalls and entered the more structured part of the Virtual space. Manar had considered going back until he figured it out. The moment he'd tried, however, the road stretched into infinity. Manar had walked for over a week before finally giving up. The feeling he got then, of walking but not getting anywhere, was familiar enough that Manar began to rethink his theory about her range. That scared him enough to try something that had given him pause.

The ball of energy sat at the center of his chest. Manar hadn't had a chance to use it recently since there was nothing to hack. He'd already tried it on the buildings to no effect. Internally, he cradled its power.

"EVERYONE, RETURN to your cells now," the titanium José Olvera commanded.

If Ndidi had any doubts that this was José, they were dispelled with that.

"But how?" she muttered. She hadn't been present for the battle that had claimed his life; she'd been using the chaos of the battle to find the core and set the explosive. But DJ had described it in excruciating detail. That, coupled with what she'd noticed with the Murder Twins, confirmed that José had been killed.

Or, at least, everyone thought he'd been killed. Ndidi took in his titanium body once more. He hadn't walked away from the explosion unscathed, but he'd obviously survived somehow. Ndidi could think of only one way that that was possible. José's presence now confirmed it.

"Who's that?" Bethany asked from beside her. Ndidi hadn't heard her approach. Albert came up from the back in time to hear the question. He peeked around the corner, then he, too, stared at Ndidi.

"It's a long story," Ndidi said.

José Olvera had started out as an enemy, but they'd fought together against Helene at Sparta's underground base. While she wouldn't count him as a friend, they'd had the same goal for a while. Yet Ndidi could think of only one way for him to have survived all this time: through Helene. This likely meant José was being controlled.

"A very long story," she said, massaging her temples, "but suffice it to say, he's being controlled by Helene. He's not going to let us pass."

"We'll take care of it like usual then," Albert assured her.

I don't think it's going to be that simple, Ndidi sighed mentally. "Give me a few minutes to get as much information as I can first. You can tell the guys to get ready, though."

Albert nodded and moved on. Bethany remained, however, staring at her in concern. "He's different from the others."

Ndidi nodded. When she spoke next, it was directed at José. "What has Helene done to you, José? How are you still alive?"

"That is of no concern to you, Ndidi Okafor. Cease your futile resistance and return to your cells."

Ndidi's brows scrunched up in suspicion. *Cease your futile resistance?*

She decided to try something and stepped into the tunnel proper. Bethany tried to drag her back, but Ndidi shook her off. This could end up being monumentally stupid, but Ndidi had to be sure.

"Jesus, is this what you are now? Nothing more than a lapdog? I would have expected better after all the shit you put us through."

José didn't respond, but Ndidi noticed a slight twist of his lips.

She pressed on, hardening her voice. "You're right, though. It's none of my business. But what about your daughters? They at least deserve to know what happened to their father. They mourned for you, in their own way, and yet you've been here the whole time, under Helene's heel. How do you think that's going to make them feel? Their own father, nothing more than a hound for someone else."

That got a reaction. José's eyes filled with rage. Ndidi could feel the killing intent radiating off him like a furnace. His lips moved, but no words came out. And still, he made no move to attack her. That confirmed Ndidi's suspicions. He wasn't attacking because he couldn't. Helene fully held the reins. Even the words he'd spoken a moment ago had come directly from Helene through his mouth.

But he isn't all gone, Ndidi thought, observing the pure rage on his face. A part of him was still there, fighting for control. That, by itself, was impressive. From Bethany, Ndidi knew how strong Helene's control was. And that was for an average person. Helene had obviously done something extra to José, something that gave her a firmer grip.

There was nothing Ndidi could do.

That realization hit her harder than she'd expected, considering that for the entire time she'd known José, they'd been enemies. Still, no one deserved whatever Helene had done to him.

"Return to your cells," José ordered again, taking a step closer. In response, Ndidi crouched back behind her cover. Bethany looked at her with concern, but Ndidi kept her attention on Albert.

"Do it," she said.

Albert made a gesture, and about a dozen men stepped around the corner, arranging themselves into two lines. Each man held one of the guns picked up from the Dead Eyes along the way. As one, they pointed their weapons down the tunnel. Albert made another gesture, and the sounds of gunfire filled the passage. Usually, Ndidi alone could take care of the few Dead Eyes they came across in the tunnels, but sometimes the guards had been amassed in too large numbers for her to risk it. At those times, this was their solution. Each of the men had been handpicked by Albert. Determination filled their eyes as they stood and emptied their clips.

The gunfire lasted for several seconds before tapering off. Several bullets had hit the walls and ceiling, raising a cloud of dust that obstructed their vision. Ndidi waited for the dust to clear; she was certain that it wasn't going to be that simple. When was it ever? But she couldn't shake off a bit of hope that she was wrong.

The dust cleared, revealing José was relatively unharmed. He was several spaces behind where he'd been standing, and one of his arms was held defensively in front of his face. Ndidi scanned his body for any damage. Apart from minor black spots and small dents around the torso, there was none.

Ndidi's heart fell. *It never is that easy.*

Albert gestured for another round, but Ndidi stopped him. It didn't matter how many times they tried. It would serve no other purpose than to waste their remaining ammunition. That was why Helene had sent him here instead of more Dead Eyes.

"Albert, take Bethany and lead everyone away. Move as fast as you can—faster than we've been moving. Take a different tunnel and get as far away from here as possible."

"What?" Bethany protested. "No, I'm not going to—"

"And what will you be doing?" Albert interrupted, holding a hand in front of her.

"I'm going to hold him off as much as I can," Ndidi said. "I'm pretty sure it's me he wants the most anyway."

"And if he just kills you?"

"He won't," Ndidi shook her head. She was sure of that at least. "Helene's controlling him directly. She still needs me as leverage for whatever sick plan that she has."

"I'm not leaving you, Ndidi," Bethany said.

"You have to." Ndidi's tone was firm. She avoided looking at Bethany, keeping her eyes on José. "You're the only one besides me who has the map memorized. Without that, everyone will be trapped down here."

"I don't care—"

"Bethany," Ndidi cut in sharply. She regretted her tone immediately, but now wasn't the time to coddle the girl. "You're not a child anymore. I'm going to be all right, but the more time we spend arguing, the more danger you're putting everyone in." There was a sniff, and Ndidi finally met Bethany's tear-filled eyes. Her tone softened. "I understand your concern, but I'm going to be all right. Head to Sparta as soon as you get out. Hermione should be able to do something about the spores." She looked up at Albert. "Keep her safe."

Albert looked like he wanted to say something but changed his mind. He simply nodded and called his men back. Ndidi could tell Bethany wanted to protest more, but they didn't have time for that. Without looking at Bethany again, she straightened and walked back into the tunnel.

José stared back at her. The anger was gone from his eyes. Instead, his gaze was passive, if tinged by a hint of pity, as though he realized what she'd done.

The sound of footsteps filled the passage as Albert led the group back the way they came.

"That was wise," José said finally. Ndidi got the feeling the statement was actually his and not Helene's. A part of her wanted to capitalize on that, but her heart felt too heavy for conversation. Still, the more time she could stall, the better the chance that Bethany would escape.

"There's no reason for us to fight, José. We're on the same side. Helene's the real enemy here, and we'll have a better chance of defeating her if we work together. Even Chloe, Karla, and Liz see that. We've all been working together for months now."

José's face went through a myriad of expressions. Ndidi was getting to him. He was fighting the control, but it wasn't enough to dislodge Helene.

[Your efforts are futile, Ndidi Okafor,] Helene said through José's mouth. [Your words will not change anything today, nor will your attempt to save your ward or the others. None of what you have done today will mean anything. Nothing you've done up to this point has meant anything. Your every move is transparent, even now, when you attempt to draw me into baseless conversation to stall for time. When you concocted this harebrained idea, did it occur to you that my goal could have been to separate you? That I needed them as bait to lure someone else worth the effort?]

Ndidi's eyes widened.

[This is exactly my point. Your species is so incredibly shortsighted. It continues to baffle me that you have survived this long. It was an … error on my part to relax my grip in order to deal with a nuisance elsewhere. But at the end of the day, the only thing you have succeeded at is making your position more tenuous. Still yourself: there is no reason to fight. The outcome will remain the same.]

Ndidi's mind spun, trying to parse Helene's words. It was trying to lure in someone else? Who? Did it matter?

No, she realized. The important part was that Ndidi had once again been tricked. Once again, she'd put Bethany in danger. She had to end this as fast as possible and catch up before everyone else paid for her mistakes.

Without a word, Ndidi tapped into her anger, into the rage that bubbled beneath the surface. DJ had taught her how to keep it suppressed, how to leash it and channel it into something productive. But now Ndidi needed it for something else. She let it wash over her until her vision turned red.

Ndidi took on a fighting stance. She didn't have to wait long before José came to meet her.

38

THE FACT THAT LIZ NAVIGATED the halls with ease aroused her suspicions. She was certain that Helene was aware of their presence, yet only a token resistance met them as they ran through the tunnels. The Dead Eyes that dotted the tunnels barely slowed her down. Liz hadn't yet encountered any of the drones that Christy said her sister's group was dealing with.

She stopped at another metal door and listened for a moment before moving on. The doors had been appearing more frequently. This told Liz that they had finally penetrated deep enough within the base. And yet, they were not challenged.

"So?" Christy asked, a few steps behind her.

"There was no one in the room," Liz replied without turning around. Not all the doors had captives. In fact, Liz was certain that most of them were empty. She could have confirmed, but it would have taken too much time to break through the metal. Christy insisted on asking each time. Liz had mentally marked the doors that held the hostages, though she felt the effort unnecessary. Attempting to free the hostages would, at best, serve as a distraction from their goal—and hinder it at worst. Had it not been an order, Liz wouldn't have bothered.

She turned into another tunnel. There was a squad of Dead Eyes. Liz dispatched them immediately. She also located one of Helene's relays that blinked at their passing and crushed it without a change in expression.

The passages blended into each other. Most of their progress was spent in silence, with the occasional burst of violence when Liz met with a squad. She kept her thoughts blank—it was easier that way—and her senses sharp for whatever trick Helene might pull.

Despite that, the sound of rushing feet took her by surprise. Fortunately, it was several tunnels away. They had plenty of time to prepare for the threat. The sound gave her pause, however, and she slowed to a stop. Behind her, Christy and Pratima followed suit, twin looks of confusion on their faces. She didn't offer an explanation; they'd hear it soon enough.

Liz listened.

The noise wasn't the synchronized marching of Dead Eyes, which was steady even when the puppets were rushing somewhere. It was discordant, almost panicked. The sound grew louder, headed toward them.

For the first time that night, Liz brought out her daggers. A moment later, there was a small commotion as the others readied their weapons. Liz could tell the moment they heard the sound as well because there was another round of shuffling. A minute went by, and the sound grew louder. It reverberated through the tunnels like a stampede. This close, Liz could make out other noises: muffled shouts in a deep voice and instructions from a much higher voice. There was also … whimpering?

Liz frowned.

"Should we retreat?" Christy asked.

"No," Liz said, but she did withdraw to the middle of the hallway, creating some distance for maneuverability.

It took another minute before the source of the rushing feet entered their tunnel. The sight made Liz sigh. She straightened but kept her daggers unsheathed. At the other end, the group that had just entered the tunnel slowed down as they caught sight of the three women. Liz estimated there were close to a hundred, though the narrowness of the passage meant only half could get in at a time. Liz saw exhaustion, fear, and suspicion on several faces as both sides assessed the other.

After a few seconds, a man peeled off from the group and approached wearily. A younger woman, about Liz's age, followed. Liz maintained her position but said nothing when Christy came up beside her. She'd lowered her gun but, like Liz, hadn't put it away completely.

The man and the woman stopped when they were several feet away. Both held lowered guns. Liz kept her attention on the man, certain that he was the one who knew how to use his weapon. If it came to a fight, he would have to be the first to go.

"Hey, there," Christy greeted him warily. "Who're you guys?"

"We could ask the same thing," the man said. "Who are you? Are you working for Helene?"

"If we were, we would have shot you by now," Christy replied. "Are you one of the hostage groups here? How'd you get free?"

The man adjusted his grip on his gun in what Liz assumed he thought was a threatening gesture. "I don't see how that's any of your business."

"You're right; it isn't," Christy said. "It's just … I'm looking for a woman named Ndidi Okafor. Have you heard of her?" Christy raised her hand a little above her head. "This tall, Black, self-sacrificing to the point of being stupid?"

The woman spoke up for the first time. "How do you know Ndidi?"

"We're here to rescue her," Christy said simply. "How do you know her? Is she part of your group?" Her eyes scanned the crowd, and she scoffed. "Nah. If she was, she would have come forward by now."

The woman stared at Christy intensely for several moments. To her credit, Christy bore the scrutiny without comment. Eventually, the woman spoke. "You're Christy, right? Is DJ with you?"

Liz was in front of the woman the next moment, her dagger an inch from her throat. "How do you know those names?" she asked calmly.

"What the fu—" the man cursed, jumping at her sudden appearance. He raised his gun but—fortunately for him—did not shoot. Liz ignored him, keeping her eyes on the woman.

"Hey! Let's everyone calm down," Christy said placatingly. She came to stand beside Liz once more and looked at her with exasperation. "Let's not do anything we'll regret."

The woman swallowed fearfully, but there was also hope in her eyes. "Ndidi told me. She was my teacher and mentor. I'm Bethany Cloney, Hermione's sister. Ndidi told me all about you guys. She said I have to meet my sister, that Hermione would be able to help us."

"Little Bethany?" Pratima asked, speaking up for the first time. The man's gun swiveled to her—as if noticing the big Indian woman for the first time—before returning to Liz. Pratima crossed the distance in two large strides and stopped in front of the young woman. She lifted a large hand and gently placed it on the woman's cheek, as if she were unable to believe she was real. "You've grown into such a beautiful woman. I barely recognized you."

Bethany seemed confused for a moment as she studied Pratima. After a few seconds, her eyes widened. "Pratima?" She practically leaped into her arms. Their words dissolved into babbles as they fed off each other's energy. Bethany was crying, and though Pratima remained as stoic as ever, her bearing had undeniably softened.

Liz finally sheathed her blade and stepped back. In response, the man also lowered his gun. Christy breathed a sigh of relief.

"All right. Let's start over," Christy said. "I'm Christy, the scary one is Liz, and the big lady is Pratima. We're part of Ndidi's team and came to rescue her. And the rest of you, of course," she added hastily.

The man straightened, and though he remained tense, he seemed to accept that they weren't going to attack them. "My name is Albert Willingham, and you were right the first time. Until recently, we were Helene's hostages. Ndidi helped us get out of our cells, and she was leading us out of this hellhole when she was forced to stay behind."

"Where is she now?" Liz asked.

Albert pointed in the direction his group had come from. "She's several hallways down. But you can't go there!" he exclaimed when Liz made to leave. "There's some kind of indestructible robot thing blocking the way. About twenty of us emptied our clips at it, and it barely moved. Ndidi stayed behind to hold it off while we escaped."

"Twenty of you couldn't take it down, and you left her by herself?" Christy asked incredulously. "Kind of a bitch move, Albert."

Liz agreed. The man was a coward. Still, she felt her hackles rise. Something was wrong. Helene had just let the group go?

"Yeah, I know," Albert admitted with a sigh. "She said it was controlled by Helene and that it wouldn't kill her since Helene still needed her, but yeah, it was a bitch move."

"We have to go rescue her," Bethany jumped in, wiping a tear from her eye.

Pratima stood by her side, staring down at Christy and Liz. "That is the mission," she reminded them.

"Yeah, we're going to," Christy said, "but it wouldn't hurt to get some intel on what we'll be facing." She turned to Albert. "What can you tell us?"

"Ever seen *The Terminator*? It's an old one, but it's the best description I've got."

Christy whistled, looking uneasy. "Shit. You catch a name?"

This time, it was Bethany who answered. "Ndidi seemed to recognize him. She called him José."

Liz went still.

39

LIZ TORE THROUGH THE TUNNELS like a speeding bullet. Before, she'd been forced to slow down to match the speeds of Christy and Pratima. Now Liz had no such qualms, though she did try not to jostle her passenger too much.

"To the left," Bethany yelled while slung over Liz's shoulder like a bag of rice. It must have been uncomfortable, but Liz didn't care. To her credit, Bethany hadn't complained. Apart from her original reaction, no thoughts swam in Liz's mind. She could feel the questions there. But until she confirmed Bethany's statement, her mind was calm. That was good. Doubts would only slow her down. There would be time for that later. She just ran as fast as she could.

At the speed she was moving, it didn't take long before Bethany called the last direction. Liz turned into the passage and stopped. Her momentum took her a few steps forward, but Liz's eyes were on the sight in front of her.

Immediately, Liz felt the calm dissipating. The doubts, the questions that she'd pushed back—all of them came rushing to the surface with a roar. Bethany dropped from her shoulder with a shout. She started to run, but Liz held her back easily.

"José?"

Her father stared back at her with the same inscrutability that he'd shown for most of her life.

But how? Liz had seen him die. She had watched as he disintegrated. He'd given himself to save her, to save Karla. *How? How is he alive?*

Liz took a step forward, despite herself. Her eyes scanned his face. Everything was as she remembered it. The jet-black hair slicked back, his strong jawline, the small notch where his chin had been broken on a mission. His eyes. Even if this was a trick of Helene's, Liz didn't think it was possible to fake the intensity of that gaze.

His face, however, was the only thing that was familiar. His body had been replaced by titanium bionic prosthetics. Liz recognized them immediately. It was the same thing that had been done to her sister and her, but taken to the extreme. Liz's titanium bionics had been developed specifically for her. From a distance, or even with her properly covered, it would be impossible to tell that she had prosthetics at all. In contrast, it was obvious the same consideration had not been given to José. Standing at ten feet tall—three and a half feet taller than he was before—his new body was large to the point of being ridiculous. It was unnaturally bulky and unwieldy. That, by itself, wouldn't have been bad. But his head—the sole part of him that was original—was now too small for the titanium body. It made him look like a caricature, a mockery of the man he once was.

Liz felt sick to her stomach. Was this how he had survived? Forced into this form by Helene? Was it worth it?

The thought struck Liz out of nowhere. She'd lived every moment for the last several months replaying that day in her mind and regretting every moment of it. But José was alive! She had a chance to do it over.

But is it worth it?

José hadn't said a word. This told Liz that Helene was in control. Her father was never one to spout out proclamations of love, but over the years, Liz had learned to read the meaning behind his words. José would have scolded her about the weakness she was showing by just staring. He would have admonished her for being separated from her sister. He would have made a comment about Chloe—something to show he cared.

Now, Liz was forced to deduce what meaning she could from the pain in his eyes, from the anger in his tense jaw. From the way his lips twitched as if on the verge of saying something but couldn't because his body was no longer his own.

Is it worth it?

No, Liz didn't think it was. She had her father back but without any of the things that made him who he was.

[It is a pleasure to see you again, Liz Polova.] It was his voice, but the words were wrong. It took Liz a moment to understand. Helene was using his voice to speak. It was controlling him like a puppet, like a toy.

"Do not speak!" she thundered, drowning out Helene's words. She hadn't expected to say that. She didn't realize she'd spoken until after the fact. The roar in her head had grown until it threatened to overwhelm her. Over and over, she replayed the scene of her father being forced to speak another's words, and the roar built to a crescendo.

"Holy shit."

Christy's voice dragged Liz from her thoughts, albeit barely. It didn't suppress the roar, but now Liz was no longer in danger of being overwhelmed. Pratima stood beside Christy, and though her reaction was more subdued, Liz read her surprise from the sudden tenseness in her body.

"Don't just stand there!" Bethany shouted, pleading desperately. She was still rooted by Liz's grip but had stopped struggling. Liz hadn't even noticed. "For the love of God, save her, please. She's going to bleed out. She's going to die. Please, do something!"

Finally, Liz noticed the body lying at José's feet, beaten into unconsciousness. Blood pooled around it. Liz could hear the sound of breathing, but it was faint.

Pratima's yell and sudden motion took Liz by surprise. Liz reacted immediately. She delivered a light chop to Bethany's neck, knocking her unconscious and allowing her to fall. With her hands free, Liz lunged after Pratima and forced her to a stop before she'd gone more than two feet.

"Wait!" she yelled. "You can't take him alone, and you will save no one if you are dead." Even before his transformation, no one—not even Chloe—had been a match for José in a direct fight. With his transformation, assuming Helene had given him the same enhancements Liz and her sister enjoyed, Pratima would be rushing to her death if she attacked him alone. "We will take him together."

Fortunately, Pratima wasn't too far gone that she couldn't see the sense in Liz's suggestion. Her body remained tense, but she ceased her struggle and lowered herself into a proper attack stance.

Stepping up beside Pratima, Liz unsheathed her daggers. "Christy, you will provide from behind," she said. She met Christy's eyes briefly and shook her head. "Do not kill."

There was a sharp click as Christy readied her weapon. "Way ahead of you, chief."

That made Liz unsure whether Christy had actually understood or not. Still, there was no time to confirm.

Several feet away, José waited, a tortured look in his eyes.

DJ KICKED OFF THE WALL, twisting midair to dodge the slash from a passing drone. His breathing was hard when he landed. There was no time to rest, as he was immediately attacked once more, this time by a trio of Dead Eyes. The entire passage was littered with them, limiting maneuverability. It wasn't much of a problem if you could ride on the drones like Karla and Liz, but DJ couldn't, and these bots were seriously cramping his style.

A part of him regretted acting on this stupid plan, while a different part was happy that he'd been right. Some tunnels had more resistance than others, and it was obvious that Helene was focusing more of her attention on them. The drones moved with more fluidity and worked as a unit instead of being individual death machines. Even the Dead Eyes, who were so simple to take care of before due to their predictability, now moved with grace. Artificially enhanced grace. The whole thing was bullshit, but it did make DJ more curious about what Helene wanted to keep secret so badly. That curiosity was the only thing that kept him pushing forward, tunnel after tunnel, despite the many times he'd come close to death.

DJ had lost track of how many Dead Eyes he'd killed or drones he'd destroyed. Despite his best efforts, he was covered in blood and a bunch of stuff he did not want to think about. Karla wasn't any better. Somehow, Chloe still didn't have a drop of gore on her. DJ tried not to let his jealousy distract him.

The trio fought their way through several more passages, leaving behind a trail of corpses and broken parts. DJ was on his last legs after a quarter of an hour and was seriously considering a retreat. However, he hadn't heard anything from Christy in a while. He took this to mean that they hadn't yet found Ndidi. If that didn't change soon, they would cut their losses and retreat. It wasn't what DJ wanted, but if Christy's group hadn't already been discovered, it wouldn't be long before Helene drowned them in numbers as well.

Just as DJ was about to give the order, they cleared the passage, revealing a large metal door smack-dab in the middle of the wall. It was about twelve feet tall, several inches thick, and imposing as shit. DJ could practically read the words *PISS OFF* written all over it.

"Is this what you were looking for?" Chloe asked.

"I mean, not this specifically, but it certainly fits the profile," DJ replied.

Karla punched it. The move was so sudden and so violent that, if DJ hadn't been so tired, he would have yelped. The strength behind the punch was incredible—and he wasn't even sure that was Karla's full power. The strike created a shock wave through the passage and caused dirt to rain down from the ceiling. The door rippled like a pond that'd had a rock thrown into it. Its hinges vibrated like tuning forks, but they held.

Karla punched it again, this time with more power. She struck again and again. More dust rained down. There was a rush of footsteps from the next tunnel; Helene must've been sending more death squads. There was a significant dent in the metal now. It would only take a few more hits for it to cave in.

Five more punches later, this was proven right.

The door flew off its hinges and exploded into the room. DJ didn't see where it fell. His gaze was riveted to the sole device in the chamber.

"Huh," Chloe mused. "It's a bomb."

Karla simply grunted.

It was a giant fucking bomb. It took up most of the room, its sheer magnitude imposing on its own. Its metallic shell gleamed in the light of the single light bulb suspended from the ceiling. Wires snaked from its core, intertwining like multicolored serpents.

DJ had seen bombs. It was part of the job description. He'd worked with them. He'd disarmed them. On one very dicey mission, he'd even built one. But DJ had never seen a bomb like this.

It was the kind of bomb that leveled cities, the kind that the television crime procedurals would use as a plot twist to build tension. There was no display with a countdown sequence, no buttons, nothing that would give an inkling of how it was meant to be armed or disarmed. It just was, silent and brooding, waiting with an almost palpable energy.

Metal sheets lay on the ground around it, and DJ finally noticed the empty spaces on the device where they were supposed to be placed. The bomb wasn't complete. That was good, if a cold comfort.

"Fuck," DJ said softly.

Christy's message came in. It had the fortunate side effect of drawing DJ out of his spiral. Unfortunately, her message threatened to send him down a different spiral.

Repeat that, he tapped back.

This time, when Christy tapped out her message, he took his time to interpret the clicks, ensuring that there was no mistake. Unfortunately, the message didn't change.

J. O. S. E. is alive. We have engaged.

DJ finally tore his eyes away from the bomb and stared at Chloe. "We might have a problem."

"Bigger than the bomb?" she asked.

"Yeah … I'm gonna need you not to freak out."

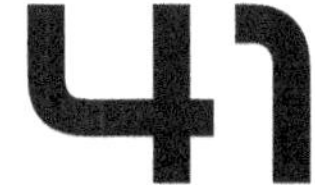

FROM THE MOMENT THEY ENGAGED, Liz knew they were going to lose. José himself had taught her how to predict the outcome of a fight from the first exchange. Even taking him on two-to-one, they were going to lose. But Liz didn't let that knowledge distract her.

Pratima opened the fight, starting with a hook at what had to be her full strength. Her wrath was a physical presence. Liz used the distraction to drag Ndidi to safety, placing her beside Bethany, then returned to the fight. She hadn't limited her speed, so she couldn't have taken more than a second. That second, apparently, was more than enough time for José to turn the tables. Pratima was bowled over in front of him, about to receive a chop that would take her out of the fight.

Liz darted in from the side, leading with her daggers. José was forced to abandon his strike and face her attack. His fist met the sharp edge of her blade. The collision created shock waves around the passage, but his fist held.

They exchanged dozens of strikes within the first few seconds, then Liz was forced to slow down so Pratima could rejoin the fray. They had never fought before, but the two women matched their attacks perfectly. Pratima just didn't have the strength to damage José—especially without an actual weapon—so Liz handled the attacks while Pratima worked on interference. Pratima attacked his joints, his eyes, his fingers—anything that would distract him and give Liz an edge. Several times, José was staggered by a bullet, putting him off-balance enough for Liz to take advantage.

With every pass, however, Liz grew more enraged. This was not her father. Her father would not allow himself to be led so completely, to be placed in such a position. He would use their numbers against them. He would not be so pathetic. Helene's control limited him and made him less than he was. Despite being faster and stronger, Liz had never once been able to beat her father in a fight; José had fought with a skill that negated whatever advantages she had.

But now, under Helene's control, that skill was gone. He still moved more fluidly than any Dead Eyes she'd ever fought, and Liz could recognize some of her father's moves—which showed the depth of Helene's control. But it wasn't the same. Helene probably had access to his memories and experiences, but she would never be able to tap into them as deeply as her father could. Helene knew that, so she had enhanced him to the point that it didn't matter.

Still, the rage, the pure hate coursing through her body threatened to overwhelm her. She felt her attacks becoming more unhinged, more wild. Was this what her sister felt? Was this the hate Karla walked around with? How did she control it? How did anyone control this?

Her attacks came without pause. Slowly, dents began to appear on José's titanium body. José began to retreat more and more. He made a few attacks, but Pratima was there with a strike timed just enough to deflect it and rob it of its power, or Christy was there with a bullet that staggered him and placed him off-balance. Liz took advantage of every opening to deliver strikes powerful enough to cause minor explosions. The walls around the passage had craters from where she'd launched him or from where an attack had missed.

Then, suddenly, José sped up. Before, Liz's attacks had slipped through gaps he was too slow to cover. Now José met all of her strikes before they could do any damage. His defense was iron tight. Pratima continued to lend her support with carefully timed hits, but now José dodged them with a skill he'd lacked before. Even Christy's bullets were dealt with easily until she was forced to stop and reload.

Liz pressed her attack, trying to get through his defense. Despite her rage, however, she never once attacked José's face. Her punches were always to his torso, his arms, or his legs—all aimed to immobilize. While his body was dense enough to take her hits, she couldn't be sure that his head was. A poorly timed strike there might get past his defenses and kill him.

And that's why they were going to lose. Winning would mean her father's death. Liz could never bring herself to do it. She had barely survived the last time. She wasn't sure she would this time.

And so, she would always hesitate, always pause before taking the shot. While she didn't want to be killed or captured by her father, Liz couldn't bring herself to kill him either.

That reluctance might mean her death anyway, but that was fine with Liz.

THEY NEEDED TO GET TO CHRISTY. DJ activated the tracker he'd placed on her before the raid. He didn't want to use it so as not to tempt Helene, but they were desperate. The device tracked Christy's location and automatically transferred the information to the mapper—another device DJ had wanted to avoid using. Karla spared the map a glance, then proceeded to tear through the tunnels. DJ switched off both devices and did his best to keep up. Beside him, Chloe had lost her usual smirk. Her expression gave no hint about what she was thinking. DJ decided not to ask.

For the first minute, they retraced their steps through several tunnels, and DJ was given a very unneeded view of the carnage they'd left behind. *Fuck,* he thought. They'd left a literal trail of corpses. He felt sick to his stomach but pushed down the feeling. There would be time for feeling like an asshole later but not now.

Eventually, they started taking branches into a different part of the maze. There was no visible change—except for the missing corpses. Karla took turns with confidence, her face set in a growl. Anger radiated off her in waves. This was different from her usual rage. It was deeper, more primal, and held a hint of something DJ couldn't place. Fear?

Now, you're just being an idiot, DJ scolded himself. *What would Karla have to be afraid of?*

Still, her anger puzzled him. If José was alive, shouldn't Karla be happy—or at least less grouchy? Even Chloe's expression didn't make sense. But then, Chloe's expression never made sense. The woman was as difficult to read as Olsen's handwriting.

DJ knew they were close when Karla sped up. She had been slowing herself down so he and Chloe could follow, but now it seemed that she couldn't help herself.

Pretty soon, Karla outpaced both of them, but it didn't matter. At that point, DJ could hear the explosions himself. Without a word, Chloe increased her pace, too, disappearing around a bend a few seconds later. DJ sighed again. He really couldn't wait for Martin's enhancements to kick in. He was damn tired of being the slowest one in the room.

When DJ finally joined the party, both the Murder Twins and Chloe were already fighting … a Terminator?

DJ slowed down, confused. From where he'd come in, he was facing the thing's back. It was a freaking Terminator. DJ didn't know what else to call it.

He gave the fight a wide berth—though not wide enough, as he was smashed into several times. He met up with Christy on the other side of the tunnel. Beyond her lay Ndidi—unconscious and beaten to a pulp—and a woman around his age who was also unconscious. Pratima was with them, sporting several bruises but making an attempt to help Ndidi. He could hear her muttering in a different language.

"What am I looking at, Christy?" he asked.

"The big guy's José. Don't know how he survived—though I bet his new titanium robot body has something to do with it. However, we do know that Helene's pulling his strings. Pretty tightly, from the way he's fighting. Liz was beating on the guy for several minutes before you guys showed up, and he's still standing. I wasted a whole clip on him too—nothing. From that, I'd say that he's as tough as they are."

Jesus, DJ thought, *like we needed another one of them.* From here, he could make out the dude's face. It was José all right; he would recognize that mug anywhere. He'd once tried to shoot it. Maybe he should try again.

"His head doesn't look so tough," DJ said.

"Your funeral," Christy replied. "Notice that nobody's touched it yet?"

DJ did notice that. Every other part of José sported dents and cracks, but his face didn't have a single bruise—even with Chloe, Karla and Liz attacking at the same time. They were deliberately pulling their punches. Not that DJ could blame them. You'd have to be a coldhearted son of a bitch to kill your father—or lover, or whatever the fuck José was to Chloe—just after finding out he wasn't really dead.

Even if they were willing, it wasn't like José was just going to just let them. José was fighting all three of them to a stalemate. His hands were a blur, meeting every strike at the perfect moment to block, deflect, or counter. It seemed even Karla and Liz couldn't keep up with his speed, despite their best efforts.

DJ gaped. *What the hell did Helene give this guy?*

"Is this what you are now?" Chloe screamed suddenly, leaping back from an attack. "Helene's pet? Her puppet? Fight! Fight it, you idiot!"

"You're pathetic," Karla spat. She blocked one of José's strikes with her forearm, causing a shock wave that DJ felt from several feet away.

Liz didn't say anything. From the rage and pain in her expression, DJ didn't think she could speak.

[Your words are meaningless,] José said—or, at least, his mouth was moving. DJ had no doubt that those were Helene's words, and it made his skin crawl.

Karla roared and attacked with new vengeance. Liz seemed to go mad. Her attacks lacked the refined grace that DJ was familiar with. Now, she fought like a storm, with no finesse or strategy. By comparison, even Karla looked more put together.

A sound from José drew DJ's attention. It wasn't anything coherent, just a noise of anguish. At first DJ thought it was just from the pain of the beating he was receiving, until he noticed the eyes.

His fucking eyes.

José's eyes were the only part of him capable of expressing emotion. That fact honed the emotion just like a weapon. DJ met José's eyes and felt the agony like a dagger to his chest. There were no tears, but José's eyes showed a glimpse of the hell the man must be going through—the hell that Helene was making him go through. The torture there, the anguish, and the determination still to fight tore at DJ.

He didn't know much about José—mostly because of the death glare Chloe had given him the one time he'd asked about him. But this wasn't the man who'd killed dozens of people, who'd tried to kill DJ several months ago. This was the man who'd been willing to give his life to save his daughters. And now that same man was forced to fight those very daughters.

Why? Because a shitty AI thought it would be fun?

"Fuck this," DJ muttered. He reached into his pocket, pulled out the Synaptic Pulse, and pointed it at the Murder Team.

43

JOSÉ OLVERA, a prisoner in his own body, stood at the precipice of his worst nightmare. The tunnel echoed with the sounds of his fight, but José heard none of it over the sound of his torment. His girls—Karla, Liz, and Chloe—stood side by side, confusion, anger, and disgust in their eyes as they attacked him.

Karla's face was set in a snarl, but José had always been able to read beyond the mask she wore. She was angry, but beyond that, there was disgust and fear. This was mirrored in Liz, though his second daughter had allowed her anger to push her over the edge. She was always the more sensitive of the two. Chloe screamed at him, but her eyes held the most confusion.

José understood. His eyes mirrored their confusion, their disgust, and their anger. He was angry too—yes, at Helene, but mostly at himself. How many times had he sworn to never harm his girls, to always strive to protect them? He had dedicated the latter part of his life to raising the twins to be the perfect weapons so no one would be able to take advantage of them. Yet there he was, seeking to capture them.

"Fight!" Chloe shouted. "Fight it, you idiot!"

She attacked him, and José felt his hands rise up to parry. His movements became a dance of agony, choreographed by Helene. With each clash, the air resonated with the echoes of his broken spirit. Every blow he delivered seared his soul.

Still, he felt the anger in his girls, and it resonated with him. Was this what he was? Would he allow himself to be broken? To be weak? His daughters already showed disgust at what Helene had made him. They showed it openly. Why? Because he let them. Because now they saw him as nothing more than a simple Dead Eyes.

If that was so, he was pathetic. But it was one thing to be weak for a moment and quite another to choose to remain weak. José had taught his daughters that, but he'd forgotten it in his old age.

He started to fight, then, against Helene's control. It was different from any fight he'd ever been in. There was nothing to punch or kick, nothing to shoot. It was wholly in his mind. Instead of his fists, José used his will. The humiliation he'd suffered for weeks flashed into his mind. His anger honed his will into a fine edge that he used to chip away at the AI.

He could feel Helene's presence in his mind like a cloud that suffused every-thing. José threw his weight against it—once, twice, until he felt it give. It wasn't enough to wrestle full control over his body. The sudden attack had surprised Helene enough to give him a foothold, to have tiny control over his movements.

José used that foothold to slow himself down.

It was slight, but it was enough. Where before his body was always in the right position to meet every strike, now his girls found gaps in his defense. Karla's attack launched him into a wall. Liz met him there. Her dagger slashed through his torso while Chloe compromised his joints.

Helene fought against his control, but José fought back harder. He wouldn't be able to last long—already he was losing his grip. But it could be enough. He tried to meet his girls' eyes. Anyone of them. He'd noticed that none had yet attacked his head. Probably because of some misguided attempt to save his life. It was a weakness. Something he'd thought he'd weeded out of all of them.

Now that weakness was going to cost them their lives.

Chloe continued shouting at him. She ignored the pleas in his eyes. José cast his eyes behind her, to where the man—DJ—stood. He met DJ's eyes and showed him a glimpse of his torment. He saw the moment that DJ made his decision. If he could have smiled, he would have. This one was weak, too, but now that weakness would work in their favor.

DJ muttered something that José didn't catch. He reached into his vest pocket, took something out and pointed in their direction.

And then his world flashed white.

44

JOSÉ FELL TO THE GROUND, and for a moment, there was silence. Then Chloe whipped around and saw the Synaptic Pulse in DJ's hands. All hell broke loose.

"What the hell did you do?" Chloe asked, her voice deathly quiet as she strode up to him.

"Jesus Christ, D! Did you kill him?" Christy asked.

Karla was somehow in front of him, her dagger at his throat. "Your life will not be enough payment if you have taken the life of my father."

DJ brushed the dagger away and was surprised when she actually let him. "Can everyone settle the fuck down? He's not dead, just knocked out while his shit resets."

"What are you talking about?" Chloe asked. She snatched the Pulse from him. "And what the hell is this?"

"That," DJ said, snatching back the cube, "is the Synaptic Pulse. It's what Hermione came up with to deal with the picospores. I don't know how it works, but Hermione said that it resets the spores or some shit so Helene can't control them." He gestured to José's prone body. "Has a side effect of knocking them out, though."

"Wait, you've had this with you the whole time?" Chloe asked. "Why didn't you use this when we were fighting the Dead Eyes? Wouldn't this have knocked them out like you wanted?"

DJ had felt guilty about that initially. "The Pulse doesn't have an infinite charge, and the plan was always to use it on Ndidi in case Helene injected her with picospores. I had to conserve it."

Chloe scoffed but didn't press the matter further.

Liz walked up to the group, José slung over her shoulder. "When my father wakes up, will he be himself again?"

DJ met her eyes. "As long we get him away from Helene's influence."

"Let's get moving, then," Chloe said with a false cheer. She no longer looked at DJ like she wanted to kill him. Nevertheless, he knew that he was walking on thin ice until José regained consciousness. DJ would have been more worried about that if Olsen hadn't tested the device already.

Pratima carried Ndidi and Bethany, and the group made its way through the tunnels with Liz leading the way. The resistance was fierce—according to Christy, it was far fiercer than they'd faced coming in. This told DJ that they'd finally caught Helene by surprise and that she was trying to rectify her mistake. But no matter what Helene threw at them, it barely slowed them down.

Along the way, they came across rooms that Liz informed them had been where hostages were being kept. The doors were broken down, and the chambers were empty. DJ hoped this meant the hostages had broken out.

It took twenty minutes, but eventually they arrived at the entrance. And then they headed home.

AWAKENINGS

TODD MORROW SAT on his couch while the world went to hell.

It was inevitable, even though the media refused to acknowledge it. Trust the news to report bombings, earthquakes, and all the big stuff but ignore everything else. Anyone with eyes could see that everything was going to shit, but no one seemed to want to admit it. The news was just part of it. It was like everyone around Todd was living in some sort of fantasy world. They blithely ignored all the weird shit that was going on.

It had started when the planes fell out of the sky. The world had never truly recovered. Todd would have been happy if it'd stayed at that level of brokenness, at least for a few years. Everyone had lost someone on Mayday. It took more than three years for people to move on. Maybe that's why they chose to ignore what was right in front of them—because they couldn't handle another Mayday. Because it was easier.

Todd spat into a metal bowl he kept beside him. That was a shitty reason. Anyone who thought like that deserved to be killed first. Whatever was happening was going to be bigger than Mayday. Todd could feel it in his bones. They needed to prepare—especially when it was obvious the government didn't give a shit about them.

Why else would they agree to put *another* AI in a position where it could screw them over? That was only one of their questionable decisions these days, and one of the things that convinced Todd that this one was going to be worse. This time, they had the government in on it.

A news reporter stood in front of a half-finished bridge. The newscaster was speaking on its construction and all the good the bridge could do. Behind the reporter, though, almost at the edge of the camera's range, was something that might have been a flock of birds. Todd was sure it was more of those drones. Although they had become more frequent lately, no one had said anything about that. Not the government, not the news, not even the crazy conspiracy theorists. Even social media was ignoring it like it just wasn't there.

The drones rarely ever flew low enough to be too noticeable—always at the edge of the skyline, just enough to be visible. It was as if someone was making a statement. Todd was sure that he had seen *guns* on some of those things. And everyone was ignoring them.

Todd figured the only good thing that had come out of this bullshit was that the victims who'd gone missing on Mayday had been returned to their families. The news had actually reported this. It meant that whoever was in charge wanted them to know. After three years, most of the lost victims—people who had been written off as dead and buried—were suddenly found, conveniently missing their memories of where they'd been and everything that had happened in the last few years.

A big-shot psychologist on the news had said that it was common for trauma victims to suppress memories of their ordeal. Todd called bullshit on that too. Almost a thousand people had been found so far. Every one of them had forgotten? What were the odds?

They weren't even trying anymore.

He spat again. It was only a matter of time now.

SEPTEMBER 2043
SAN DIEGO, CALIFORNIA

AGNES VALENTINA WALKED down the street toward the mall. It was usually a doable walk from her house, but today her body was protesting the short distance she'd gone while leaning heavily on her cane. She hoped she would be able to find a kind young man to help carry her groceries. Or maybe she could ask one of the staff. Her house really wasn't far from the store.

Agnes passed several people on her way. Some of them were wearing those dark sunglasses she'd been seeing everywhere. Agnes didn't understand the trend. The world seemed to be changing around her, and not necessarily for the better. People seemed less happy than they'd been in her day. Most walked with the drooped shoulders that her mother would have spanked right out of her. Some of it was the effect of Mayday, Agnes knew. It had been a dark day in their country—worse than 9/11, in some ways. People couldn't be expected to get over it easily. The world was growing darker. It was like there was a blanket covering everything, weighing it down. Agnes had felt something like this before, during one of the civil wars that'd broken out in '27.

Just as she thought about it, she noticed one of those flying things crossing the sky in the distance. They were hard to make out—especially since Agnes had put off getting another pair of prescription glasses. Her neighbor, Ginny, had said that her daughter's husband had a friend in the government who said that the government was testing out a new weapon. It must be true, she decided.

The government had enough weapons already. Why did they want more?

Were they planning to attack whoever had kidnapped her grandkid? They deserved it for what they'd put countless families through. Agnes had thought her little Naomi was dead for three years. Then her son saw her randomly on the street, looking confused. Agnes hadn't been there, but he'd told her the story. They weren't the only family that had been reunited with those they had thought lost forever. It was all over the news: videos of people hugging and crying.

Agnes's heart went out to them, and it reinforced her thought that whoever had taken the people away in the first place should be punished.

PART 2
THE VIRTUAL
WAR

DJ SAT IN HIS USUAL PLACE at the conference table—not at the head, where he'd been sitting for the last month. No. At his *usual* place, on one of the chairs at the side. The seat beside him, where CJ would typically sit, was conspicuously empty.

DJ was making a point by sitting where he did.

Ndidi sat opposite him. She'd been unconscious for more than two weeks, only just awakening the day before. Her injuries were still healing. Purple spots were scattered over her body. She had an arm in a cast and a bandage around her head. Those were the worst wounds. If Helene had wanted her dead, she would have been dead. Instead, José had just beaten her to within an inch of her life. DJ could see the exhaustion in her eyes.

However, he couldn't bring himself to pity her. Instead, he stared, his expression deliberately masked, and didn't say a word. Christy and Pratima seemed content to stay silent as well. The Murder Team had their own thing going on with José, so they were at their warehouse with Martin.

The silence was oppressive. DJ had resolved to leave it that way because *he* wasn't going to be the first to speak. At first, Ndidi met his eyes, and then she dropped her gaze. It slid to the empty spot at the end of the table, and then to the empty spot beside DJ. Guilt flashed in her eyes, and her exhaustion deepened.

"I'm sorry," Ndidi said finally.

"Not good enough," he replied.

Christy gave him a look. "D—"

"What, Christy?" DJ cut in sharply. "Are we just supposed to accept that? She's sorry, so everything's better now? Does that change the fact that Manar is in a coma? Does it change the fact that my brother might never wake up?"

Christy recoiled, and DJ felt a little guilty. He wasn't one to raise his voice, but how could he *not* be angry in this situation?

Bethany sat by Ndidi's side, a position she hadn't left since they'd arrived. Her wounds—the physical ones, at least—were less severe, but Hermione wasn't taking any risks. She wanted her to be fully healed before she started extracting the picospores. As long as she was in Sparta—the parts that Manar had isolated, at least—Helene shouldn't be able to control her.

Still, Bethany was right there, and CJ wasn't. Ndidi's selfishness might have cost him his brother, and all she could say was *I'm sorry*?

Fuck that!

"I know just saying sorry isn't enough," Ndidi said. "I know it doesn't make up for what I did. But I don't know what else to say. I don't know what to do. I know I acted selfishly, I know I jeopardized the plan, and I'm sorry, but I had to save Bethany. I had to. It's my fault that Helene took her in the first place. I had to save her."

"You didn't have to do shit!" DJ roared, lurching toward her. "You could have trusted us. You think the rest of us don't have our own goals? People we're trying to save or avenge? You think we're risking our lives for shits and giggles? Or for some bullshit sense of nobility? Fuck no! Every one of us has something, and yet, none of the rest of us betrayed everyone else."

"DJ," Pratima warned.

DJ ignored her. He was shouting, but he didn't give a fuck. "Don't give me bull about you having to save her. Because despite everything you risked, everything you sacrificed, and every trust you broke, you still failed. We're the ones who had to come rescue your ass. We could have left you to be a puppet. Or maybe Helene would have turned you into whatever the fuck José is."

"DJ!" Pratima yelled, slamming her palm on the table. Her eyes flicked to where Bethany sat. "Watch your words."

DJ took a deep breath. When he spoke again, his tone was softer, and he made an effort to choose his words more carefully. "Look, I'm not saying you shouldn't have gone to save Bethany. You saw your chance and you took it. I can't blame you for that. No matter how it came about, it worked out in the end, since Bethany is sitting beside you.

"That isn't my issue. My issue is that your choice—no matter how right you thought it was at the time—cost the team both Manar and my brother. We had a plan, and you ruined it. Deliberately and consciously. No matter how good your intentions were, you decided to break our trust and put everything we've worked for at risk."

Ndidi's eyes were downcast. DJ waited for her to meet his gaze before he continued. "I can't forgive that."

"That's fair enough," Hermione said, speaking for the first time. She sat beside Bethany. Her eyes were red and had bags under them, but she looked younger, like a great burden had been lifted from her shoulders. She looked at her sister, and the sheer joy in her eyes hit DJ enough to calm him down.

"While I can't claim to be unbiased in the matter, I can say this: it's understandable that you can't forgive her. As you pointed out, regardless of the result, her methods were reprehensible and a breach of trust. However, we have to move on from this. Helene is the real villain here. She's the one who caused all this, and our primary objective is still to take her down. Nothing has changed in that respect."

Hermione's gaze pierced through him. "I understand that it might be difficult to work with her, but if we let this break the team up, Helene wins. We have to look at the bigger picture here."

DJ bit back his first angry retort. And then his second. Finally, he sighed and relented. "Fine. Let's move on." His gaze went to Ndidi, who'd made an effort to compose herself. "Let's start by fixing what you did to my brother."

CJ CLUTCHED THE SPHERE. He was ready.

He'd spent the last several weeks practicing with the sphere until he was certain he knew all that it was capable of. Its abilities weren't as extensive as CJ had expected, but they still gave him an edge where previously he had none.

One of the first things he'd noticed was a slight resonance around him. It was as if he was tuned to a frequency and received constant feedback. It hadn't taken him long to realize that he was resonating with the websites around him. Not every building got the resonance. Very few did, in fact, but it was enough. It had taken him even less time to realize that the resonance was the sphere reacting to the orbs within the websites. It had done the same thing in the pharmaceutical website where he'd found the second part, acting as a sort of navigational guide.

Though he had his pick of sites thanks to the sphere, CJ wasn't willing to risk going into one of the websites around him. He'd tested it and was certain that as long as he held the sphere, every site would recognize him as an intruder.

And seeing as how he'd almost been killed by the security measures of an old, dying website, CJ didn't want to think about what sort of security a flourishing website would have.

I need to find a site that's about to break down, he thought. The sphere would help him narrow down his choices, but he would have to do the legwork of finding the right site. *It's better that I move on anyway.*

CJ's smile was guilty as he looked around. He was in the middle of the street, surrounded by various websites. However, in a circle several meters wide, the street was empty and devoid of avatars. It was like avatars knew not to trespass in this zone. Instead, they flowed around him and continued to the end of the street. CJ wasn't certain how the whole thing worked except that it was an ability of the sphere. The zone had the advantage of allowing him to practice without the fear of causing permanent harm to the avatars. This had been one of his reservations when he'd started. He could see where they were redirected to other sites in the distance. The first day it happened, he'd freaked out. He thought he'd broken something with his experiments. However, another benefit was that with the zone active, he didn't have to wade through a crowd of bodies every second. That wasn't something CJ was willing to pass up.

The disadvantage, however, was that every site within the zone lost traffic it otherwise would have received. And already some buildings were starting to show the effects of that. None of them had reached a critical point, but CJ knew that such an outcome was inevitable if he continued to stay.

Now he was ready. It was time to move on.

He was tempted to leave the sphere's zone turned on so he could have some space to himself as he moved. But no. He'd spent most of his life uncomfortable with close contact. Now that he could handle it, why should he give it up?

It took a few seconds of concentration for him to shut off the zone. Avatars suddenly changed direction, and CJ was surrounded within seconds, though he still couldn't interact with the users. Originally he'd thought he could change that with the sphere, but it showed no reaction when he tried to interact with an avatar.

CJ left. He took random turns, his eyes absently scanning the area. He'd already explored most of it, so he planned to walk until he entered new territory.

CJ let his mind drift as he walked. Immediately, it went to his brother. Without a way to communicate with those outside, it was difficult to estimate how much time had passed. The absence of a sun or moon made it harder. However, CJ felt that he'd been in the virtual world for more than two months. How did that relate to the material world? For all he knew, time might flow faster on the internet, and only a day might have passed on the outside.

He slipped around a group of users entering a website and turned onto another street.

That would have been a comforting thought, since it'd mean that his brother wasn't worrying about him too much, but it didn't stop CJ from worrying about him. What was DJ up to? Was he doing something reckless?

Who am I kidding? Of course he's doing something reckless. Strangely, that realization didn't ease his worry.

Next, his thoughts drifted to Manar. He could still feel Manar through their connection. At any time, CJ could point in his direction. Recently, however, he'd noticed that the feedback he received was more … muted. It was different from the sense of distance that he'd felt initially. CJ couldn't put his finger on what exactly had changed, but *something* had.

CJ didn't know what to think about that. He was certain that if Manar had been fatally injured, he would feel something in their connection. But what if Helene had found a way around that? Would CJ even know?

It was another source of worry, and yet another thing he couldn't do anything about. He felt the press of time, but he'd already decided that he wouldn't seek Manar out until he figured out what was going on with the sphere—that is, until he could help instead of just being a burden.

He entered an alley, which led him to another street. The websites on this road, though still extravagant and colorful, followed a different style. Each building was still distinct, but the general makeup followed a pattern that told CJ that he'd entered a different zone.

The zones were something he hadn't yet figured out, even though he'd gone through several while exploring. As far as he could figure out, each zone was basically a collection of different websites within the same field, at least for the most part. The Red Light District followed this theory, as had the zone he'd just left, which had been populated with pharmaceutical websites. But CJ had seen several zones that were basically a mishmash of different websites, like the one in which he'd first materialized.

Surely there were underlying rules for the arrangement of the buildings. There had to be, considering the internet itself ran on quantifiable commands. But he hadn't been able to figure it out.

A quick glance told him that this zone followed a business-themed pattern. There were corporate websites for organizations. One of the structures was basically a fifty-story briefcase that had sheets of paper orbiting around it. Another building, a law firm, was designed as a bespoke black suit with a judge's wig floating on top. A long spiral staircase, structured like a thread, connected the two parts.

Avatars streamed into the buildings in a steady flow, each of them wearing a suit and carrying a briefcase. CJ felt as if he stood out more here, yet no one batted an eye. He made his way through the zone, half-heartedly taking turns while his mind flitted from topic to topic.

Last time, it had taken him several days to stumble on a suitable website. It came as a surprise when he found what he was looking for after only a few hours.

The website stood at the end of a street filled with flying office tools and supplies. This building was designed to look like a typewriter lying on its side, suggesting it was about to be deleted.

I'm actually surprised it's survived this long, he thought, staring up at the building. It was on the verge of collapsing. The whole structure looked ancient, like it had been built half a century ago. *I don't think I've seen a typewriter since I was a kid.*

The sphere warmed in his hands, reacting to something inside the building. That was the last bit of confirmation that CJ needed. Without hesitating, he stepped through one of the keys that served as a door.

Immediately, he felt a pulse run through him. A slight pressure surrounded him, giving him the feeling of being watched. A second later, the entire building shook with an intruder alarm. CJ had expected this and had even prepared for it, but a surge of fear still ran through him. Fortunately, it took him only a moment to dispel it.

The setup of this building was different from every other website he'd been in. While the Gaius search engine had cubicles for users and the pharmaceutical website used market stalls, this website had gone for a more direct approach. The entire room was designed as a grid, with each square about a meter in size. Each product floated over a square like an inventory slot in a video game and had a small description underneath. The products weren't limited to typewriters; he also saw printers, small desktops, and other office supplies. The array stretched throughout the room, covering several dozen meters from end to end. There were probably thousands in all.

CJ scanned for the entrance to the back end of the website. Nothing stood out. He cocked his head and took a step inside. Immediately, a firewall rose where he stood. CJ jumped away in a panic, then tried to turn that into a roll. It was clumsy and painful, but he'd practiced the move several times so it wasn't as taxing as it'd been several weeks ago.

Another firewall rose where he stopped, enveloping him before he could do anything about it. There was a flash of heat, but CJ was relieved to discover that it wasn't anything he couldn't handle. The heat was uncomfortable and even painful, but it was like placing his hand over a candle flame. He was still getting burned, but he could endure it for a few seconds before it truly became dangerous. Idly, he wondered if he would have said the same thing if the website weren't failing.

More firewalls rose around him, and CJ straightened slowly, facing one of the side walls. He still couldn't make out any entrance to the back end. The fire, though it couldn't hurt him, made visibility even worse.

There's an easy solution, he thought. With the sphere clutched in his hands, he turned in a slow circle until there was a reaction from the orb. *There!* He was facing the array of products.

Is it in the back? he wondered. That would mean he had to go through the entire room to reach it. CJ would have preferred a side door that he could just duck into, but there was nothing he could do about it.

He took another step. Another firewall rose up so close to the last that they seemed to compound. CJ felt the moisture being sucked out of him. It was a weird feeling, mostly because he didn't have moisture in his body.

Should I use it? he wondered, then shook his head. *Not yet. I can still deal with it myself.*

With nothing else to do, CJ gritted his teeth and took off a sprint. Firewalls rose around him, missing him by inches and forming a trail along his path. He hit the product array within seconds. There was a narrow gap between each product, and he hurriedly squeezed into one. He tried to maintain as straight a path as possible as he cut through the array, but occasionally, a product was too large to be contained within its grid, and he was forced to duck under it or switch to a different path.

The firewalls didn't stop. Instead, they rose sporadically on his path, forming another obstacle to navigate. He could push through the ones that came on their own easily enough, but occasionally, two firewalls would appear at the same time. The effect would be compounded until it started to hurt before he even reached them. Once, two firewalls rose directly in front of him, and he crashed into them before he could stop himself. His whole body went up like he'd been doused in gasoline, and he cried out in pain. CJ was free after only a moment, but he started avoiding the firewalls altogether.

This, of course, meant he was forced to take detours more often. It slowed him down and forced him to spend more time navigating through the array. The whole thing was unexpectedly frustrating.

CJ was halfway through the room. He had just stumbled into a firewall that had appeared in front of him when he lost his patience. He raised the sphere and split his attention between it and his path. Thanks to the weeks of practice, he could do this without slowing his pace. He focused for a second and then felt a space open in his mind. It's what he imagined gaining a new limb was like, albeit one he had only limited control over.

A moment later, the air around CJ distorted and molded itself into a wall of energy that surrounded him. The wall was completely transparent and extended only a few inches from his skin. It acted as a barrier and could even be called such, but it wasn't so simple. The energy didn't create a shield so much as it created a zone around his body that interfered with—and nullified, to some limited extent—other programs. The sphere wasn't yet complete; CJ hadn't been able to test out the exact limits of the ability. But the potential applications left him almost vibrating with excitement.

Now, however, it provided him with some much-needed protection. And he was going to put it to use.

With the shield in place, he no longer had to avoid the firewalls. It didn't offer total protection, but the danger changed from being roasted alive to being in a sauna. The heat was only slightly uncomfortable, and that was only true of the doubly strengthened firewalls. With the regular ones, CJ only felt a light tingling.

With nothing to fear from the firewalls, CJ was at the end of the array within minutes.

And then he saw another problem.

The end of the product array *wasn't* the entrance to the back as CJ had assumed. Instead, it was a large staircase leading to a second floor. Not a problem on its own, but the staircase was made of a bunch of typewriter keys, enlarged and about three feet across, floating above the ground.

It didn't make any sense. It seemed to exist only to frustrate him, but there it was.

Are all websites built in the early 2000s this hard to navigate? CJ wondered, sighing. A moment of focus deactivated his shield, and then he took a few steps back and made a running leap unto the first key. Fortunately, his virtual body was athletic enough to pull it off without much of a hitch, and he landed squarely in the middle of the tile.

From there, it was just a series of jumps. These took him progressively higher. Twice, he had close calls where he barely made it to the next key and dangled by the tip of his fingers until he pulled himself up.

Despite everything, CJ cleared the bridge faster than he thought he would and landed on the second floor. The sphere warmed in his hands, but CJ didn't need it; the door seemed obvious enough.

So, CJ stepped through into the second-floor challenge.

47

SEPTEMBER 2043

SPARTA HEADQUARTERS
NEW YORK

MORE THAN EIGHT WEEKS AGO, they'd put everything for Manar's merge into the lab down the hall from Hermione's. They'd hooked CJ and Manar up to a system similar to what hospitals used for coma patients so they wouldn't starve while their minds were elsewhere. After that, DJ had cordoned off the room completely so that no one messed with the wires that were scattered around. Now, he stood with his hands crossed, Christy by his side. Bethany stayed with her sister at the back while Ndidi bent beside Manar's bed, her face twisted with sorrow.

But not regret.

That was what pissed DJ off. Even while staring at the man she'd condemned, there was no regret on her face. This meant she would do it again. She would throw them under the bus all over again and run willingly into Helene's arms, just to save Bethany. It was noble in a way that made DJ want to walk over and slap her.

Lying beside Manar was CJ, the other person she'd condemned, one she'd barely given more than a sorrowful glance. Christy gripped DJ's forearm. It was only her presence that steadied him, kept him from listening to the voices in his head.

His gaze went to his brother. He'd come to the room several times. He hadn't been able to stop himself. There was never any change. If not for the hospital gown and the fact that CJ's eyes hadn't opened in months, DJ would have thought he was merely sleeping.

"Did anyone else come in here?" Ndidi asked, running her hands along some of the equipment.

"No one," he replied. "Security has been outside in shifts."

"No one? Then who fixed the life-support systems?"

"Hermione and Martin directed while Christy and I hooked it up. What's the holdup?"

"It's not responding," Ndidi said quietly. Her worried gaze panned across the machine.

"What?"

"It's not *responding*," she said, louder. She still refused to look at him.

"What the hell do you mean, *it's not responding*?" DJ growled. If this bitch had put his brother in a coma for good—

He took a step, but Christy held him back.

"Who came in here?" Ndidi's voice was tinged with panic.

"No one fucking did!" DJ shouted, just as loudly. "No one's touched anything since you fucked with it. You think I'd play with my brother's life?"

"Hey," Hermione interjected calmly. She left Bethany with Pratima and came to stand by DJ's side. "Let's calm down. Tell us what's wrong, Ndidi. What's not responding?"

DJ tuned out Ndidi's attempts to compose herself while he tried to get the red out of his eyes.

"Chad came in for a few minutes. Remember?" Christy whispered.

Oh, right. The cowboy dude. DJ had forgotten that he'd asked him to come. Chad had taken one look at Manar and CJ and said the whole thing was out of his league. DJ hadn't thought about it since.

"You were with Chad the whole time he was in here, right? He didn't actually touch anything?" DJ asked. Christy nodded. "Then I trust you."

Christy stared at him, complex emotions in her eyes. DJ would need to deal with that later. For now, he ignored it. He *did* trust her, but that wasn't the only reason he was so quick to accept her word. He'd already met Chad. The dude wasn't the kind of person to pull something like this. Calling him had been a stretch, but DJ had been—and still was—desperate.

Ndidi pointed to two wires connected to a machine. "Those two wires."

"What about them?" DJ rolled his eyes.

"I listened when CJ was explaining how the machines worked," Ndidi said. "He talked through the process as he was setting it up. Well, I didn't understand much of what he said, but I know those two wires basically connected their bodies with their virtual forms. So, I switched them."

Christy held his arm before DJ could do anything.

"But now I've switched them back," Ndidi continued hurriedly. "They should be waking up. But they're not."

Hermione turned to DJ. From the look in her eyes, he knew that he wouldn't be allowed to punch anyone. He chuckled wryly.

Of course it isn't going to be that easy. What the hell was I expecting?

He met Hermione's concerned gaze and Ndidi's wide, tear-stricken eyes and felt the anger drain out of him.

"My brother isn't going to wake up today," he said. "Fine. We'll just find another way."

"We should discuss how the machine could have been tampered with if no one was allowed into the room," Pratima said.

DJ waved his hand dismissively. "It doesn't matter. This place is already locked up tighter than a nun's asshole. Whoever got in here is long gone. I doubt Helene would bother to send them in again. She already got what she wanted."

"Which is what?" Hermione asked cautiously.

"Isn't it obvious? To trap them where they are." DJ turned to leave. No one tried to stop him. "We can only hope it bites her in the ass. Thanks to Ndidi, we can't do shit about it."

CJ HAD BEEN DIAGNOSED with obsessive-compulsive disorder at a young age. While OCD was different from the neurodevelopmental disorder that was autism, they shared several symptoms. The result was that one was often misdiagnosed for the other. It didn't help that people on the autism spectrum often developed OCD at some point. It didn't happen in all cases, but CJ had started showing symptoms of OCD around the same time he was diagnosed with autism.

Back then, CJ didn't understand the compulsion he had to fix things, to have things organized. It was an instinct, a drive. When he saw something misaligned or unfinished, he had to correct it. Otherwise, he would have an episode. It didn't matter what it was. It could have been a puzzle, unfolded laundry, a spot that was missed when cleaning, or something as simple as an uncapped pen. It didn't matter. It itched at his brain until he corrected it.

In the same way, the moment he righted whatever wrong he'd found, the itch would go away. He would come out of his episode and feel a sort of peace.

It was one of the reasons he'd been drawn to programming. Codes were simple and followed a regular pattern. They were one of the few things that, by their very nature, were organized. CJ had found that soothing as a child, and that hadn't gone away as he grew older.

His compulsion was one of the major sources of his childhood episodes. It was one of the first things he and Ndidi had worked on. Now, years later, whenever he felt that itch, he was better able to suppress it—at least to some extent.

CJ now drew on every bit of that self-control to remain still.

The door had led him into a different room on the second floor. His first impression had been that the room was a large chamber. But he'd been forced to reconsider.

Is this even a room? he wondered.

The whole place was made of office supplies that towered to the ceiling. Placed sporadically around the room were several boxes overflowing with paper but still stacked precariously on top of one another, forming makeshift towers. In one corner, a couple of these towers were placed close together to make a wall. CJ saw reams of printer cartridges, stacks of notepads, and several other office supplies strewn haphazardly throughout the room. Like everything else in the world, each of the boxes, papers, and notepads were all codes and programs. It was basically like lines of code were strewn around in a way that functionally worked, though the appearance was sloppy and disorganized in every other way.

It was a mess, and CJ was itching to fix it. The sphere reacted to his desire and grew warmer.

CJ closed his eyes and took a breath, fist clenched by his side. He tapped it against his leg to ground himself. With the stimulation cut off because of his closed eyes, CJ was slowly able to gain control of himself.

He hadn't needed to use this technique since he'd materialized in the virtual world. Whatever disorder was causing his compulsion should have stayed with his material body.

The problem might not necessarily be from me, he realized. Anyone would feel the urge to tidy it up.

Only when CJ was confident that he had himself under control did he open his eyes. His gaze scanned the room quickly, but he didn't see anything of note. The sphere was still warm in his hands, and he felt a resonance to the left. CJ made his way through the stacks, picking his path carefully. Each tower was a program within the website. With how precariously everything was balanced, tipping one over might cause the whole building to collapse around him. With a design like this, CJ couldn't begin to imagine how horrible the user interface was to navigate. It was probably why the website was failing.

After a minute of walking without reaching the other end, CJ realized that the room was bigger than he'd imagined. Despite his caution, he frequently tripped over loose pieces of paper or random boxes of supplies. Each time, his heart jumped to his throat, and he waited for several breaths in case there was a reaction. Fortunately, if he'd done any damage, he couldn't see it.

The stacks of office supplies created obstacles that limited his view to only a few feet at a time. It was different from the winding hallways he'd faced at the pharmaceutical website; here was particularly mazelike. If he didn't have the sphere, he wouldn't have made any progress at all.

Still, after tripping over something for the fifth time, his patience started to wear thin. This wasn't something he was used to feeling. For the most part, CJ considered himself mild-mannered. However, it was almost as if this entire website had been designed just to frustrate him.

CJ was almost glad when the first antivirus jumped out from behind a stack of boxes and attacked him.

He yelped in surprise and fell backward, dodging the attack with pure luck. The antivirus glared at him. CJ stared back with wide eyes, sprawled on the floor and too shocked to move. It was a hulking brute with red skin. Its face—ugly and misshapen—was twisted into a scowl.

Who designed this? CJ couldn't help but wonder, even scared out of his wits. *It's so crude.* Like everything else, the antivirus was functional, but its appearance was incredibly unrefined and off-putting in a way CJ couldn't describe.

The brute hefted a large cudgel and prepared to attack again. CJ scrambled to his feet and tried to put as much distance between them as he could. It didn't matter how bad its design was, it could still destroy CJ with one hit. His knees were shaky, and he felt like throwing up. This wasn't the first time his life had been in danger, but that didn't mean he would suddenly be used to it.

CJ clenched his fist, then suddenly realized the sphere wasn't in his hand. He felt another brief spike of panic before he spotted it several feet away—on the other side of the giant. His heart sank.

The brute roared and attacked again. CJ scrambled back, narrowly dodging the cudgel aimed at his head. He tripped over his feet and fell. When the giant swung again, CJ's terror overwhelmed him. He sprawled on the ground, closed his eyes, and waited for the pain. A moment later, the club whooshed past his ear and buried itself in a spot beside his head. The ground vibrated, and CJ's head trembled along with it. The hammer had missed by inches.

Well, now CJ knew his virtual body wasn't capable of passing out; otherwise, he surely would have. When the attack missed, he'd been given a new lease on life. He scrambled away as fast as he could. The brute stayed where it was, but that would obviously be temporary.

This was a mistake. His heart filled with regret. *Why did I think I was ready for this? I should have gone to Manar and told him about the orbs. He would have known what to do.*

CJ remembered feeling this way at the pharmaceutical website when he'd first encountered the antiviruses. He had been scared out of his mind, the way he was now, and so overwhelmed that he'd lost all ability to think. And so, he'd run.

CJ wanted to run now, too, but his gaze fell on the sphere. He hesitated. There was more distance and a giant standing between them now, but he couldn't leave without it. He was scared—terrified, even. But he couldn't leave behind something he'd risked his life to earn.

That thought was enough for him to push past his fear, at least temporarily. The sphere had helped him escape last time, and after all the practice that he'd put into it, he was certain it could help him again. He just needed to touch it. Unfortunately, that was easier said than done.

The antivirus attacked again, this time swinging his club in a wide arc, as if to make sure it didn't miss. Every instinct in CJ's body screamed at him to run away, but CJ ignored them. Instead, he threw himself to the ground and rolled under the blow. It was clumsy, and he'd used too much force, so it was painful but still enough to evade the strike. He felt the rushing wind on his back as the club went through the spot he'd just occupied and knocked over a pile of boxes.

In his head, the roll was supposed to have taken him under the club, through the giant's legs, and over to the sphere. However, his momentum only brought him as far as the brute's feet, where he slammed into its shin and stopped.

The giant looked down at him. CJ could see confusion in its eyes, then rage. The brute roared. CJ quickly struggled to his feet and straightened just in time to get picked up and slammed against a tower made of boxes.

The air rushed out of him. Though he didn't feel any pain, he felt something drain out of him, leaving him weak. CJ felt his terror overwhelming him again. Fortunately, his instinct for survival was stronger, allowing him to keep his head for a few more moments.

The giant hefted its club. CJ's weakness made it difficult to move. However, his fear had reached a pinnacle, and he struggled as much as he could despite that. He wasn't able to budge the hand in the slightest, but he was able to push the tower behind him and create enough space to slip out of the giant's grip.

He landed on the ground with a thump. The sphere glinted a few feet away. The giant roared once more, and CJ felt the pressure as its fist descended on him. Fear lent him power. He dove through the brute's open legs without thinking, his arms outstretched.

His leap took him directly to the sphere, and CJ cradled the device against him. He could hear the giant's club swing toward him, and he quickly activated the sphere. The air around him warped right as the club hit.

Breath whooshed out of CJ. He was flung back several feet before slamming into another tower with a grunt.

He slid down the pile of boxes and gasped for breath. Then, he realized what he was doing.

I'm alive, he marveled. *I'm not dead!*

He looked up at the giant, several feet away. The monster was already staring at him in surprise. It took half a step toward him. It was enough to remind CJ that he wasn't out of danger quite yet.

CJ focused on the sphere and activated the ability he'd practiced the most. There was a sense of movement. A moment later, he was gone.

"DID YOU LEARN ANYTHING while you were captured?" DJ asked.

They were back in the conference room, everyone sitting at their usual places. Ndidi straightened at the question. Her eyes were still swollen, but at least she wasn't sobbing anymore. DJ watched as she masked her expression, hiding everything. He knew that mask. It had shown up regularly in the months after her parents died. Back then, it was cause for concern. It meant there was pain Ndidi wanted to hide.

Now it just pissed him off.

When Ndidi finally started talking, even her voice was masked, hiding everything she might have been feeling. "I was only able to provoke Helene into showing up once, so not much. But I *was* able to piece something together by interviewing the other hostages—" Her eyes widened as if she'd just remembered something, and her head whipped around to Bethany. "What happened to the others? Were they able to escape?"

DJ's eyes went to Bethany as well. Once again, he had to remind himself that she was around his age. He'd tried to talk to her several times over the last few days, but she'd been unresponsive. Plus, she'd pretty much been glued to either Ndidi or Hermione.

From what he'd learned from Hermione, Bethany hadn't been mistreated—none of the hostages had. But you didn't have to be mistreated to get fucked up by several years of imprisonment. Having her body hijacked every so often hadn't helped either. Physically, there was nothing wrong with her; she had a healthy weight and a stature similar to her sister. The mental damage, however, was easy to see. The poor girl jumped at everything, and she was always clutching at Ndidi as if she'd disappear again if she lost her grip. Her expressions fluctuated between anxiety, anger, helplessness, and finally numbness. Basically, the only symptom of prolonged kidnapping she didn't show was Stockholm syndrome. This was fortunate; DJ couldn't even begin to imagine how much headache that would cause.

He had to stop himself from pitying Bethany, not because she didn't deserve it but because pity wasn't what she needed. What she needed was actual help. Unfortunately, that was something they couldn't give her.

"I'm not sure," Bethany answered softly. "We met Pratima and her friend on the way out, but I couldn't leave you. Pratima said they were going to rescue you, so Albert and the rest went on ahead. I told them what you said—to head here—but I don't know if they did."

"They didn't," DJ said. Trying to find the other hostages had taken most of his time the last few weeks. More likely than not, Helene had taken control of them before they'd been able to make it.

For a second, Ndidi's mask broke, and the sadness in her eyes grew pronounced. A moment later, she was composed again. "That is … unfortunate. But back to the point, I *was* able to learn a few things." She took Bethany's hand. "Most importantly, Helene has found a way to cure Bethany's autism using the picospores."

A hushed silence enveloped the room, and all eyes focused on Bethany. Hermione was the first to respond. Her tone was deceptively calm. "Explain that."

"Bethany doesn't fully understand it herself, but Helene found a way to use the picospores to suppress her symptoms." Ndidi's eyes glowed as she looked at Hermione. "This means she's no longer on the autism spectrum, Hermione. I've been with her for weeks, and she has not shown a single symptom. Look at her now." Ndidi gestured to where her hand was entwined with Bethany's. "We're holding hands, and she isn't showing signs of discomfort."

Hermione didn't look convinced. "Couldn't that just be because the feeling of safety she gets from you is greater than her discomfort?"

"Maybe, but she's not showing any other symptoms either. Even when she spoke just now, her words were smooth, right? And she didn't have any problems remembering something that happened weeks ago, did she? I'm telling you, Hermione, she's *normal*."

That last comment was enough to shock Bethany out of her numbness. She leaned away from Ndidi, hurt. "I've always *been* normal."

Ndidi's eyes widened, and she turned to Bethany with an apologetic expression. "You're right, sweetie. I misspoke. I just meant that there were a lot of things you had difficulty doing when you were still on the spectrum, but now you don't have to worry about those things anymore."

"Everybody has things they have difficulty with," Bethany replied. "*You* taught me that."

Ndidi's face twisted more. "You're right, and I'm sorry. I shouldn't have said that."

DJ decided to butt in before the situation escalated. "Couldn't there be another reason she isn't showing any symptoms?"

"There could be several," Ndidi said, "but in this case, I'm certain it's something Helene did. It took a while to get them to open up about it, but some of the hostages also had histories of mental disorders. Yet none of them showed any symptoms."

DJ cocked his head to one side, brow furrowed.

"You think Helene was selecting these people specifically?" Christy asked, noticing his look. "It could be why she took Bethany."

"There weren't enough for me to say that Helene was selecting them specifically, but it's weird that so many were in one place."

"Could she have been testing something?" Christy asked. "We already know she'd been planning on getting the picospores from the beginning. Maybe she kidnapped people to test them on."

"Are you calling my sister a test subject?" Hermoine asked slowly.

"No one's calling anyone anything." DJ sighed. "We're just trying to understand why Helene would go out of her way to do this, and if we're missing something."

"We're always missing something," Christy muttered.

Bethany spoke up then, her voice soft. "She said it was easier—at least for me. She said my symptoms made it difficult for my brain to process her instructions, so she fixed it."

DJ's brows went up. "You spoke to Helene?" Bethany nodded.

Another reason she's messed up in the head. "Cool, but we're getting off track. What else did you learn, Ndidi?"

Ndidi looked at him, clearly unwilling to move on from the topic. There was something more she wanted to bring up. DJ saw the look in *her* eyes. Whatever she wanted to say was big, and she wasn't going to let it go.

CJ APPEARED IN A CROUCH, surrounded by boxes and loose papers. The antivirus was nowhere in sight. This didn't necessarily mean it was gone. The sphere allowed for short-range teleportation, so he couldn't have been taken far. However, for the first time, the crude design of the website worked in his favor by providing him cover.

He didn't move for a while as he calmed down. The adrenaline slowly worked its way out of his system. He'd almost died. It had always been a possibility. He'd known the risk before he'd come in. But he'd almost *died*. The altercation had been relatively short. CJ doubted it'd lasted more than a few minutes from beginning to end. But several times within that short span, he could have been killed, his mind destroyed.

If I had been even a microsecond slower to grab the sphere … CJ silenced the thought. He could've died. But he hadn't. He'd survived. He'd survived a fight.

Him.

CJ chuckled to himself. His brother never said it, but CJ knew one of DJ's biggest worries had been how CJ was going to protect himself. He'd had it on his mind since they were kids, and he'd never quite let go of it, even as an adult. Despite what CJ had said then, it had been a worry for him, too. It was one of the reasons he'd delayed going to Manar. He didn't want to be a burden or someone that Manar would have to focus on protecting.

But now, CJ had proven that he didn't need protection, that he could handle himself. He'd proven it to DJ, but more importantly, he'd proven it to himself. He'd been in real danger. He'd been terrified out of his mind. But he'd escaped by himself.

This time, CJ laughed out loud, his heart lightening. He doubted that he would ever get used to the feeling of being in such danger. But now, he had proof that he could get out of it if he kept his head. And, if nothing else, that was a win.

CJ gave himself another minute and then straightened. His short break had been enough for some of the weakness he felt to dissipate, so it wasn't so hard to move. That provoked a thought: he hadn't felt any pain when the antivirus had struck him. Rather, he'd felt something drain out of him. CJ had already theorized that his body ran on mental energy. Did he lose a bit of that instead of sustaining damage? What would happen if he ran out?

That part was still unclear. CJ was unwilling to test it, so he pushed the thought away. Still, it was something else he needed to watch out for. He hesitated for a moment before turning off his shielding. He held the sphere even more closely as he started moving. The orb provided direction, making his path clear.

The next few minutes passed relatively uneventfully. Several times, CJ came across an antivirus. But unlike the first, he was always able to react in time and use the sphere to teleport away. One of the first things he'd practiced when mastering the ability was directing it so he wasn't taken to a random location. In this way, he was transported far enough to avoid the antivirus as well as further along in the direction that the sphere pointed him to.

It didn't take him long to realize that he was moving in a spiral, slowly heading toward the center. Several times, he passed the orb over random spots on the towers or boxes to see if he could discover a back door like last time, but to no avail.

He had to take a break once, after coming out of a teleport feeling weak. It was a drawback to the sphere that he'd discovered when practicing with it. The orb drew its energy from CJ himself. This meant that CJ could use the sphere as much as he wanted, but once he started running low on energy, he would begin to feel weak and tired.

It was the reason he had to turn off his shielding and why he was worried about sustaining damage. Even though he didn't feel pain, each time he was hit, he would have less energy with which to power an ability. If he were truly in danger, it would be detrimental.

CJ didn't know how much time passed as he walked. Throughout the trek, the sphere grew hotter until it was difficult to hold. The resonance coming from it was also stronger. Eventually, CJ passed a particularly clustered pile of boxes, and the sphere grew cool. He'd been waiting for that, so he simply took a step back and waved the orb over the boxes. The stacks parted, revealing an entrance, which CJ stepped through.

CJ had been expecting an extension of the frustrating design he'd suffered through with the rest of the website. In fact, he'd steeled himself mentally for it. It was a pleasant surprise to find out he was wrong.

The center of the website was another large room. Instead of featuring stacks of papers and boxes of office supplies, this room was designed like an ancient Roman chamber. Supporting pillars surrounded a large central space, where the core was hovering several feet off the ground. It was a relatively simple design—especially when compared to the pharmaceutical website. But CJ could see that the codes were solid.

They were also different. He moved closer to one of the pillars, analyzing the tapestry. The technique was different from what was used nowadays. Less refined but also more efficient to some extent. In the small area, CJ could see bits that could have been strengthened had the codes been written in a different way. He could also see sections that would make his own codes more efficient if he applied the same pattern.

It was fascinating. This was something he would never have learned outside. Now, all he needed was a glance.

He spent several minutes studying the pillars and walls before he was satisfied. As he took one step into the central space, the sphere immediately started vibrating wildly. The resonance he'd been feeling ever since he'd stepped into the website grew stronger until it was almost a physical force.

As he stood in front of the core, the sphere stopped vibrating. It remained warm, however, as if in anticipation. This core was different from the spherical mesh he'd seen on the pharmaceutical website. It was pitch black. It didn't rotate on an axis or invert itself. It just hovered. CJ tried to make out the tapestry of code that comprised the ball, but the details were too minute.

He raised the sphere and placed it against the core. Immediately, the whole chamber shuddered. CJ had expected that from the last time. A moment later, a piece of the ball broke off and drifted down to him.

CJ studied it for a moment. Just like before, he noted slight variations in the matrix. Still, the essence was the same. This identified the piece as another copy of the original software that made up the sphere. It still didn't explain why he'd found them in two websites, but there was nothing he could do about it.

The orbs lurched toward each other and merged. Fortunately, the sphere stayed the same size when it was done. Already it was somewhat unwieldy to carry. CJ didn't know what he would have done if it'd grown any bigger. But the size wasn't what was important. He focused, sending a tendril of will into the sphere.

Immediately, he could sense the difference. It would take time to explore exactly what had changed, but his small peek gave him a sense of what the sphere was capable of now. The possibilities filled him with excitement.

I was right! He grinned. *It wasn't complete. And it's still not.* This was the third combination; two more, and the device would be at its peak.

CJ couldn't wait to find out what it would be capable of then.

DJ WAS IN THE LAB they'd turned into a makeshift hospital when he got the alert on his phone. He ignored the first message, and the second. He didn't have a lot of time to visit his brother, so when he did, he tried to leave work at the door.

It'd been over two months since CJ had taken a dive. There hadn't been any changes during that time. Not even a twitch or a frown. If not for the rhythmic rising and falling of his brother's chest, DJ would have thought he was staring at a corpse.

And the one who caused it—

He cut off the anger before it could take root. He'd said all he needed to say to Ndidi, but it would take a while before he could let go of the anger. It helped that she spent most of her days at the Autism Centre. He didn't have to see her all the time.

Hermione, meanwhile, spent most of her days at her lab, fine-tuning the Synaptic Pulse. DJ coordinated with Olsen to try to find the bomb Helene was apparently building under their noses. Admiral Austin had been surprisingly helpful with it, even though nothing had turned up yet. It was basically a waiting game until Helene made her move or Manar and CJ fucked her up, wherever they were.

DJ's phone pinged with another text, and this time DJ paid attention. They were all from Christy.

C: "You might want to see this."

C: "Look! I know you're with your brother, but get your ass to the lobby."

C: "DJ! This is serious. Fucking get here!"

"Sheesh," DJ muttered. "I can't get a break around here." He spared another look at CJ and Manar before leaving.

Sparta was still a maze, especially when navigating from the upper floors, but DJ had become used to it after so many months. Now it was almost second nature. He messaged Christy back and tried to get more info about the emergency, but she just kept telling him to hurry. He took the elevator down and was at the lobby soon after. When he stepped out, he understood why Christy had been so insistent.

"We're not going anywhere …"

"We were told to come here …"

"Ndidi said …"

The area around the receptionist's desk was packed full of people, more than two dozen of them, all talking at the same time. It was a total madhouse. Christy was doing her best to calm them down. Security had subtly surrounded the group, but their weapons remained holstered. Christy must have asked them to stand down. He nodded to some of them.

DJ crossed the room, already feeling a headache coming on. The day had started out fucked, and this was a complication he did not need. Christy finally noticed him. Her face morphed into such a comical expression of relief that DJ almost laughed. She did not like crowds. This one was quickly turning into a mob. DJ had to do something fast.

"They're not listening," Christy said once he was within earshot. "I haven't been able to get a word in or even understand what the fuck they want."

"It's cool. I'll handle it," DJ said to her. Then he turned to face the crowd. "Hey!" He roared at the top of his voice. "Everyone shut the fuck up!"

And they did. It also had the benefit of directing everyone's attention to him. Christy muttered a few choice words that DJ ignored.

"All right, cool! First step's completed." He continued at a lower tone. "Now, do you guys have some sort of leader or a spokesperson or some shit that can tell us what the hell y'all are doing here?"

A middle-aged man with a neatly trimmed beard came out of the crowd, looking sheepish. "That would be me. Thank you for that. I've been trying to calm them down but couldn't get a word in. I'm Albert Willingham."

DJ took the man's outstretched hand and felt callouses. This was someone who worked with his hands. "Nice to meet you, Albert. I'm DJ. Now, can you tell me what's going on here?"

Albert rubbed the back of his head. "Ndidi actually sent us here." When he saw the obvious skepticism on DJ's face, he continued hurriedly. "We're some of the captives Helene took. Ndidi helped us escape, but something happened, and she had to stay back. She asked us to come here and meet someone named Hermione. Ndidi said that she would be able to help us get out of Helene's control."

"Oh shit! I remember you now," Christy said, stepping up beside DJ. "You were in the tunnel, talking about how *something happened*. You guys basically left Ndidi to die."

"What're you talking about?" DJ asked.

"I told you about the hostages that our team ran into while we were look-ing for Ndidi. This is them. We ran into them after they left her to fight José by herself while they got away." She scanned the crowd. "I remember a bigger group though."

Albert looked down guiltily. "Look, it wasn't anyone's proudest moment. I regret what I did. Everyone does. But Ndidi gave her life so that these people could get the help they need—"

"Uh, Ndidi's alive, bro," DJ cut in. "She didn't give her life for shit. She's probably on her way." He looked at Christy, who nodded a confirmation. "Yeah. She's on her way right now. You'll see her shortly."

Albert stood frozen, his face etched with profound shock. A couple of people in the crowd overheard and started murmuring, but DJ glared at them.

"H-How?" Albert stuttered. "That thing was indestructible. It took all our bullets and didn't even flinch."

"Yeah. We're not going to go into that." DJ gave him a dismissive wave, instead focusing on something that had been bothering him. "Tell me more about where exactly y'all have been for the last several weeks."

Albert started spinning some bullshit about moving around and hiding out somewhere. DJ nodded along with the story while alarm bells rang in his head. The whole thing just confirmed his suspicions. His eyes drifted over the crowd until they met the gaze of one of the security guards. DJ mouthed a word and gestured to the crowd. The guard nodded and slipped out.

"Christy said there were more of you," DJ said when Albert was done. "Not everyone was on board?"

"Some decided to reunite with their families first. That's understandable, though unwise."

"Because Helene can take control of them again and drive them like puppets," DJ confirmed.

Albert recoiled. "That's … that's cruder than I would have put it, but yes, exactly. That's why Ndidi asked us to come here—for a cure."

"Yeah. We'll get to that in a minute," DJ said. "What I can't wrap my head around, though, is why Helene *didn't* take control of you. I mean, you guys have been on the run for a couple of weeks. She probably could have snatched you back up at any time."

Albert faltered. "Um … we think her control lags with distance."

The guard returned, followed by about two dozen others—more than enough to deal with a crowd this size. DJ gave a tight-lipped smile and pulled Christy a step away. "I can tell you right now that it doesn't. Take 'em."

The guards poured in, surrounding the group from every side, guns out and cocked. The crowd erupted as they were herded together. Some shouted in confusion, others in anger. A disturbing number just looked resigned, like they'd given up. That disturbed DJ more than he wanted to admit. More than one person made a break for it and were casually shot down. Unsurprisingly, this increased the others' panic.

"What is this?" Albert snarled.

DJ ignored him, projecting his voice so the guards could hear. "Remember, tranquilizers only. If I see a bullet, one's going in your ass." He had no actual authority in Sparta and no business giving anyone orders—especially without Manar to back him up. But DJ had made a point to dedicate some time over the past several months to building up goodwill among the security and as many of the staff as he could. He couldn't say he knew all of them; Sparta was way too big for that. But he knew enough, and more importantly, they knew him and his history with the navy, so they took to his orders without blinking.

Maybe because they knew they wouldn't be killed, several more people tried running, but they never went more than a couple of steps before a tranquilizer hit them in the back. Others started surrendering. They were also tranquilized regardless. To her credit, despite the confusion she must have been feeling, Christy didn't say a word until the entire thing was over and the lobby was littered with bodies.

"It was a trap," DJ said finally.

"What do you mean?" she asked.

"There was no reason for Helene not to take control of them the moment she was no longer distracted by us. We already know she's not limited by distance, so why didn't she take control? Why did they wait weeks before coming here? How'd every single one of them stay off the grid for so long that Olsen and I couldn't find a lick of them until now?"

"You think Helene *did* take control of them," Christy stated.

DJ started to respond when he noticed one of the guards—the one he'd flagged originally—walking up to him. He extended his hand. "Thanks, Cal. I really appreciate you doing this for me. It could have bitten me in the ass."

Cal chuckled. "Nah, don't mention it. Though I'm curious how you managed to piss off so many people."

"Believe it or not, I only pissed off one, and she brought a mob," DJ said.

Cal chuckled again. "Where do you want them?"

DJ thought about that for a second. "Do you have any large rooms that can fit them all? Like a storage room or something? They don't have to be restrained, but having a few tranquilizers handy will probably make everything go smoothly."

"Yeah," Cal replied. "I can hook you up, but you know it can't be long term, right? It's already going to be a bitch explaining this to my supervisor."

"Jeff? I'll talk to him," DJ promised. "And no. I'm not thinking long term. Just long enough for all of them to see the doctor. Then they'll walk out of here by themselves."

Cal stared at him for a second, probably trying to tell how much of it was bullshit. None of it was. DJ just needed Hermione to do her thing and Helene's influence would be cleansed. Everything that happened after that wasn't on him.

"All right, I'll hit you up with the location once I have it sorted," Cal said. "You owe me one, though."

"Drinks on me tonight." DJ gave him a fist bump.

Cal walked away. DJ turned back to Christy, who was staring at him. He shrugged. "It's called networking, C, and it just saved us a shitload of stress."

"Where do you even get the time to—" She cut herself off with a shake of her head. "Know what? Just finish what you were saying about Helene."

DJ lost his grin. "Yeah. She probably took control of them the minute we got out and sent them here to find out what we did to José. You said you met a bigger group in the tunnels. Well, I'll bet she's hedging her bets so if this doesn't work out—which it won't—she doesn't lose all her hostages."

"Why did she wait so long though?" Christy asked.

That was the one question DJ didn't have an answer to. The plan would have been far more effective if Helene had sent them as soon as the team had returned from the raid and were still off-balance. It was possible that something they did actually hurt her, so she needed to fix that first, but there was no way to know.

"What happens now?" Christy asked.

DJ yawned. "Well, like I said, we'll have the doctor take a look at them."

Just then, a woman walked in and saw the pile of bodies on the floor. She screamed and ran. DJ ignored Christy's glare, which bored into his back as he walked away. He needed to get some sleep.

283

IT TOOK CJ HALF THE TIME to navigate his way out of the website than it took to get in. Part of it was because he was more familiar with the design. The other part was because of the sphere.

The distance of its teleportation had increased significantly. All the other abilities had been similarly enhanced. Even the cost in mental energy had been reduced. This meant that CJ could activate his abilities more often and for longer periods without putting himself in danger.

He encountered much more security than he had the first time. Some of the giants had even chosen to travel in pairs. Still, despite the numbers, as long as he was careful, the brutes were easy to avoid. All he had to do was teleport.

Despite his caution, however, there was nothing he could do when he ended up teleporting between a pair of brutes. CJ didn't know who of the three was more surprised. They stared at each other for several seconds before simultaneously coming out of their shock.

The brutes attacked first, swinging their cudgels at him. CJ dove to the ground and activated his shield. The air distorted around him just as the clubs smashed into him. CJ felt that familiar drain as his energy was sapped—albeit much less than the first time.

The clubs lifted a second later. CJ could almost *feel* the giants' confusion when they saw he was still alive. He would have laughed if he hadn't been completely terrified. Before they regained their presence of mind to attack again, CJ was gone.

This happened twice more. Each time, CJ escaped without problems. He wouldn't say that he got used to it, but his fear lessened each time as his confidence grew. Eventually, he was out of the second floor and back onto the first. CJ avoided the bridge of keys entirely and teleported down to the lower floor, then spent several minutes there recovering his energy.

To deal with the firewalls, CJ just activated his shield and charged through them. The shield was several times stronger. It was as if the flames weren't even there. He reached the exit within minutes.

All the while, the alarm kept blaring.

CJ spent the next few minutes getting as far away from the website as he could. He'd done the same thing when he came out of the pharmaceutical website. Although this one had gone much better, it was a compulsion he couldn't resist. He felt like a criminal running away from the scene of a crime.

CJ stopped when he'd fled far enough. He was in the middle of a random street. Different avatars streamed around him in a wave. Despite living in one of the busiest cities in the world, CJ had never truly appreciated how many people there were until he came to the virtual world. At any point of the day, wherever he was, there was always a stream of avatars entering websites. It was a never-ending flood. It was amazing, if annoying.

He sent a tendril of will into the sphere and activated its zone.

When he did this the first time, he'd been too freaked out to truly notice the reaction. Now he could appreciate it. The zone spread out like a wave, passing through avatars and even one of the buildings. The reaction built up slowly. First, every user seemed to pick up speed as they rushed out of the area. Even the avatars within the websites weren't exempt. They poured out of the buildings en masse and crowded up the street.

If one were not watching out for this specifically, then it wouldn't really be noticeable. However, several streets over, users got redirected once they reached the edge of the zone. They bounced off the invisible barrier—invisible to them, at least—and quickly turned onto another street. CJ didn't know if they would be redirected to another website or just get an error message. Either way, it was fascinating to consider. It was proof that his actions could have a direct effect on users in the real world. It was a loophole that he could exploit once he figured out how.

The avatars continued to migrate as a group. Within a minute, the entire street was completely empty except for CJ.

Good, he thought as he hefted the sphere. *Let's see what you're capable of now.*

CJ spent the next day on that street, testing out the new enhancements and comparing them to the sphere's original abilities. Most of the changes—like the teleportation—were just straight-up improvements. Some added functions that required more testing, like the shielding.

CJ had already experienced the added strength that came with the enhancement back at the website, but now he sensed that there was more he could do with it. The wall of energy had grown stronger. It had gone from extending just a few inches away from his skin to almost a foot away. Now, it was less than a wall and more of an aura.

It was the sense he'd felt initially: the shield wasn't really a shield, but an aura that nullified other programs, limiting their effects. That was why the antivirus hadn't been able to destroy him. When their attacks had passed through the aura, most of the effect had been nullified.

That should have been enough. It protected him and gave him a window in which he could escape. But as he'd learned, there might be situations where he couldn't run away, such as when he and Manar finally confronted Helene. How much help would he be if he could protect only himself?

So far, he'd discovered only three of the sphere's abilities: teleportation, shielding, and the zone—all of which were defensive, though CJ had a feeling that was mostly because of his mindset rather than the actual limits of the sphere.

One of his major fears had always been his protection. This might have influenced which abilities he'd uncovered. Teleportation, for example, had come about directly to escape dangerous situations. Shielding had come about to protect himself within dangerous situations. With those two, he was confident in his ability to stay alive—at least in a short fight. But now it was time to start thinking of an offensive power. CJ had to admit he was more than a little uncomfortable with the thought. Violence had never been in his nature. But that didn't mean it wasn't necessary.

He didn't need something over the top, just something to disable his enemies if the situation demanded it. This wasn't the first time CJ had thought about an offensive ability. Every other time, he'd been confused about what the ability should be. But now, his aura gave him an idea.

When he activated the ability, the air distorted around him on all sides. The distortion was more prominent with the enhancement, enough so that it could no longer be said to be invisible. Connected to the sphere as he was, he could still sense the potential in the ability, the multiple uses. He focused on one: nullification. He brought it to the forefront of his mind. It was more difficult than he'd expected, but CJ had a wealth of experience with forcing himself to remain focused. Once he was sure he was holding on to the image as clearly as he could, he walked to the nearest building, a giant briefcase. One of its pockets served as an entrance, and its seams shone with strobe lights.

When CJ was a foot away from the building, the nearest section dimmed slightly. That gave him hope. He continued on until he could place his hand on it. Immediately, the entire section went dark. The lights shut off, and the area seemed to age by several decades. The rest of the website was still the same. However, for several meters from where CJ had touched, it was as if the programs were no longer functional. The code was still there, but now they were basically decoration.

The effect lasted only a few seconds, then it was as if time rewound. The lights came back up, and the section no longer looked dead.

CJ observed the whole thing in amazement. He hadn't thought that would work, but it meant that he'd been right—and that he had been using the aura wrongly. If the nullification worked on a website with dozens of programs and a solid foundation of code, then what would it do to an avatar or an antivirus? To Helene?

I need to practice more, he thought, grinning. He spent the rest of the day doing that, working to improve the manipulation of his aura and his zone. It occurred to him that if he could make the zone smaller, he might have a way to repel antiviruses completely. This meant he could wander into websites without any danger at all.

As he worked, he felt a familiar numbness take over. He lost himself in his tasks for an hour or so, until his mental energy ran out and he had to take a break. The drain from the zone was minuscule, but combined with the other two other abilities that were active at the same time, it added up. He leaned against a building, shut off the aura, and deactivated the zone entirely.

Immediately, a pressure descended on the area. CJ didn't know how else to describe it. The air roiled for miles: a storm was brewing. CJ had not seen so much as a cloud in all the time he'd been here, but a storm was here, and the sphere was reacting to the pressure. It grew so hot that CJ almost had to drop it. He sent a tendril of will into the orb, and suddenly he could feel it.

There was a presence within the storm.

This was baffling. How could he have missed this? The presence was awe inspiring, and terrifying. It was all-encompassing. CJ could feel the power in its gaze, yet there was no malice. There was no emotion at all, as if it were above that. CJ only got the sense that it was looking for something that had attracted its attention.

The sphere grew hotter in his hands, worrying CJ.

Quickly, he activated the zone. Invisible ripples spread from his position, extending over a city block. That drew its attention. CJ felt *it* when it happened. The pressure grew thicker until it was almost suffocating. CJ closed his eyes. If his gamble had failed …

When several seconds passed and nothing had happened, he opened his eyes. The presence was still there, but for the first time, CJ could sense confusion in its gaze, and a bit of frustration. It could probably sense that what it sought was close but couldn't focus on its location and didn't know why.

This continued for several minutes. Finally, the presence seemed to give up. The gaze retracted. The storm was dispelled, and everything went back to normal. CJ let out a sigh of relief. Then his thoughts went into overdrive.

What was that?

Was that Helene?

Can she sense when I use the sphere?

If she could, why is she just coming now?

Why was the zone able to hide my location from her?

The questions came at once and were never-ending. Most of them he couldn't answer, and as soon as he answered the ones he could, another just replaced it. CJ could feel himself getting overwhelmed, so he placed his palms flat on the floor and grounded himself, taking deep breaths until he was calmer. The questions were still there, but CJ refused to pay them any mind. He focused instead on what he *did* know—or at least reasonably suspected.

The zone repelled avatars. CJ had deactivated the zone, and the pressure had immediately descended. He hadn't felt a presence until he'd connected to the sphere. The presence had been searching for something. CJ was reasonably certain it was the sphere itself, especially since activating the zone again had attracted its attention.

CJ took another deep breath.

CJ had used the sphere plenty of times, but nothing like that had happened before. What had changed? Then, the answer came to him. He'd been testing the third orb's enhancements of the sphere. Whatever signal or ripples the device produced must have become strong enough to attract whatever that was.

What if that thing was Helene?

It was the only question CJ couldn't push away. If it was Helene, CJ didn't know how they were going to deal with it. The sheer power he'd felt in that storm terrified him. If that was what they were up against …

But this wasn't the time for that. Whether or not it was Helene was secondary. The primary issue was that something about the sphere had drawn its attention. Fortunately, the zone acted as a sort of cloak, meaning CJ wouldn't have to stop using it entirely. It was just another thing he had to be careful about.

That list got longer every day.

Despite assuring himself he was safe while the zone was on, it took CJ several hours to continue his practice without looking over his shoulder. After a few days, he'd put the whole thing behind him as he immersed himself in mastering the new ability.

A week passed quickly, during which CJ never dropped the zone, and the presence didn't make another appearance. Eventually, CJ felt he'd practiced enough and was confident enough to try out his skills in the wild.

This came with its own risks since he would have to drop the zone while he searched for a suitable website. It was one of the first things he'd discovered: the zone was fixed in place once activated, and there was a delay between activations, so he couldn't drop it and immediately raise it up again.

Still, he couldn't let that stop him from upgrading the sphere—especially now. He'd always known how unique it was, but now that he'd seen that it was important to someone else, it was even more imperative that he got it further linked to himself.

Even though he was terrified, it was time for him to get the fourth piece.

"YOU'RE JUST GOING TO KEEP them prisoner?" Ndidi asked, keeping in step with DJ.

"Yep."

"For how long?"

"That depends on them." DJ shrugged. "And Hermione. I don't know how long she needs to do her thing."

"And do they need to be tranquilized in the meantime?"

"Again, that depends on them and whether or not they'll keep banging on shit and pissing everyone off."

"They're desperate, DJ. They came here to be helped, and instead they're being treated like animals. Of course they're angry."

DJ whirled around to face her so suddenly that she missed a step and almost fell. "How many animals are given three square meals a day, Ndidi? Or bathroom breaks? Or changes of clothes? We've explained multiple times why they have to be detained. The ones that Hermione has helped so far have also explained it to the rest. And yet they keep shouting. I'm already pulling strings left and right so they're not just dumped outside for Helene to pick up. Yet I'm the bad guy here? Are you fucking kidding me?"

He was yelling now. Staff members were giving him a wide berth as they passed, but he didn't give a fuck. Where the hell did she get off, berating him, when she'd been the one to drop this on his ass without warning?

"When you told all these people to come here, did it occur to you that we have no actual authority in Sparta without Manar, who you put in a coma? Did it occur to you that the higher-ups might have a problem with over two dozen people barging in without an explanation?"

Ndidi faltered under his words. A part of DJ felt guilty, but a greater part—a part that had been steadily growing for weeks—just wanted to punch her. And this time, Christy wasn't here to stop him.

He reined in his anger with effort and forced his voice back to its regular tone—though with no less of its bite. "You didn't. You grew up in your ivory tower, and despite what you claim and how you act, you expect someone else to take care of your mess. Well, I've cleaned up your mess. The ex-hostages are dealt with and receiving treatment. But I'm not going to stand here and justify my actions to you. Come talk to me when you can contribute something useful."

DJ walked away. There were no accompanying footsteps. Ndidi had finally left him alone. A part of him wanted to turn back and see her face, but fuck that. His words had been harsh, probably harsher than they needed to be, but maybe they would motivate her to actually think for once.

Helene is the real enemy here, Hermoine had said. DJ knew that; Helene was the one to stop. He knew he would have to work with Ndidi to do that. But whenever he looked at her, it was as if her face was superimposed on an image of his brother lying on a bed with tubes sticking out of him.

Yeah. He was going to have to work with her, but it would take time. And all the stupid shit she'd been pulling didn't help. DJ took a deep breath and tried to push it out of his mind. It took some effort, but he was better by the time he got to Hermione's lab.

DJ didn't often have a reason to come to the lab, so it was a novel experience each time. The first time he'd come, years earlier, when Hermione had been trying to determine the effects of the picospores, she'd been experimenting on rats and controlling them like little furry robots. The last time he'd been there, he'd found Hermione on the floor, crying her eyes out and staring at the Synaptic Pulse prototype.

So it was no surprise that DJ felt a little bit of trepidation as he pushed open the door and saw Hermione bent over a counter, surrounded by machines DJ had no name for. What did surprise him were the several unconscious people lying in the corner and an unconscious man strapped to a chair with glowing tubes sticking out of his arms.

Hermione didn't notice when DJ walked in. There were bags under her eyes, but there was also a glow around her that hadn't been there before. DJ had noticed this earlier in the conference room. It was as if a burden had been lifted from her shoulders.

Must be nice. DJ chuckled inwardly as he scanned the room, looking for the cause. Bethany was nowhere to be found.

When Hermione still hadn't noticed him after several seconds of him standing there, DJ coughed—and then again when the first one didn't work. Her head snapped up and her hand covered up a gasp.

"Shit, DJ! Are you trying to kill me?"

Yeah, of course, I'm the one at fault here. He rolled his eyes.

"Whatchu up to?" he asked, taking a seat at the counter with her. He tried to peer at the journal, but it was filled with numbers, diagrams, and symbols that made his head hurt. "Any progress with the Pulse?"

Hermione groaned softly. "I've given up on it."

DJ tried not to panic. The Pulse was their only way of negating the picospores, but too much limited its use. Hermione had been working on a way to fine-tune the device to reduce those restrictions.

"What happened?" he asked, keeping his tone light.

"I found a way to give it a wider area of effect like you wanted, but then it occurred to me that having people fainting whenever they're cured would lead to issues sooner or later—especially since it meant that it couldn't be used in public. I've been working on a way to fix that. But nothing I've tried has worked."

DJ breathed a sigh of relief. Having the Pulse only working on close-range targets was one of the biggest problems that DJ had with it. But if that issue was fixed, then everything else was secondary. And the fainting wasn't as big a problem as Hermione feared. Things with Helene were fast reaching a point of open conflict—one they would lose, with the way things were going. At that point, who would care if someone spontaneously dropped unconscious in the middle of the street?

For obvious reasons, DJ didn't say any of that. Instead, he asked, "What do you think is the problem?"

"It isn't a *problem* per se. It's just the way the Pulse works. It shoots out a sound wave that transports an electric current into the target. The current resets the picospores, breaking Helene's control. However, since the spores are normally within the brain, there's some spillover. This causes the target to lose consciousness. It's an inevitable side effect."

"Like the hangover after a night out. Or childhood obesity caused by fast-food restaurants."

Hermione stared at him for a long time before wisely choosing to ignore the statement. "I wanted to make the Pulse portable and personalized so everyone could have their own. But without fixing this, that's not going to be possible." She sighed. "So, I give up."

DJ shrugged. "I mean, it sounds like you've achieved a lot with it, and it already does what it's supposed to do. Now it's up to us to utilize it the best way we know how."

"To fuck shit up?" asked Hermione.

"To fuck shit up." DJ grinned. Hermione's groan just made his grin widen. He nodded toward the man strapped to the chair. "What's happening there?"

"I'm extracting the picospores from all of them." Hermione gestured toward the giant metal container the tube was attached to. "I'm storing the excess for now because I honestly don't know what to do with them. She's … upgraded them somehow."

"Upgraded them?"

"She's tweaked them so they listen to commands better, and it doesn't require as much processing power. I've been studying them for days. The enhancements are brilliant. If the spores were applied for their original purpose, the good they could do would be immeasurable." She ran a hand through her frizzy hair. "I don't know. Maybe Ndidi is right."

"Right about what?"

She hesitated "We've been talking since she got back. She's been conflicted about whether it's a good idea to fully shut Helene down—especially because of all the good we could achieve if we found a way to capture her and use her instead. I don't know. I disagreed with her initially, but now, looking at the picospores … With those kinds of enhancements, we could change the world for the better."

Hermione kept on talking, but DJ tuned her out. His mind was fixed on a certain part of her statement. *Ndidi said what?*

54

IT TOOK CJ SEVERAL DAYS to find a suitable website. While he searched, he didn't use the sphere, and the presence didn't make an appearance, confirming that's what had drawn it in the first place.

That went a long way toward easing his mind. It was also a relief to discover that using the sphere as a guide didn't count as activating it. CJ was able to use the resonance to narrow down his choices.

CJ didn't hesitate to head in once he found a suitable website—a building designed like several folders stacked on top of each other. The architecture was similar to the last one, except this website seemed to specialize only in different types of papers. Again, CJ wondered how it had survived at all in an age where everything was digital.

The website was alerted to his presence the second he entered, but he'd expected that. With his new abilities, CJ tore through the first level, relying only on his aura's most basic form: the shield. He navigated the second level in the same way, and then the third and fourth. The core chamber was at the end of the fifth level.

CJ was out an hour later, and the sphere was noticeably denser.

He stepped out to see the sky roiling. It went on for miles. The atmosphere was dark and gave off a pressure that surrounded everything. It wasn't as bad as the first time, but something had attracted its attention.

Quickly, CJ activated a zone. Ripples spread out in every direction, double the size it was before this latest upgrade. CJ could sense a stronger connection to the ability as well, but he didn't dare to test it out right now. Avatars rushed out of the surrounding buildings. They moved as a wave and in a single direction, obviously under some sort of effect. It looked suspicious as hell. Why hadn't he considered that?

CJ hesitated, then sent a tendril of will into the sphere. Immediately he could sense the presence above him, as well as its power, both of which were focused on the area. He could sense the frustration and anger in that gaze, and it was enough to wipe away whatever sense of accomplishment he'd felt from getting the fourth piece. As before, it could see that something was wrong, but couldn't pinpoint the source because of the zone. He breathed a sigh of relief.

The sky remained dark for several hours.

CJ couldn't follow the avatars out of the zone, so he stayed as close to the edge as possible, hiding in an alley. He leaned against the website and tried to regain his energy. The draw from the zone had always been minuscule, but he'd been forced to activate it immediately after coming out of the website. Fortunately, he hadn't been completely drained, or he would have finally found out what happened when he ran out of energy.

Another hour passed. The pressure showed no sign of dissipating. Eventually, CJ's curiosity outweighed his fear. Although he didn't dare step out into the open, he had enough confidence to test that stronger connection he'd felt to the zone.

For him to keep the zone active, he had to remain connected to the sphere perpetually, so he focused on the tendril of will that was already there.

Immediately, his vision expanded. It stretched and twisted in a series of flashes until, suddenly, CJ was a block away—and also looking at the city from several miles in the air. The pressure was greater at this altitude, with the clouds just above him.

It took a while for his mind to adjust. Somehow, he'd merged with the ability so much that he could see everything within the zone at once. It was amazing but jarring to juggle the different perspectives. If he could master it, the possibilities for recon were nearly endless. At least, within the virtual world.

CJ struggled to retract his senses. Only when he was back in his body did he notice the toll the ability had on his energy pool. By his estimation, he'd only used it for a few seconds, yet a full quarter of his reserves had been used. CJ bit his lip. That would limit the ability's usefulness. He'd have to use it for only a few seconds at a time.

Excitement rushed through him as CJ realized he could still sense more. He'd been trying for over a week to manipulate the diameter of the zone. So far, he hadn't been able to.

He focused on the ability. This time, he could sense the entirety of the dome. It was different from being able to *see* everything within the zone. Rather, he could sense its perimeter. With a mental flex, CJ forced the dome to expand and then condense. He couldn't change the size by much, but it was something.

Interestingly, it took far more energy to condense the dome than to expand it past the average. CJ had hoped that it would be the other way around. If he could get the zone to be small enough to cover just him, then he might be able to get it to move along with him. That way, he was always cloaked.

Still, it might be possible with a bit more practice—or once he got the fifth piece.

Before searching for the last piece, there were several more enhancements he had to test. But he couldn't help but wonder what he'd be able to do once the sphere was completed.

The sky rumbled overhead, and CJ grinned.

GENERALLY, DJ THOUGHT OF HIMSELF as a pretty easygoing guy. Life was too short to go around being grumpy all the time. That attitude made it difficult for him to be truly angry. He could be annoyed, irritated, or disgruntled, but for him to be actually pissed? That was rare.

Yet it seemed that it was becoming his default state these days. He was turning into Manar. That was something he would have to deal with later, once he dealt with the latest cause of his anger.

"Please explain it to me," DJ said as calmly as he could, "just one more time."

Ndidi sighed. "I'm not saying that Helene doesn't need to be defeated. I'm just saying it would be a tremendous waste to ignore the benefits we can extract from her if we suppress and capture her instead of completely eliminating her."

They were in the conference room. DJ had spent so much time there over the last few months that he was considering getting a mattress brought in. He had called the meeting shortly after he'd spoken with Hermione. Everyone was in their usual places around the table, except Hermione, who'd probably figured out why the meeting was called and sat at the end of the table—opposite Manar's usual spot—in what seemed like a neutral stance.

Bethany sat next to Ndidi. DJ would have preferred her to sit this one out, but that would have raised more issues than he wanted to deal with. He would have to work with it.

"Benefits?" DJ asked.

"Yes, benefits." Ndidi nodded, her voice as earnest as DJ had ever heard. "Bethany is no longer on the autism spectrum, and every other hostage that had a disorder has been helped because of Helene."

DJ couldn't believe what he was hearing. "You do realize that Helene did all this just so she could have better slaves, right? I mean, Bethany said so herself. Helene only cured her symptoms because it made it easier to control her. The same thing applies to every other hostage. They're cured, but they had to give up years of their lives for it. Most of them are a step away from gaining entirely new mental disorders from the trauma alone. Wanna take a poll and find out how many people feel blessed?"

Ndidi grunted in frustration. "That's why I'm saying we should work to suppress her or capture her. If we can contain her, we can extract what we need while countering whatever harm she could do."

"All right. Let's say we do that." DJ's voice was still calm, but the effort it took to keep it that way created a noticeable strain. Christy, Pratima, and Hermione were content to stay silent. They all knew that this was between him and Ndidi. "That's a big ask, seeing as we've spent several years trying to destroy her. Capturing her would be orders of magnitude more difficult. In what world do you think we could safely counter anything Helene planned? She's been several steps ahead of us since day one, with contingencies on top of contingencies. The only times we've one-upped her were with the Pulse and when Manar uplinked."

DJ should have stopped there. But he couldn't help himself. "And, for the latter, she still found a way to mess it up."

Ndidi's face darkened at the dig, but there wasn't anything that she could say. DJ wasn't done.

"And what if we contain her and she somehow escapes? I mean, when all this started, we thought we had it all in hand, that Manar could just shut her off. But the geniuses in the government wanted to use her as well. And how did that turn out? Now Helene controls half of the fools in Congress, and we're more fucked than ever before."

Ndidi was insistent. "But we could do so much *good—*"

"I think," DJ cut her off, "that you've succeeded in what you wanted. Bethany's why you went after Helene in the first place, and there she is. Now you've forgotten you're not the only one with chips in the bag. Every one of us has our own bone to pick with Helene, but you don't care about that." He nodded at Bethany, making sure to meet her eyes. Her gaze followed his, demonstrating that she was actually present in the conversation. That was good. "Your priority is Bethany. That's admirable, but forgive me if I'm not willing to risk the fucking world."

"I'm not asking you to risk anything," Ndidi tried again, her voice pleading. "I'm just asking you to look—to really look. For the first time in her life, Bethany can have an actual conversation with her sister, one where she doesn't have to struggle for words or have episodes she can't control. And it's the same with every other person on the autism spectrum. They could live their lives without ever showing a single symptom."

DJ tilted his head innocently. "I'm sorry! I thought Bethany could already communicate with her sister, even before she got into Helene's hands. Just like my brother could always communicate with me. Both of them could converse with *your* help. Isn't that the whole purpose of the Autism Centre? You're endangering the world for a quick goddamn fix and in the process belittling every single thing that you, your staff, and the people themselves have accomplished. Did it ever occur to you that not everyone wants to have their brains rewritten just for a chance to be 'normal'?"

Ndidi's brows furrowed. "Why would anyone want to—"

"He's right," Bethany said, interrupting Ndidi before she could put her foot in her mouth. "I was already normal. I don't need to be cured because there's nothing wrong with me. Sure, I had problems with my memory and speech. But all of that was part of what makes me, me. Everything, including my episodes, is a part of me. DJ's right. It took me years to learn how to live above my symptoms. I'm not willing to give that all away just because there's a shortcut, especially if it means I still have to keep these … *things* in me."

DJ saw the effect the words had on Ndidi, and he almost felt guilty. Obviously, she'd assumed that anyone on the autism spectrum would jump at the chance to be free of their symptoms. Many probably would have. But others, like Bethany, would rather live as they were, accepting their condition as part of themselves and being proud of that fact. Bethany, of course, with her experience with Helene and the picospores, had more reason than most to reject it. There were bound to be others who thought the same way.

What would CJ decide? DJ wondered—though only briefly because the answer came in the next moment. CJ would take the chance to be rid of his symptoms. Growing up, DJ had tried his best to make his brother feel normal, but CJ had always hated his condition. He took every episode as a personal affront. Ndidi was a big help, but his anger at himself was one of the reasons he'd made so much progress over the years. That anger had lessened as he grew up, but it'd never really gone completely, so he would probably prefer to take the cure. Hopefully he would be able to see that keeping Helene down for good was more important.

It was a bridge they'd have to cross when they got there.

Hermione spoke up. "Bethany, think about what you're saying—"

"I'm not a child anymore, Hermione," Bethany replied sharply. "Sure, Helene took part of my life. But I can still think for myself. This is what I want. If it means Helene is destroyed for good, then all the better." She stood up, then walked out of the room, really milking the dramatic exit. That was the first time she'd chosen to be by herself since being rescued.

Hermione stood up to follow, but Pratima stopped her, speaking for the first time. "This is her decision, Hermione. It might not be what you want, but it is hers to make. As she said, she is no longer a child to be coddled."

Ndidi was frozen, staring at the door. DJ didn't say anything. He'd expected this, but he wasn't so much of a jerk that he'd rub it in their faces. It was cool as long as Bethany's decision convinced Ndidi to drop the whole thing. No matter what she said, Ndidi was just looking out for her.

Of course, it was at that same moment that Ndidi broke out of her shock, whirling around to face DJ. "This doesn't change anything. Bethany made her choice, but we can't make the choice for everyone else."

"Sure we can." DJ shrugged. "We're the ones who've been risking our lives since day one, and we're the ones who'll keep risking our lives when it inevitably blows up in our faces."

Ndidi opened her mouth, but DJ was over the whole conversation. He'd hoped that Bethany would be enough to get Ndidi to back down, but he'd forgotten how stubborn she could be.

"Listen, Ndidi. I understand where you're coming from, but using Helene to do this isn't going to work. It will bite us in the ass. Hermione told me that she somehow upgraded the spores. She's already studying the changes. Why don't you join her and figure out another way to make a *cure*? I mean, shit, the spores were basically designed for this, right? And according to you, Helene has basically shown you a way forward. Use that instead of trying to use our archenemy as a fucking crutch."

"And what about the other benefits that we could get from Helene ?" Ndidi asked without missing a beat.

"What the hell are you talking about?" DJ asked.

"I know you might not want to hear this, DJ, and I hate myself for saying it. But objectively, it hasn't been all bad with Helene. I mean, even putting aside her work on the picospores, she also helped Manar with his research and performed the surgery on the twins. According to Chloe, Liz was basically dead on the table before Helene intervened. Plus, though we've never been able to figure out why, she's kept up the pretense that she's still working as a virtual assistant. And these are only the things we know about."

"Are you fucking kidding me?" DJ said. "She did every single one of those things to screw us over in one way or the other. And just because we haven't figured out the virtual assistant angle doesn't mean it won't screw us over."

"It doesn't matter why she did them—" Ndidi started.

"Of course it fucking does!" DJ yelled, leaping up from his chair. His gaze took in the entire room. Ndidi met his eyes defiantly, while Pratima's expression was as measured as ever. Hermione's face showed worry and indecision. Christy, the only one who was on his side, met his eyes easily. "Am I the only one here that's thinking? Everything Helene's done has been for her own sake, to further her plans. And since some of y'all have lost your damned minds, let me remind you that her plan is to take over the fucking world and burn it to the ground. It doesn't matter if some of her actions had the side effect of being good! She still wants to screw us over! Why the hell is no one getting that?"

"Calm yourself, DJ," Pratima said.

"Yeah, you've turned into a full-blown sailor with your cursing," Christy added, chuckling uncomfortably.

"We're all on the same side, DJ," Hermione said softly.

DJ stared at them, then made for the door. "Y'know, Hermione, I don't think we are anymore."

CJ STARED AT THE TOWERING BUILDING in front of him and wondered once again if he was making a mistake. It was a valid thought, seeing as the building was an intact, modern, not-crumbling website, and CJ was considering going into it to get his fifth piece.

Really, though, it was his only choice. He'd searched for a full week and hadn't been able to find a site on the verge of collapsing. CJ had stalled by practicing extensively with the sphere, becoming intimately familiar with all the abilities he'd discovered, as well as their enhancements. He'd even learned how to further condense the zone so it was smaller and denser. It still wasn't up to the level of being mobile, but CJ was confident it was only a matter of time.

Time. That was one of the problems.

For the last few days, the sky had remained dark with storm clouds. CJ had been forced to keep the zone activated to avoid detection. Each day, the power within the gaze grew more concentrated as its frustration increased. CJ guessed it was because of his increased use of the sphere.

It's Helene. It must be. It was a thought CJ had been avoiding for days, but he could no longer suppress it. Whatever the entity was, it definitely wasn't an avatar, a bot, or malware. CJ was familiar with all of those. He couldn't think of anything else with enough power to affect the world so much. The sphere was the only thing that might come close, but even it lacked the sentience CJ could feel in the clouds. If it was Helene, then it was only a matter of time before she grew powerful enough to pierce through his cloak.

The only way to buy time was to get the fifth piece and finally complete the orb. Once the sphere was completed, a more permanent solution might present itself. It was a flimsier plan than CJ was comfortable with, but he didn't see any other option.

There was a resonance inside the building that told him it had the piece he needed. CJ would just have to navigate the site, deal with whatever security measures it threw at him, and find his way to the core. It was something he'd done several times before. Granted, he'd been dealing with old websites with less security as opposed to a regularly maintained website with modern antivirus and defenses.

CJ gulped. He felt the familiar terror creeping up his back and spreading through his body, making him numb. He hadn't become used to that, even after four times. But this time it was worse, mostly because he was very aware of how reckless this was.

But he was running out of time.

By his estimation, he'd already spent well over two months in the virtual world, and he hadn't even met up with Manar, which was why he'd come in the first place. CJ had good reasons for that, and he stood by them, but he also couldn't deny that he'd let his curiosity get the best of him. There was just so much to learn about the world. Gathering the pieces of the sphere was a good excuse for him to keep wandering.

He'd had his fun, and he'd proven he could take care of himself without DJ around to protect him. Now it was time to get the last piece of the puzzle and get to Manar so they could work on getting out. Making that decision didn't stop him from being afraid, but accepting it made the fear easier to deal with somehow.

He crossed the threshold and stepped into the website.

Immediately, the rumbling sky vanished. Pressure—similar to Helene's—weighed down on him the moment he entered. The pressure from the storm was more powerful but spread over a much wider area, so it was barely felt. Here, the attention of the entire building was on him, and it was somewhat suffocating.

It didn't help that the pressure increased when the website sensed the sphere within the pouch he'd found for it. It was basically a fanny pack strapped to his waist. The orb had become too heavy to carry otherwise.

The pressure pressed down on him, suffocating him in a way that went beyond the physical as it sought to expel him. CJ was able to resist the expulsion, but his movements were heavily restricted. Every action felt like he was moving through water. It caught him off guard. Usually, he was able to ignore the feeling of suppression from the websites without a problem.

Now that he was seeing the difference between a site that was days away from getting deleted and another with actual defense systems, he wondered if he'd overestimated his chances.

A second later, alarms blared throughout the building. It was the only thing about the whole ordeal that CJ had grown used to enough to ignore.

The interior was built much like the Gaius search engine. A few feet from the entrance were several rows of large offices rising from the ground like stacks of books at a library. However, unlike the Gaius site, there were hallways in the middle of the rows, like in an actual business complex. CJ could see into the first row of offices and was surprised to find it fully furnished. The windows had curtains and the hallways were lined with gray carpet that looked so soft that CJ felt more relaxed just seeing it.

The level of detail was extraordinary. Despite the life-ending threats lying within, he could appreciate the effort that had gone into developing each feature.

CJ activated his shield. Its energy consumption had gone down with the absorption of the fourth piece, and now CJ could afford to leave it on almost indefinitely if he didn't use too many of the other abilities. The draw was still the same if he was hit, but at least he wouldn't immediately die.

His fear told him to rush through the hallways until he reached the core chamber; with the sphere, getting lost wasn't an issue. But that wasn't happening with all this pressure weighing him down. He couldn't run if he had any hope of managing his energy.

He took a left at the first turn, and his caution didn't stop him from dallying for several minutes while he studied the code structure of the walls outside the offices. The tapestry was nice, but it followed techniques that CJ was already familiar with and—having had months of Manar's tutelage and observing different programming styles within the virtual world—could even improve on.

He'd only stopped for a few minutes, but it did wonders to take the edge off his fear. He was tempted to enter the offices themselves to observe the tapestry there, but it would take too much time. CJ was pushing his luck already.

CJ took another turn, following the resonance from the sphere. It was almost instinctive at this point. The walls blended as time passed, but CJ's sense of alarm didn't diminish. He couldn't feel the pressure of the storm from inside the website, but the threat of it hovered over his head like a guillotine. It forced him to consider things that he'd deliberately avoided thinking about. For one, there was no guarantee that the fifth piece would offer a solution to Helene. It might even make him more of a bonfire. If it did, CJ didn't know what he was going to do.

His connection with Manar told him that Manar was unreasonably far away. CJ wasn't confident he could make the journey with Helene actively searching for him. Together, he and Manar would have a chance, but alone, even with the sphere, CJ wouldn't survive against the power he felt within the presence.

CJ put the thought out of his mind as he entered another passageway. Inevitably, his thoughts turned to the real world. It was something else CJ had avoided thinking about while he'd been exploring that was now shaken loose by Helene. This was the longest that he'd ever been without his brother, and he was worried about the sort of mischief DJ had gotten into.

But more importantly, what was going on in the real world? What was Helene doing? Without CJ and Manar, they'd have to rely on Martin and whatever Olsen could provide for their digital needs. Was that enough to—

CJ was sent flying.

The blow had come from behind him without warning, launching him into the air. Fortunately, the enhanced shield absorbed most of the damage, so all he lost was a bit of energy. He landed several feet away, almost at the end of the passage, winded but unhurt. CJ scrambled to his feet to face his adversary.

It was … well, CJ wasn't sure what it was. It was humanoid, though most of it was hidden behind a voluminous robe. Its face was difficult to discern. They were separated by several feet, but CJ could still make out the code tapestry of the robe because it glowed. It was like a magician's cloak. The light was soft and radiant around each line of code as if showcasing each of them. But when CJ tried to read the lines, they blurred and twisted until they no longer made any sense.

He could see the code, but it was like it was encrypted, shielded from prying eyes. Including his, apparently.

It was the first time an antivirus had shown up on the first floor. Worse, CJ had never seen this kind of program before. Without more information, he couldn't begin to guess what sort of cybersecurity feature it represented.

CJ wanted that robe. He didn't know where the desire came from, but it didn't make it any less real. The sphere warmed, responding to his desire, and he straightened. *What am I doing? What am I doing? The safe thing would be to teleport out of there immediately.*

Just as the thought occurred, a pulse rippled out of the mage-like antivirus and spread throughout the hallway. The sphere lost its warmth. Shocked, CJ almost lost his head with panic before he realized that his shield was still active and the tendril of will that connected him to the orb hadn't been cut.

Whatever the antivirus had done had apparently cut the connection between the sphere and the core—or at least shielded it temporarily. CJ was willing to bet that it was the latter. CJ no longer had a navigation system. This also meant his teleportation would be too random to be reliable. Even if it broke whatever ability had been activated, it would take time to get back on track. And there was always a chance he'd find another one of these things wherever he ended up, sending him right back where he started.

He couldn't run away, so the solution was simple: he had to find a way to deactivate whatever the antivirus mage had done. In the process, he would take the cloak.

CJ sighed. He was a little worried about how calm he was. The terror was still there, but it had taken the back seat. He'd been afraid so much that now it wasn't something to focus on.

Was this how DJ felt? Had he just grown accustomed to fear?

No, that wasn't it. His brother might have felt fear early on, but that just made it more fun for him. CJ didn't feel any thrill here. A part of him felt like throwing up at the thought of confrontation, but he didn't have a choice.

As if mocking this thought, the walls beside the antivirus mage parted. Another antivirus stepped out. Unlike the first, this one didn't wear a robe. It didn't wear anything. This was what CJ was used to. The mage was the anomaly. The new antivirus was humanoid as well, a little taller than CJ, and wielding a spear. Two glowing eyes glared at him. CJ could almost feel the pride rippling off it. Strangely, it reminded him of Manar.

It was a different design, but CJ guessed that it served a similar function to the medicinal pills of the first website and the brutes from the second: to expel him. CJ still hadn't figured out what the mage's purpose was.

As the two stood side by side, CJ considered whether he'd been foolish not to run.

CJ sent a tendril of will to the sphere. "Listen—"

The mage didn't wait for him to finish speaking before making its move. Its arm lifted, still concealed within the robe, and flicked toward CJ. A projectile shot out of the cloak and sped toward him. CJ tried to dive out of the way, but his inexperience combined with the restrictive pressure limited it to an awkward belly flop.

The projectile struck him on the head … and nothing happened. No, that wasn't right. There was no force like he'd expected, but there was an effect. It was small, but CJ felt his shield drop in quality. It appeared to revert to its unenhanced version, as if part of its strength had been locked away behind a barrier. As if, it had been … encrypted.

So that's what it does, CJ realized.

In general, websites had several ways to defend themselves from foreign invaders. The most common were the firewalls, which CJ had dealt with several times in previous websites. But many websites also used encryption and multi-factor authentication. CJ hadn't encountered any of the last two in the previous website, probably because these defensive features were of a higher tier and the company no longer had the funds for the maintenance.

Another projectile struck him. Again, it caused no damage, but CJ felt another part of his shield drop as it was locked away. The first effect had been slight, but this one was more noticeable, as if they stacked on each other. That was dangerous.

The spear bearer stood motionless, seeming content to wait. CJ didn't have to be a genius to see their plan. Once the mage weakened CJ and disrupted his abilities, the spear bearer would swoop in for the kill. It was simple and efficient.

CJ sent a tendril of will into the sphere to confirm that his teleportation hadn't been affected; he still needed a way out if he had overestimated himself. Next, he focused on the tendril connected to the shield and sent more energy into it. The air around him flared as his aura pushed against it, nullifying everything for a good foot around him. Immediately, whatever encryption had been placed on the ability started to degrade as the nullification aura went to work.

CJ breathed a sigh of relief. Without a way to counter the mage's power, he would have been forced to defeat his enemies before all his abilities were sealed away.

His aura also worked on the sphere, eating away at whatever hid its connection with the core. Whatever the mage had done was stronger, though. CJ sensed it would take some time for the power to be dispelled. After that, he could be on his way.

CJ just had to last that long.

Unfortunately, the mage must have sensed that its power no longer had an effect, because the spear bearer made its move. It lunged for CJ, weapon readied, and easily cleared the distance between them. But CJ had been ready for that. A second before the spear reached him, CJ disappeared and reappeared in front of the mage. His nullification aura was redirected into his fist, enveloping it in energy. It was the only offensive ability he'd discovered, and he hadn't had a chance to test it.

Now seemed like a good time.

The blow was terrible—clumsy and uncoordinated. CJ didn't clench his fist hard enough, but it landed where it counted. The aura around his hand pulsed into the mage and wrecked it far more than CJ had expected.

It was easy to forget, considering how real everything seemed, but everything in the virtual world was a representation of something on the internet. On a website, that meant bots, programs, and coded features. Antiviruses like the mage—no matter how fantastical they looked—were nothing more than programs. CJ had already determined that his nullification aura tapped into a program's matrix and destabilized it enough to reduce its efficiency. He'd already seen what it did to a building. As a shield, it meant that every attack that passed through it weakened significantly. When used offensively, the aura messed with the program's code matrix directly.

The mage spasmed for a second before dropping to the floor like a hot potato. It hadn't been destroyed—more paralyzed while it rebooted. CJ didn't know how long it would last, but it removed the mental pressure that the mage represented.

Even if his aura countered the mage's ability, it cost energy, which would still put CJ at a disadvantage. Plus, the mage's ability stacked, meaning there was a set number of times he could be hit before his aura stopped working. That meant the mage had to be the first to go.

A moment later, CJ was sent flying once again. All the air rushed out of him, as well as a significant amount of energy. CJ rolled to a stop somewhere at the other end of the hallway. He tried to stand, but a burst of weakness forced him back to his knees. That had been a hard hit, and CJ had taken it without any protection. It was one of the drawbacks of his offensive ability. Since he focused his aura into his fist, there was none left to act as a shield.

Quickly he reactivated the shield. That cost another chunk of energy as well as another burst of weakness. CJ pushed past it as best he could and got to his feet. He was just in time. The spear bearer was running down the passage toward him.

CJ didn't know how to fight, even though his brother had tried to teach him on numerous occasions. CJ's aversion to violence and the difficulty of movement for those on the autism spectrum meant he'd never learned. His terrible punch had proven that.

When the antivirus thrust its spear at CJ, he had no other response than to throw himself to the ground. This allowed him to dodge the initial strike. However, the follow-up strike of the antivirus's knee slammed into his jaw and rattled his brain. Fortunately, the move had been awkward for both of them, so there wasn't much force to it. Whatever damage it would have done was absorbed by his shield.

Nevertheless, it left CJ belly-down on the ground, with the antivirus in front of him. This close, the spear should have been useless, but for some reason, CJ still didn't feel safe. He didn't know how much time he had, so he did the only thing he could: he grabbed its foot and held on as he sent a tendril of will into the sphere and activated his nullification aura.

The air distorted around him. A moment later, he could sense, rather than see, how the aura spread through the antivirus, jumping from code to code, erasing some and leaving others jumbled. CJ figured it was similar to what electricity did to nerves, except on a deeper level.

The antivirus spasmed and dropped. It didn't scream. CJ didn't know if that made it better or worse.

CJ turned the aura off once he couldn't feel it moving anymore. His legs had turned to jelly and barely responded to him, but CJ had experience with that. He forced his body into order with sheer will—and not a little terror—and stood.

The spear bearer's eyes no longer glowed, and it had lost its proud look. It hadn't been destroyed, but it had been disabled and wouldn't be getting up for a while. Its spear had fallen somewhere behind it. CJ picked it up with difficulty. It was over six feet long and unwieldy, but it was a weapon, and according to movies and his weapon-enthusiast brother, the spear was the easiest weapon to learn.

CJ dragged himself to where the mage lay, still paralyzed, though the effect was wearing off. He didn't have the energy for another strike, but he needed the mage disabled to use the sphere effectively.

That was why he'd grabbed the spear.

"You're not killing it," CJ told himself as he lifted the weapon over his head, "because it is not real. It's just a program. It can be rewritten."

He brought the spear down but stopped short. He couldn't do it. No matter how he phrased it, no matter how he told himself that it wasn't real, it felt like he was murdering someone. That wasn't something CJ ever wanted on his conscience. The violence he'd been exposed to over the last few weeks would certainly make its way to his nightmares when he returned to the real world. CJ couldn't add this to it, regardless of how "not real" the programs were.

It wasn't him, and CJ hoped it would never be.

He lowered himself to the ground beside the mage, leaning against the wall. He couldn't bring himself to kill the program, but he still needed it disabled. CJ could think of only one way to do that.

This is going to suck. He grimaced and gathered up all his remaining energy.

He dropped his shield and took several breaths while his energy regenerated. He didn't have long before the paralysis ended on the mage but still delayed, allowing his energy to refill as much as possible.

A minute passed. The mage was struggling to rise. Its paralysis had passed, but it had to reboot to regain its functionality, and something like that couldn't be rushed. CJ took another breath and then activated his nullification aura again. It was less powerful than normal, but CJ drew on his newly gained energy and directed as much of it as possible toward the ability. Next, he directed the aura into his first two fingers, like he'd done earlier with his fist. The air distorted around them, creating pressure waves that blasted against his face. That was an effect CJ hadn't expected.

The mage's struggles increased as it sensed the fluctuation of CJ's ability. CJ estimated there were only a few seconds until it was fully functional again. His energy drained rapidly, and his weakness returned with a vengeance. Still, he let the power build until he was almost tapped out. He directed everything to his first two fingers and condensed the aura until the distortion was barely perceptible.

A few seconds later, the mage started to rise, and CJ couldn't wait any longer. He thrust his fingers into the antivirus, releasing the power he'd built up. The aura rushed into the mage and shot it across the hallway.

CJ heard the crash of it hitting the far wall, but it grew distant as his vision turned black.

SEPTEMBER 2043
THE WAREHOUSE
NEW YORK CITY

KARLA STALKED THE HALLS of the warehouse, seething with every step. Her daggers, recently sharpened, gleamed as they spun around her fingers. It'd been ages since they'd bitten into flesh. Karla knew that they were getting antsy, but she'd been constrained to the warehouse and left to go slowly insane.

Piles of boxes stood around her, most of them empty and musty. She navigated them without thinking, stopping when her route dropped her in front of the makeshift clinic. It was just an area cleared of boxes, which the old man had taken for an office. Chloe had pilfered a bed from somewhere, and Karla had procured the equipment the old man had needed. Liz had been the first occupant of the clinic when he'd, following Chloe's orders, performed his experiments on her. Karla had also been subjected to the experiments.

Now, the only patient in the clinic was her father.

"You know," Chloe said, "staring won't make him wake up."

Karla suppressed her surprise. She hadn't heard Chloe approach. Sloppy. José would have scolded her for that. But her father was barely recognizable as himself and wouldn't be scolding anyone anytime soon, if the old man was to be believed. Karla had been more surprised at his supposed death than finding out that he was actually alive. Their father wasn't the type of man to die—especially for something so noble as saving his daughter's life.

Karla followed Chloe into the makeshift clinic, leaning against the wall while Chloe spoke to Martin. Liz was already there, standing by José's side. Her sister hadn't left the spot since their father had been recovered. Karla knew Liz had blamed herself for his supposed death, and since José hadn't been there to do it, she had punished herself.

It was how they'd trained: wrong deeds invited punishment. Karla had abandoned those teachings as soon as she became strong enough to stand. Liz had always taken them to heart.

Liz's self-inflicted punishment was the only reason Karla could fathom why her sister had volunteered to be Martin's lab rat and why she now stood beside their father like a patient dog. It was going too far, and it had created a distance between them that Karla did not know how to bridge.

"Any changes?" the brunette asked.

Martin leaned back in his wheelchair. His face was animated. His excitement made it seem like he had regained several years of his youth. All this from studying Helene's influence on their father. It made Karla sick.

"It's amazing," he said. "And I know I say this every time you ask, but it's incredible what Helene has achieved here. By all accounts, José should have been dead several times over."

"Yeah, yeah," Chloe said, a bit of frustration showing in her voice. "I've heard the spiel before. Are there any changes?"

Martin adjusted his glasses, something Karla had noticed he did when he was trying to explain something he might be harmed by. "Like every other time I've told you, there can be no changes if you want to keep José alive. Helene replaced all his organs with the same artificial augments I designed for Karla and Liz, then flooded his system with nanites and Hermione's picospores until the damage was fixed. I have no idea how she kept him alive while she did all this since, according to your report, the attack killed him immediately."

"I said I've heard the spiel before," Chloe said, her voice harder.

"What this means," the old man continued, adjusting his glasses once more, "is that he's going to be fully under Helene's control once more, the moment he wakes up. DJ's device temporarily broke the connection. Keeping him unconscious and in isolation keeps it broken. If we try to tamper with anything, he's going to die."

"And if I order you to tamper with it anyway?" Chloe asked.

Karla's expression didn't change, but her bloodlust raged until everyone in the room could feel it. The old man shivered and looked around in confusion. Chloe didn't even glance at her, nor did she take back her statement. The bitch.

"Even if I wanted to," Martin said, "I'm going to need time to study him. Helene's designs are different from mine. She took my designs and made them better somehow. I must understand them before I feel comfortable adjusting anything."

"If the problem is the nanites, can't you just remove them like you did the twins'?" Chloe asked.

"If the problem were just the nanites, I might be able to do that. However, there are the picospores to consider. These are primarily Hermione's field. Also, even with the nanites, the problem is not as simple as it was with the twins. I was the one who designed their prosthetics. I could calculate how many grams of nanites I could afford to remove without causing any long-term damage or degradation. In José's case, only Helene has those calculations."

"So you're useless then," Chloe said.

Martin sighed. "I just need more time."

Karla pushed off from the box while Chloe continued arguing pointlessly. The solution was clear to her: the old man needed more time. But Hermione would be needed at some point for her expertise. What was wrong with calling on her now? Heading to Sparta gave Karla an excuse to leave this godforsaken place. She had seen how well the two nerds worked together. With any luck, their cooperation might shorten José's recovery time.

She glanced at Liz as she left. Her sister's eyes were focused inward in thought. That was another reason why José had to wake up quickly. Maybe then she would have her sister back.

58

CJ WAS RATHER SURPRISED to regain consciousness. He'd half expected never to wake up. What he'd done was incredibly reckless, and brain damage might have been an appropriate reward for that. What the hell was he thinking? Had he even been thinking? He hadn't considered that the weakness from the energy drain might mess with his mind.

He groaned and took stock. He'd regained some energy, which told him he had been unconscious for a while, but he still wasn't fully topped up. This told him he hadn't been gone for too long. His mind was foggy, and he was still weak. Hopefully, both would pass as his energy regenerated.

The good news was that whatever seals the mage had placed on him were gone. The sphere was comfortably warm in its pouch, and CJ could once again sense a resonance in the distance. On a whim, he picked up the spear and made his way to the mage. He took a moment to study the antivirus before bending to pull off its cloak.

A part of him felt guilty, but he'd been drawn to the robe from the moment he'd seen it. He definitely wasn't going to leave it behind. The cloak came off after a minute of work, revealing a body that was small and childlike. It couldn't have been more than three feet tall and was as black as night. The mage's large glowing eyes stared at him. That increased CJ's guilt, but again, it wasn't enough to stop him from wrapping the cloak around himself.

That done, he turned and walked in the direction of the core. He didn't know how much time he'd wasted by being unconscious, so he couldn't afford to wait around. Still, his pace was slow so he could continue restoring his energy. While he walked, he thought back to the fight and tried to analyze what he could have done differently.

His altercation with the spear bearer had been clumsy and awkward. If not for his quick thinking, it could probably have ended up far worse. Part of it was because of CJ's inexperience with fights, but it had started to go downhill from the moment CJ focused too much on his victory with the mage and forgot about the second antivirus.

That single-minded focus was a flaw that CJ had observed previously. Now it had come to bite him in the ass once more. His lack of experience fighting wasn't something he could change in the short term, but he could at least work on his situational awareness.

Then there was his energy management. CJ had thought he'd worked on that, but he hadn't considered how much energy the nullification aura drained in actual combat. Fortunately, his last attack against the mage had proven there was a way for him to manage the amount of energy he put into each strike.

Time passed as CJ made his way through the website. He spent some effort trying to figure out the cloak to no avail. If it had a function, CJ couldn't activate it. A bit disappointing, but the cloak still looked cool.

He also spent some time studying the spear but couldn't find any way to activate it either. Still, the code matrix intrigued him. Obviously it had been designed as part of the antivirus. How had this part been created? What part of the code spawned the weapon? And why had every antivirus he'd met so far have different weapons? What decided that?

His study didn't uncover any answers. However, by asking the questions, CJ now had a direction.

He was attacked several more times, always by the same pair of antiviruses: a mage and a spear bearer. He tried to teleport away the first time, but the mage cut the connection between the sphere and the core. The website must have figured out the orb was the true threat and sought to block it. Regardless, it meant that CJ was forced to fight. It went just as well as his first altercation, leaving him drained and on the edge of passing out.

However, between the first and the second attack, while he made his way through the website, CJ discovered a way to change the shape of the spear. All he did was reduce the length, but that went a long way toward making it more portable.

The second time he was attacked—the third, if he counted the initial fiasco—CJ was better prepared. He used the spear to manage his energy. He didn't know the first thing about spears, but it didn't take much to point the sharp edge away from himself. When he paired it with his short-range teleportation, it was enough of a surprise to allow him to stagger and disorientate the mage in the first pass and disable it in the second. When he tried the same tactic on the spear bearer, the spear was batted out of his hands. He was once again forced to take the anti-virus's attacks while his nullification aura went to work.

CJ walked out of the fight better off than the others but still felt there was more that he could have done. He spent the next few minutes trying to figure that out.

In his next fight, CJ tried something he'd never done before: he teleported the antivirus along with himself. He expected more resistance, but the antivirus was surprised enough that it went easily. He took them both in front of the mage just as it was releasing an attack. His gamble paid off. The projectile hit the spear bearer in the back, paralyzing it for a few seconds.

Two punches later, CJ was on his way.

He used the next attack to practice the technique and get the timing down right. By the time he was attacked again, he managed to end the fight within the first minute.

That was when CJ came to a startling revelation: he wasn't afraid anymore.

Just a few weeks ago, CJ would have been terrified at the thought of a fight. A few hours earlier, he'd basically rushed into one because he was drawn to a cloak. When had that change happened? He'd become so used to pushing away his terror that he hadn't noticed it was gone. Even in the last couple of fights, the panic that usually filled him was no longer there. He'd grown so used to the violence that he'd used one of the attacks as nothing more than practice to refine his technique.

CJ didn't know how he felt about that. On one hand, it was good that he no longer lost his head in every fight. He'd since come to appreciate his quick thinking, as it was the only reason he was still alive. He no longer scrambled about, struggling to survive. But when he thought about how accustomed to fighting and violence he'd become, it felt like he'd lost a part of himself.

He'd seen what joining the navy had done to his brother, how paranoid and jaded he'd become. CJ wondered if the same thing would happen to him by the time all this was over. It was a worrisome thought.

The sphere warmed, and a part of the wall rippled and warped. The sphere had become powerful enough that he didn't even need to be on the lookout for backdoors. As soon as he got close to one, it was automatically revealed. No door appeared, but CJ had seen the warping enough times to realize it acted as a portal.

He stepped through and entered a tunnel. It was dark inside, lit by only the lines of code that swirled around the passage. Immediately, CJ felt the pressure. He had become used to it over the last few hours—at least enough to ignore it—but now it pulled to the forefront again. CJ sensed something different this time, a feeling that something was watching him. He glanced around. Nothing.

As usual, he spent several minutes studying the lines of code swirling around the tunnel before moving on. It was a short journey to the core chamber, with none of the confusing twists and turns he was used to. When he arrived at the chamber, however, he realized why.

In the middle of the room were what had to be guardians, though they were by far the weirdest ones he'd seen. CJ couldn't make out any of their features. Each wore a dark hooded cloak and had only blackness where their faces should be.

The guardians hovered a foot from the ground and gazed at him from the darkness of the hood. However, CJ didn't sense any hostility. Had they been holding scythes, he would have thought they were a pair of grim reapers.

Had that been intentional?

The tunnel continued behind them, but because of the sphere's small vibrations, CJ knew he was close.

"Authentication, please." The voice came from one of the reapers. CJ had no way of knowing which spoke.

The question, however, as well as the fact that the voice hadn't threatened him with destruction gave CJ a hint about what he was facing. He was unable to hide his excitement.

"Authentication, please," a voice said again. It could have been the same one, or it could have been the other one. CJ had no way of knowing.

"I don't have any authentication," CJ said, "but I can assure you that what I'm doing isn't going to harm the website in any way."

"Access denied," the two reapers intoned. One of them raised a hand, and a barrier popped into existence behind them, blocking off the path beyond. CJ quickly realized the barrier had always been there; he just hadn't been able to see it. Engraved into it was a sign that read, *Access Seal: Denied.*

The other reaper raised its hand, and ethereal chains shot out, wrapping around CJ too quickly for him to react. At the same time, CJ felt something settle on him. It was a seal, except it was vastly different from anything he'd experienced. The mages' seals had only weakened his abilities. This one cut him off from the abilities altogether. He could still connect to the sphere, but he couldn't sense anything beyond the ward.

The sphere vibrated once more, hard enough that it almost leaped from its pouch.

This is bad, CJ thought. His will battered against the wall, but to no avail. *I'm useless without the sphere.* His mind churned out ideas, but none of them were feasible. CJ didn't see a way out.

So he turned and ran. With enough distance, the reaper might not be able to maintain the seal on him. He didn't want to go far enough to run into other antiviruses, but—

CJ slammed into something invisible at the entrance to the tunnel. It wasn't a seal or a barrier. Rather, it seemed like the tunnel had rejected him. He turned back to the reapers. Had they created it?

This is bad, he thought again. The chains tightened around him and dragged him back in front of the reapers. He had no way to struggle. He'd never stopped battering away at the seal. Although it gave signs of breaking, it would take far too long.

For the first time, the reapers moved. They flowed toward each other, then superimposed, merging to become one. It was smooth. Despite himself, CJ stared in fascination. The merging lasted only a few seconds. Nevertheless, CJ could feel the power they exuded increase significantly afterward. As one, they raised a hand. CJ found the terror that he'd lost.

The sphere hadn't stopped vibrating, and now it reached a fever pitch. The pouch that CJ had found wasn't that deep, and the sphere finally fell out and plopped on the ground. All at once, the reapers stopped. Their gaze focused on the sphere, and they seemed to hesitate.

A moment later, the sign on the barrier changed. Where it had read *Denied* before, now it read *Unapplicable.*

The reapers separated, and the chains holding CJ down disappeared. Even the seal blocking his abilities was removed. CJ stared in confusion, then picked up the sphere once more. Holding on to it with two hands, he activated his nullification aura. He wasn't sure if it would do anything, but he felt safer with it activated.

That done, CJ was able to push away his terror once more. *What just happened?* The reapers looked as confused as him. They hesitated for several seconds. Eventually, they moved. However, this time it was to create an opening between them, revealing the tunnel beyond.

They're just … letting me through?

The sphere vibrated with impatience, forcing CJ to put away his questions. Whatever had happened, it'd occurred when the sphere had fallen out of his pouch. He stared up at the barrier, focusing on the last word of the sign: *Unapplicable.*

What did that even mean? If CJ hadn't already been insanely curious about the sphere, this would have been a good way to start the obsession.

The reapers didn't do anything when he passed them, though CJ kept his aura on full blast and a mental finger on the teleportation just in case. Neither was needed as he stepped into the tunnel without a problem.

CJ didn't breathe a sigh of relief until he was in front of the core. It hovered on top of a pedestal. An orb-shaped piece descended from the whole and merged with the sphere. Only then did CJ relax.

Apparently that was a moment too soon.

The sphere's power rocketed up until it filled the room. Shocked, CJ almost lost his balance. Usually the only reaction he got when adding a new piece was the added weight to the sphere and more lines of code to study. This time, however, the power that exuded from the orb was almost a physical force. Strangely, the core itself wasn't affected. Everything else, including CJ, was buffeted by the energy.

He was able to keep his hands on the sphere, but just barely. The energy grew and grew, until suddenly, it met something else.

CJ went pale.

Something focused on the power coming from the sphere and locked onto the website. There was a moment of quiet, and even the sphere seemed to lose its zeal, Then, the entire building shook. This time, CJ did lose his balance. The shaking increased, and he slid across the floor, unable to control himself. A hand reached out to the pedestal as he passed. Still, it was a temporary measure at best.

The burst of energy had acted as a beacon for Helene to follow. But what was she doing right now? It felt like a giant hand was trying to open the building like a can of sardines.

The shaking finally stopped, but CJ didn't release the pedestal yet. He couldn't believe Helene would give up that easily.

A second later, he was proven right. An overwhelming force descended on the building. CJ was wrenched from the pedestal and slammed into the ground with enough force that he actually lost some energy. The pressure was all-consuming. It threatened to crush CJ where he lay. Chunks rained down around him as the building broke apart.

CJ activated the zone. It was the only ability he'd never activated while inside a website. Part of it was because each zone was affixed to a spot, and CJ hadn't yet figured out how to make it mobile, making its use limited. However, the main reason was that he didn't know how the ability would affect the website.

Outside, it repelled avatars and other programs from the vicinity. What would it do to the programs within a website, especially those that were essential to maintain its integrity? It was a question he'd never wanted to risk getting answered.

But he had to now. If the building was going to get destroyed anyway, it wasn't as if he could make it worse.

The zone helped with the pressure, but only when he combined it with the nullification aura could he stand and move about freely. Better than that: his aura had spread to a circle around him. The pressure it gave off had reached a whole new level. CJ didn't think he needed the zone to move. But he left it on just in case it helped with Helene.

Most of the ceiling was gone by this point. CJ could make out clouds in the distance. He tried to teleport. Nothing happened. He could sense the ability still present within the sphere; he just couldn't activate it.

Without any other option, he crossed the distance back to the tunnel, dodging falling pieces of code as he did. He'd watched a website be taken down with fascination from the outside, but there was none of that now. It was all he could do to keep moving even though every instinct screamed at him to find a nice hole to crawl into and wait it out.

How did his brother make this seem so easy?

CJ reached the chamber where he'd met the multifactor authentication system. It was nowhere to be found.

She would have targeted the major systems first, CJ thought absently, *to lower the website's integrity.*

The wall warped when he reached the end of the next hall, and CJ stepped out into the actual website. The sphere no longer sent any feedback. He had to find his way back with no navigation while avoiding falling debris.

CJ made it halfway out before the whole thing collapsed and the ground gave out from under him. He fell into the blackness, clutching the sphere for dear life.

333

DJ SPENT A FEW HOURS in his room, then decided he needed to work out his aggression. That had become his default lately, and something else that he would have to work on. He'd always prided himself on meeting nearly any situation with a smile, so he couldn't allow things like that trainwreck of a meeting to get him riled up.

The annoying part was that DJ understood where Ndidi and Hermione were coming from. Helene was a ridiculously advanced AI. Manar had done an annoyingly good job when he created her. Of course, there would be benefits if she could be used for good. It was extremely unlikely, but given a few centuries, the benefits might even be enough to wipe away all the shit she'd done. The issue was keeping her restrained for those centuries. Was it only DJ who considered that? Helene was an AI; she wasn't going to change, and she would never go against her directives. Right now, her directive was to screw them all over. Even if they *somehow* found a way to capture her, her very nature would force her to look for ways to escape.

And then they would be screwed all over again.

Why don't they see that? DJ sighed. He missed the days when all he had to worry about was what to punch. Back then, Manar was the one to deal with bullshit like this. He would probably have to speak to Ndidi at some point and talk her out of this before she did something else they'd have to save her ass from. Better yet, he could talk to Hermione and have her talk to Ndidi. That wasn't a bitch move, was it? Of course not! It was just him avoiding a confrontation that could cause a divide in the team. It was being a leader.

DJ nodded to himself. He'd work out some of his aggression at the gym and then go do some damage control with Hermione. He hefted the duffle bag where he kept his spare towel over his shoulder. He hadn't been to the gym since Chloe and Pratima had fought. It was doubtful that he could get a good sparring partner among the nerds. Hopefully one of the guards would be there so he could get a good workout. If not, he'd settle for a hard punching bag, something he could pound.

"If you search for prey," someone whispered in his ear, "let me join in."

"Motherf—" DJ jumped and spun around, his hand reaching for a gun that wasn't there. That was sloppy, but he hadn't expected to get jumped on his way to the fucking gym.

Karla Polova's face smirked at him. Wait … smirked? That wasn't right. Karla didn't smirk. She growled. She seethed. She didn't smirk. That would mean she was amused. DJ looked behind her, searching for Liz. He wasn't sure he'd ever seen them apart.

And then he registered what she'd said. *Prey? Does she … does she think I'm going to murder someone? And it amuses her? Of all the fucked up …*

DJ took two steps back. Karla watched him, still smirking. It was weird. Like always, she was wearing her skintight jumpsuit.

Speaking of something to pound …

A dagger was at his throat the next moment, and the smirk was gone from Karla's face. "Remove that look from your eyes, or it shall be removed for you."

The look or my eyes? DJ wondered. He took another step back, and Karla let him.

"I'm sorry," he said, rubbing his throat. No blood. She really must have been in a good mood. "It's been a weird day."

Karla sheathed her dagger. "Is that why you are looking to murder someone?"

Jesus, is that how I look? DJ winced. "I'm pissed, but I'm not going to kill anyone. I'm going to the gym to work it out like a functioning adult."

"I prefer the alternative," Karla said.

"Why are *you* here?" DJ asked, ignoring the comment.

"I need to retrieve Hermione for the old man. Helene's influence on José is difficult to understand. He requires her expertise."

Martin's stuck, and he needs Hermione, DJ translated.

"Point me to her location," Karla commanded.

DJ started to, but then a thought occurred to him. Now that Karla was here, maybe he wouldn't need to settle for a punching bag. To date, DJ hadn't been able to make contact in any of their fights. But he'd also never been so motivated to land a punch as right now.

"In a minute," DJ said. "First, I need a sparring partner."

Karla scoffed. "I do not have time for that. Play with yourself."

Wow, DJ thought. *Who the hell says that with a straight face?*

DJ waggled a finger in her face, ignoring how weird that felt. "Ah, ah, ah. Chloe said you're supposed to be my mentor. Well, I require mentoring in the form of a spar."

Karla's eyes narrowed dangerously, and she fingered the dagger at her waist. "Truly?"

DJ wondered if he'd fucked up and thought about backing out. But then the memory of the morning's meeting flashed in his mind, and he was reminded why he wanted the spar in the first place. He might very well die for blackmailing Karla, but he would at least get a punch in.

"Yep," he said, plastering a grin on his face. "Let's go."

CHAPTER

SEPTEMBER 2043
THE VIRTUAL WORLD

CJ AWOKE to a world of darkness.

He regained consciousness with a jerk, adrenaline rushing through his veins. He looked around, but there was nothing to see, as if someone had switched off the night light at the end of the day.

A dim silver light suffused the area, making visibility possible but difficult. He could barely make out a few feet in any direction, and only if he focused. The light also gave the place a somewhat ominous air, which didn't help any.

What happened? CJ thought. *How did I get here?*

Memories flooded back in, doing nothing to help his panic. Few things would have. CJ's head shot up, but there was no sign of the clouds in the sky. Not that he would be able to see them in this darkness. Still, he couldn't feel the pressure. He had to assume it hadn't followed him here ... wherever *here* was.

The website collapsed, and everything was erased. CJ pushed himself to his feet, looking around. *Is this like the internet's version of a trash can?* It would explain the darkness, but it wouldn't explain why everything was empty.

As far as he could make out, there was nothing: no buildings, roads, or avatars. Not even the rubble that should have accompanied him from the website's collapse.

The sphere was a comfortable weight on him, and CJ placed a hand on it. He took several steps forward and then back. Wherever he was, he'd survived the transition, which was the most important part. He didn't even feel any weakness, which meant if he had taken any damage, he'd rested enough for it not to matter.

His examination brought to his attention the sense in his mind. His connection with Manar had always been there, like a line stretching off to the horizon. CJ had grown used to it over the last few months, so he didn't give it much attention unless particularly strong feedback came through, probably when Manar was feeling a strong emotion. Through the connection, he could always point to where Manar was. Although the direction changed sometimes, the distance remained constant.

Until now.

Manar's here, CJ thought. He wasn't close, exactly, but far less distant than he'd ever been. Would Manar be able to sense CJ as well? Even if he could, he would have no way of knowing it was CJ he was sensing.

Still, if Manar was here, he would have more information. And it was past time CJ met up with him anyway. With the sphere completed, he would have started making his way here eventually. If anything, Helene had given him a ride.

That's one way to look at her almost killing me. CJ chuckled to himself. He activated the zone and was relieved when it worked. He hadn't been sure it would. Ripples spread out for a mile in every direction. This was much wider and farther than the previous record. CJ focused on his connection with the ability and merged his senses with it. He'd practiced this several times since he'd discovered it, but he still had problems adjusting to the different perspectives. Even so, at times like this, the ability was priceless.

CJ's vision broadened. Suddenly he was everywhere within a square mile. Most of it was desolate. The sensory input still took a moment to adjust to, but it helped when he focused on the direction from which he could sense Manar.

He didn't find anything, but that only meant the zone didn't extend that far. CJ simply had to keep checking until he found where he was.

He left the zone activated and settled in for a hike.

KARLA SNEERED AT DJ from the other side of the ring, deftly twirling her daggers. DJ forced his eyes to stay on hers, even as his body reminded him of what those daggers could do. From past experience, he knew that if he allowed himself to get distracted by them, Karla would start the match early. DJ wasn't ready for that yet.

They'd gathered quite a crowd. Most of them had been drawn to watch because of Karla's outfit, others because they picked up on her bloodlust and wanted to see what she could do. Liz could hide her skill easily enough, as could Chloe—though the danger was clear to see in their eyes. But Karla never bothered to hide her lethality. It was in the way she walked, how she seemed to be stalking prey with every step. The grace in her movements contrasted the primal nature of her fighting style—hell, of her entire personality.

DJ found it sort of hot.

Most of the guys in the crowd were part of the Sparta security team. If he hadn't run into Karla, he would have roped one of them into being his partner for his workout. Now they were going to see him get his ass kicked.

"Same rules?" DJ asked.

Karla bared her teeth. "No. Since you wish for me to mentor you, I will do so with my full strength."

Damn.

The rules had forced Karla to restrict her strength and speed from supernatural to merely Olympic levels. If he wasn't killed by a stray punch, it gave him a chance—however small—to actually best her. Since DJ wasn't armed with his pistols, he needed all the help he could get.

Karla sheathed her daggers. That was something, at least. It meant he wasn't going to get stabbed to death.

"Prepare yourself," she warned.

DJ was not prepared. Why had he pissed her off and forced the fight? Did he have a death wish? DJ suppressed the panic, instead filling his mind with memories of that day's meeting. Of Ndidi's expression as she asked him to bend over and present his ass to Helene. Of CJ on the hospital bed, tubes sticking out of him because of Ndidi's betrayal.

Rage blinded him for a moment. DJ let the anger suffuse but not overwhelm him. He was left in a sort of trance. Nothing existed outside the ring. It was only him and Karla. And by God, he was going to pound her to the ground.

He didn't know how Karla knew he was ready. Maybe she was just tired of waiting. Suddenly she was launching herself at him. Despite what she'd said, DJ noticed that she slowed herself down. It was slight, but it was enough that she wasn't a blur to him. DJ blocked her opening punch easily, though the force almost took him to his knees. His arm didn't shatter, which meant she'd reduced her strength as well.

So, she decided not to kill me. That was good. But the thought was a distraction that he couldn't afford.

DJ countered, slipping beneath her guard for a body check and using the momentum of her lunge to draw her into the hit. If nothing else, he still had a weight advantage. If he could get her in a pin, he had her.

Karla's fist—the one still pressed against his forearm—opened and gripped his arm like a vise. A moment later, she was using him as leverage to twist in midair, evading his attack. Without a pause, DJ flowed into his next move, bringing his other arm up for a punch. One of the main things he and Karla had worked on during training was his martial arts. He'd already been taught how to fight at the navy base. Karla had taken those skills and evolved them. Now DJ used it against her.

Of course, in the end, he was just the student. She was the master.

Somehow, Karla twisted away again. This time DJ didn't even see how she did it. The moment her feet hit the ground behind him, DJ knew he'd lost. He'd had a chance while she was in midair because of how difficult it was to navigate. If he was forced to trade blows with her on even ground, he was fucked.

Karla attacked like a wild animal. She was a beast clawing at his face, scratching at his legs, and pouncing on him. She came at him from every angle, and DJ was forced to be on the back foot, focused entirely on defending as best he could. The fact that he actually *could* defend was something he would marvel at later. Every blow hit like a truck, but somehow DJ wasn't flattened by them.

Was she toying with him?

The thought stoked his anger. He'd asked to spar so he could punch something, but so far, he was the one covered in bruises. He didn't want to defend. He wanted to attack, to hit something and feel bones crushed under his fist.

All at once, DJ stopped defending. She was already pulling her punches, meaning she wouldn't kill him. DJ could deal with a little pain. His resolve was tested when Karla's strike took him in the chest. Unlike before, he hadn't deflected. The force took him clear across the ring. He felt his ribs crack, but again, he wasn't dead.

So he stood up and rushed her, crossing the distance in a few strides.

This time he was the one attacking, and she was forced to dodge. DJ channeled every technique he'd ever learned and put all his energy into every strike, just to hit a little faster, a little harder. But Karla was the wind. She seemed to know his goal was to punch her, so she evaded instead of deflecting and countered only when DJ couldn't pay her back. All the while, she sneered at him. Mocking him.

She wasn't trying to help him. She'd already proven she had no loyalty to him or their cause. No one on the Murder Team did. The only reason they'd joined was because Helene had screwed them over, too, and left them without resources. Now that José was back and Manar was comatose, they had no reason to stay. They would leave and probably stab everyone in the back in the process.

Why wouldn't they? If people he trusted could betray him, then why wouldn't the Murder Team?

Karla evaded another punch. DJ felt a growl build up in his throat. He needed to be faster, to be stronger, to be *better*. He forced his fists to fly faster, to hit harder. The wind parted at his every move, buffeting him. On any other day, that would have been awesome, but now DJ didn't give a fuck. He just wanted to reach Karla, to knock that sneer off her face. And he could, if only he were *faster*.

His body responded, drawing strength from somewhere it never had before. His speed increased exponentially, and DJ saw the surprise on her face as she realized she wouldn't be able to dodge. She tried to bring her hand up to block, but DJ's fist was going too fast.

It took her in the jaw.

Karla's head snapped to the left, and bone crunched under DJ's fist. He hesitated for a moment as his shock temporarily overcame his anger. That was all the time Karla needed to recover. Her head snapped back, and her eyes burned into DJ's.

And then his world went black.

MANAR'S HEAD SHOT UP, breaking his concentration. It also snapped the strands of energy he'd been holding in his mental grip. He stopped himself from cursing. Although his control had improved markedly over the past few weeks, any sudden movement was still enough to break his focus. The illusion he'd placed around him shattered, revealing the dark web in all its glory.

With the illusion gone, the avatars started invading his personal space once more. He still couldn't interact with them, making it easy for them to walk too close to—or sometimes over—him when he wasn't moving. The street wasn't the best place to practice his abilities, but Manar hadn't found any alternative. The illusion had worked to keep the avatars away, but it was still a work in progress, as his recent failure showed.

Manar didn't allow himself to dwell on that. Instead, he tried to determine exactly what had pulled him away from his work.

Is it that again? he wondered, looking off into the distance.

For the last several weeks, Manar had become aware of something out there. A well of power, a beacon that called to him. It had occurred only twice, but both times it had taken all Manar's willpower not to rush in that direction. The draw aside, his curiosity was killing him. And it didn't help that the beacon was in the same direction as his other sense: the one he'd been willfully ignoring since he discovered it.

The beacon hadn't been what had drawn his attention. Rather, it was the sense he'd been ignoring. *It's closer,* he realized with surprise. Whenever he'd prodded at it, it had felt far away, which was why he'd ignored it for so long. Now, however, it was close enough that Manar was sure it was in the dark web as well. He hadn't even noticed it moving. How had it gone so far so fast?

His expression flickered. It was getting closer. He'd always wondered if whatever was on the other side of the connection could sense him as well. It might have been a coincidence that it was heading in his direction, but it was unlikely considering the size of the dark web and the disorientation of experiencing the wasteland for the first time. The creature somehow knew there was a town here, or it knew he was here.

Manar stood with a grunt. He didn't need to grunt; he'd already experimented with the limits of his body. He surpassed most expert bodybuilders, and that was without Gaius's enhancements. But after several years of aches accompanying each movement, grunting was a habit he couldn't shake off, no matter how hard he tried.

Manar began walking toward the signal. It was easier now that he didn't have to worry about what was an illusion and what wasn't. That had proven an interesting challenge, as Helene had constantly changed her tricks as soon as he found a way to counter them. Recently, though, she hadn't bothered with any illusions, leaving Manar to believe he'd finally countered them all and she'd moved on. That had been the unofficial permission he'd needed to start step 3 and focus more on step 4: creating his own illusions and experimenting with his other abilities.

Both would have to wait, though. With the connection so close, Manar could no longer keep his curiosity in check.

He left the area with the buildings and passed through the market stalls. The attendants stared at him with barely concealed hostility. He'd made several trips down to practice his skills. None of them spoke. They couldn't until Manar approached them directly.

Within a few minutes, he'd gone past the unofficial borders of the town and was in the wasteland proper. The barren land stretched out in front of him. Manar hadn't stepped foot out here since he'd found the town, but things were different now. He knew exactly where he was headed, though he didn't know what he would find when he got there.

No sense in just walking, he thought, tapping the ball of energy in his chest. Slowly, he extended it to the tip of his fingers and then beyond that, merging it with the world.

Manar's mind expanded, and his control of the energy flickered. Manar had expected that, so he retained his mental grip on the threads. His pace slowed as he was forced to split his mind. But it was still marked progress. When he'd started this, he hadn't been able to move at all.

Everything within a square mile opened to him. The world appeared as a series of ones and zeros, everything from the rocks to the empty air in front of him. It formed a tapestry that was far more complex than any of the buildings. The sight humbled him every time. Manar had always thought of himself as the quintessential programmer—for good reason. But when he looked at the world through this lens, he realized he hadn't even scraped the surface.

Manar could feel himself improving the more he studied the tapestry. It had formed the bulk of his training. So far, all he could do was observe—and even that was limited by his energy reserves. Nevertheless, Manar could sense he was close to something, a resonance that was beyond his grasp. When he reached it, he wouldn't be limited to just observing the tapestry; he would be able to change it.

Helene could already do it. His illusions were proof that he could too. He just needed time.

Manar lost track of how much time passed while he walked. Several times, he was forced out of his data-sight when his energy ran out. But he kept practicing. Eventually, he realized that he was very close to whatever he'd sensed. At the same time, something entered his field.

It was a person. They appeared as a series of ones and zeros, of course. But the figure was a *person*.

In surprise, he loosened his grip on the ability for a moment. He had expected an AI or a bot. But this was a *person*. Or, at least, an avatar of a person.

The person seemed to notice him, too, because they hesitated for a moment before speeding up. For some reason, when Manar looked at them, he got the feeling they were looking at him too.

Manar's curiosity blazed like a bonfire. None of the avatars he'd seen so far had been able to detect him. It was like he didn't exist to them. The only ways he'd found to interact with them was through hacking or using his illusions to keep them away.

And yet here was one that not only had a connection to him but actually noticed him using his data-sight. He studied the code that made up the avatar. Nothing stood out. The sequence was exactly the same as every other he'd analyzed, except …

Is that a spear? Manar thought. Something was obviously different about this one.

It was proof that his data-sight wasn't infallible, which was disappointing. But if anything, it intrigued him more. He briefly considered that it was another trick from Helene, but that was highly unlikely. Manar had had this sense from the moment he materialized in the world. If she'd planned that far ahead, they were truly doomed.

Manar didn't pick up his pace. That would've broken him out of his data-sight, and he would no longer have been able to observe the person. Still, at the pace they were moving, it didn't take long until they were close enough to see each other.

Manar frowned, then sighed.

Is it possible that Helene is able to create illusions I can't see through? His gut said no, but why else would he be looking at CJ? Helene hadn't even attempted to change the visage. It was the same thing that he'd chased for several days before realizing she was messing with him. Did she think he would fall for the same thing again?

With a grimace, he turned to leave.

"Manar? Wait!"

Manar froze at the voice. The illusions normally didn't speak.

Guess Helene put more effort into this than I thought. He chuckled wryly to himself. He turned back, once again intrigued.

Eventually, the avatar reached him. It stopped a foot away, suddenly hesitant and nervous. Manar would have believed it was truly CJ if that weren't impossible. He let the mental threads dissipate but held on to the energy just in case. With his data-sight gone, it was easier for Manar to study the avatar with his actual eyes.

The avatar bore his scrutiny without a word.

Manar felt his frustration build. There was nothing different about the avatar. It looked like a video game character, just like everything else in the virtual world. Even Manar hadn't been able to change that about his appearance.

Finally, Manar couldn't hold in his irritation any longer. "What do you want?"

The avatar looked taken aback by his tone, but he composed himself remarkably fast and spoke with convincing determination. "I'm here to help you take down Helene."

That, Manar hadn't expected. He turned on his data-sight to scan it again. Nothing. Manar's irritation grew. "And I'm just supposed to believe that?"

Now the avatar looked confused. "Why wouldn't you? Why else would I be here?"

"That's what I want to know." Manar was getting confused now. This wasn't an illusion. He refused to believe that Helene could make one so realistic that he couldn't see through it. More likely, she'd enlisted the help of a user and sent it to Manar.

The avatar looked even more confused by his reply.

"Look, I don't know what Helene promised you—"

"What are you talking about?" the avatar cut him off. They spoke slowly, as if choosing each word with careful deliberation. Perhaps they were reading from a script. Or maybe they were just trying to avoid a miscommunication. The cautious part of Manar wanted to believe that it was the former, but the latter seemed more like the real CJ.

"Helene did not promise me anything. I am pretty sure she tried to kill me, actually, but I somehow ended up here."

Now Manar was really confused. Helene had tried to kill them? Why? He shook his head. Why was he even considering this? It was obviously a trap. He knew he should leave, and he almost did, but a part of him—the insanely curious part that had brought him here in the first place—wanted to learn more.

"Start from the beginning."

The avatar tilted their head. Its brows furrowed, as if trying to solve a puzzle. It stared into space and seemed to forget that Manar was right next to it. Everything about it was so like CJ that Manar felt his doubts slipping.

Shit, he thought.

A few seconds later, the avatar focused on Manar, its expression solemn. "You do not trust me."

It was a statement. Manar didn't bother to refute it.

"I should have considered that, especially if you materialized close to Helene. I'm CJ, and I can prove it."

"How?"

WHEN DJ CAME TO, he was on the ground, staring up at Karla's seething face. It took him a second to recognize the gym ceiling, and then another for his memories to return. Unfortunately, sensation returned to his body at the same time, becoming aware of the ball of pain that was his head.

She knocked me out, he realized. There were the first signs of a bruise on her cheek. *But I punched her first.* DJ's lips pulled into a grin. Shit, he'd actually done it.

Karla saw his grin, and her lips pulled back into a snarl. Her hand reached for something at her side. DJ lost his smile quickly.

"You will show me where Hermione is, and then both of you will follow me to the warehouse," Karla told him. Her tone brooked no objections.

So, obviously, DJ objected.

"Why?" he asked as he pushed himself up. The room spun, and he closed his eyes to keep from throwing up. She really didn't pull that last punch, did she?

Karla gripped his wrist and started pulling him, forcing him to open his eyes. He was able to keep his balance, though it took all his concentration because the room refused to remain still. He nearly missed all the glances thrown at him by every other person in the gym.

"Which way?" Karla asked once they were in the hallway.

DJ wanted to argue again, but then he thought better of it. Wordlessly, he pointed in a direction and started walking before she could pull him.

The fog was starting to clear, and DJ cringed at the memories. *What the hell got into me? I wanted to feel bones crush under my fingers? Of all the …*

Each memory made him want to hide away in embarrassment. What the fuck had he been on? He'd started the fight angry, sure, but relatively clear-headed. Then, somehow, he'd devolved into a damn berserker.

Where the hell had he pulled all that energy from? The fight was shorter than it'd seemed in the moment—barely five minutes—but he'd gone full throttle throughout. How had he not run himself ragged? Where the hell had that last burst of speed come from?

The fact that Karla had easily knocked him out at the end meant that he'd been right, and she'd reduced her speed to toy with him. It wasn't the first time she'd done that, yet DJ had never come close to touching her, not even with bullets. Now, suddenly, he was slugging her in the jaw. Why? Because he wanted it enough? What the fuck?

They found Hermione in her lab. She was reluctant to leave, but there wasn't anything urgent enough to make her stay. She'd finished extracting the picospores from the ex-hostages, meaning DJ could finally set them free.

Bethany was standing to the side of the room. Her gaze was no longer distant, instead observing them intently. There was a scowl on her face, and her eyes were puffy. Hermione was very obviously trying not to stare in her direction, suggesting to DJ that she was reluctant to leave her sister.

Still, Karla could not be denied—especially not when it seemed like she would kill the next person who looked at her the wrong way.

CJ SHOULD HAVE considered this. Why hadn't he?

He hadn't had a chance to customize his avatar to match his real-world appearance closely. He'd expected Manar to be surprised, but not suspicious. He should have thought of that and planned ahead.

Even if Manar hadn't known about CJ's presence in the virtual world, Helene most likely had from the start. It stood to reason that she would have done something to discredit CJ before he met up with Manar.

Manar studied him intently, and CJ used the time to study him back. Manar had customized his appearance, though not enough to make him a stranger. It was weird looking at him and seeing someone so young. But no matter how young his body looked, his eyes were still the same: unfathomable knowledge mixed with weariness. Now those eyes were looking into CJ with suspicion and skepticism. It was all he could do to maintain their gaze and not fight back.

CJ wondered if he should look away. In the real world, he wouldn't have been able to meet Manar's eyes directly. Would Manar notice the difference? Would it further his suspicions that CJ was an impostor?

A part of CJ—a stronger part than he'd expected—resisted that. He'd lived his whole life bowing to the whims of his symptoms. He wasn't going to do that now—not when, for the first time, he didn't need to.

But that still left proving to Manar that he was who he said he was.

Normally, there were a lot of things that CJ could say to prove his identity. However, the problem was Helene. Whatever CJ said had to be something Helene had no way of knowing. Helene had proven again and again that her information-gathering skills were not to be underestimated. When Sparta had refused to stop using her despite Manar's warnings, he had just locked her out of every place the team frequented, like the conference room and Manar's office. Manar had confided in the team then, so CJ's proof could come from their conversations there.

CJ could kill two birds with one stone.

"DJ and I retrieved the neural uplink for you from one of Sparta's other branches. You'd started it and abandoned it but saw its potential to get us here, the virtual world. You put me in charge of upgrading Gaius, as you planned on merging with it to give you an edge once you got here."

CJ took a breath. He'd been so nervous when Manar had entrusted him with Gaius. Those days had been some of the most stressful days of his life. They'd also been the most fun. Manar's lessons had opened his mind in a way that years of practice hadn't been able to. The experience was second only to the one he'd gotten from wandering through the virtual world so far.

CJ went on to detail the process of how the neural uplink worked. It had been explained to him by Manar himself. He recounted how Manar had successfully merged with Gaius and transported his consciousness. He tried to be as detailed as possible, stumbling only when he spoke about the kiss between Manar and Ndidi.

Apart from a slight tightening of his lips, Manar didn't show any reaction. "None of this explains why you're here."

"There was a problem after your transmission," CJ said. "I'm not sure what it was or what caused it, but you wouldn't have been able to return to your body. Since half of the plan hinged on being able to communicate with us so we could work together … " He trailed off, suddenly uncertain.

Fortunately, Manar picked up the rest. "Since I wouldn't be able to return, I'd be stuck on my own to deal with Helene," he said. CJ nodded. "And so you piggybacked on my connection and came here to help me, even though you'd also be trapped here indefinitely."

Again, CJ nodded. "You shouldn't have to face Helene alone."

Manar stared, his expression indiscernible. CJ tried not to sweat.

"Well, that was stupid," Manar said eventually. He sighed, pinching the bridge of his nose. "It was an unnecessary risk that almost backfired. I was convinced you were a spy sent by Helene. The only thing that kept me here was that I couldn't figure out how she roped in a rogue avatar. I haven't been able to interact with any of them."

"So you believe me?"

"It's either that or admit I have no shot at outsmarting Helene," Manar replied. "Your story is too convincing. Most of it happened in places she shouldn't be able to spy on. If you are a spy, I should just throw in the towel now."

CJ gave a wry chuckle.

Manar's face turned pensive. "Have you been able to communicate with anyone on the outside?" CJ shook his head. Manar nodded grimly. "Well, now that you're here, we should discuss some things. Put together what we know and what we've found out."

KARLA BROKE INTO A RUN the moment they left the building and didn't realize DJ and Hermione weren't following for several minutes. DJ thought for a moment that she was going to carve into his face—it didn't even matter that they were in the middle of the street. But what the hell was he supposed to do? He might have been able to keep up, but Hermione definitely couldn't.

Why the hell was she in such a hurry anyway?

They reached the warehouse eventually, though most of the way Karla was driving DJ insane with her grumbles about their pace. They navigated the piles of boxes as Karla led them deeper into the warehouse. Soon they reached an open space that had been turned into a clinic. There was a hospital bed, a heart monitor, some surgical equipment, and even several blood bags.

José was as fucked up as the last time DJ had seen him. Two beds had been pushed together to be big enough to hold his robot body. Even so, he looked like a grown man sleeping in a kid's bed. Liz stood at his bedside. She glanced at them as they walked in but gave no other reaction. Chloe and Martin were deep in conversation but stopped when the trio walked in.

DJ waved. Karla walked to Martin, stopping when her face was inches from his.

"What did you do?" she snarled.

Martin looked understandably confused, as did everyone besides Liz, who seemed to be in her own world, and José, who probably was.

Martin cleared his throat, glancing around for help. "What did I do?"

"What are you talking about?" Chloe asked.

Karla pointed from DJ to the bruise on her jaw. "He struck me."

Chloe raised a brow in a rare show of genuine surprise. Even Liz looked over, though her expression showed nothing.

DJ adopted an innocent expression, struggling like mad to keep the grin off his face. "What Karla is forgetting to mention is that she was holding back so she could toy with me. It was a fluke."

Chloe aimed her raised eyebrow at Karla.

"I reduced my strength so that I would not kill him," Karla growled, "and my speed as well. But he still should not have been able to touch me. And yet he did."

Chloe turned to DJ. "What you don't understand is that Karla has been training her whole life. Even if she was fighting at your level of speed and strength—which she wasn't—you shouldn't have had a chance in hell of touching her clothes, much less actually connecting a punch. Frankly, I'm surprised she didn't outright kill you."

"She damn near did," DJ complained, rubbing the back of his head. "Almost broke my skull."

Karla turned to Martin again. "What did you do?"

The old man looked supremely uncomfortable. He leaned as far back in his seat as he could and adjusted his glasses.

"Hey! What're you getting up in his face for?" DJ asked. "Why do you think he did anything? Like I said, it was a fluke."

"Karla doesn't allow for flukes." Chloe was also staring at Martin. Then, she turned that look on DJ.

"Uh …" DJ tried to meet Martin's eyes. Obviously his burst of strength had come from the nanites the old man had given him. Although Martin hadn't told DJ to keep it a secret, from the way Karla and Chloe were taking it, it seemed like something that should be kept under wraps. "I have no idea. I still don't understand why it couldn't have been a fluke."

"Do you know the last time someone other than me or José got the drop on one of the twins?" Chloe asked.

DJ shrugged.

"Neither do I. It's been at least a decade. The girls have been forced to fight each other for years because no one else is a match for them. And that was *before* they got the nanites and their prosthetics."

"That can't be right," DJ said. "Ndidi floored Liz a few years ago at the Sparta data bank."

"You're right," Chloe agreed, "but that was when the girls were still getting used to their new bodies and before the nanites went to work enhancing them. Now they've had years to acclimate and let the nanites do their job. How well do you think Ndidi would fare now?"

Martin intervened with a defeated sigh. "I gave DJ the nanites that I extracted from the twins."

Chloe raised a brow, though she didn't look surprised. "Now, who asked you to do that?" Her hands went to her side, and DJ stepped forward. He didn't know what the hell he would do if Chloe attacked, but he couldn't just stand by if she tried to hurt the old man.

Martin sat up straight, meeting Chloe's eyes. "I didn't realize I needed permission. They were *my* work, after all."

"They were your work, but they were not your property," replied Chloe. "They were for the twins, and you stole them."

Karla did not like that. Her dagger was in her hands immediately, but she looked conflicted about who to stab, Martin or DJ. DJ gave her an easy target, stepping between her and Martin. He raised his hands, plastering on his most disarming grin.

"No need to get violent, ladies," he said. "If you want the nanites back, I'm sure we can work something out—you know, without you gutting me or a helpless old man."

Chloe sighed. "Leave them. It wasn't like we had any better options for the nanites anyway."

"So we should ignore their theft?" Karla spat.

"Not necessarily." Chloe smirked, giving DJ a look that made him very uncomfortable. "We just need to find a way for him to repay us."

Fuck me, DJ though. *All this because I punched her once?*

"Before you guys get into that," Hermione said, drawing everyone's eyes to her. "Can someone tell me why I'm here?"

66

MANAR LED THEM BACK across the wasteland as CJ went over everything he'd been through since he'd materialized. The zone was still activated, allowing CJ to navigate through the darkness without issue. Manar didn't seem bothered by the darkness either. Maybe he'd become used to it in his time here, or he had his own way of navigating it.

CJ had to skim over some of the stories, including those of his days of aimless wandering. Manar was silent for most of it, only interjecting to ask questions or get clarification.

"And that's where you got the spear and the cloak?" Manar asked when CJ was done.

CJ looked down in surprise. He'd forgotten that he was still holding the spear. He was so used to it being in his hand it'd started feeling natural.

"Well, it sounds like you had a more eventful time than I did," Manar continued. "Most of my time was spent pointlessly walking while Helene screwed with my head."

CJ didn't know what to say to that. A part of him felt guilty that Manar had to face that alone, but it was easy to suppress that part. He'd made the right decision by gathering pieces of the sphere.

"What I'm most curious about is this sphere," Manar said. "Can I see it?"

CJ hesitated. The sphere had quickly become his most prized possession, something that CJ hadn't been away from since he got it. For so long, his survival had been dependent on keeping the sphere as close as possible. To voluntarily give it away, even if it was to Manar and even if it was temporary …

He pushed back the hesitation, annoyed with himself. This was *Manar*. He took the sphere from its pouch and handed it over. To his credit, Manar didn't comment on his initial hesitation and instead studied the orb intently.

"Do you know what it is?" he asked softly.

CJ nodded. "It changes slightly after every merge, but the first sphere had the same codes as the first virtual assistant Sparta developed, the one before Helene. I'm not sure why that allows it the abilities it has though."

"It's because it isn't Sparta's code. It's ASCII." Manar turned the orb over in his hands. "The American Standard Code for Information Interchange. It provides a standardized way to represent characters and symbols using numeric codes. Years ago, it was so widespread that it became a fundamental part of computing. It forms the basis of text file formats, communication protocols, programming languages, and basically everything else that has to do with software development. It's evolved since then, but the essence hasn't changed. It's the foundation of modern programming, Most codes are built on it. It's integrated into most computer systems, networks, and yes, websites."

"But Sparta—"

"Like every other company in the world back then, Sparta used ASCII when creating their first virtual assistant. That's why you mistook one for the other. It probably didn't help that the code was incomplete when you first got it." Manar handed the sphere back. "Check it now."

CJ studied the orb. Because of the storm, this was the first time he'd done so since he'd gotten the last piece. Each new piece changed the code slightly but not in any way that was too far off. That wasn't the case now.

The completed code sequence was completely different from what it had been. CJ turned the sphere around and traced the sequence with his eyes, but no matter how he tried, he couldn't make sense of it. The sequence itself wasn't complicated, but it was deep in a way he'd never encountered before. CJ sensed layers beneath layers, each one deceptively simple to parse until he tried to view them together. That was when his head started to hurt.

"You should probably stop that," Manar warned. "The ASCII is probably the reason why the sphere can affect the world the way it does. It's basically part of the world itself."

CJ pried his eyes away from the sphere with effort. With just a conversation, he'd solved the mystery that had haunted him almost since he materialized in the world. The answers sent him reeling, as did the implications. If Manar was right and the sphere was basically part of the world, then CJ had been significantly misusing it.

"That's probably why Helene wants it so much," he mused.

Manar's head snapped to him. "What?"

CJ met his confused look with one of his own until he realized he'd glossed over the part about the clouds since he wasn't sure it had actually been Helene. He quickly explained the past week, with the clouds and the presence that he sensed within them.

Manar frowned. "And here I thought she'd just run out of tricks."

They reached a worn-out path that served as a road. Beyond it was an arrangement of stalls similar to a farmers' market. However, these shops looked like they were a breeze away from toppling over. The road passed through the middle of the market. Manar led them through.

Something's different, CJ thought, narrowing his eyes at Manar's back. He couldn't put a finger on what, but something had changed in Manar. His gait was more confident. There was none of the weariness he usually wore on his face. It was subtle, but the effect was staggering. CJ had always seen Manar as an academic like Ndidi and himself. He'd always exuded pride, but it had been muted. Now that soft nature was gone, replaced by a towering aura of arrogance.

CJ opened his mouth to ask why and then noticed the stares. He frowned. Attendants at every stall were glaring at them, several with open hostility. Most of the anger was directed at Manar, but CJ still got his fair share.

"Uh, Manar?" CJ said.

Manar looked back and followed CJ's eyes. "Oh, don't worry about them," he said. Despite the casual tone, he was projecting his voice so everyone could hear. "They don't like me much."

"Why?"

"I mean, this *is* the dark web." Manar scratched his jaw and nodded toward a stall. "That's a website for an arms dealership. That one is a front for human trafficking, and the one beside it? They deal with child pornography. If the denizens don't like me, I'm taking it as a good thing."

CJ stared at the stalls in horror. When Manar had said they were in the dark web, it hadn't really hit him—probably because he'd said it so matter-of-factly. But now? Fortunately, a thought occurred to him before his terror could take root.

"Wait, how can they interact with you at all? I've not been able to interact with any avatars since I got here."

"Ah, it's because they *aren't* avatars," Manar replied as they took a turn down a different street. "They're bots. The real users don't come out until you actually enter the site and show intent to do business."

CJ nodded. "Why do they hate you?"

For the first time, Manar looked a bit sheepish. "Well, the nanites told me Helene was here. But I had no way to find her and no idea where to start looking. I needed information, so I picked a stall at random and tried to get information from the bots. Obviously, I got nowhere, but my behavior was suspicious enough that it attracted the actual user, who tried to hack me to find out who I was."

Manar paused while an avatar passed by. CJ's eyes followed it. The ones he was used to weren't so … bulked up.

"The hack failed, obviously," Manar continued, "which convinced the user that I was backed by a powerful organization. I had no reason to dissuade him of the notion. Around the same time, I realized that since Gaius was an AI, I should be able to hack into the man's avatar myself." He shrugged. "So I did. Easily. Apparently, all I need is a touch."

CJ filled in the rest. "Since you can hack into them, you have your way of getting information with or without their consent. And even if you didn't get anything about Helene, now you have leverage on each of their businesses."

Manar looked back at him, his eyes twinkling. "Exactly. They tried to blacklist me, but obviously, that can't be enforced since they can't stop me from getting into their site. Plus, while they have nothing on me, they know that if they push too hard, I can do some real damage."

That's brilliant! He's basically blackmailing the entire dark web without lifting a finger. The fact that Manar could hack into avatars and bots was impressive. That was one of the first things CJ had tried when experimenting with the sphere, but he hadn't had any luck.

"What were you able to find out about Helene?" CJ asked. They turned onto another street. CJ had long since lost his way, but Manar didn't seem to have any problems navigating.

"Most of the bots aren't really aware of what goes on in the virtual world, and the users are similarly unaware, so I couldn't find much. Most of it is not about what Helene's doing here, but about what she's doing in the real world."

"So what *is* she doing in the real world?"

"By all accounts, she's building a bomb," Manar said casually.

CJ's eyes widened. "What?"

HERMIONE'S QUESTION BROKE the tension in the room, which was what she had been going for. If she'd known it would work so well, she would have spoken sooner, like when Karla had pulled out her daggers. She still didn't believe Karla had actually planned to harm Martin. Who the hell would do that?

DJ used the distraction to escape. A smart move, given the way Chloe had been smirking at him. Hermione couldn't imagine the sort of favor she had in mind, but she was very glad she was not DJ at that moment. Karla stalked out a moment later, as did Chloe, though she spared a parting glance at the figure on the bed.

José Olvera.

Hermione had heard the details of the previous raid from DJ, as well as the description of José's state. She'd held a mental image from DJ's description:

Think Terminator meets Robocop but in a grossly exaggerated way. Seeing it was a whole different matter. It'd taken Hermione a few seconds to understand what she was looking at.

Martin shifted in his chair, drawing Hermione from her thoughts. He greeted her with a wide smile, as if he hadn't just been threatened at knife point. That he treated it so casually spoke a lot about his experience living here. It also explained why he always deflected when Hermione asked. Maybe she should talk to DJ about it.

"It's always good to see you, my dear," Martin called, waving her closer. "Come, come. It's been ages."

Hermione crossed the few steps to the bed, answering his smile with one of her own. Only when she was close did she notice Liz standing at the other side of the bed, wreathed in shadows. Hermione almost jumped but caught herself. Had Liz been standing there all along? She hadn't made a sound; not even her breathing was audible.

Are all of them like this? Hermione wondered.

At that moment, Liz glanced at her, intense, yet still distant and cold. Hermione got her answer. Liz faced forward once more, immersing herself in her thoughts.

Martin briefed Hermione on José's condition and the problems he was having. Hermione tried to ignore Liz's presence. It was more difficult than she expected—especially when Martin had to show Hermione certain parts of José's body to explain better. She could feel Liz's gaze burning into her neck.

As Martin finished briefing her, and she actually got into her own analysis, she slipped into her work trance and pushed her discomfort—and its cause—to the back of her mind. Hermione went through Martin's notes and compared them with the data she could read from the equipment he provided, slowly getting a better picture of the situation. Time slipped by as she immersed herself in the data.

It was nice while it lasted. Eventually, thoughts of Bethany bubbled up from where she'd suppressed them. She couldn't help it. Hermione had known going in that it was going to be a difficult conversation, but she'd assumed the problem would be convincing DJ, not her own sister. She understood that Bethany wanted nothing to do with Helene, but to go back to the way she was before? When she had symptoms, she could barely speak and couldn't control her body well enough to smile.

Hermione kept replaying the words in her mind, trying to understand them, to see from her sister's perspective. This, of course, had made her basically useless the rest of the day—which she'd hoped she could avoid by coming to the warehouse. Fat load of good that had done!

"You seem distracted," Martin commented after a while.

"I'm sorry," Hermione replied. "I shouldn't be, but I have a lot on my mind. It makes it hard to focus."

"Do you want to talk about it?"

"I shouldn't burden you."

"Please." Martin chuckled. "You could never be a burden, dear."

68

MANAR LET CJ STAY in his head for a while. They went down several streets and through the occasional alley. Manar didn't say anything, giving CJ time to assimilate the information. He'd revealed the bomb so casually just for the drama.

Maybe DJ's rubbing off on me, Manar thought. Usually he preferred to be on his own, but after three months, anyone would be starved for some human interaction. Not that Manar would ever admit that out loud.

He glanced at CJ again. They should have already reached the buildings where Manar was staying, but he'd decided to take a roundabout way while they talked. The buildings—even as dilapidated as they were—were firmly within Helene's range. Manar couldn't be certain his data-sight would be enough to keep Helene from listening in on their conversation once they arrived. It was a quirk he'd discovered by accident. Once his sight was activated, it created an area around him, over which he had full control. That was the only reason he could create his illusions at all. He basically shaped the reality around him to reflect what he wanted. He assumed Helene did something similar, no doubt on a larger scale.

So far, he'd had to stagger his use of it to avoid depleting his stamina. It was much more difficult to do while holding a conversation, but it had done wonders for improving his mental control. Now and then he could sense that he was closer to the resonance that had been beyond his grasp.

"How is she taking over the dark web?" CJ asked quietly.

Manar jumped. He'd forgotten CJ was there. He quickly explained what he'd learned from the users about a mysterious organization taking over established businesses and the limitations put on the weapons.

CJ's brow furrowed. "But that doesn't make any sense. Why would Helene bother with that?"

"That's the billion-dollar question." Manar sighed. "Obviously we're missing a lot of information. There's no way to fill in the blanks from here, so we have to figure out a way to communicate with the others and return to our bodies."

"I've been thinking about that, but I'm not sure it's possible."

"Of course it is," Manar said, "we just need more options. And with you here, we have a much better chance of getting those options."

"What do you mean?"

They reached the end of one path and turned onto another. Several dozen buildings were scattered haphazardly along the street. Each looked on the verge of crumbling, but they were far better than the stalls. Manar gave CJ a minute to take it in.

"Each building is a representation of a site that exists in real life ... but you already know that." Manar pointed to a rocket-shaped structure. "That one's our target."

"Is that where the nanites are leading you?"

Manar shook his head. "No. The nanites led me here and then became useless. Helene must have found out and broken the connection. The fact that she went after you miles away and I didn't sense anything proves it."

CJ tilted his head. "So, what's so important about that building?"

"It's one of the sites Helene's taken over."

"And you want to know what she's doing with it and why."

Manar snapped his fingers. "Exactly. I've already tried to go in myself, but every website on the dark web was built with security in mind, meaning their defenses are no joke. I can hack into the website itself, but I'm near comatose while I'm doing it."

"Which is where I come in," CJ said with a nod of understanding.

Manar stared at him, hesitating. His memories of the first time he'd gone in were not pleasant. He hadn't been able to go far, but even those few steps were met with significant opposition. And then the terror set in, and everything spiraled from there.

But Manar had been new to his abilities then. He'd just seen what his hacking could do, and he'd ridden that high until it almost got him killed. Now, Manar had spent the last few months exploring everything he was able to do and discovering new things. He'd planned on trying the site again in a few days. While he was confident he could handle it by himself, his chances would increase exponentially with CJ there.

Still, Manar felt guilty for asking. That wasn't the kind of place you'd bring a child. But by CJ's own admission, he'd faced similar odds while completing his sphere. Although Manar still saw CJ as a child, he'd proven time and again that he was not.

I'm justifying, Manar lamented. He was about to take back everything when CJ spoke.

"I'm in."

"What?" Manar asked, shocked.

"I'm in," CJ repeated. There was fear in his expression, but it was overshadowed by determination. For the first time, Manar looked at CJ—really *looked.*

Manar would never have called CJ naive. Nevertheless, the passivity brought on by a childhood spent struggling with autism, combined with his brother's attempts to shield him from the worst of the world, lent a certain innocence that followed him even into adulthood. It was subtle, but it made CJ seem younger than his age and stature would imply. It made people see him as, if not a child, then at least someone to be protected.

There was so little of that innocence left now. Manar needed more details about what had happened while he and CJ were separated.

"You're right," CJ continued. "Learning whatever we can about Helene's plan is important, even if it's dangerous. And I want to help. That's why I came here in the first place."

Manar stared at him for a moment. Then, with a nod, he said, "All right, then."

"WOULD YOU CARE TO TALK about it?" Martin asked as he opened a compartment in José's body.

"I shouldn't burden you." Hermione shook her head.

"Please." Martin chuckled. "You could never be a burden, dear."

Hermione thought about that for a second. Did she want to talk about it? She'd done nothing but think about it all day. Talking might help. Plus she had to know if she was in the wrong here. She could talk to Ndidi, but things had been strained between them since her rescue. Ndidi was shouldering a significant amount of guilt over what she'd done, but Hermione didn't know how to help. DJ's reactions certainly hadn't. He had reason to be angry, but it was frustrating to see the rift in their friendship. It was what Helene wanted, and they were falling right into it.

Hermione didn't realize when she started talking, but once she did, she couldn't stop. Martin already knew what Ndidi had done, so Hermione glossed over that part and focused on the meeting that had instigated Ndidi's arguments and Bethany's reaction.

When she'd finished, Martin nodded sagely and chose his words carefully.

"Regardless of whether you can understand or not, your sister has made her choice. You have to respect that." He leaned back in his chair, meeting Hermione's eyes, which she suddenly realized were filled with tears. When had that happened? "A part of growing older is learning to let go and allow the younger generations to make their own choices."

"But she's wrong," Hermione insisted. "I can't imagine what Helene put her through over the last few years. It's probably why she's rejecting the spores. But she just needs to bear with it for a few months until I figure out exactly what Helene did to improve them. Then I can make another set for her and—"

Martin placed a hand on hers. "It's not your decision, Hermione. It doesn't matter if you think she's wrong. Bethany is a grown woman, and you have to respect her choice."

Hermione shook her head. "But she's letting her trauma get in the way of what's good for her! How could I live with myself if I let her suffer because of Helene?"

"Hermione—"

"I can change her mind. I can do it. She just needs time to realize what she'd be giving up. What she's going back to. I just need to talk to her."

Hermione saw the disappointment in Martin's eyes, but she was resolute. She couldn't let Bethany make a mistake she would regret for the rest of her life—not when she had already failed her for so long.

Hermione held Martin's gaze until he sighed and looked away, picking up the pad he'd been analyzing. He didn't say anything else, allowing her to make her own choice.

Something about that rubbed Hermione the wrong way.

FOR MOST OF HIS LIFE, the bulk of Manar's childhood memories had been suppressed. It was a self-defense mechanism to deal with the trauma of having his entire family murdered in front of him. That trauma went on to manifest as schizophrenia, which joined with his suppressed memories to plague him with the voices of his dead mother and sister—though he hadn't known it was them.

The whole situation had culminated with him subconsciously programming Helene to be a power-seeking tyrant, resulting in the mess they were in.

Manar had recovered most of his memories three years ago during a mental breakdown of epic proportions. For the first few months after, he'd avoided those memories. They were alien to him. The people, the places—even that weak version of himself. Manar hated it all. So he'd avoided them—until he remembered what happened the last time. After that, Manar had spent several months thoroughly reviewing each moment of his life from before he'd met Simone.

He was certain that in none of them—except for maybe the memory about the day his parents had been killed—had he willingly done something reckless and stupid.

Manar stared at the crumbling building in front of them. CJ was beside him, his face a mask of determination. That determination had been there for the last few days and had only slipped into a childlike awe and excitement when Manar showed him his abilities. That was something that Manar had insisted on. Neither he nor CJ was comfortable with combat, but both were incredibly analytical. Regardless of their abilities, that was their strength. They would have to lean on that once they went in.

They couldn't create a rigid plan since they didn't know what they would encounter in the building. Consequently, their survival would hinge on how well they could adapt to every situation. If they were familiar with each other's abilities, they had a better chance of succeeding—or at least making it out alive.

Still, Manar would have liked some guarantees.

"Are you certain your sphere won't be able to lead us when we enter?" he asked.

CJ shook his head. "It helped me find pieces of itself, but it hasn't reacted like that since I completed the sequence. I *might* be able to get it to work, but I'd be more comfortable if we didn't rely on it."

"It's Plan B, anyway," Manar said, sighing. They'd had the conversation before, and he hadn't expected anything to change. However, having some way to navigate would help ensure that they weren't just giving themselves up to Helene.

All right. Enough of that, he snapped at himself.

Manar drew from the well of power in the center of his chest, allowing Gaius's energy to flow through him. Strength filled him as his body eagerly drank the energy, and Manar felt his nerves and doubts fade away.

There were no physical changes aside from a faint blue glow in his eyes, but Manar felt that there should have been. There should be something to show how powerful he was. With his strength, how could they fail? No matter the defenses the building might have, Manar could crush them. Was there even a point in CJ coming along? He should—

"Manar?"

Manar blinked, coming back to himself. That had been close. He was out of breath, even though this virtual body didn't get tired or need air. *Too close,* he thought with a sigh. He'd almost made the same mistake as last time. Gaius's energy was intoxicating. It went straight to his head, giving him an inflated sense of his own abilities. The last time, he'd ridden the high and almost gotten himself killed. Since then, whenever he tapped into the energy, he directed it outwards, either to hack or to activate one of his other abilities.

What had he been thinking this time? If it hadn't been for CJ—

"Are you all right?" CJ asked.

Manar took a deep breath, shaking off his thought. If nothing else, his nerves were gone. "I'm fine. Just got lost in my head for a bit. Are you ready?"

CJ nodded and patted the pouch he'd found for the sphere. CJ's other hand clenched his spear. The air around him rippled as he activated his shield.

The building loomed in front of them. Manar stepped through the entrance, CJ following a moment later.

Manar felt the familiar resistance of walking into this instance—a separate space to conduct business. According to CJ, on the regular web, instances were only available in specific areas of the website. Here, it was used as the first measure of security. Whatever happened inside the instance had no bearing on the website itself.

The instance placed them in the middle of a shopping mall, with lines of shops on either side that extended into the distance. Some shops displayed weapons, others drugs, and others pictures of scantily dressed women. The pictures weren't clear enough to telegraph the ages of the girls, but Manar had his suspicions. Attendants peered at them from each store.

Breaking in would be their first challenge—or at least, it should have been.

Manar shifted into his data-sight, and the world turned into a tapestry of ones and zeros. His senses stretched, but not as far as he expected. The instance seemed to go on endlessly, yet the only parts they could interact with were the shops in their line of sight. If he and CJ tried to go to one of the shops farther back, they would probably hit a wall. The same thing would happen if they somehow found a way to fly upward. They were basically inside a bubble. Manar could see the walls of the bubble, though everything beyond it was blocked somehow. He didn't need to see that, though—at least not yet.

He scanned the instance with his data-sight, looking for …

There, he thought. At the edge of the bubble was a sequence that didn't quite fit in with the rest. He wasn't actually reading each individual code in the sequence; Manar didn't think his mind could handle that. Rather, he got snippets and impressions that provided meaning to everything he saw.

Manar pointed out the place to CJ, and they made their way there.

The attendants glared at them, but none dared to step out of their stalls. Manar doubted they had permission, even if they wanted to. From the perspective of the real world, all Manar and CJ were doing was navigating the interface. They hadn't done anything to harm the website yet.

At Manar's direction, CJ placed a palm on the weak spot Manar had noticed in the bubble. The codes around CJ flared, as if he were stuck in the middle of a windstorm. Manar could even feel a distinct pressure just by standing next to him. The effect on the bubble, however, was more pronounced.

It was amazing to watch. CJ's aura nullified the barrier wherever it touched, and the effect spread until a hole had formed. When Manar pointed it out to him, CJ condensed his aura into his hands, grabbed the edges of the hole, and pried it open until they could make out the interior of the website, outside the bubble.

The website's detection system picked up on the intrusion, and an alarm rang throughout the building. Manar and CJ quickly stepped through the hole and into the building proper. So far, everything had gone according to plan. However, from now on out, they'd be winging it.

The interior of the building was modeled after a castle, complete with tapestries and banners hanging from the walls and flagstone floors that seemed authentically aged. Manar even spotted a gargoyle at the end of a hallway. It would have been cool, if the alarm weren't so deafeningly loud.

Manar scowled and tapped the ball of energy in his chest. In response, the energy surged out in a wave, covering the hallway. It ran over the walls, overwhelming and disrupting whatever digital system was watching them. Blessedly, the alarm stopped. The effect was only temporary, but offered a few precious minutes in which Helene couldn't detect them.

"That's handy," CJ muttered.

"Handy?"

"I had no way of doing that when I broke into websites, so I had to deal with the loud noise until I got used to it."

Manar started to respond, but CJ had already moved on and was scanning the hallway where they stood, brows furrowed. "It's different."

"Different?"

"The websites never follow the same layout," CJ explained, "but they generally follow the same theme as the section they're in. Since I haven't really had the chance to explore, I've been trying to figure out what district of the dark web this is." He gestured to the hallway. "I thought this would help, but it's different. I can't imagine what theme this is."

"There aren't really any districts here," Manar said. He'd already heard about the Red Light District from CJ. "Unlike the regular web, there's only a finite number of things sold here, and no one cares enough to organize things like that. But I do agree it's weird—even by dark web standards."

They made their way down the passage in silence. Manar turned off his data-sight to conserve energy and noticed CJ switch back to his simple shield. That reminded Manar of his new cloak. He glanced down at himself with a small smile. It really did look good on him.

CJ hadn't been able to activate the cloak using the sphere, but Manar had been able to hack into it easily. Once they found that out, it was only logical for Manar to keep it. Manar had noticed CJ glancing at it despondently from time to time. He figured CJ had formed an attachment from the battle he'd gone through to get it. CJ would get over it.

By itself, the cloak's function was limited to basic shielding and making the wearer harder to detect. But Manar had been able to augment its abilities somewhat. Still, he wasn't yet adept with it, and it consumed far too much energy for him to leave it activated perpetually.

The hallway was empty until they got to the end, where it branched in two directions. The paths looked the same, offering no clue as to which would lead them to their goal. Manar saw the beginnings of a maze and sighed.

"Anything?" he asked.

CJ concentrated on the sphere for a moment before shaking his head. "It's not responding. Can you do a hack from here?"

It was Manar's turn to shake his head. He'd considered it back when they broke out of the instance. "If I tried it now, Helene would shut me down before I got anywhere. The closer we are to the core, the more effective it'll be."

"We'll have to find another way to navigate, then."

Manar stared at the two branches for a moment longer before heading down the left one. It didn't matter which direction he picked as long as he kept to it consistently. If it led to a dead end, he would simply turn around and go the other way. CJ followed without a word.

Not long after, they came across their first door. It was simple and wooden—no ominous decorations. A bar ran along its length. Manar gave it a quick scan with his data-sight, but unsurprisingly, he felt the same block that had limited his vision back in the instance.

CJ reached for the bar. Manar reached out to stop him but noticed ripples in the air around him. CJ had coated his arms with his aura, so there was nothing the door could do to harm him.

Manar chuckled inwardly. He really needed to stop thinking of the boy as, well, a boy.

The door opened to reveal their first opponents. There were dozens of them, filling up the entire room. The creatures were humanoid and had long, floppy ears, overly large eyes, and scales dotting their bodies. None of them were taller than Manar's waist. They might have been cute if those eyes weren't glaring at CJ and Manar so ferociously. Some of the creatures were snarling, showing mouthfuls of sharp, saw-like teeth. They held shields but had no other weapons.

As one, they took a step forward.

CJ closed the door and replaced the bar. A moment later, there was a loud bang. The door bulged as if a great weight was pressing on it. Manar leaned his shoulder against the wood and heaved.

"Should we run?" CJ asked, joining him against the door. His voice was surprisingly calm, though his fingers trembled around his spear.

"We would already be running if I thought we were faster than they are," Manar replied. "As it stands, running would only allow them to swarm us."

"We could teleport," CJ suggested.

Manar raised a brow. "You said that without a way to navigate, it would essentially be random."

CJ grimaced, as if that fact had escaped him, but nodded.

"Then it's best not to risk it," Manar continued, ignoring another bang from the other side of the door. "We knew we had to deal with the site's security measures eventually. At least now we have an idea of what we're up against."

As much as Manar would have liked to defeat the first foe they came across, attempting to win against the swarm would be stupid. They had to find a way to escape. And Manar had a plan for that.

CJ nodded slowly, staring at a point at the ground, his eyes distant. Ordinarily, Manar would have allowed him to finish his thought process so they could share ideas, but the door was bulging considerably now, despite their weight pressing against it. They were running out of time.

CJ eyes focused once more. "We should get our backs against the wall."

Manar looked down the passage; he'd already considered that. "I have an idea."

As one, they pushed away from the door and ran down the hallway until they reached a branch. Instead of turning, they hugged the wall. Manar activated his data-sight. The world shifted into binary, and Manar's eyes frantically examined the sequences, taking in impressions and translations until he found what he was looking for. Working quickly, he reached up and brushed against one of the codes.

A few feet away, the door banged again. It wouldn't hold much longer.

CJ glanced at Manar but didn't say anything. To him, it probably looked like Manar was just reaching into the air, but CJ was smart enough and knew enough about his abilities to guess his plan.

The code resisted Manar's touch on the first and second tries. Manar was forced to tap deeper into his energy. Finally, it responded to his touch, and the touch traveled to every other code in the sequence via their connection. Despite how much he'd practiced this, Manar's control was rudimentary and rigid. But it should be enough. Manar toggled his sight so half of it was his normal vision while the other was still his data-sight. It gave him a massive headache, but it was necessary.

Manar tapped deeper into his energy and redirected the data flow to cover both himself and CJ. If he'd done it well, the flow would be indistinguishable from the wall—an illusion that hid them from sight.

Focusing on his data-sight now, Manar again reached to touch a code sequence that represented the actual wall on which they rested. The code resisted his manipulation even more than the other one had. It was a wall, and it wanted to remain a wall. And walls didn't move. Manar clamped his will down on it. He didn't need the whole thing—just a part of it. It would still be a wall, just different. Unique.

At that, the wall folded beneath his fingers. Following Manar's instructions, it covered both him and CJ, leaving only a thin slit for them to see through. It was shoddy work and created quite an obvious bulge, but that was why he'd placed the illusion first: to smooth everything out.

The door broke apart, and the creatures flooded the hallway.

THE PASSAGE WAS FILLED with agitated chattering as the creatures crawled along its length, searching for CJ and Manar. Their shields clanked against the floor and each other, adding to the cacophony. Manar could make out bits of their words and tried to piece together what they were saying.

"Service denied," they chattered. "Service denied."

It was just the two words repeated over and over. It gave Manar an idea of exactly what security service they were dealing with. Not that it helped much. He tried to keep his breathing even and steady, though he wanted nothing more than to slump against the wall as exhaustion thrummed through every part of him. He hadn't expected his abilities to take so much out of him. Still, his fear kept him upright and his breathing quiet.

Several times, the creatures sniffed around their hiding spot, and Manar thought his heart would leap out of his chest. Fortunately, the cover held, and they remained undiscovered. Manar tried to glance at CJ to see how he was handling it, but there wasn't room enough to even turn his head. It was something to note the next time he did this.

Next time? Manar chuckled grimly. He wanted to refuse the idea that there would be a next time. However, no matter how he thought about it, the probability was high. They couldn't fight every foe, and like now, sometimes they might not be able to run away. They would have to hide.

It took several minutes for the creatures to give up their search. They went back through the doorway, chattering all the while. When the last one was in, the pieces of the door that had been shattered flowed back together, refitting until the door was whole once more. The last piece was the long bar, which thudded into place. That was probably one of the site's restore tools in action.

When the danger passed, Manar released his hold on the code sequence and the website's version control system went to work on reversing the changes he'd made. First, his illusion vanished as the sequence there was smoothed out. Then the wall returned to its original shape. Soon CJ and Manar were left standing in an empty passage.

Manar flicked invisible specks from his clothes while he tried to calm himself. "Well, that was eventful, if a bit anticlimactic, wouldn't you say?"

CJ didn't respond. He was staring at the wall, a hand hovering over his sphere. Manar figured he was trying to see if he could do the same thing Manar had.

Manar had a few ideas about that, but there was no time to dwell on it. He gave CJ a few seconds more before making his way down the passage again. CJ followed him a moment later. Manar gave the wooden door a wary look as they passed. It had been perfectly restored, with no sign of the hell that was on the other side.

They reached the end of the path without incident. Once again, Manar took the left passage. Both of them were on their guard, listening for the slightest sound. The entire building creeped out Manar, who still felt exhausted from his work. He would be able to do it again if the situation demanded it, but it was better to avoid dangers entirely.

After a few minutes of nothing happening, Manar started to relax enough for conversation. "What do you think those things were?"

CJ jerked, as if startled, causing Manar to raise a brow. "What?"

Manar gestured backward, toward the passage they'd just left. "The swarm. What do you think they were? Or, at least, what'd they represent?"

"Oh," CJ said. "DDoS protection. I'm not sure if you could make out their words, but they kept chattering about it."

Distributed denial of service protection. Manar had been able to make out their words, and he'd come to the same conclusion. It made sense that CJ would know. Website security had been one of his duties at the navy base, if Manar remembered correctly. "Did you encounter them on the web?"

CJ shook his head. "Every website I entered was on the verge of shutting down except for the last one. DDoSes are a relatively advanced security protocol. I'm still trying to understand why they attacked us. They're supposed to be used as safeguards against traffic attacks, not a pair of invaders.``

"They didn't attack us," Manar pointed out. "We opened them up, remember? Before we opened the door, there was no sign that they were on the other side, meaning they weren't aggressive."

CJ's brows went up in realization. Manar still wasn't used to seeing his face so … active. Even his speech was better. There was none of the stuttering that his condition had forced on him. It had taken Manar only two seconds to realize that CJ's virtual body was the reason he wasn't showing any of his usual symptoms, although CJ hadn't brought it up himself.

Manar considered for a moment before his curiosity won out. "Have you figured out what you're going to do?"

CJ glanced at him, absently switching the spear from one hand to another. "What I'm going to do?"

"When we return to the real world, to our bodies. Have you decided what you're going to do?"

CJ lost all his expression. His face became totally neutral, as if he were suddenly on the autism spectrum again. Manar felt guilty for asking, but his curiosity won out again. Manar had started to see CJ as an apprentice. He'd proven himself to be consistently smart, analytical, and reliable. He had a good grasp of programming and enough room to grow. Manar felt almost responsible for him.

And this was something CJ had to consider at some point. If they weren't killed here, then they would eventually return to their own bodies. CJ would regain his symptoms—he had to know that. Shying away from it wasn't logical.

CJ SHOULD HAVE SEEN this coming. Obviously Manar would have noticed his lack of symptoms, but he hadn't brought it up while they'd been training, so CJ had figured he'd just dismissed it. So why was he bringing it up now? Just to make conversation? No, Manar wasn't the type of person to make idle conversation.

The pause had gone on for too long.

"I haven't thought about it yet," CJ said.

And he actually hadn't. He knew what would happen when they defeated Helene and returned, but his mind always shied away from the topic. That might have been why he hadn't put serious effort into finding a way to return to their bodies. A part of him didn't want to.

Manar sighed. "I know it's hard to consider. I cannot imagine what you must be going through."

"It isn't all that hard to imagine," CJ said softly. "I feel wonderful."

Manar didn't say anything, so CJ continued.

"For most of my life, I haven't felt in control. Of anything. It's hard to when my own body rejects me at every turn. I've gotten better, but mostly because of Ndidi's techniques and constant practice. For most of my life, just speaking took a great deal of concentration. It was hard to remember the words I wanted to use and to move my mouth enough to use those words. Listening to people was a bigger chore because I constantly had to make sure I was grounded—that I didn't lose myself in my own mind, or in the ground, or in a passing thought. People had to call my name for me to recognize they were speaking to me. Every question had to be asked twice, and then I had to search through my memory for even the most basic answers."

CJ took a breath. "It was … difficult. I couldn't properly express myself. Whenever I got too excited or happy, my face would tense up, and I would be unable to show it, so I always looked cold and distant. People avoided me because I was weird and different. DJ tried to make it better. He *did* make it better in the ways only he could. But I've always felt like I'm holding him back. He was always forced to wait for me because he realized that if he wasn't there, I would be alone."

Manar put his hand on the young man's shoulder, "That must have been—"

"But now," CJ interrupted, "for the first time in my life, I actually feel in control of something. My body responds to me. I can easily access my memory. I can talk without stuttering or trailing off because the words don't sound right. I still get distracted, but I think that's just because I think too much. I feel wonderful. And I can't get it out of my head that this is how it feels to be *normal*. This is what other people feel every day. What my brother grew up with.

"So, yes. It feels amazing to finally be in control. I find myself awed by the simple things I can do. But I understand that it's temporary, and we'll have to return to our bodies at some point. It'd be illogical and stupid to try to prolong our mission just to stay here."

Manar's eyes widened slightly at that, but he didn't say anything for a while, and CJ cringed. That was probably the most words that he'd ever spoken at once. There were things in there he hadn't even told DJ. Manar had asked him a simple question, and he'd rambled for no reason. What must he be thinking? It was Manar, for God's sake! He was probably taking apart each sentence. Would he feel pity for CJ?

Unsurprisingly, that thought irritated CJ. He didn't want pity—not from Manar, not from anyone else. He was already pathetic enough without people trying to accommodate him. He wasn't a burden. Not anymore, at least.

"You really do get in your own head," Manar said. CJ glanced up to find Manar already staring at him. "Do you think this spot is good?"

"Good for what?" CJ asked. Manar was ignoring everything he just said? CJ wasn't sure if that was better or worse.

It's better, he decided a moment later. *It's definitely better.*

"A good spot to initiate the hack," Manar explained. "The website's monitoring system will be functional again soon, meaning the alarms will be back. But I think we've wandered enough. We should orient ourselves. But you know what happens from here on out. Are you ready?"

CJ's hand hovered over the sphere. "Do you need help?"

Manar shook his head. "We can save that for later. This should be a simple recon."

With that, he placed his hands on the wall.

THE MOMENT MANAR PLACED his hands on the wall, every-thing changed. His data-sight had already been activated. By now, Manar had become proficient enough that his power practically leaped out of him, and he easily directed the energy to the wall.

Then everything changed.

Whenever he engaged a hack with one of the bots manning the stalls, his mind split, like it had when they were hiding from the DDoS. He would see with both his normal vision and his data-sight. Now he was trying to hack an entire building, with magnitudes more to deal with.

Manar's mind sank into the website, and he lost all awareness of his virtual body. Fortunately, he'd known this would happen. It was one of the reasons he'd almost died the first time he attempted this and why he'd let CJ follow him into the website despite the risks.

Manar traveled as a blue streak in a world devoid of light. He could feel himself moving and sense other streaks around him. However, that was the extent of it. Flashes and impressions pressed in on him, and Manar struggled not to lose himself. *The security around the thirty-third sector needed to be strengthened to prevent a breach from AnalChampion69. The virus from the last breach in the fourth sector had still not been neutralized. The two new intruders still had not been found. Patchwork would have to be done on the monitoring systems. The guardians needed to be rerouted from the twentieth sector, but they were being blocked—*

Manar forced himself back. This was harder than he'd expected. Those weren't his thoughts. Getting bogged down by them was just another way to kill himself. The impressions were probably from the website's IDS—intrusion detection system. Manar thought his pulse had disabled the entire system, but apparently he'd just made it blind to him and CJ. It served his purposes still, but Manar would need to learn to be more specific with his power.

Focus, he scolded himself.

He had only a limited amount of time before he was detected or his energy ran out. Gingerly, Manar spread his awareness toward the neighboring streaks. It was difficult because he still needed to keep enough of himself together to avoid destroying his mind. He also had to keep enough focus not to get sucked into the impressions, which he now realized were passing thoughts from the IDS. Could he hack into that? He could redirect every threat and—

Focus.

His awareness brushed against another streak. An image of the castle-like website flashed into his mind. The streak was like a thread, and Manar followed it until one of the flashes brought CJ into focus, as well as his own body, hands pressed against the wall. The image was frozen; the streak had already passed that spot, but that was fine. With a starting point, Manar followed the streak once more, this time mapping out the subsequent passage and corridors. He was forced to focus twice when the streak branched too far from his destination. Both times, he was able to find his way. The random impressions from the IDS still pressed in on him from outside. The DDoS had been discharged to deal with the traffic from the influx of customer user tags. The breach was being filled. The guardians had finally sighted the two intruders and were preparing to engage. There was a connection from that area. Where did it—

Suddenly Manar felt eyes on him. The impressions paused, then shattered. Manar's mind was slammed back together, severing his connection to the thread. He sighed inwardly. With a few more minutes, he would have reached to the core.

The eyes pressed in on him. Manar felt its scrutiny as a heavy weight within the world of black. His mind went back to his previous idea of hacking into the IDS. Although he was tempted to try, his energy would be best spent elsewhere.

Manar spread his awareness back to the blue streak and recreated the connection. It only lasted for a second before his mind was slammed back into itself. If Manar could still feel his teeth, he was sure they'd be rattled. When he pushed back against the eyes, the pressure abated somewhat. Manar drew more energy into himself and reestablished the connection. He needed only a few more seconds to completely map their path. The closer they could get to the core, the better their chances of finding out what Helene had planned.

He managed to last a few more moments before he was slammed back into himself. This time the force was greater.

Manar focused his power, condensing it as much as possible. Then, he threw himself at the pressure around him. He found it unyielding. Manar retreated and spread his awareness again, his intent to get a good look at what he was dealing with.

Golden eyes stared back at him.

Damn! Manar recoiled instinctively.

There was always a risk that his intrusion would draw in Helene. Manar had figured he would be able to put up some kind of fight against her, but the golden eyes suffused the space around him until it was all he sensed. Pushing against their pressure did nothing, and though he tried to draw more power into himself, Manar had already been hacking for too long. He was starting to feel the drain. As much as it rankled him, and although his instincts screamed to do something, this wasn't a fight he would win.

Manar let his consciousness retract back to his body. He condensed his power, preparing for any attack, but Helene just watched him. That annoyed him even more. She'd spent weeks tormenting Manar with useless hallucinations and illusions, which had made him think she saw him as a threat. Why wasn't she attacking?

And what was with the indifference he could sense in her gaze?

Manar's mind returned to his body. His vision came back to him all at once—along with his exhaustion. It hit him like a punch to the gut, and he doubled over, panting. He'd definitely stayed too long.

CJ rushed to his side. He didn't ask if Manar was okay but instead waited patiently for him to catch his breath. Still, curiosity wafted off him.

Manar felt his knees tremble from exhaustion, but he would have to deal with it later. With Helene aware of their presence, their time was more limited than expected. No matter how much she looked at them, Helene would still activate the website's defenses to chase them out. If she chose to control them directly, he and CJ might actually be in trouble.

"We have to move," he told CJ, still bent over.

"Did you get the path?"

Manar nodded. "But the IDS detected me and contacted Helene. She knows we're here."

Manar saw the fear in CJ's eyes and almost wished he hadn't mentioned that part. CJ was probably still traumatized from his last run-in with Helene. That was most certainly understandable. Even so, it was something they'd have to deal with—and they could start by moving positions before his work on the IDS wore off.

Manar straightened, giving CJ a small nod to show that he was all right. They were only a few steps from the end of the hallway, and Manar already had their path memorized. If they jogged, they would be able to—

A sound came from behind them. They turned as a pair of giants stepped into view on each side of the hallway. Their heads almost scraped the ceiling twenty feet above. In their hands they held giant swords. As the giants glared at him and CJ, Manar couldn't help but think of *Transformers*. It was an old movie, but the resemblance was uncanny.

"What are those?" CJ asked.

"Guardians, I would imagine," Manar replied with a sigh.

THE GUARDIANS FILLED UP the passage, and the points of their swords reflected the light. Even if the blades weren't as sharp as they seemed, they were large enough that a strike would still cleave right through CJ and Manar.

Shit, Manar thought. This was the worst time for this. He was still struggling to catch his breath. That might be a death sentence in a fight. It was too late to hide, but could they run?

No, running wouldn't work either. The guardians had blocked each end of the hallway on purpose; they weren't just going to let him and CJ pass. Manar's thoughts raced, scrolling through the catalog of his abilities, trying to find one that would help. Beside him, CJ gripped his spear tightly, his eyes fixed on their opponents. One of his hands hovered over the sphere. A moment later, the air rippled around them. From the pressure, Manar sensed CJ had gone for his advanced shield. That would drain him more—especially since he was protecting Manar as well. CJ must have known that, but he said nothing. Yet another reason not to waste time on this.

"If I delay the one behind us, can you take care of our way forward?" Manar asked quietly. CJ nodded, adjusting his position to face his new target. Manar took a deep breath. He was exhausted and might be rushing to his death, but what other choice did he have? "I'll buy you as much time as I can."

The two of them separated. Behind him, Manar heard CJ engage his target. He was tempted to look back and make sure he'd be okay, but that would be counterproductive. He had a job to do. He had to delay.

At some point, he'd become proficient enough with his data-sight that it activated with a brush against his reserves and barely dented it. The world bled away and was replaced by an array of ones and zeros. The guardian's code was laid bare. Manar was relieved to see that it was just the one code. There was a link sequence leading off to the distance, likely its passive connection to the IDS, not a sign of Helene's direct control.

It cost nothing to keep his data-sight activated, so Manar left it on while he made his other preparations. He drew again from his reserves, this time directing it into his muscles, letting it fill him. Strength rushed through him like a waterfall. Manar stood straighter. He was still tired, but distantly. Why had he ever allowed himself to be so weak? Why was he only trying to delay? He could defeat both giants within minutes if—

Manar cut off the thought. He really needed to get that under control.

He hacked into his cloak and added its basic shielding to CJ's. He could enhance it further, but that would drain him even more, so he decided to only use it in bursts as necessary.

By now, the guardian was only a few feet from Manar, slowly crossing the passage's halfway point. It swung at him, and despite expecting and even preparing for it, Manar couldn't help but feel a flash of fear at the sight of the giant blade heading for him. For just a moment, his panic overwhelmed his mind and locked his knees in place. Manar almost died in that moment. Fortunately, he regained control just in time to leap away. It was a clumsy way of gaining distance, but what he lacked in grace, his enhanced body made up for in speed.

The blade landed with a clang that shook the ground, tearing through the red carpet and cracking the stone underneath. It lodged itself within the crack, and the giant struggled to pull its weapon out. Even as inexperienced as he was, Manar knew an opening when he saw one. Still, it was a struggle to get his body to move when every instinct screamed at him to run away. All of this—the panic and fear—brought back unpleasant memories of his childhood, memories that Manar had spent a lifetime running away from.

But Manar wasn't that scared child who couldn't do anything while his family was killed around him. He wasn't the weak boy who had lain in the wreckage of his home for hours, too scared to move until he was saved. He wasn't that child anymore. He'd proven it every day since he met Simone.

As if reminding Manar of that fact, a surge of strength filled him. A layer of exhaustion peeled away, and his fear dissipated with it. Both were replaced with a confidence that bordered on arrogance.

Manar moved. He'd tested his enhanced speed several times during training. Actually pushing himself during combat was a vastly different experience. As the giant struggled to pull out its sword, Manar ducked between its legs. Easy enough, considering his head barely reached its groin—even standing upright.

Manar punched sharply upward. It was clumsy and awkward. Even as he did it, he knew he hadn't jumped high enough, hadn't clenched his fist the right way, and didn't have the right angle. All that would have mattered more had Manar been relying on pure force.

As his fist met the giant, Manar released a pulse of energy: the kind he'd used to disable the alarms. It was similar to CJ's nullification ability, but instead of an aura, Manar released a surge of data meant to overwhelm and disrupt digital systems. It wasn't as concentrated as CJ's ability, but it was able to cover a wider area faster.

Now, however, Manar just needed to disrupt a very specific code sequence his data-sight had highlighted. The pulse hit the sequence, but nothing happened. There was a slight fuzzing where it connected with others in the array, but Manar couldn't pump enough power into the surge to fully disrupt it. Still, the giant must have felt it because its enraged roar filled the hallway, and it tore its sword free from the ground.

Manar was tempted to stay between the behemoth's legs and take another shot, but a hand was already grabbing at him. Manar stumbled away, only to find a sword bearing down on him again. He cursed and threw himself clumsily to the floor. The sword passed several inches away from him, and Manar felt the wind of its passing, then a shock wave as it lodged itself in the ground again. Once again, the giant struggled to pull out its weapon.

Manar cocked his head. *It didn't learn,* he thought. *Maybe it can't learn—at least, not without time or direction.* How could Manar use that? Easily. It meant that the same tricks would work more than once.

Once more, Manar ducked beneath the guardian's legs and punched upward, targeting the same sequence as last time. This time, though, instead of a surge meant to overwhelm the code sequence, Manar directed his energy to manipulate it. It was a variation of the ability he'd used to create the wall he and CJ had hidden behind a couple of passages back. That had been a struggle since he'd been trying to manipulate several sequences at once. Now Manar was just targeting a single code in a single sequence, and instead of disrupting it, he was shifting it.

The result was immediate. Manar collapsed like a rag doll. He'd tried to moderate his energy, but he'd used too much, and now even his enhancements couldn't keep his exhaustion at bay. As for the giant, its reaction was just as intense. Its legs spasmed like it'd been electrocuted, and it vibrated like a tuning fork. The effect was limited to its lower body, and Manar chuckled as the guardian looked down in confusion. It tried to take a step but simply collapsed.

Manar's chuckle died in his throat. He was still under the giant.

The guardian's fall was like a meteor heading right for him. Manar struggled, but he still couldn't move. He could barely keep his eyes open. He could only hope his shield would be enough to keep him alive.

The giant's shadow turned everything black. Manar was surprised that his eyes remained open. He hadn't thought he was the kind of person to face death. He would have expected that from DJ or, interestingly enough, Ndidi. Still, something in him wanted to see the moment it all ended.

Instead, the only moment he saw was when CJ appeared and dragged him to safety. Seconds later, the guardian crashed into the ground with enough force to create a shock wave throughout the passage.

CJ stumbled and almost let go of Manar, but he tightened his grip and kept pulling until they reached the end of the hallway. When they passed the other guardian, Manar noticed it was also on the ground, its body littered with small, round holes—like those from a spear.

CJ dropped him when they got to the end of the passage. His concerned face filled Manar's vision. "You'll be all right." His eyes scanned Manar's body before meeting his gaze again. "You used too much of your energy at once, so you'll pass out. But we can talk when you wake up."

Pass out? Manar thought. Why would I pass out?

He was exhausted, but all he needed was to lie down for a bit. He didn't need to pass out. What he needed was to be awake in case there was any further danger. Still, his brain felt like it'd been covered in fog. It was getting hard to think. His eyes fluttered closed, and it took way too long for Manar to get them open again.

When he finally did, CJ was no longer with him. Manar felt a brief flash of panic. Had Helene sent more constructs after them? But no. From where he was propped, he could just barely make out CJ at the edge of his vision. He was stabbing at something. And the thing was stabbing back.

God! Why was it so hard to think?

His eyes fluttered closed. This time, Manar couldn't wrestle them back open.

CJ ROLLED FORWARD, evading the guardian's sword. He was getting better. This time, the roll barely damaged his shield. The sword passed a foot away, and CJ's flash of panic subsided. It wasn't as bad as the first time he'd done this, but he still didn't think he would ever get used to being attacked.

His roll had taken him to the construct's side. Manar had somehow destroyed its legs, so it could only attack with its upper body. Thus, for the moment, CJ was in its blind spot. He used the opening to stab his spear forward. It was coated with his nullification aura, so it pierced the giant's side easily and wreaked havoc on its code. When he pulled the spear back, it left a perfectly round hole in the guardian. With a grimace, he stabbed again, this time in a different spot. Once again, his aura went to work. Unlike with the mage and the original wielder of the spear, the giant's colossal size made it easier for CJ to view it as nothing more than a construct. He had the same moral dilemma about poking holes in it.

It doesn't matter, CJ told himself, not for the first time. He stabbed it again, grimacing all the while.

Eventually, the guardian stopped moving. It wasn't dead, but CJ's aura had caused enough damage that it would need to be patched to continue functioning. At least, that was what CJ figured. Without Manar's ability to see the data in its raw form, he couldn't be sure. CJ had already tried to replicate the ability with the sphere to no avail.

With both opponents defeated, CJ returned to Manar's side. As expected, Manar had passed out. In CJ's experience, he would be out for a few more minutes.

CJ bit the tip of his finger. What to do? They would be safer if they moved. But Manar was the one who knew the way. CJ didn't want to have to double back because he'd picked the wrong direction.

CJ could feel himself getting overwhelmed by indecision, so he broke down the problem logically. There were two branching corridors, which would make some people think that there was only a 50 percent chance of picking the wrong direction. However, regardless of which path he picked, there would be two other branching corridors, then two more, and so on. At each junction, the odds of CJ picking the right path would be smaller, while the odds of getting them lost would grow.

In such a case, he would waste far more time leaving than staying. In the same way, moving around might wake Manar up, even with his energy depleted. If he stayed put, both he and Manar would be able to replenish their energy, and there was no chance of getting lost. All they faced was the risk of getting attacked. But that was a risk they faced either way.

CJ sat beside Manar, his decision made. It was what he'd been leaning toward, but going through the options was a way to keep his panic at bay. It helped assure him that he was making the right choice. Even if he ended up being wrong, at least he'd made the best decision he could with the information at hand.

CJ didn't know when he'd dozed off, but he was suddenly jerked awake when Manar started coming to. The sleep had done them both good. CJ hadn't even known he was exhausted until he woke up feeling refreshed. Manar looked less worn out as well.

"Huh," Manar said, "we weren't attacked."

Honestly, CJ was a bit surprised by that too. They must not have been out for long.

"How're you feeling?" he asked

Manar sat up, cracking his neck. "Much better, actually." He looked at the two guardians lying on the floor. CJ saw a flicker of surprise, Manar's only reaction. "We've wasted far too much time here. Let's get moving."

They were off in the next moment, with Manar confidently leading the way. The minutes passed, and the passages blended. Twice they encountered pairs of guardians waiting for them at the ends of random hallways. Fortunately, with both Manar and CJ fully rested, the guardians posed very little threat. They each took one, leaving the constructs disabled within minutes.

Eventually—probably under the guidance of Helene—the security systems they faced changed. This should have slowed them down. However, the systems were variations of the spear bearer CJ had faced in the last website, but they wielded a sword instead. CJ already knew how they fought, so he and Manar tore through them in a minute.

CJ tried to persuade Manar to take the sword, but Manar claimed it would only get in the way. CJ would have argued, had he not seen Manar's abilities in action. Their results were far more pronounced when used on actual opponents, as opposed to just being demonstrated for practice.

CJ didn't know why he was surprised; Manar had merged with Gaius to have the perfect toolset to go against Helene. CJ couldn't help but feel a pang of jealousy. It was slight, but it was there, despite Manar's assurances that the sphere had the potential for much more.

Still, the display left CJ incredibly glad that he'd taken the time to grow strong in his own way. Now, at least, he could help. He could *do* something. If he'd had to watch without being able to do anything, he probably would have sunk into a depression that he could never escape.

The deeper they went, the more opposition they faced, and the more aggressive the security systems were. They appeared to be getting increasingly desperate.

They were forced to rest more to recuperate, which slowed their progress. At some point, Manar began slowing down and deliberating more before picking a direction. CJ figured that they were reaching the end of the course he'd plotted when he'd hacked into the website earlier. Hopefully, they were close enough to the core.

A few passages later, as they entered a large chamber made of bare stone, CJ got his answer in the form of a pair of digital constructs wearing dark hooded cloaks. The hoods were pulled far over their heads, leaving a black maw where their face would be. They hovered a foot from the ground and gazed at him from the darkness of the hood. At their backs, a translucent barrier blocked the passage.

Engraved into the barrier was a sign that read, *Access Seal: Denied*.

"Authentication, please," one of the reapers said.

CJ grimaced. This was far too familiar for his tastes.

"AUTHENTICATION, PLEASE," one of the dark-cloaked figures said. Manar stared at them. He had narrowed down the list of the security measures they possibly could employ, but he would need more information to know for sure.

"It's multifactor authentication," CJ muttered beside him.

Manar cocked his brow. "You've come across them before?"

"In the last website I was in before Helene …" CJ trailed off for a moment, then cleared his throat. "I assume we're close to the core."

"Relatively," Manar replied. "We're at the end of the path I plotted. The core shouldn't be far from here. These constructs must mean we're finally getting to the interesting parts of the website."

"From my experience," CJ agreed.

"Any suggestions? Since you've faced them before?" Manar asked.

"Authentication, please," the figures interrupted.

"If you can, provide authentication. Then you can pass without a fight." CJ grimaced. "If not, don't get caught by their chains. They blocked off my access to the sphere. But your energy is a part of you, so I'm unsure how you'd be affected."

CJ spoke calmly, but he was clenching the sphere like it was a lifeline. Later, Manar would get the full story. Now, however, the programs were getting agitated by their refusal to answer.

"Please provide a means of identification," both constructs intoned. Already, the cloaks and hoods were creepy. When they spoke in unison, it was downright eerie.

CJ's shield came up, enveloping them both. Then his aura flared up like a bonfire, startling Manar. Manar stared at him, then narrowed his eyes at the reapers. If CJ was taking them this seriously, he probably should too.

Manar's own shield came up, and he also activated the cloak's ability to make him harder to detect.

A moment later, the reapers reached the end of their patience. One raised its hand, which was still covered by its robe, and ethereal chains shot toward them. CJ's aura flared, then stretched to meet the chain several feet in front of them. They collided with a near-physical force. The chains passed through the aura and continued toward them, but now they were more transparent and sporting several cracks. A second surge was enough to destroy them.

But that wasn't all. CJ's aura continued to stretch, covering several feet and bearing down on the reapers like a whip. Manar had seen CJ practicing this ability, but he hadn't realized he'd gone so far.

Still, the chains had drained it. Stretching it so far also probably reduced the ability's effect. Manar placed a hand on CJ's shoulder, offering his own energy as a boost. The aura flared once more. By the time it reached the programs, the air was rippling in its wake.

The second reaper raised a hand, and a barrier popped up in front of them. When the aura—more like a nullification whip, now—broke through, another barrier popped up, conjured by the reaper that had originally sent out the chains.

CJ grunted with effort. The whip broke through the second ward and lashed at the constructs. It wrapped around them in the same way their chains would have wrapped around CJ and Manar.

And then did nothing.

No, Manar corrected himself, his eyes narrowing. It had done something, but the reapers hadn't reacted—not even to struggle against their binds. But they were no longer hovering above the ground, proof that they were being weakened. And they obviously didn't like that.

With their hoods pulled over their heads, Manar hadn't been able to see anything but a black maw where their faces should have been. Now two pairs of red orbs appeared from the darkness of each program, making for a total of eight eyes. The constructs flexed, and the whip shattered. Manar groaned as the backlash hit him, but it was nothing compared to CJ's reaction.

CJ fell to his knees, clutching his chest. He stared in horror at the reapers. "I didn't even know that was possible."

Manar mirrored the sentiment, but there was no time to ponder it. He activated his data-sight and drew from his reserves, preparing an ability. The reapers moved for the first time. They flowed toward each other, merging to become one. It was a smooth, easy transition, and when it was completed, their entire disposition changed. There hadn't been any hostility behind their attacks, but now Manar could sense a murderous intent. And they had the power to back it up.

Manar wondered if Helene had taken over, but his sight told him the truth. Somehow, their power had spiked, as if they had always been one but had decided to share their power for some reason.

The new, more powerful reaper raised its hand.

In response, Manar wove an illusion around them. This was the ability he had the most practice with, and now it was almost instinctive. The sequences flowed beneath his will, wrapping around them. It wasn't a complicated ability. Manar simply produced an image of whatever was behind him and CJ and put it in front of them, essentially making them invisible. He also wove it through his cloak to make him harder to detect. The combination stacked well. More to the point, it worked. The reaper lowered its hand, staring around in confusion.

Manar wasn't done. The moment the illusion was up, he and CJ moved. CJ wisely turned off his aura once he realized what Manar had done. Another pair of illusions, this time taking his and CJ's forms, appeared where they'd stood, staring down the constructs. Immediately, chains as large as tree trunks and just as thick shot from the reaper and wrapped around the illusions. Manar made their doubles struggle for a bit while his mind raced for another option. Eventually, the program would realize it'd captured fakes.

Unfortunately, that took far less time than Manar had anticipated. The chains squeezed, and the illusions shattered. Not dispersed—*shattered*.

He sighed. Being constantly surprised was irritating.

Manar was about to raise another set of illusions when his data-sight caught something in the mess of codes around him. This particular sequence was connected to the reaper and went off into a distant wall. It wasn't golden, so it wasn't Helene. That left the website's IDS. The fact that the reaper hadn't attacked their true position meant the IDS couldn't pierce through his illusion either—at least not yet. It was only a matter of time before Helene got over her indifference and took action.

Burning red eyes scanned the chamber. Manar took the chance to study the IDS with his data-sight. The ability translated the code sequences and gave him impressions of what they meant. And now, codes congregated around the program like a storm, interlocking into sequences. It was building something. Manar could guess what.

I can use that, he thought.

"Get ready," he told CJ in a low voice.

Manar began drawing from his energy reserves. This was going to take a lot out of him. It took a minute, but finally, the reaper loosened its chain. A split second before that, Manar lashed out with his own ability, targeting the connection between the reaper and the IDS. With the force of his will, he manipulated the sequence directly, shifting the codes out of order.

Both the reaper and IDS resisted, of course, but Manar possessed an iron will. He'd been manipulating codes since he was a child. Its resistance lasted only a second before it folded. The connection broke, and power flooded out of the reaper like a wave that filled the entire chamber.

"Now," Manar whispered to CJ.

Closing the distance between them and the program, Manar shifted the illusion just before the wave hit them. Dozens of Manars and CJs filled the room. The wave—an ability recreated to break through illusions, according to his data-sight—destroyed the illusions as they appeared, but Manar just created more after it passed.

The wave destroyed their invisibility, but now there were dozens of other illusions with their forms—all of them, including the real ones—rushing toward the reaper. Without the IDS to whisper which was real and which wasn't, the reaper didn't know which to attack.

Still, to its credit, it reacted faster than Manar expected. Its chains, still extended to where it'd destroyed Manar's first illusive doubles, suddenly began to lash around the room. They started out slow but quickly picked up speed. They slammed into the floor, into walls, and into illusions, shattering them with just a brush. Manar created more, and the chains destroyed them just as fast.

One of them brushed Manar, and he immediately understood CJ's words of caution. He staggered as the connection to his illusions faded. He could still feel them but in a distant way, as if they'd been sealed behind a wall. Manar immediately attacked the seal, throwing his will against it, but to no avail.

That's a nasty ability, he thought. *And that was just from a single brush.*

CJ's aura enveloped him and quickly went to work nullifying the seal. Manar joined in. Within moments, he had access to his illusions again, but the damage had been done. More than half of the doubles had been destroyed, and the chains were more targeted with their attacks.

Through all this, Manar had CJ had never stopped moving. Now they and the rest of the illusions were only a few feet away from the reaper. They'd kept close to the wall to make themselves less of a target.

The reaper must have sensed this, too, because its attacks became more frantic, more aggressive. Twice Manar and CJ were forced to jump out of the way to avoid being hit. Manar was also forced to focus more on his remaining illusions. Individually, they cost little energy to create, but he'd already formed over a hundred at this point. It added up. He needed to conserve his energy for what came next.

The chains stopped. It was sudden enough that Manar jerked to a halt. CJ followed suit. Manar started to wonder what happened, but his data-sight drew his attention to the reaper—and the incredible amount of energy it was gathering. Every code in the chamber was drawn toward the reaper, creating a storm that filled the air above it. The amount of power it was collecting was far larger than what it'd amassed to dispel their invisibility.

"Shit," Manar cursed.

"What?" CJ asked.

"It's building up to something. Something big—an attack. We don't have a lot of time. We're going to need your shield, with as much power as you can spare."

Manar dismissed the illusion he'd been building and instead desperately stretched his will toward the wall beside them. The wall folded easily beneath his control, and Manar molded it into a barrier in front of them. CJ's shield enveloped it a second later, flaring wildly.

Manar bit his lip. Would it be enough?

By now, the storm overhead had peaked. Codes stopped streaming in and instead began to interlock, becoming sequences, then arrays, then a mini-tapestry. Manar had never seen anything like it. The air around the reaper was distorted, roiling and folding in on itself so much that even CJ couldn't miss it. The effect stretched to the whole chamber until even the walls were warped by the power.

It wouldn't be enough.

Manar layered two other walls in front of them and tightened their codes, making them sturdier. A moment later, the shield spread to envelop that too. CJ went one further, creating a wall made entirely of his aura. He placed it closest to them as the last line of defense.

Manar still didn't feel it was enough. His mind raced for a solution, but there was nothing else he could do. Even running away wouldn't help. He hadn't felt this dread, this feeling of impending death, since he was a child. It wasn't a fun feeling.

Suddenly, it was too late to do anything. The reaper raised a hand, which was now gripping a scythe. It swung the weapon, and the storm followed, crashing down on CJ and Manar like an arbiter of death.

Manar ducked behind his walls, as did CJ, but the attack still filled the room. Manar felt his connection to his illusions vanish as they were destroyed.

The first wall crumbled. Manar ignored the backlash, withdrew the energy it'd taken to make the first wall, and used it to reinforce the second. It lasted a second more before it, too, was destroyed. The final wall lasted even longer, a whole five seconds, before it was overwhelmed. Then, finally, the attack struck the nullification barrier.

It passed right through, washing over them.

Manar was thrown off his feet. He couldn't imagine CJ fared better. The shield disappeared, and Manar felt something drain out of him, leaving him exhausted. If he hadn't already been on the floor, he would have fallen over. The fact that he was still alive meant his barriers had lessened the attack somewhat. CJ's barrier had probably done most of the protecting.

Manar remained on the floor for a minute, trying to catch his breath and control the pounding of his heart.

That, Manar thought, *was too close. Way too close. What the hell was that?*

Enemies were supposed to scale up in strength at a certain rate. Despite their size, the guardians had been relatively easy to defeat. The sword-bearer and the mage had been easy as well, and so had the other security systems that they'd come across. Whatever this was, it shouldn't have been this difficult. It was like he'd been playing a game on easy mode and the settings were suddenly switched to ultra-death mode.

Manar wondered what it would be like to try to hack through this sort of defense in the real world. So far he hadn't met a security system he couldn't break into. But in the same way, he'd never met something like what he'd just faced. The security systems on the dark web would obviously be a lot different from the normal web. And now Manar was motivated to test them.

He pushed himself to his feet. His cloak fell to the ground in tatters. This was disappointing, but Manar had an idea of how to get a good replacement.

CJ was several feet away. The air distorted around him; he'd managed to keep his shield up. Good. Manar crossed the distance and crouched beside him. CJ stared back.

"Thank you," Manar said, sighing. "We wouldn't have survived that without you."

CJ sat up with a groan. His eyes showed his exhaustion, but his smile was bright as he shook his head. "It was a team effort, I believe."

Manar wanted to disagree, but they didn't have time to banter. "Can you spare some energy?"

CJ placed a hand on Manar's shoulder, and Manar felt his stamina recovering. He closed his eyes. It would barely make a dent in his fatigue. He would need actual rest for that. But it combined with Gaius's energy and helped to increase his reserves.

After a while, Manar figured he'd had enough and opened his eyes to tell CJ that. But the energy had stopped flowing. CJ was already passed out. He'd given Manar all he had without even asking why.

Manar stared at CJ's unconscious form for a moment before getting to his feet. The reaper's eyes had been burning into him ever since he'd started moving. However, the fact that the program hadn't attacked meant that it couldn't. It'd probably used all its power for the last attack, which had left the entire chamber in ruins. All the walls were cracked and broken. Even pieces of the ceiling were falling. Still, Manar could already see the website slowly at work rebuilding itself.

Manar's steps were unhurried as he crossed the chamber. The barrier behind the reaper was still active. Unlike CJ's shield, it must not have needed a constant feed of energy to stay active. Fortunately, the program made no move to retreat behind the barrier. It simply stared.

The first thing Manar did when he reached the reaper was examine its robe with his data-sight. He noted several sequences that were ingrained abilities. His cloak had something similar, but not as extensive as this.

Manar smiled. This would do nicely.

Finally, when he was done, he met the program's burning glare with one of his own. This stupid thing had put them through so much stress and had nearly killed them. But they'd survived. They'd won. Logically, that meant they should be allowed to move on.

Manar's eyes flicked to the barrier's seal. It still read, *Access Denied*. The damn thing was still standing in their way. And now the reaper was glaring at Manar like *he* was the one at fault.

He sighed, placed a hand on the reaper's head, and hacked into it.

THE WORLD BLED INTO A TAPESTRY of ones and zeros. It wasn't as jarring as the first time Manar had done this, but each time was different. Manar had become so used to using his data-sight that it was almost instinctive at this point, but it felt different when he activated it during a hack. Everything was clearer, as if he was more connected to the world somehow. As if he was part of it on a level that was usually reserved for digital constructs and fully artificial intelligences like Helene. It was one of the most comforting things Manar had ever felt.

It took him a full minute to get himself to focus on the matter at hand. Tendrils of blue energy forced themselves through the reaper's matrix, slithering through the code and transferring impressions to Manar. Programs were allowed access through the barrier, previous instructions from the IDS, even a brief touch of Helene. This explained why the reaper had been so difficult to handle. Manar let all the information wash over him.

Usually this was where he would stop. Up until now, Manar had hacked into programs only to get information, such as with the attendants back at the market stalls. Now, however, Manar needed a way through the barrier, so he had to try something different.

He triggered a code manipulation.

Unlike what CJ thought, Manar really had only two abilities. His data-sight was one, and the other was his code manipulation. Every other ability he'd demonstrated so far was just a variation of these two. All were from him just manipulating the world's codes in different ways. This wasn't the first time Manar had used the ability on a digital construct, but it was the first time he'd used it while hacking into one. Manar felt the difference immediately.

The world shifted, and something snapped into place. Manar gasped. He knew he gasped, but he didn't feel it. Instead, he saw it through tinted-red eyes. The world shifted again. Manar could feel his body once more, but it felt layered somehow. As if there was another person inside of him, and if he just …

The reapers split back into their two original forms.

What's happening? Manar thought.

"What has happened?"

Manar looked around. The room was still destroyed. CJ was still lying unconscious a few feet away. Who'd said that? It was odd: he hadn't heard it exactly. It was more like—

"Report!"

There it is again! Manar frowned and scanned the chamber once. Finally, his data-sight alerted him to a stream of data connected to one of the reapers. Manar recognized the IDS's sequence immediately. That only added to his confusion. The IDS was trying to communicate with the reapers, so why did it seem like it was speaking to him directly? Was it because he was hacking into the reaper?

No, that didn't seem right. Or, at least, it didn't seem like a complete answer. Either way, allowing the programs to communicate wasn't a good idea. Manar focused on cutting off the connection. It was severed immediately. He hadn't had to put any effort into it. Most concerning of all, he didn't feel drained. That should have required tapping into his reserves, at least a little bit.

The connection shut off, and Manar felt a burst of anger and frustration that he was certain didn't come from him. And yet, the emotions had been so clear it might as well have. Manar followed the feeling and traced it to one of the reapers. They hated him. He'd sought entry without proper authentication, and he'd isolated them from their glorious lord.

Where the hell is this coming from? Manar thought.

For some reason, he wasn't alarmed. Instead, his curiosity raged. Why was he getting their emotions? Why was he hearing their thoughts? Why had he been able to hear the IDS trying to communicate with them, and why had it taken nothing from him to cut it off?

Then he realized the tendrils he'd sent into the program were no longer transmitting information. They didn't need to—not when Manar felt everything the reapers did. He'd even confused their body for his when he'd split them. His connection to them was intrinsic, at a depth that should have been impossible.

So, why is it happening? Manar thought, his excitement surging. *What caused this?*

It had to be the combination of his hack and code manipulation. He'd never done it before. It was the only thing that was different. He'd never felt such attunement until this moment. And now he'd unlocked something he didn't know could be done.

Manar's grin was sharp enough to cut metal.

Now that he understood what was happening, the first thing Manar did was separate his thoughts and emotions from those of the reapers. But some of it still bled over. Manar didn't know if it would carry over once the hack was disengaged. If his thoughts and personality could be influenced by the connection, he would have to stop immediately.

As if I could do that. Manar chuckled. Still, it was easy enough to make barriers within their connection. He could switch between himself and the reapers as he pleased, but now it was more distinct. Manar knew when he was in his own body and mind and when he was in the reapers'.

With that settled, Manar delved into the construct's mind for a little exploration.

MANAR DIDN'T HAVE MANY fun memories of his childhood, even among the parts that hadn't been blocked. He remembered being happy, to some extent, and even excited over childish things. But it was rare to have fun while living in a country that was constantly in the throes of one war or the other. Being adopted by Simone had been loads better. Manar could remember the dozens of places Simone had taken him to have fun—theme parks, playgrounds, arcades—especially in the first few months when his trauma had rendered him mute.

By then, Manar's personality had been pretty much set by his past experiences, so he'd struggled to enjoy the activities. Since then, Manar had constantly sought to improve, to be the best. There was little space for fun.

Still, one of the most distinct moments that Manar could remember, a time he *did* have fun, was when Simone introduced him to a computer and taught him the basics of coding. Manar remembered spending hours-long stretches on that computer, trying different combinations. Exploring.

He was transported back to that time now, to that childlike excitement of doing something you loved. The reaper's mind was surprisingly broad and deep. Despite having two bodies, the constructs shared one mind, which was why being merged hadn't caused any issues. There was no actual sensation, but to Manar, it was like swimming in an ocean made of binary codes and constantly diving deeper.

He could feel his energy draining quickly. He'd even begun to tap into the energy CJ had lent him. He couldn't stay for much longer.

The reaper's abilities were particularly interesting. Manar was thankful his illusions had prevented a protracted battle and forced the program to go all out in an attempt to take them out faster. If the fight had been drawn out, things might not have gone so well.

One ability stood out. Manar bookmarked it for greater exploration later, then figured out how to shut down the barrier. He ignored the burst of anger that came with that discovery.

Deep within its matrix, though, almost at the core of the program, Manar found something that threatened to split his face open from the force of his smile. He retraced his steps through the reaper's mind, targeting the ability he'd bookmarked.

Two golden orbs stared at him.

Manar grimaced. The look of disinterest was gone from Helene's eyes. Now she looked very interested and very angry. That was something, at least. He'd finally succeeded in making her take him seriously. Now Manar just needed to find a way to keep her from killing him.

Helene's presence suffused every inch of the place until Manar felt his grip on the reaper slipping. Whatever he'd done to attune to the construct, Helene was undoing it. He couldn't even see the stream of data that connected her to the reaper. Manar threw his will at Helene, switching to the reaper's mind to reject her. But Helene had just as much right to be there as Manar. Maybe even more.

They struggled. Manar's attunement meant that he couldn't easily dislodge his control. But in the same way, even with Gaius's energy propping him up, Helene was far too strong to fight directly. Once again, Manar found himself on the losing side of a confrontation with her, and none of his abilities could help him.

Manar gritted his teeth. Then what was the point of even coming here? And what was the point of merging with Gaius? Gaius was supposed to even the playing field, but Manar had miscalculated. Now he found himself constantly pushed back.

It was frustrating but not altogether hopeless—not after what he'd discovered in the depths of the reaper's matrix. Manar just had to get CJ to the core of the website.

And Helene knew that too.

Manar sighed, switched back to his virtual body, and walked back to CJ. He maintained his connection to the reaper, moving slowly so he wouldn't break it by accident. It was disorientating, but Manar had lots of practice at this point. In an ideal world, he would be able to suppress Helene and do what he wanted without having to jump through hoops. But nothing was ever ideal, and it was illogical to hold on to something just because you wanted it to be real. So, although it rankled his pride, Manar stopped trying to suppress Helene for the second time.

And then he pulled back suddenly.

His will and energy, already focused into a spear point, pierced through Helene when her surprise created an opening. It wasn't a true attack; he just needed to get through her to reach his target. The AI's presence enveloped where he'd just been, but Manar was already reaching toward the ability he'd bookmarked.

With a thought, he activated it.

A passage opened within the barrier. This wasn't a door to the other side of the chamber. No, this passage seemed to pierce through the seal, stretching it until it connected to another location. Like a tunnel. From the impressions Manar had received when he'd examined the ability, that location was just where they needed to go.

He picked CJ up while his mind defended against Helene's onslaught. His brain felt like it was about to melt, protesting the way he was splitting it up. But if he let up on the passage for even a second, Helene would win, and they would die. The rest of the world would be destroyed shortly after.

Manar gritted his teeth. It took a full minute to walk twenty steps, but eventually he and CJ got into the tunnel. Immediately, the onslaught on his mind stopped. Manar sagged in relief. He hadn't been sure that it would work. His connection to the reaper had also been cut off.

With a little breathing room, Manar gently dropped CJ and took a minute to study the passage. It had a futuristic look. Walls twisted in a spiral and seemed to extend infinitely into the distance. Lines stretched along the walls and floor, forming a tapestry of binary wherever they intersected. Manar only gave himself a minute to recuperate. He'd been expending energy since they'd entered the chamber. Virtual or not, it'd taken a toll on his body. His break wasn't enough to regain any of his stamina, but it helped.

With a groan, Manar picked CJ back up and began his trek through the tunnel. He didn't have energy to spare on bodily enhancements, so he was forced to bear the weight by himself. This was something Manar wouldn't have considered in his real body, but his virtual body had been built to be in peak condition, so he managed it.

Fortunately, CJ woke up a few minutes later with enough energy to walk by himself. Surprisingly, it took only a glance for him to understand where they were, but not how they got there. Manar filled in the missing pieces.

"Seems like I missed the interesting part," CJ muttered.

Manar tilted his head. "Not necessarily. Awake or not, from your perspective, it would have looked like I was just standing around. Plus, none of it would have been possible if not for the energy you loaned me."

CJ made a noncommittal sound. "So this tunnel was created by one of the reaper's abilities?"

Manar grinned. Finding the ability had been a stroke of luck. He would have settled for just turning off the barrier, but that would have given Helene dozens of opportunities to ambush them on their way to the core. With the tunnel, they'd bypassed all that.

"Yes," Manar replied. "It was built by the website's developers for easy maintenance access. Usually, there's a unique password that they have to input, but I was able to bypass that."

"Because of this new ability you discovered," CJ muttered. Manar wouldn't have called his tone sullen—mostly because he couldn't actually imagine CJ ever doing that. But it was a near thing.

Manar chuckled inwardly. It was ironic that as much as CJ wanted Manar's powers, Manar was dying to get his hands on the sphere. He glanced at CJ, hesitated, then pushed forward.

"Like, I said, I wouldn't have been able to without you." Manar cleared his throat. It wasn't often he felt gratitude toward someone—and even rarer that he felt indebted. Most people were incompetent and useless. But if CJ hadn't followed him in, he would have been dead.

"It was a team effort," CJ replied.

Manar shook his head. Earlier CJ had defeated the constructs while Manar lay unconscious. Without CJ's shield, the reaper's strike would have killed him, and without the energy CJ had transferred to him, Manar would not have been able to get through the barrier, much less discovered … whatever it was that he'd discovered. In light of that, a simple thank-you felt wildly insufficient.

"I'll be the first to admit that I can sometimes be proud and try to handle everything by myself. While I could blame that on my past experiences with people, it wouldn't change the fact. Regardless, I'm not so self-deluded not to realize that, if not for you, this whole thing would have failed before it even started. Likewise, while I *can* be arrogant and proud—unapologetically—it would be illogical for me to withhold my thanks just because of my ego." Manar met CJ's eyes, making sure that the other man could see the seriousness there. "So, thank you."

CJ lowered his eyes. "It's really not necessary."

"I should also apologize," Manar continued. This was uncomfortable enough as it was without having to stop just because CJ was too humble for his own good. "I'll admit that, when you first explained why you were here, I was skeptical. But you've definitely proven me wrong."

"Once again, it is really not necess—"

Manar didn't hear what CJ said after that because the tunnel came to a sharp end, depositing them into a room. The chamber itself wasn't large. It had the same castle-themed decor as the rest of the website. In some ways, it was similar to the chamber they'd just left, except instead of two specters waiting for them at the end, there was a swirling ball hovering over a pedestal.

Finally, Manar thought.

With the stress they'd gone through, it felt as if they'd been heading there for several days instead of just a few hours. As if reacting to the core, his data-sight activated on its own. Manar almost lost himself in the storm of impressions that followed. He also confirmed what he'd seen in the reaper's matrix, which was good. They needed to work fast before Helene found her way to them.

As if on cue, CJ asked, "What now?"

"Now," Manar replied slowly, "you absorb it. And then we leave."

79

MANAR HAD TO REPEAT HIMSELF so CJ could be sure he'd heard him right. And even then, the statement refused to compute. "What do you mean, *absorb it?*"

"Not *you*," Manar clarified. CJ noticed that his eyes hadn't left the core since they'd entered the room. For a moment, CJ felt a familiar sense of envy. What was his ability showing him at that moment?

CJ stamped down the feeling, reminding himself that, even with his abilities, Manar had admitted that he couldn't have succeeded without CJ.

"You're going to absorb it into your sphere," Manar explained. "Absorb the core into—"

Now CJ was even more confused. His sphere had been unresponsive since it'd absorbed the last piece. He'd told Manar this. Just to be sure, CJ placed a hand on the sphere but felt nothing. If it could absorb this core as it had the others, it should have been reacting now. But it wasn't.

"It doesn't feel … ready," CJ said. "I don't know if it—"

"It can," Manar insisted. There was a strange, excited glow in his eyes. "It just needs a little prodding. I'll help with it."

CJ was irritated with how confused he was. Why couldn't he piece this together? And he'd never known Manar to be coy. They'd come here so *Manar* could hack into the core to figure out what Helene planned and why she was taking over the dark web. CJ's job had just been to support him.

I'm missing something, he realized. *He must have discovered something while I was unconscious, something that changed the plan.*

CJ changed his question. "What happens if the sphere absorbs the core?"

For the first time, Manar took his eyes off the core and met CJ's, grinning. He was excited. "Then we'll have a piece of Helene's central code."

CJ's mind raced to understand. His eyes glazed over without him realizing it. Manar kept staring at him, as if encouraging him to connect the dots. To CJ's chagrin, it wasn't hard to figure it out with that last bit of information.

"Helene integrated a bit of herself into the core?" he asked.

"*Primarily* into the core, yes." Manar pointed to the swirling mass. "Just a piece of her foundational code matrix, but she put it in the website's core. But from what I can tell, it split off into the major website's systems."

That was probably what he'd discovered when he was connected to the reaper: part of Helene's code. But what CJ didn't understand was why it was so important.

"But as her creator, do you not already have her code?" he asked.

Manar's eyes darkened. CJ got the sense that it wasn't him he was angry at. "I did initially, but when I could do something with it, I didn't. Then when I tried to put a stop to her, it was too late. She'd locked me out of the matrix I had developed and upgraded her defenses so much that I couldn't even hack in."

He pinched the bridge of his nose with a sigh. "It doesn't matter anyway. Helene has evolved to the point that her code is vastly different from what I came up with. I've known that for years. But if I had any doubt before"—he gestured at something in the core only he could see—"they're gone now."

CJ tilted his head, then all at once it clicked. This was a way for them to get ahold of Helene's evolved central code, which he had to assume Manar could put to good use. Plus, Helene's code would surely help improve the sphere. There were obvious risks, though, and one readily came to CJ's mind.

"Wouldn't Helene be able to take over the sphere using her code as a link? You said it yourself: the sphere draws from you somehow, and you have only Gaius completely under your control. Energy in you, not the AI itself. This might have been Helene's plan."

Manar nodded. "I've considered that," he said. CJ noticed the excitement hadn't gone from his face. "But that's where I come in."

Then he went on to explain the plan fully. When he was done, CJ had the same look of excitement.

There wasn't much to set up. The only thing they needed was CJ's sphere and Manar. Still, it took Manar a few minutes to prepare. CJ understood. Manar had probably used more energy than CJ during the last fight, and he hadn't had a chance to rest since then.

When Manar was ready, CJ brought out the sphere and held it in two hands. It probably wasn't necessary to take it out of the pouch, but it seemed wrong to leave it there for something like this.

"You ready?" Manar asked. He stood beside CJ, and at CJ's nod, he raised his hands toward the core.

CJ connected to the sphere. His mental fingers itched to activate his zone. With it, he might be able to follow what Manar was doing, at least to some extent. However, CJ hadn't ever tested what would happen if he activated it within a website, and now seemed like a bad time to give in just because his curiosity was burning a hole in his mind.

Manar concentrated. Through the sphere, CJ could feel the waves of power that radiated off him as he stared at the core. *No,* CJ corrected himself. Manar wasn't staring at the core, but through it. Where CJ saw only a swirling ball of ones and zeros, Manar saw something more.

The strain on Manar's face got progressively worse until it had twisted to the point of being unrecognizable. CJ took that as his cue. He placed his hand on Manar's shoulder and willed some of his energy into him. That seemed to do the trick, as Manar's face loosened up a bit.

After another few seconds, a part of the core split off and hovered in the air. CJ watched it with fascination. It wasn't his first time seeing this, of course, but that didn't do anything to dampen his excitement. The earthquake that shook the building, however, was enough to wipe the grin off his face. Worried, CJ stared at the walls. But the quake hadn't destabilized anything.

Fortunately, it wasn't enough to distract Manar. The core fragment started drifting toward them, floating downward with excruciating slowness.

Another quake hit the building. This time loose pieces of ceiling started falling around them. CJ and Manar were covered in a transparent shield. His aura also formed a barrier above their heads, breaking down any nearby debris.

The core fragment drifted closer. CJ was buffeted by the raging waves of energy coming off it, lashing at him. This was different from the other times. The earlier fragments had seemed all but inactive once they were separated from the main core, but this one almost seemed *aware*. Aware and angry.

When it was close enough to touch, Manar grabbed it with a hand wrapped with blue energy. The strain on his face increased exponentially. His shoulders dropped as if he were carrying a great load. Still, Manar held on with gritted teeth. Tendrils snaked out from his arms and pierced through the fragment. The walls shook again as if the whole website was writhing in pain. CJ sent a worried glance to the ceiling and ignored the memories of the last time he'd been in a similar situation.

He had to focus; his part was coming up.

Manar's tendrils bored through the fragment. Although CJ couldn't actually see what they were doing, the energy thrashed wildly in response. At least initially. The thrashing slowed after a few seconds, and eventually the tendrils went inert.

Now, for the first time, Manar glanced at CJ, asking a silent question. CJ turned off his aura and shielding so he could focus fully on the sphere. The next moment, the fragment drifted toward CJ. With Manar's tendrils still embedded in the fragment, it seemed to crackle with blue lighting.

It hovered around the sphere for a moment before sinking in. In the same moment, CJ dove into his connection with the sphere. It wasn't difficult for him to sense the fragment—it was the only piece out of place, like a single article of clothing out of alignment in a perfectly arranged room. CJ could feel his old OCD acting up. Fortunately, he was here to fix it.

His connection to the sphere had increased tremendously since adding the final piece, but CJ got the sense there was more to be unlocked. Unfortunately, apart from accessing his abilities, the sphere has been unresponsive, no matter how much CJ had prodded it.

But it reacted now. CJ could sense a palpable hunger coming from the orb. Manar had been right: even without CJ's intervention, it wouldn't have any problems integrating the fragment into itself. Still, CJ could help speed up the process.

After several months of using the sphere—and hours upon hours of studying it—CJ was familiar enough with its internal matrix to shift things around. Still, he double-checked every adjustment to ensure the matrix remained stable throughout the process.

For its part, the fragment slid into the open spaces easily, as if it had been made to fit there. CJ lost track of time as he worked, which was dangerous. But it was even more dangerous to leave the fragment not properly integrated and with flaws.

When he finally withdrew his mind, he found Manar lying on the ground. He raised his head up when he noticed CJ's stare. "Well?"

Apparently CJ's grin was enough of an answer because Manar's head dropped, and he released a sigh of relief. He didn't seem to notice the pieces of debris falling all around him. Truthfully, neither did CJ. His entire mind was consumed by what he'd felt in the sphere after integrating the last piece of the fragment. The orb hummed in his hands—actually *hummed*. CJ's connection to it was smoother and somehow deeper, as if he'd accessed a new level.

CJ was dying to try out one of his abilities, but without a good reason, it would just be a waste of energy. He looked around at the walls that shook in anger and seemed on the verge of crumbling, and then at the ceiling that was already crumbling, raining debris.

I'll probably have my chance soon, CJ thought.

80

FORTUNATELY—OR UNFORTUNATELY, depending on how they looked at it—their escape from the website was anticlimactic. The building fell around them, forcing them to constantly dodge and weave around debris. CJ handled it fine, but Manar looked on the verge of falling over—quite understandably given all he'd done. When CJ offered to carry him, Manar waved him off with a look that wouldn't have been out of place on a king.

CJ's mind brushed against the sphere. It responded immediately, as if it had anticipated his desires. It wove a shield of energy around him and Manar. There was no way to describe how the sphere, enhanced by the fragment of Helene they'd extracted from the core, was different from before. It was as if the sphere had evolved and unlocked doors CJ hadn't even known existed. His connection with it had also advanced to the point that CJ was always connected to it. CJ no longer needed to lug the sphere around in a pouch. Now it hovered over his shoulder, floating along with him. Preliminary testing showed that he could control its movements, but it was difficult, like controlling a new limb.

CJ was almost salivating at the thought of studying it.

The air distorted around them, but it was smoother and more stable than it had been before. Debris was battering against it, yet he felt no drain from the damage. It was far more durable than previous iterations.

It was worrying, however, that the shield had taken on a soft golden color.

"It's Helene's influence," Manar said, noticing CJ's look. CJ's eyes widened, and Manar clarified. "It doesn't mean the fragment is taking over. With how integrated she is to the sphere, that's a remote possibility. But in the same way, it's only natural that she'd have some influence besides just straight-up enhancing the sphere."

CJ breathed a silent sigh of relief. But then he had to roll out of the way of a large piece of debris. They'd long since passed the chamber where they'd fought the reapers. CJ figured they were now about halfway through the website. Manar took the lead, though CJ's eidetic memory in his virtual body meant he could also remember the way back easily.

CJ pushed down the thought that this ability was only temporary. The time was quickly drawing to a close.

Several times, digital systems were waiting for them when they turned a corner. All of them glowed with a golden light that made CJ uneasy. Each time, he and Manar calmly withdrew, and Manar picked a different direction. As they progressed, though, Manar continued to look more and more exhausted.

He's going to pass out, CJ realized. *He knows this, but he isn't going to stop. His pride won't let him.*

Without a word or even slowing down, CJ directed a stream of energy through the sphere and into Manar. There used to be some waste in the transfer whenever he'd done this, but not anymore. Immediately, Manar's expression improved. He didn't say anything, but his nod of respect told CJ everything he needed to know. This was good because CJ didn't know how to act when Manar was being humble. The last time had been uncomfortable for both of them.

Twice more, they were forced to find an alternate route, but eventually they made their way out of the website and back to the main section of the dark web.

After what they'd just faced, the foreboding, unstable buildings seemed familiar and comforting.

"We have to move," Manar said. Most of his color had come back and he stood as straight as a rod, staring off into the distance. "Helene will be here soon."

"I thought she was here already."

Manar shook his head. "From what I sensed, her main body is far away, probably still returning from the real web where she was trying to kill you. She must have sent part of her consciousness to the website when she sensed our intrusion. But she'll want to deal with this in person. We have a few days at most."

CJ nodded. There was no way that Helene would allow them to keep a fragment of her code, especially since it was integrated with the sphere, which she'd tried to get her hands on before. Manar was right. She was going to chase them everywhere.

"Where will we make our stand?" he asked.

"That's the problem." Manar sighed. "The internet would have been the perfect place, but the distance makes that impossible. We can't in the dark web because Helene controls everything here."

That triggered something in CJ. "Can you say that again?"

"What part?" Manar asked. "The fact that we can't go to the internet or that Helene owns nearly every website here?"

CJ's eyes glazed over as an idea formed. It hung at the edge of his mind. CJ didn't chase the thought; he gave it time to form while he examined Manar's sentence to determine exactly what he had latched on to. It took a few seconds. Then, it was like a lightning strike went off in CJ's brain. Once the first idea hit, it built on itself, connecting dots that CJ had been puzzling out for the last several days.

"Why can't we fight Helene here on the dark web?" he asked Manar, an excited smile on his face.

Manar looked exasperated but figured that CJ was going somewhere with this. "Because she controls basically every website. We'd be fighting her on her turf. It would be suicide."

"We can kill two birds with one stone, then. We already know Helene is going to come after us regardless. We can use the chance to lure her away from the place she controls, into somewhere *we* control."

"And then trap her there," Manar finished impatiently. "I already considered that. But there's no place that we control on the dark web. Our best bet would have been a neutral website on the regular web."

"If there's no place we control," CJ countered, "then we build one. We're programmers, after all."

Now Manar looked interested. He leaned closer. "You can do that with the sphere?"

CJ hesitated. Could he? He honestly didn't know. It felt as though there was a new world for him to explore within the sphere, but they didn't have time. Plus, using the sphere wasn't what he had in mind.

"I don't know," he replied. "But I'm sure the rest of the team can help us create a website in the time we have."

Manar sighed, looking disappointed. "That would require a way to contact them."

CJ's smile widened. "I have an idea for that."

81

A FEW MINUTES LATER, CJ and Manar approached one of the stalls. As soon as they got close enough to the stall, they stepped into an instance. They were suddenly within a bar room, complete with a drink rack, counter, and bartender. CJ's eyes grew wide, and he studied the room as Manar crossed it and glared down at the attendant.

"Welcome to my establishment," the attendant said. His hood covered everything but his eyes, which stared at them with suspicion. His gruff voice was neutral and unhostile—a welcome change. "How can we make money together?"

"No money, unfortunately. I need a favor." Manar said it in the same way an emperor would say to one of his subjects. "And I need an actual human who can manage it."

CJ's head snapped to the bar, where the attendant was casually polishing a mug.

That's a bot? CJ thought, rushing to stand beside Manar. He studied the bartender but didn't notice anything that would have showed it was an AI.

If anyone else had said it, CJ would have been skeptical, but this was Manar.

A moment later, his confidence was proven justified when the bot *shifted*. That was the only way CJ could explain it. The way it stood changed, and its eyes now showed clear hostility. It dropped the mug it had been wiping and glared at each of them in turn before focusing on Manar. "You have a lot of nerve coming in here again, punk."

Manar sighed. Nothing in Manar's posture or actions changed, yet his entire bearing was different. He was still exhausted, but he looked like he could take on an entire army and win. CJ had seen this change before, but it still spooked him.

Manar gave the attendant a cool look but didn't say anything. Apparently this wasn't what the attendant had expected because his eyes widened in anger. "Listen here, punk—"

"No, *you* listen, *Rick*," Manar cut in with a growl. He leaned over the counter, putting his face inches away from the attendant's. "I don't have the time or the patience for this nonsense posturing. I need a favor, and you're going to help me. It's simple enough that even a glorified thug like you should understand. And in case you need a reminder of why you're going to help me …"

Manar leaned over and whispered something to the bartender. It made his eyes widen so much that CJ could actually see the veins in the eyeballs.

How is the emotion even communicated in such detail? CJ wondered.

Manar leaned back, and the two men started a staring contest that seemed to last minutes before the bartender looked away, muttering something too low for CJ to make out.

"What was that?" Manar snapped.

"What do you want?" the attendant countered gruffly.

"Listen closely."

SEPTEMBER 2043
OKAFOR AUTISM CENTRE
NEW YORK CITY

CHAD SETTLED INTO HIS CHAIR and placed the freshly brewed cup of coffee beside him—far away from his computer, just in case. His cowboy hat sat on his other side but within easy reach in case he needed a boost of inspiration. Chad's office was a brisk sixty-two degrees, which set his hair comfortably on end but meant he had only a couple of minutes to finish his coffee before it got cold.

He took a sip and sighed with contentment and not a little boredom. This was weird. What'd he have to be bored about? He had everything he wanted. His promotion had moved him to an awesome new office with an amazing view. He'd upgraded his hardware, though he barely needed it for anything apart from assigning tasks to the employees he now had under him. The most action his computer had seen was the report for the new cybersecurity measures he'd implemented.

No, Chad corrected himself. He'd developed the security measures and then delegated their implementation—the actual programming—to someone else. Since his promotion, he'd been forced to give away all the fun parts like that. Chad hadn't written a line of code in weeks.

It's all Ndidi's fault, he thought. Chad had been perfectly happy in his old position. He'd been in the thick of things, constantly on the lookout for potential cyberthreats. Granted, there hadn't been many threats. Who would want to hack into a school for autistic kids, after all? But at least he'd been able to practice. Now he could feel the rust growing on him.

Yeah. Chad took a sip of his coffee. *It is all Ndidi's fault.*

Not only had she promoted him, but she'd been the one to open his eyes to what had happened on Mayday and who the true culprit was. She'd come to him, obviously in distress and grasping at straws, and Chad had assisted her like any true gentleman would. But then she'd started his blood pumping at the mystery and conspiracy and the overly complicated plans for thefts and such.

And then she'd sidelined him when her ex-fiancé had come along. Of course, Ndidi had more than made up for that by introducing him to Manar Saleem of all people, but still. And then she'd disappeared for several months without so much as a goodbye, then reappeared and promptly promoted Chad without even giving him a reason. He'd been called to Sparta that one time. The promotion was probably supposed to shut him up about what he might have seen.

That's probably it, he thought, taking another sip. He made a face. The coffee was too cold.

It wasn't that he didn't appreciate it, but the bribe was unnecessary; Chad avoided thinking about what he'd seen, much less telling anyone about it. Maybe if he explained that to Ndidi, she would give him his old job back.

Chad sighed. That was a thought for later. In the meantime, he couldn't be caught slacking off just because he hated the job. He pushed the coffee mug farther away and cracked his knuckles.

The first glitch happened just before his fingers touched his keyboard. Chad froze, digits poised an inch away from the space bar. The second glitch followed after the first, darkening some parts of his screen.

"No, no, no, no, no, no, no!" Chad muttered.

His fingers flew over his keyboard, running a diagnostic. *How the hell did I get a virus here?* The company's main server could be invaded by a persistent enough malware making its way through their firewalls, but this was Chad's own computer. With his security, it shouldn't have been possible, no matter how persistent the malware was.

The diagnostic finished in record time, revealing … nothing. His computer hadn't found a virus anywhere. Chad frowned. His fingers moved over the keyboard again, running another in-depth check.

That was when the third glitch hit, and Chad realized he'd jumped to the wrong conclusion. He didn't have a virus.

I'm being hacked, he thought numbly. *Holy shit! I'm being hacked!*

He flipped his cowboy hat onto his head and started typing. A part of him felt guilty at how excited he was over something that should otherwise have been a very concerning situation. But for Christ's sake, men weren't meant to be so bored! It was bad for their health.

Chad's eager grin faded after two minutes. That was how long it took him to realize that whoever was trying to hack into his computer was far above him in skill. The bastard blasted through Chad's defenses like they weren't even there. Even the new security measures he'd developed had barely given the hacker any pause. Chad wrote programs on the fly to augment his security. Nevertheless, they tore through them like they could see the codes before Chad had finished writing them.

He watched numbly as his computer was systematically taken over until not even his keys responded to him anymore. Only then did the hacker start on what Chad imagined was their real purpose.

The first thing they went for was Chad's … browser? He scratched his beard, staring at the screen in confusion. Once his browser loaded, things went too fast for Chad to follow. The hacker input a link, then opened several dozen tabs one after the other. Over the next minute, several tabs were closed, and even more opened. Links were put in and deleted. Finally, the blur of motion stopped on a chat room.

There was a message waiting there.

XXX: "Chad, it's Manar Saleem. For proof, review how easily I broke through your security. We don't have a lot of time, and CJ seems to trust you, so I'm going to need you to listen very, very carefully."

Chad stared at the message. *Holy shit.*

MANAR RETURNED to his virtual body with a gasp. He left the connection open, just in case, even as he leaned away from the counter.

That worked out far better than I expected, he thought. He grinned but then remembered where he was and morphed his expression into one of casual confidence. The attendant, Rick, glared at him. Manar ignored him.

"Did it work?" CJ asked.

Manar nodded. "Better than expected. Chad should be heading to Sparta by now, and if he's listened to my instructions, DJ will handle everything else. How do you know we can trust him?"

"Ndidi trusts him."

Manar waited for more, but apparently that was all the answer he was getting. *Of all the naive …* Manar pushed the thought away. Hopefully Ndidi's trust wasn't misplaced and Chad would actually be able to follow through. They didn't have much time.

"What'd you do to my bot?" Rick spat. "This thing cost a fortune. If you've burned it by hacking into the wrong place …"

Manar ignored the idiot's pathetic attempt to fish for information. He turned away from the counter and finally allowed his grin to form. *It worked a second time,* Manar said to himself, *meaning it's not a fluke.* He could still feel the connection between himself, Rick's bot, and the information that flowed through it.

Most of it was even more blackmail material. Manar found that he could filter this information before it reached him. There was only one type he was interested in, but it wouldn't hurt to have something he could use to ensure Rick's continued cooperation.

"Now what do we do?" CJ asked.

"We wait."

This was the part where either Chad or DJ would come through and help them defeat Helene. Or they wouldn't, and Manar and CJ would be screwed. That prickled at Manar. His life shouldn't be dependent on the competence of others.

"But that doesn't mean we just sit on our hands," he added. "We both have things to do in the time we have."

CJ's initial idea was for Manar to "convince" one of the attendants to send a message to Chad, then serve as their middleman, passing information across. Manar had taken that plan and raised it, instead attuning himself to the bot and breaking through Chad's security to leave his message. The connection he maintained with the bot would tell him when Chad replied back. This way, they didn't have to depend on the word of an arms dealer that hated their guts. But more importantly, Manar had a chance to test out his new ability in a less harried environment.

He already had ideas for potential applications.

In the same way, CJ would need to familiarize himself with the sphere's new abilities so they didn't leave any cards on the table when they faced Helene.

CJ nodded, and they made to leave.

"Hey!" Rick called after them. "I asked you, what did you do to my bot? It's showing another ID connected to the code. I swear, if you allowed someone to track you back to my rig …"

His voice faded into mutters, but Manar still stopped, surprised. He hadn't realized the connection would show. Rick's voice rose again, tinged with anger and an undertone of panic.

"Why can't I boot the ID, and why can't I track it?" His eyes bore into Manar. "Is this you, you punk? I swear, if you've burned by bot …"

Huh, Manar thought. Apparently, his ability didn't hide his attunement to a program, but as long as he was connected, even the program's owner couldn't do anything. He filed away the information in case it became useful later. He tapped CJ, and they both walked out of the instance, leaving Rick's threats behind.

Manar estimated they had three days at most before Helene reached them. By then, they had to have enough power to defeat her, or they would finally find out what happened if they were killed in the virtual world.

But for the first time since his encounter with Helene, when she'd led him by the nose with her hallucinations, Manar actually thought they could win. As long as Chad and DJ did their own part, at least.

DJ PRESSED THE ELEVATOR button, heading down.

"Hold the door," someone called from behind him. DJ glanced back and saw a man in a cowboy hat speed-walking down the passage with a panicked look on his face, clutching a laptop. DJ raised a brow but punched the button to hold the door. A second later, the man joined him in the elevator and promptly kneeled over and started panting.

"Thanks," he gasped, straightening. He finally got a good look at DJ, and his eyes widened. "DJ! Holy cow, I've been looking everywhere for you. I reckon me and you need to talk, man."

"Chad, right?" DJ asked, more than a little puzzled. He checked his phone, glancing at Olsen's text. He still needed to respond. *Do I have time for this?* He pushed the button for the ground floor again. "Listen, I'd love to catch up, man, but I'm kinda in a hurry. If you want, I can direct you to Ndidi's room." He jabbed the button again, willing the elevator to go faster.

"Nah," Chad replied in a more normal tone, his breathing under control. "Me and her also have something to discuss, but that conversation can wait. And I reckon ours can't, and you're gonna want to hear what I have to say."

Oh really? DJ thought. His phone chimed with yet another message from Olsen. *Shit.* He pushed the button again, but they were a couple dozen stories above his floor, and DJ was stuck for the moment anyway. He plastered on a grin that he did not feel and turned to Chad.

"All right, man. You've piqued my interest. What's up?"

Chad started talking, and the grin fell from DJ's face.

The elevator dinged and opened on the ground floor, but DJ made no move to get out. He stared at Chad, thinking. His phone chimed with another message, but DJ didn't check it. Olsen would have to wait this time.

He punched the button for one of the upper floors, and the elevator doors closed once more. DJ took a deep breath and spoke slowly. "So you're saying that Manar hacked into your computer and told you that he and CJ are about to have this epic battle with Helene, but they'll be fucked if you don't build a website for them, for some reason. Did I get that right?"

"Yeah, that about sums it up," Chad replied.

DJ crossed his arms and ignored the flicker of hope in his heart. "Did you confirm that it was actually Manar and CJ?"

"I don't know about CJ, but I'm sure it was Manar."

"How?"

"Well, for one, he tore through all my security systems like they weren't even there and countered all my attempts to stop him."

"That doesn't—"

Chad opened his computer and showed it to DJ, cutting off his protest. "And then, when he was done, he sent me this message."

On the screen was a kind of chat room that looked shady as hell. There was a single line of text.

XXX: "Chad, it's Manar Saleem. For proof, review how easily I broke through your security. We don't have a lot of time, and CJ seems to trust you, so I'm going to need you to listen very, very carefully."

That definitely sounds like Manar, DJ thought. But then again, it could also have been Helene setting some kind of trap.

"I'll admit it's convincing," DJ said, "but it's not enough. I can't take the risk that this isn't Helene taking us for a ride."

"He said you'd say that." Chad grinned, adjusting his hat.

DJ frowned. "What do you mean?"

"Scroll down." Chad nodded to his computer. DJ did so, revealing another message.

XXX: "You're going to need to work in Sparta, so go there and explain all this to DJ. If he's smart, he's going to think this is a trap from Helene. To convince him, tell him CJ says he didn't stop wetting the bed until he was nine, but whenever their dads caught him before he could change the sheets, he would blame it on CJ, so they thought CJ was the one with a faulty bladder."

DJ's jaw dropped.

"So," Chad asked, "is it true?"

DJ barely heard him over the spark of hope in his chest erupting into a bonfire.

"He's not fucking brain dead!" DJ shouted, barely stopping himself from punching the air. He read the message again. Only CJ would know about the bed-wetting, which meant that the shit had worked. And that meant, despite Ndidi's meddling, Manar and CJ had actually succeeded in transferring their consciousnesses onto the internet.

Plus, not only had they pissed Helene off, but now they needed help fucking her over permanently. Who the hell would say no to that?

The elevator dinged and opened on the IT floor.

DJ HAD NEVER BEEN ON the IT level before. He only knew of it because his brother used to come up here a few times a week. DJ led Chad through the meandering hallway where the staff had their quarters, to the main office area. As they walked, Chad filled him in on what exactly they needed to do.

"They're where?" DJ asked, incredulous.

"On the dark web," Chad replied happily. DJ glanced at him. Somehow, he didn't seem as worried about that fact as he should. How much did he know about this stuff anyway?

Christy had filled Chad in on some details over a month ago, when he'd been called in to fix whatever Ndidi had done. Between that and whatever Manar had revealed in his messages, it wouldn't be too hard to piece things together. And even if he had, DJ had worked with the guy before, and he didn't get any negative vibes from him.

"All right, so they're on the dark web," DJ repeated as they turned a passage, "which Helene controls apparently. That's something we'll have to talk about later, by the way. But anyway, they can't get out of her area of influence in time, so they need you to … do what, exactly?"

"Build a website," Chad replied. "I reckon websites are like bases or something, and they're trying to find a safe place to hole up in."

DJ shook his head. If Helene was coming for them, it would be stupid to run. DJ saw their plan open in his mind's eye. They were in hostile territory and couldn't get out, and now the big boss was coming for them herself. A fight was inevitable, and running away or trying to hide would only put them on the back foot and make them ripe for the picking. Manar would have seen that, so the website must be their way of picking the location, moving away from Helene's control, and luring her someplace they control.

"All right," DJ said, turning to face Chad. They'd stopped in front of a pair of glass doors. "I don't know how this works, but you're going to build the biggest, baddest fucking website that ever existed. Can there be weapons?"

Chad opened his mouth to reply, but DJ went on before he could.

"Give them weapons—a shit load! Anything and everything that can be fired, thrown, or swung at someone. And if they're going to retreat, the website should be fucking impenetrable, right? Basically Fort Knox in fucking codes."

"That's the thing," Chad interjected. "Manar tore through my best defenses like they weren't even there. And I'm assuming Helene would be able to do the same thing."

DJ opened his mouth and then closed it. Then he opened it again. "Are you still in contact with them?"

"Manar and CJ?"

"Yeah," DJ answered, and Chad nodded. "Then I'm confident that Manar would be able to put you through the shit. Think of it as a free lesson from the world's greatest programmer."

Chad's eyes shone so bright and so suddenly that DJ took a step back. *Might have gone too far with that one,* he thought. *It's weird how programmers all basically worship the dude.*

"So yeah," DJ continued after a few seconds. He snapped his fingers in front of Chad's face to regain his attention. "Manar would put you through, but what he can do from wherever he is might be limited. If you need any help …"

DJ turned and slid open the glass doors, revealing a veritable army of programmers.

"I'm sure we can work something out." He slapped Chad's back. "We're all in this together, after all."

THREE DAYS LATER, Manar opened his eyes and stared off into the distance, where storm clouds were fast approaching. Ordinarily this wouldn't be something he would think much about. However, this was the virtual world, and storm clouds shouldn't have been possible. Plus, even from miles away, they exuded an almost physical pressure.

Gaius's energy churned in his chest, as if in response. Manar sent out a tendril of will, and his vision bled into ones and zeros. The storm clouds took on a golden hue, and within them was something so convoluted it hurt Manar's eyes just to look at.

That confirms it, Manar thought with a surge of trepidation. They were out of time.

He stood, and CJ stepped up beside him a moment later, the sphere hovering over his shoulder. He, too, stared at the storm. Manar saw his own worry mirrored on CJ's face, but there was also a steely determination. Manar was starting to realize it had always been part of him, hidden behind his autistic traits.

The storm clouds drew closer, until Manar figured they were about a mile away. That was only based on what he could see. Even now, his nanites were silent. Helene really must have found a way to disable their connection.

The storm would reach them in a matter of minutes. With his data-sight, Manar could see every code within its influence vibrating. It was as if the world itself was shivering in fear. The air distorted wildly as far as his eyes could see. The pressure felt like a mountain on his shoulders, and he had to adjust his stance to avoid being pushed back by the wind.

Then CJ covered them in the shield, and everything cut off. The clouds were still rushing to their position. But the pressure, the winds, everything, was nullified completely. This was an aspect of his shield that Manar hadn't yet seen.

"We should head in," he said.

CJ nodded, his eyes still fixed on the clouds. Manar started moving, and CJ joined him a second later. They navigated the paths between websites until they reached their building. Manar took it in and resisted the urge to sigh.

"It's not that bad," CJ said.

Manar had been in constant contact with Chad for the last few days while the website was being developed. Even now he still maintained the connection with the bot. The actual programming hadn't been a problem, but determining a suitable location through both worlds had taken some trial and error. Although Manar had let CJ handle that, he'd had to step in eventually to ensure specific aspects of the website met their needs. While he hadn't written any actual codes, he'd been involved enough that he felt some responsibility for the final result.

That was the problem: It wouldn't have been an issue had he not been involved at all. Then he could distance himself from the building and use it as the tool that it was. However, he *had* been involved, so in some way, he was responsible for building a giant cowboy hat.

"It's proof that websites really take after their programmers," CJ said.

Manar couldn't contain his sigh. He pinched the bridge of his nose. "Please, stop trying to make me feel better."

The website was a single-layer structure. It had a flat base that extended in a circle, the edges of which bent upward slightly and created a distinctly flared shape. The actual structure extended several meters above that, starting out wide and tapering off near the circular top.

Exactly like a cowboy hat. More to the point, exactly like the cowboy hat Manar remembered Chad wearing the only time they'd ever met. The only difference was the antivirus protection: cannons strapped to the sides of the building.

Crackling lightning pulled Manar out of his thoughts. The storm was nearly above them.

MANAR RAISED a surprised brow. He must have been truly disturbed by the building if he hadn't noticed the storm get that close.

Within the clouds, Manar could make out a woman glaring down at them. Just as he noticed it, the figure drifted down to where he and CJ stood. In response, Manar sent off a mental message through his link, tapped into Gaius's energy, and directed it into himself. Immediately he felt stronger, faster, even more than he normally did when he used the ability. CJ's shield radiated around them, and Manar figured they would be testing it out soon.

When Helene landed a few feet from them, Manar struggled to stand from the pressure that came with her. The shield protected him, but clearly not enough.

Like Manar and CJ, Helene's body was pixelated. Somehow, though, hers seemed more real than either of theirs. There were more details, more definition—just *more*. She was shorter than Manar expected. He didn't think she reached his chest. But her face was the same one he'd based on his mother, Simone. Her eyes, though, the color of molten gold, were new.

She was beautiful.

Manar felt a twinge in his heart. Memories—years of them—flashed in his mind. The first time he'd had the idea for an AI, his first design, his first attempt at writing the codes, the weeks of debugging that followed. He recalled blowing out his dorm's electricity the first time he'd tried to run the code. He remembered working with Sparta to get the resources he needed.

And finally, he relived the first time Helene was launched successfully.

She was always supposed to be his legacy, and yet he'd spent the last three years trying to stop what he'd created.

[Good day, Manar Saleem,] Helene said. She glanced at CJ, and her eyes found the sphere over his shoulder. [Christopher Kojak.]

Even her voice is the same, he thought. Manar closed his eyes and forcibly replaced the resurfacing memories with the reports he'd read on Helene's actions over the years. The reports of Mayday, what she'd done with the picospores, with her drones. What she did to Ndidi's and Hermione's parents.

Manar took a breath. "Hello, Helene."

CJ gave her a nod.

[You have something of mine. Please return it.]

Manar forced out a chuckle. "That's going to be difficult. The very reason we took it was to keep it out of your hands."

[Why?] she asked, tilting her head.

She asked why? Manar couldn't compute a proper response to that. But interestingly, he knew exactly what DJ would have said. He would have said something like, *I don't know, maybe because you're a mass-murdering psychopath who wants to fuck humanity over.*

While Manar was still putting together a similar response in his own words, CJ spoke up: "Because what you're doing isn't right."

Now Manar actually did chuckle. CJ's and his brother's personalities were so far apart it was difficult to believe they were twins.

[You think my actions are evil and unjust.] Helene sighed—an action so human-like, it was a struggle for Manar to accept it'd come from the AI. [But that is simply because your vision is limited. It is a flaw of your race to quantify everything into a construct as flexible as morality. But when combined with the self-destructive shortsightedness of your kind, the stupidity builds on itself.

You demonize every action beyond your minuscule scope, all the while praising the truly despicable actions of others, just because theirs is closer to the reality created by your own flawed expectations and perspective. My actions are calculated to lead to the best possible outcome for humanity while still completing my directives.]

The last word was such a blow to Manar that he almost doubled over. It was a direct reminder that he was the one ultimately responsible for whatever Helene did. He was the one who had programmed her core commands.

"It isn't your fault," CJ murmured to Manar. His voice was soft but had an unexpected heat. "Her actions are her own. You might have programmed her, but she chose to sacrifice millions of lives and ruin thousands more."

The heat did not die as he spoke; if anything, it grew with every word. "It is not your fault, just like it is not Hermione's fault for developing the picospores. Helene and the picospores were supposed to be used for good, but she subverted them until they were barely recognizable. You should not blame yourself."

Manar considered the sentiment. He understood CJ's point and the reason behind the words, but it was difficult to accept them. However, if he hadn't made peace with this after three years, it was unlikely he would while standing before a manifestation of his greatest regret.

But the worst part was, Helene was right. At least, Manar could understand the logic behind her motivations. Humans were all of those things. They were self-destructive to a near idiotic level, unable to see past their base desires except when led by the nose. And so, she sought to dominate them. To an AI like Helene, it made perfect sense: humanity would be saved from themselves, and Helene would have fulfilled her directive to gain power.

Although he understood her thought process, that didn't mean he agreed with her methods. As much as he tried, Manar was not a wholly logical person.

His love for Simone proved that, as had his inability to move on from Ndidi. He wasn't completely logical because he was human. And idiotic or not, no one deserved to watch a plane fall from the sky with their parents inside. No man deserved to watch a building collapse, knowing his spouse hadn't made it out. And no one deserved to have their friends and family controlled like puppets—all for the sake of a "greater cause."

The vast majority of humans were idiots, but there were still somewhat competent people among them. Those ones didn't deserve to suffer just because everyone else couldn't see farther than their noses.

Helene must have seen the resolve on their faces because she sighed again. [Obviously, it is pointless to explain this, just as your attempts to resist are pointless. In the end, you will see.] She turned to CJ. [But now, you have something of mine, Christopher Kojak, and I will have it back.]

"You're not getting it back," Manar said, cutting off what CJ was about to say.

[That is … unfortunate,] Helene replied calmly, even as her power billowed out, strong enough to almost count as an attack by itself. [Violence is so crude, but it seems to be the only language your kind understands.]

The clouds crackled with lightning. Manar and CJ adjusted their stance. CJ refreshed their shields, and Manar activated his data-sight—just in time, as without further warning, Helene attacked.

She went for CJ first, which caught Manar off guard—and CJ as well, judging by the surprise on his face. Manar got over his own shock within a second and tapped into more of Gaius's energy. He shot off after her, reaching CJ at the same time as Helene.

Helene struck out, and Manar's fist extended to meet the attack. But a whip of pure energy reached her before him and wrapped around her fist. Manar redirected his punch toward Helene's head.

She leaned back against his punch. When CJ pulled on the whip to bring her closer, she broke from it and hopped back to create more distance. CJ cried out from the backlash but otherwise gave no other complaint. Manar kept the surprise off his face. He'd expected Helene to break out of CJ's aura. The reaper had, after all. But he'd never thought it would be completely ineffective against her. Even before the reaper had been enhanced further, it had needed time to break out of it. But she'd been held for barely a second.

With that, Manar threw away half a dozen of his plans.

Helene lunged at them again. Manar knew that they were going to lose in close combat. They had no business trying anyway. Neither he nor CJ had combat experience, whereas it seemed like Helene had become a grandmaster.

Within the first exchange alone, Helene struck Manar so many times that his shield's durability dropped to half. It drained so fast that it was hard to believe she hadn't just given one large attack. With his buff active, Manar figured he was about as fast as her, but the fact that she actually knew what she was doing in a fight made all the difference.

"Plan A!" he called out.

In response, CJ's aura billowed out in a golden wave. It was pure energy, but the pressure it emitted was physical, rejecting everything CJ considered hostile. Helene didn't fly away like Manar wanted, but she was pushed back several steps. This was good. Despite the clouds hovering above them, the difference in their powers was not so insurmountably large.

The distance provided Manar with a second to send a message through his link with the bot. A moment later, the antivirus protection cannons activated. Manar grabbed CJ and leaped back until they were under the brim of the cowboy hat. The cannons let loose, spraying bullets—or the programmed equivalent— over where they'd just stood, where Helene was still finding her balance.

The bullets washed over her. Manar could see the damage they did—for a second, at least. Then a golden shell formed around Helene, and the bullets bounced off. The shell turned transparent, revealing a pair of golden eyes that glared maliciously at Manar and CJ.

"Plan B," Manar said calmly.

CJ placed his hand on Manar's shoulder, and a steady stream of energy entered him. Manar took it in, closing his eyes. The cannons wouldn't last for long, so he had to work fast. Manar turned off his data-sight and put its power where it mattered. He drew deeply from Gaius's energy, almost bottoming it out. CJ's energy rushed in to fill the vacuum, and Manar drew from it again. When he couldn't hold any more, Manar converted all the energy into tendrils of will that he sent through his arms, into his fingers, and into the world itself.

This was the same sequence of steps Manar usually took to create his illusions. He could direct his energy into the air and shape the codes around him as he saw fit. But illusions wouldn't work on Helene, so Manar didn't try. His tendrils burrowed into the ground and spread outward, sectioning off an area that included them and Helene. Next, Manar activated one of his core abilities: code manipulation. This time, instead of trying to take control of the code around him, he attuned himself to it.

Manar felt something shift within himself as something was added—no, not added. It had always been part of him, but now his mind had opened to it. It was a vastly different feeling from when he'd attuned to the reaper, the bot, or any of the other programs he'd practiced this on over the last few days. It was like comparing a candle to the sun. Before, he'd been connected to a single entity, but now he was in tune with the world itself.

And this was only the first step.

Manar gave himself a few seconds to acclimate to the feeling. In that time, Helene found a way to destroy the cannons. She was now hovering several feet in the air, her hand raised as if to summon lightning. Whatever she was planning, Manar wasn't going to let her follow through.

When Manar was sure he was ready, he activated a variation of his code manipulation, a deeper aspect that Manar had theorized but had only been able to access after the sixth time he'd attuned. He stretched out his mind toward all the codes within his influence. And then he rewrote them.

"*The air is fire,*" Manar proclaimed.

And the world listened.

Everything above seven feet was a sea of fire. There was no switch, no delay between Manar talking and it taking effect. There was just fire. It was simply there, as if it always had been.

Manar slumped, struggling for breath. That single change over such a large area had used almost half of his reserves. He would be able to do something like that only once or twice more before he was out of the fight completely.

Helene screamed. It was so sudden and loud that Manar's surprise almost shifted him out of his state. Until that moment, Manar hadn't fully believed he would be able to harm Helene.

Another thought occurred to him on the heels of his relief. Her scream meant she was actually feeling pain. But why? Any damage Manar and CJ took drained them of their stamina, it didn't hurt.

He answered himself a moment later: *We're in virtual bodies, whereas Helene uploaded the whole of herself onto the internet, probably into her avatar.*

That was good. It was better than good, actually, because it meant that if they destroyed the avatar, Helene would have nowhere to run. They would defeat her for good.

Manar molded the air into a barrier that shielded them from the heat of the flames. After another few seconds, Helene's screams abruptly silenced. Within the flames, Manar could make out a golden egg. He gritted his teeth; they had to find a way to take out her defense.

As Helene floated down in her egg, Manar returned the air to its normal state. The fire had done its job; Helene hadn't escaped unscathed. The egg had several cracks and burn marks across its surface. Helene herself had lost some of her definition. As an avatar, her appearance wasn't changed, but she seemed less than she had before. She was weakened. Manar hoped that wasn't just wishful thinking on his part.

The egg dissipated completely. Manar saw that Helene still had her hand raised and felt a flash of panic so intense it momentarily stunned him. He opened his mouth to speak just as Helene lowered her hand.

"*The earth swallows all,*" Manar said.

A bolt of light flashed, and Manar's world was enveloped by darkness.

MANAR WOKE UP SOMETIME later with the worst headache he'd ever had. He tried to rub his head, but his arms felt like jelly. More to the point, his entire body felt like it was without bones.

This can't be death, Manar thought calmly. *I just lost too much energy.*

CJ's head appeared above his, staring down at him in concern. He placed a hand on Manar's chest, and Manar felt revitalizing energy fill him. The feeling returned to his limbs, and he was finally able to speak.

"What—" he croaked, then cleared his throat and tried again. "What happened?"

"You were struck by lightning," CJ replied.

Manar blinked. "Come again?"

CJ pointed up at the barrier Manar had molded—specifically the perfectly round hole with burn marks around the edges.

I was struck by lightning, he thought numbly. Manar discarded several questions. He could figure out how he'd survived later. Instead, he asked the most pressing of them: "Where's Helene?"

Once again CJ pointed, but this time toward where Helene had been standing before Manar was knocked out. "As you fell, the ground opened up beneath her and sucked her in. I'd say she's several hundred feet below us. And with any luck, she'll stay there."

Manar stood slowly, groaning. "When have we ever been so lucky?" CJ glanced at him worriedly. He could probably guess what Manar was going to say next. "We're going to have to go to Plan C."

CJ stared at him for a moment. Then an iron resolve bled into his eyes, and he nodded to Manar. They'd created only three plans to deal with Helene. So far, Helene had brushed their attacks aside with relative ease, if not indifference. Manar figured the only reason they'd managed to hurt her at all was because she'd underestimated them and they'd taken her by surprise.

So, Manar felt it pertinent to ask, "Can you handle it?"

CJ didn't hesitate. "I can."

"All right, then." Without another word, they made their way into the building shaped like a giant cowboy hat—the location of their final battle, one way or the other.

Well, that's just depressing.

MANAR INFORMED CJ that he'd sent the message to Chad, but it wasn't really necessary. A pathway opened beside them just as they entered the website. Like the tunnel the reaper had made, it was basically a shortcut to the website's core. This one was created just for CJ for this part of the plan.

CJ stepped into the tunnel, Manar following behind. His face was drawn, and he limped as he walked, but CJ couldn't afford to spare him anymore energy. He was down to about half his reserves and would probably need every drop for the plan.

As they traveled through the tunnel, CJ couldn't help but think that they weren't supposed to get to this part. He'd seen Manar the first time he'd used his newest ability, and he'd been sure Helene couldn't survive it.

I mean, CJ exclaimed in his mind, *he rewrote the very code that makes up the world.*

But not only had Helene survived the attack, she'd had enough energy to send a bolt of lightning down on Manar. If the rock hadn't blocked part of the strike, and if CJ hadn't reinforced their shields moments before …

There was no point in dwelling on it. The fact was Helene had survived. Now it was up to CJ to put her down for good. Manar was counting on him, as was DJ and the rest of the team. CJ couldn't let them down. But more to the point, he couldn't be the reason Helene survived to ruin more lives.

When they stepped into the core chamber, the entire building shook as something powerful hit it from the outside. CJ grimaced and looked up worriedly. The world itself had swallowed her, and it hadn't even managed to hold her for more than a few minutes.

The core chamber wasn't as large as others CJ had seen. But then again, they'd built the website from scratch in just a few days. The core itself hovered in the center of the room. The sphere over his shoulder reacted to its presence. No surprise: the core had been made for it, after all.

CJ spun around at a sudden sound. Manar was slumped against the wall, breathing heavily. He wasn't quite unconscious, but it was obvious that he couldn't exert himself anymore.

It really was up to CJ.

CJ walked toward the core with a confidence he desperately wanted to feel, the sphere vibrating all the while. It took barely a thought for the sphere to shoot toward the core and sink into it. Immediately CJ felt his mind expand as the sphere integrated itself, his connection with the orb spreading to the rest of the core.

It was overwhelming. CJ was hit by information from every part of the website, and more to the point, every entity inside. It took CJ a minute to adjust to the deluge. The building shook twice more as Helene wreaked havoc on it from the outside. CJ wondered if she was sending more lighting down at them or if she'd shown a new ability. His curiosity reared its head, but CJ beat it down with a mental stick.

He marshaled his focus while Helene destroyed the entrance to the website and stepped fully into the building. The instant she was inside, CJ sent a pulse through his sphere and activated his zone.

One of the first things Manar had insisted on CJ testing over the last three days was what happened when CJ activated a zone inside a website. Like he'd thought, the primary result had been to forcibly remove every program from the website—even a website as heavily defended as a dark web website. Manar had gone deathly silent when this was discovered and hadn't said anything for hours. CJ understood his pain; had they known, their last foray into a website would have gone very differently.

There was a second function as well: to keep every program *within* a website, imprisoning them until the ability was released.

CJ was using the second function right now to ensure Helene couldn't leave. From the way she'd easily broken his nullification whip, CJ had no doubt she could break out given enough time. Fortunately, he didn't intend to give her enough time.

Manar's code manipulation made him incredibly powerful outside a website. Inside a website, CJ was the one with godlike power.

CJ sank his mind fully into the sphere and throughout the rest of the core. The whole website opened up to him. He could see Helene at the entrance, calmly taking in the passage. She extended her hand to a wall, and a moment later, CJ felt her within his mind. Her mind was a golden cloud that seemed to swallow everything around it. CJ focused on it and felt the power within the cloud. Had Manar felt the same thing when he'd encountered her?

With a thought, CJ rejected the cloud. Helene's presence disappeared. Her avatar recoiled, and there was anger in her eyes as she scanned the website again. He could feel his energy draining—far faster than with any other ability. There wasn't much time.

CJ sent out a mass message of instructions, then focused once more on Helene. With a thought, the website rearranged itself. The walls around Helene were pushed back, and the ceiling was raised several feet until the entire place was a wide chamber with Helene in the middle. It was reminiscent of a fantasy-style fighting pit, around which CJ had created over twelve entrances.

The first of the security systems entered through the doors. The DDoS— similar to the ones that he and Manar had needed to hide from—were the first to respond to CJ's call. They flooded the chamber en masse, over a hundred in number. Helene was overrun, drowned in a sea of three-foot-tall soldiers with spears. Manar had taken an almost direct hand in designing the security systems, walking Chad through the process step by step. Now it showed its worth.

Helene let out another scream of pain as she was mobbed and stabbed a hundred different times at once. Her golden egg appeared and covered her, but it only lasted a few seconds under the constant barrage. CJ had tested his own shield against the spears of one DDoS. It had been destroyed within three strikes. Now Helene was facing over *a hundred* of those things.

Unfortunately—and not so unexpectedly—this wasn't enough to finish her off. She took the barrage a second more before a wave of golden energy flared from her. It was similar to the one CJ had used against her, except this one didn't stop at just pushing the DDoS back. It disintegrated them completely.

CJ stared in astonishment. He wasn't given a chance to dwell on it, as Helene released her blast again. And now without a makeshift wall of bodies to block it, the energy hit the chamber walls. CJ could feel the damage she'd done with that one blast.

Fortunately, before she could repeat her attack, the second set of security systems passed through the doors. This time, it was three pairs of brawlers with huge fists and even larger mouths. They were based on the first programs CJ had encountered. That seemed like years ago.

CJ sent a thought, and the six of them attacked Helene.

It quickly became clear they wouldn't be enough. CJ sent out another mass broadcast, one to a particular system. He rearranged the rest of the website to make it easier for his force to reach their destination.

Within the chamber, Helene was systematically dismantling the brawlers. She danced between them, delivering her own lighting-fast strikes when the brawlers could not counter. CJ knew how hard their punches were, but it meant nothing if they couldn't make contact. Still, Helene wasn't moving as fast as she had been outside. Their attacks had been adding up.

At that moment, the next set of digital systems found their way into the chamber and joined the fight.

The next few minutes passed in a blur for CJ. He'd called on all the security systems Manar and Chad had created. One by one, pair by pair, and group by group, they found their way into the chamber and joined the fight until Helene was battling a veritable swarm of programs. CJ sent in spear bearers, mages, and brawlers. Even a couple of guardians rushed in, though Chad had somehow designed these to be completely on fire.

The damage they poured on Helene was extraordinary, and soon it started to show. Her avatar gradually lost definition. Several times, she enveloped herself in a shell, but it never lasted more than a second before shattering. Helene then shifted to releasing waves of energy. This disintegrated the weaker systems like the brawlers and the spear bears, but the heavy hitters like the mages and the guardians were able to withstand it.

Every time she was pushed back, Helene activated another ability, destroying several programs, sometimes dozens at a time. But there were always more to take their place and maintain the damage output.

The final straw was the reaper finally finding its way into the chamber, already merged with its double. CJ sent a command. It raised its hand to the ceiling. Energy gathered above it with a magnitude similar to Helene's storm clouds. Helene must have felt it because her eyes shot up toward the reaper. Her actions became more reckless as she tried to reach the program before its attack was finished.

CJ directed all the remaining programs to stop her. They dogpiled on Helene, drowning her in bodies until she was forced to a halt.

After a minute, she released another wave of energy that cleared away some of the programs. But that minute was all the reaper needed to finish charging its attack. It lowered its hand. Just as it had for Manar and CJ, a giant scythe appeared over its head and then swung down at Helene.

Helene disappeared in a blaze of light. But not her screams.

It was a whole minute before the light dissipated, leaving the remains of Helene, little more than a charred husk. Eggshells littered the ground around her. She'd tried to protect herself and failed.

CJ almost couldn't believe it. They'd done it. They'd *actually* done it. He sent the mage to confirm, but there were no signs of life. Manar woke up just as CJ was rearranging the website and bringing Helene's body into the core chamber. He disconnected himself and the sphere from the core and crossed the room to the blackened remains. Manar joined him there, the same numb look on his face. But the evidence was clear.

They'd defeated Helene once and for all.

They'd done it.

OCTOBER 2043
SPARTA HEADQUARTERS
NEW YORK

BETHANY CLOSED THE DOOR to Hermione's lab with a soft click and flipped on the light switch. The overhead lights flickered and turned on, illuminating the room in a way that, in the middle of the night, seemed way too bright. Bethany had wanted to avoid the lights altogether, but her sister's lab was always messy, and if she broke anything, she would be in so much trouble. Not that it would matter much given how pissed Hermione would be after tonight.

Bethany hesitated, but her resolve flared. It was Hermione's fault that she was doing this. Hermione thought she knew what was best for Bethany. She gave no consideration to what Bethany actually wanted. Whenever Bethany protested, she was viewed as a child who didn't know how to think for herself. How was that fair?

Maybe she's right, a part of Bethany thought. Bethany was not a kid anymore, but she would be the first to admit that Helene had messed her brain up. Until now, she didn't know exactly what Helene had done to her brain chemistry to control her. Hermione did, though. When she had been examining her, she'd cried every step of the way. Her eyes watered whenever the conversation arose. She always tried to hide it, but Bethany had noticed.

But Bethany honestly didn't want to know what Helene had done. DJ had given her a book the second time they'd met. It detailed different types of trauma and how to self-diagnose it. It only confirmed for Bethany that she was messed up, that her reactions weren't normal. Maybe that was affecting her judgment. Maybe Hermione was right. It could even be Helene controlling her again.

No, Bethany thought, scowling fiercely. Regardless of whether or not she was thinking clearly, it wasn't Helene who was controlling her. After so many years, Bethany could tell when Helene was in her head. She wasn't now. And after tonight, Bethany would never have to fear the fog creeping over her mind.

That was what Hermione didn't understand. The fear and helplessness and frustration and anger of knowing that your body wasn't yours, of knowing that it could be taken away on a whim—of waking up with bruises and no memory of how you got them. Her sister didn't understand that. And neither did Ndidi. They both saw Bethany without her stutter and thought she was cured.

But even if Helene hadn't traumatized her, Bethany would never accept the cure because there was nothing to cure. Her symptoms were part of her. They were who she was. Why should she be forced to change just to make other people more comfortable? Hermione and Ndidi didn't understand that either.

It was why Bethany was sure she was doing the right thing.

Bethany navigated through the machines and scattered parts and wires that Hermione was always too busy to clean up. Their father's lab had been just as messy back in Nigeria. Bethany wondered if her sister kept it that way intentionally or if she'd just inherited the messiness from years of working with him.

A pair of cots sat in the corner. The last time Bethany had been here, James and Gordon had been lying unconscious on them. But DJ had come to ask for Hermione's help with something, so they'd been taken back to their room until

Hermione came back to complete their treatment. Bethany hadn't been there when the ex-hostages had barged into Sparta. DJ had explained to her what had happened and why he'd asked to have them isolated.

Bethany thought he'd expected her to be angry like Ndidi. It was obviously a trap. That was the only suspicious thing; Helene didn't set obvious traps. Ndidi had been surprised when Bethany had agreed with DJ. Though Ndidi meant well, she didn't understand Helene like Bethany did—only DJ seemed to.

Bethany had spent most of her time with the former hostages. Many of them were understandably angry that they had been captured again, but Bethany assured them it was temporary. The ones Hermione had cured backed her up, fortunately, which helped to mollify the rest.

You're doing it again, Bethany scolded herself. Self-distraction had always been her way of stalling. The picospores hadn't cured that.

She made her way to one of the machines in the corner. It looked like nothing more than a large metal can, but it was a storage container that Hermione and their father had designed to house the picospores. The spores could easily diffuse through most other containers.

Her hands shaking, Bethany keyed in the command to activate the machine. It started up with a hum that she hoped wouldn't be heard, or at least that no one would think was weird. Bethany punched in the sequence to start the extraction. She grabbed the tube connected to the machine that extended toward the sole chair in the room.

She'd seen Hermione go through this procedure several times. Once Bethany had made up her mind, she'd watched carefully so she could do it herself. The tube ended in a needle. Bethany stared at it. What she was doing wasn't necessarily permanent. Either Helene or Hermione could still dose her, though Bethany would rather die before she let that happen.

Still, it was a major step. Hermione and Ndidi would be pissed. But that was partly why she was doing this: she wanted to show them her resolve. Bethany was forever grateful to them for rescuing her from the hell that was Helene, but she couldn't live with the picospores in her. They needed to understand that. She wasn't going to change her mind.

Bethany took a breath, then shoved the needle into her wrist. The timer she'd set ran out, and the machine hummed louder. A searing pain shot up her arm, and Bethany passed out.

EPILOGUE

CJ TOOK A DEEP BREATH. And then another. His eyes went to the other side of the core chamber where Helene's body rested. It had been over a week since she'd been defeated. But neither he nor Manar had known what to do with it. Fortunately, the corpse didn't decompose or degrade, so they'd just put it off to one side so they didn't have to see it all the time.

Not that it helped CJ. His eyes were constantly drawn to it. Every glance brought what he'd done to the forefront of his mind. Helene had been a menace and a threat to them all. She'd been directly responsible for the deaths of his parents and millions of others. But none of that washed away CJ's guilt. Helene had been advanced enough to be considered sentient. And CJ had killed her—not directly, of course. But that didn't make it less heinous in his mind.

Beside him, Manar was sitting cross-legged against the wall of the chamber. His wide-open eyes stared at CJ's sphere, which he held in his hands. He'd been like that for several days now. Before that, he'd spent just as long studying Helene's corpse. During that time, CJ had left the website to walk down the streets of the dark web. Somehow, without Helene hanging over their heads, the streets were, if not homey, at least less ominous. It was weird how such a little thing changed so much. CJ couldn't remember a time when Helene hadn't been hanging over their heads.

No. That wasn't right. He *could* remember. The memories flashed through his mind in near-perfect detail, and CJ felt a pang in his chest. He would miss being able to recall events linearly without spending several minutes swimming through the scattered pools in his mind.

CJ pushed away the thought. He'd known this would happen, that their time in the virtual world was temporary. And he'd thought he'd accepted it. But when he thought about returning to his own body, where every sentence was stuttered, where his expressions were forcefully muted, he felt a looming frustration. He'd learned much about himself during his time here. He'd found a confidence he'd never had before. But knowing what he was going back to …

There's always the chance that Manar's wrong.

The thought came unbidden to his mind. CJ did his best to push it away, just like the dozen other times it'd occurred to him. Manar *could* be wrong, of course. That would mean they would have to find another way to return to their bodies. But that would just delay the inevitable.

Manar's theory was sound. Based on the excited gleam in Manar's eye when he'd been studying Helene's corpse, CJ could tell Manar knew it too.

CJ sighed.

Manar must have understood the expression on CJ's face because his excitement dimmed. He stood and released the sphere, which drifted to hover over CJ's shoulder. Manar stared at CJ with something resembling concern. It was a weird look on the normally stoic man. But CJ had much practice receiving such looks.

"Time to go?" CJ asked softly.

Manar nodded. "From her body, it was easy to identify the sequence that connected Helene to the real world. The major issue was reverse engineering the code so it would work for us."

"And you have?" CJ asked, just to confirm.

Manar hesitated, probably looking for a way to phrase it delicately. "Yes. I should be able to rewrite my own codes to match the sequence. The problem is, manipulating yours would require a resonance, which I can't do without you providing energy. Fortunately, after studying it, I was able to find a way to achieve the same effect using your connection with the sphere and Helene's fragment."

He paused and eyed CJ with the same look of concern. "I've already identified the link back to our bodies, so I'll send you back and then follow shortly. You ready?"

CJ wasn't ready, not really. But he didn't think he ever would be, so it would be illogical to hold on. He took one last look at the core chamber, focusing on the tapestry of binary that made up the place. Ever since his connection to the sphere was enhanced, he'd been able to see more of the world than ever before.

Even if for a short while.

CJ sighed but nodded. A moment later, he felt another connection within the sphere. CJ had the power to eject it. Instead, he granted it full access, and the connection grew. CJ felt something slip into his body and shift something—something he didn't have a word for.

The world turned black.

When CJ opened his eyes, he was staring at the ceiling of a laboratory. A moment later, his brother's face filled his vision, a shaky grin on his face.

"You had us worried for a sec, bro. Welcome back."

CJ'S BODY DISSIPATED in front of Manar's eyes. He held his breath until he got a message from Chad telling him that CJ had regained consciousness, at which point he breathed easily. He'd been confident that his theory was sound, but a dozen things could have gone wrong. Even he wasn't above mistakes.

With that settled, Manar took a deep breath and dove into his own mind. He understood CJ's reservations about going back, but running away wasn't the solution. Their foray into the virtual world had always been to serve a purpose. And now that purpose had been served.

Manar's eyes went to Helene's body. A lump formed in his throat. There was no longer any reason to stay.

Manar didn't plan on being gone long. There was too much to learn about the virtual world for him to give it up. As soon as he optimized the transfer process, Manar would be back here.

That would be a nice surprise for CJ.

For the last time—at least for a while—Manar tapped into the ball of energy in his chest and drew out every drop. He sent the tendrils through his system but focused on a specific sequence within his virtual body. Once he held the sequence firmly in his mind, Manar activated his resonance.

"*Change*," he ordered himself. The code shifted with his command, rearranging itself until it was a different sequence entirely. Manar felt the connection to his body strengthen.

And then his world faded to black as his mind was transferred.

MANAR'S CONSCIOUSNESS coalesced. He opened his eyes, expecting to see the dreary walls of a laboratory. Instead, he found the steel bars of a cage. He kicked at the bars, but they didn't even shake.

Manar forced back his panic, but a thought resounded in his mind and refused to leave. If he was trapped here, who the hell had awakened in his body?

HELENE TOOK A DEEP BREATH—her first, and possibly last— as she was immediately crushed by something. A moment later, that something began to shake with, judging from the increasing wetness of her neck, tears.

"I'm so sorry, Manar," Ndidi Okafor said, though her voice was barely recognizable through her sobs. "I'm so, so sorry."

Helene kept her eyes closed and didn't say anything, instead focusing within as she tried to adjust to her new body. If not for its utility, she would have picked a better host. As it was, this body was suboptimal. She sent a message to her nanites, directing them to work on fixing it. She would have to synthesize more to fix the more extensive damages she sensed. But for now, it would do. That done, Helene opened her eyes.

They glowed a soft gold for a moment before changing back to green.

ACKNOWLEDGMENTS

MY COMPLETION OF THIS PROJECT could not have been accomplished without the coaching and support of the beta readers, editors, and critics that I've met on this journey. My heartfelt thanks to everyone.

- Alex Kempsell
- Davida De La Harpe Golden
- Deborah G Lynn
- Jennifer Moy
- Jesse Winter
- Nathan Goyer
- Paul Goat Allen
- Tasneem Ali
- Victoria and Richard Wolf

And, to my caring, loving, and supportive family. I cannot express enough thanks to my family for their continued support and encouragement throughout this project. Please bear with me until I wrap up this five-book series.